All day long, Hayden had been walking on a tightrope. That rope was way too close to snapping.

me I was staying at your place?"

"I did." He inclined his head toward her.

"I'm not afraid, Hayden. If he comes back, I'll be ready for him. I'll be—"

"I know you're not scared." He got that. What she didn't get. . . "I am."

She laughed. "Right, the big bad navy SEAL is afraid. You're—

"Absolutely terrified. Because something could happen to you."

A man had come after Jill. He'd shot at her.

"You aren't staying here alone tonight."

Her eyes widened. "Uh, excuse me?"

"That intruder—"

"I think I did a pretty good job of defending myself."

She didn't get it. "Do you want me to stay sane?"

Her brow furrowed. "That would probably be a good plan."

He thought so, too. Hayden nodded. "Then, you're staying with me tonight. I'll have a deputy keep watch on your place."

She crossed her arms over her chest. "Did you just tell me I was staying at your place?"

"Absolutely terrified that something will happen to you."

ABDUCTION

BY
CYNTHIA EDEN

First Published in Great Britain 2017
By Mills & Boon, an imprint of HarperCollins*Publishers*
1 London Bridge Street, London, SE1 9GF

© 2017 Cindy Roussos

ISBN: 978-0-263-92868-6

46-0317

Our policy is to use papers that are natural, renewable and recyclable products and made from wood grown in sustainable forests. The logging and manufacturing processes conform to the legal environmental regulations of the country of origin.

Printed and bound in Spain
by CPI, Barcelona

Cynthia Eden is a *New York Times* and *USA TODAY* bestselling author. She writes dark tales of romantic suspense and paranormal romance. Her books have received starred reviews from *Publishers Weekly*, and one was named a 2013 RITA® finalist for best romantic suspense. Cynthia lives in the deep South, loves horror movies and has an addiction to chocolate. More information about Cynthia may be found at www.cynthiaeden.com.

I want to dedicate this book to Elaine—the absolute best mother-in-law that a girl could ever have! Elaine, thank you so much for your support over the years.

This Intrigue is for you.

Prologue

"Stay away from him, Jill." Jillian West's grandmother pointed toward the end of the long, wooden pier. A boy was there, gazing out at the distant waves, a boy who appeared to be just a little older than Jill. "He's trouble."

But he didn't look like trouble. The boy's blond hair blew in the wind and his faded T-shirt fluttered in the breeze.

"I'll only be inside a minute," her grandmother promised as she patted Jill's shoulder. "Stay here."

And then her grandmother was gone. She'd drifted into the little souvenir shop that waited near the pier, her voice drifting back to Jill as her grandmother called out a greeting to her friend inside the store.

Her grandmother had a lot of friends in Hope, Florida. It seemed that everyplace they went she met someone she knew. Jillian's flip-flops slid over the wooden pier as she stared up at the boy with the blond hair. She'd moved in with her grandmother just a few weeks before, but she still hadn't gotten a chance to talk with any kids in the town.

Her grandmother knew plenty of people, just no one who was close to Jillian's age. No other kids around thirteen for her to chat with as she adjusted to her sudden, jarring new life.

Just then, the boy glanced back at her. She stiffened,

but then Jill found herself lifting her hand in an awkward
wave. She even took a few quick steps toward him. His
head cocked as he stared at her.

Her hand fell back to her side.

He's trouble. Her grandmother's warning whispered
through her mind once more.

But he was coming closer to her. His sneakers didn't
even seem to make a sound as he eliminated the distance
between them, and then he was there, peering down at her.
He was taller than she was, his shoulders already becoming broad, and he used one careless hand to shove back
his overly long hair.

"I don't know you," he said. His voice was deeper than
she'd expected. He appeared to be around fifteen, maybe
sixteen, but that voice was so grown-up.

"No, ah, I'm new." She tucked her hands behind her
back. "I'm Jillian, but my friends call me Jill."

His gaze swept over her—dark brown eyes. Deep eyes.
When she looked hard enough—and Jill was looking so
hard that she felt herself blush—she saw a circle of gold
in those brown eyes.

"You think we're friends, Jill?" He emphasized her
name, just a bit.

She shrugged. "We could be." She bit her lip and offered her hand to him. "It's nice to meet you."

He frowned at her hand, staring at it a little too long
and hard, and then his gaze slowly rose to her face. "You
have no clue who I am, do you?"

He's trouble. Jillian shook her head. She felt so silly
standing there, with her hand offered to him. Maybe she
should drop her hand.

"I'm not very good friend material." His lips twisted.
"Ask anyone."

She dropped her hand. She felt her cheeks burn with embarrassment. *He doesn't want to be my friend.*

"I saw you with your grandmother."

Wait, when had he seen her? She'd thought that he'd been staring at the water the whole time she'd been chatting with her grandmother.

His head cocked. "I'm surprised she didn't tell you to stay away from me."

"She did," Jill blurted.

Surprise flashed on his face. "So you're not good at doing what you're told, huh?" He made a tut-tut sound. "What would your parents say?"

Her skin iced. The pain was so raw and fresh—it gutted her. Jill sucked in a sharp breath and took a quick step back. "They can't say anything. They're dead." And she shouldn't be talking to him. She shouldn't be so desperate for a friend, for *any* friend, that she'd disobey her grandmother. Her grandmother was all she had left. If her grandmother got mad at her…what if her grandmother decided she didn't want to be saddled with a kid? What if she dumped Jill someplace else? What if—

Jill spun on her heel. "I have to go." She ran away from him, nearly losing a flip-flop in her hurry. She'd go back to the car. Wait there. And she would not talk to *anyone* until her grandmother finished her chat. Her eyes stung with tears as she fled and Jill heard the boy call out her name.

But she didn't stop.

What would your parents say?

She wished they could still say something to her. Say *anything* to her.

The pier ended. Her flip-flops sank into the beautiful white sand of the beach, sand so white it was like sugar. The first time she'd seen that sand, she'd grabbed it, laughing at how light it felt as it ran through her fingers. She wasn't laughing now.

She swiped at the tears on her cheeks. The first kid she'd met, and she'd started crying in front of him. What a way to get a good reputation in the town. *Jillian's a crybaby. Jillian's a baby.*

Her grandmother's dependable four-door sedan waited a few feet away. There were only a few other cars in the parking lot. It was late, nearing sunset, and not many folks were still out.

"Are you okay, little girl?"

I'm not little. Those were the words that rose to her lips. But she didn't snap them at the man who approached her. He was frowning, looking concerned.

Probably because I'm crying.

"Are you all alone?" He seemed horrified by the very idea.

"M-my grandmother is in the souvenir shop." She pointed behind her. The man stepped closer to her. "She'll be out soon."

The man nodded as if that were a good thing, then his hand clamped over her shoulder. Hard. Hard enough to hurt and he leaned in toward Jill and whispered, "Not soon enough, Jill."

How does he know my name?

She opened her mouth, but Jill didn't get to scream. He slapped his other hand over her mouth and yanked her against him. She kicked out, struggling, but he was big and strong. So much bigger than she was. And he was running with her, heading toward a van a few feet away.

No, no, this can't happen!

"Don't make me kill you now," he growled.

Jill froze.

He opened the side door of the van. He threw her inside, but Jill lunged forward, ready to jump back out again.

He hit her. A hard punch right to her face. It was the first time in Jill's life that she'd ever been hit. For a moment, she was dazed. Her gaze slid away from the man before her—a monster—and...

She saw him...the boy from the pier. The boy with the too long blond hair. He was running toward her.

"Jill!" the boy yelled.

But the man who'd grabbed her...he jabbed something into her neck. Something sharp. *A needle?*

She fell back into the van, her head hitting the side panel, and darkness flooded Jill's vision.

"JILL? JILL!"

Her eyes flew open and Jill sucked in a quick breath so that she could scream.

"No, don't." A sweaty hand flew over her mouth. "If you scream, he'll hear you and he'll find us."

Us?

Jill blinked as she became aware of her surroundings. She was in a room with no furniture, just wooden walls. Her hands—her hands were tied together and so were her feet. She was on a dirty, dusty floor. Light burned from overhead, too bright, too stark.

"We can't let him find us, Jill," the boy said.

Boy. It was the boy from the pier. He had scratches on his face and his eyes were wide and intense as he stared down at her.

"I'll untie you, and then we're going to run. We're going to run as fast as we can, got it?"

She nodded, tears stinging her eyes.

His hand slipped away from her mouth and he began to work on the ropes that held her. The ropes at her feet

gave way quickly, but the ones that bound her wrists—
they were knotted, stuck.

"Forget it," he said and yanked her up to her feet. "We'll
get them later, *after* we're out of here."

She didn't even know where *here* was, but she wanted
to leave. She wanted to leave right then.

He pushed her toward the window. It was open and the
scent of the salty ocean blew in toward her. "I'll give you
a boost. You get out, and you go, got it? You *move*. You
don't look back at me. Trust me, I'll be coming. I'll be right
behind you. *You just go.*"

Jill nodded. She'd go.

He pushed her through the window and she fell out on
the other side, hitting her shoulder with a jarring impact,
but Jill pounced back to her feet and she started running.
Only...there didn't seem to be anywhere to run to. It was
dark and there were trees shooting up all around her, a
marshy-like area and she looked back, scared—

He was there. The boy with the too long hair. He
grabbed her bound wrists. "Come *on*, Jill."

She didn't see the man who'd taken her. She was afraid
he was out there, watching them. That he was going to attack them. Going to hurt them both.

Kill them.

They ran into muddy water, and it was cold, chilling
her. Her teeth started to chatter, not from the cold, but
from the terror clawing at her. "H-he...hurt me." Her jaw
still ached. "He...took me..." Kidnapped her from right
out in the open. A parking lot.

"I saw him." His fingers fumbled with the ropes that
bound her wrists. The knots came free and he rubbed at
her skin, being so careful with her. "I wasn't going to let
you vanish."

Vanish.

That's what would have happened to her, Jill knew it. She just would have vanished without a trace. "I want to go home," she whispered.

Home…

The house she'd shared with her parents in Georgia. Her haven. Her safe place. She wanted her mom. She wanted her dad. She wanted this to be a terrible nightmare.

But the boy wrapped his arms around her and he held her tight. "It's okay. We're going to be okay."

She believed him. He'd found her, someway. Gotten her out of…there. He saved her. "I don't…I don't even know your name."

He pulled back and stared at her. "I'm Hayden. Hayden Black."

Hayden. Such a good name for a best friend.

They ran until they reached the road. They ran and ran, but each time a car came by, Hayden made her hide.

He was afraid the kidnapper was coming for them.

Hours ticked by and then they finally made it to the small sheriff's station. Lights blazed from inside the square building and patrol cars filled the parking lot. Hayden's fingers were laced with hers as they walked up the wooden steps that led to the station. He opened the door, and they slipped inside.

There was instant silence. Every eye turned toward them.

Jill looked down at herself. Her clothes were torn and muddy. She'd lost her flip-flops. Her feet were raw and blistered.

And she was sure her jaw was bruised. It still hurt so much.

"Jillian!" Her grandmother ran to her and yanked Jill close in a crushing hug. "My little Jilly!"

Jilly. Her mother used to call her that, too. *Jilly went up the hilly...* Her own version of the rhyme.

The tears were falling again. Jill couldn't stop them. Her grandmother wasn't mad. She wasn't going to send her away. Her grandmother smelled like sweet vanilla. Like apricots.

Like home.

"What in the hell did you do, boy?" It was a man's voice, rough and demanding. And that voice...the man...he was nearby. A big, bearlike man wearing a sheriff's uniform and sporting a gleaming badge. "You took that poor girl? You hurt her?"

No, no, of course Hayden hadn't hurt her. Jillian struggled out of her grandmother's desperate embrace. That big man had grabbed Hayden. His face was angry as the sheriff snarled, "You're just like your father."

All of the color bled from Hayden's face.

"You pulled the wrong stunt today," the man snapped. "You—"

Jill pushed her way between the sheriff and Hayden. Her whole body was shaking. "Hayden is my friend."

Pity flashed on the sheriff's face as his gaze peered down at her, lingering on her jaw. "Sweetheart, why don't you just relax with your grandmother? You don't have to be afraid. You don't—"

"Hayden saved me." Her dirty hand reached back and grabbed Hayden's. She held him tight. "A man...took me... from the pier parking lot." Her words were whispered and terror clawed at her as she remembered those desperate moments. "H-he hurt me. Tied me up. But Hayden got me out... Hayden helped me." *Hayden saved me.*

The only sound she could hear was the ticking of the big clock on the wall. Jill's desperate gaze flew around the room.

Her grandmother was crying.

The sheriff who'd been yelling at Hayden was staring at her in shock. And...

"I can take you back to him," Hayden said, his voice oddly calm and still sounding so deep and...strong. "When he took Jill from the pier, I followed him on a bike. I wrecked it near the cabin, smashed it good. So we had to run on foot to get back, but I remember everything about the place. I can take you there."

AND HE DID.

Hayden led the cops back to that little cabin that was nestled near the marsh. The authorities went in with sirens screaming and guns blazing. Jill sat huddled in the back of a patrol car, her grandmother's arms constricted around her. Hayden was beside them looking watchful, intense.

The sheriff and his deputies searched the cabin. They brought in dogs to track the man who'd been there, but he was long gone...

"It's okay, Jill," Hayden whispered.

Her head turned toward him.

"I'll make sure you stay safe."

Such a big promise but...

She believed him.

Hayden Black wasn't trouble. Her grandmother had been wrong about him.

He was a hero.

And he was her friend. Her very best friend in the whole entire world.

Chapter One

The world was dark and twisted. It was filled with monsters and evil.

FBI special agent Jill West kept a strong grip on her service weapon as she rushed into the little house at the end of Clover Lane. Her teammates were with her, moving quickly, efficiently. They were the agents on the Southeastern Division of CARD, the Child Abduction Rapid Deployment team, and their job was to find missing children.

Or in this specific case…one missing child. A sixteen-year-old girl named Jessica Thomas. Jessica had been gone for three days, but they'd tracked her abductor to this location, they'd followed their leads, they'd raced against time and now…

Be alive. Please, please, be alive.

There were too many cases that ended in tragedy, in funerals with grief-stricken families. Funerals with mothers and fathers who were too devastated to even speak. Her team needed a win…because those tragedies were pushing them all too close to the breaking point.

"Stay the hell back!" A man ran from the back room of that little house, a bloody knife gripped in his hand. "You ain't taking her from me! No one's taking her from me!"

In that instant, Jill realized three very important things.

One…the knife had recently been used on someone.

The screaming man before her showed no injuries, so odds were high that the perp had attacked Jessica.

Two…the jerk was definitely on something. His speech was slurred, and he was weaving as he staggered toward her and the other agents in their bulletproof vests.

And three…this man wasn't going down easy. He was lunging forward to attack her—

"Stand down!" Jill yelled. "Drop the weapon, *now*!"

He didn't. He just screamed louder and lurched toward her.

Jill fired. Not a kill shot, she'd never taken that shot yet, but a shot that blasted into the man's right shoulder. The knife fell to the floor with a clatter as he screamed and his blood soaked his shirt. "Perp down," Jill snapped. She was wired—all of the agents were—and her earpiece had a microphone that would pick up her words so she knew the agent monitoring the team would immediately dispatch medical personnel. Then she hurried forward, kicking the knife even farther out of his way.

Agent Henry Shaw was at her side. He kept his gun leveled at the man howling on the floor. Henry, a tall, distinguished African-American agent, was the leader of their team. A damn good leader. "I got this guy, Jill," Henry told her, his eyes never leaving the perp. "Find the girl."

Jill gave an abrupt nod and hurried to the back room. She kept her gun at the ready. All of their intel had indicated that they were only looking for one assailant, that Neal Matthew Patrick had become obsessed with the sixteen-year-old victim after first meeting her in an online chat room. He'd abducted her, determined to live out that obsession.

But just in case the guy did have a partner, in case someone else was waiting to attack in that back room, Jill didn't lower her guard.

The door was partially open. She used her foot to swing it all the way inward and then—

"Help...me..." Such a weak whisper, completely at odds with the desperate howling coming from Neal.

Jessica was on the floor, her hands pressing to her stomach—trying to stem the heavy flow of blood that had already soaked her shirt. Her face was stark white, her eyes so big and scared in her young face.

"Victim needs assistance!" Jill called out, knowing the monitoring agent would act immediately. "Get help in here, now!" And Jill ran to the girl's side. She needed to see just how bad the damage was but the fear in her heart already told her...

Bad...it's too bad.

"I—I want...m-my mom..." Jessica whispered.

Jill looked at the wounds—multiple stab wounds. So deep. A pool of blood was under Jessica's body. "We'll take you to your mom, don't you worry, okay?" She applied pressure, fear nearly choking her.

"I'm sorry..." Jessica's voice was even softer now. She was starting to shake. "T-tell her...s-sorry...n-never... should have...g-gone..."

Because Jessica had made a date with Neal. She'd snuck out of her house to meet him at her high school football field. She hadn't realized she was going to meet a man who'd long gone over the edge. She couldn't have known how dangerous that meeting would be for her. *Just a date. A sixteen-year-old going on a date.* That was all it had been, to Jessica.

"It's all right," Jill told her. "You'll be with your mom soon and you can—"

Footsteps rushed behind her. Help, finally coming. The EMTs ran into the room and pushed Jill back. She watched them, hoping, praying, so very desperate.

Jessica was shaking even harder now.

Jill looked down at her hands. The girl's blood covered her fingers. Her hands fisted. Her breath heaved in and out. Every heartbeat that passed seemed to echo in her ears.

Jill was still standing there, still watching them, when Jessica's eyes closed, when the girl took her last breath. The EMTs didn't give up, they kept trying to work, kept trying to bring her back but…

Jessica's body had gone still.

She had just…

Another victim. Another child taken.

Jill stumbled outside, her stomach in knots. The night air hit her face, slightly chilled, making goose bumps rise on her arms. The cases weren't supposed to be like this. She was supposed to help, not arrive in time to see a young girl die.

Tears pricked her eyes. The perp—that jerk Neal—was in the back of a nearby ambulance. He was alive. He was yelling at the agents with him.

Jessica was gone. Life was so unfair. So cold and dark and violent. She looked at the scene around her, the chaos, the pain, and then Jill glanced down at the blood that covered her hands.

I have to get away. I can't do this. Not anymore.

"Jill?"

She put her hands behind her back and glanced over to see Henry frowning at her. Henry had been her mentor from the moment she signed on to the team. He'd trained her from day one when she joined CARD. As he stared at her, she saw the pity in his dark eyes.

He knows I'm close to breaking.

"We'll need to tell the parents," Jill said, trying to make her voice sound strong. The mother. They'd have to tell the mother. Jill swallowed.

"I can do it," Henry offered. He always handled the families so well. He seemed to know exactly what to say to them. How to give them sympathy. How to let them grieve. "You did good work on this case," he told her, his voice soft. "You were the one to find the house, to trace Neal here, you were—"

"I was too late." That was the stark truth.

"*This* time," Henry said, his jaw tightening. "But there will be other cases, other children. You of all people know how important our job is."

Because of her past, yes, she knew. She also knew... "I have to talk to Jessica's mother." She needed to look the woman in the eyes and tell her that at the end, Jessica had been thinking of her. That her daughter had loved *her*. When she took a case, Jill saw it through to the end. But after she met with the Thomas family... Jill's breath shuddered out. "Then I think I'll take some of that vacation time I've been saving." Hoarding, more like. Work had become her life in the last few years. Only now, that life seemed to be tearing her apart.

"Good idea," Henry murmured. "Maybe you can go someplace warm. Someplace where you can forget about this coldness for a time."

She thought of Jessica's last words. "I think I'm going home," Jill said. Home. The spot of her greatest happiness...

And her most desperate moments.

HE SAW HER the instant she came into town. It wasn't as if it were easy to miss a woman like her. Jill West had always been able to stand out in a crowd. The sunlight hit her dark red head, making it gleam. She wore a pair of jeans that hugged her long legs, and she walked with an easy grace as she headed toward the pier.

Hayden Black stood inside of the bait shop, watching her as she moved with such purpose. It had been far too long since he'd seen Jill... *Too damn long.*

What were the odds that when she came back to Hope, he spotted her on that same damn pier? He hadn't thought that she *would* come back. Hell, he'd been planning a trip to see her in Georgia, but for her to show up now...in that spot...

He'd never been a particularly lucky guy. The luckiest day of his life had been when he'd met a cute redheaded girl on that same pier.

A girl with the greenest eyes he'd ever seen. A girl who'd turned one of the most hated punks in that town into a hero.

"You gonna watch her all day?" Jeff Mazo, the owner of the bait shop asked. "Or are you actually gonna go over there and tell that woman hello?"

Jeff didn't get it. The woman in question might not exactly be thrilled to see him. He and Jill hadn't ended things on the best of terms.

I lusted for her during my teens. When I became a man, she was all that I could think about...

Then she'd joined the FBI and he'd become a SEAL. Two different paths. Two different lives.

Now they were back. Both back in Hope.

Maybe it's not luck. Maybe it was more than that. Maybe.

"Never realized you were the nervous sort," Jeff snorted, as if he'd just found this discovery incredibly amusing. "Bet that made for some real interesting missions, huh?"

Hayden just shook his head, refusing to let the guy needle him. "Don't worry, Jeff, I'm just planning my move." More like hoping that Jill didn't tell him to get the hell away from her. He gave a little wave. "See you later, buddy."

He headed out on the pier, and the old wood was sturdy beneath his feet. The scent of salt water tickled his nose. *Hope.* The town was gorgeous, a sweet little hideaway on the Florida Gulf Coast. It was early spring, so the place hadn't gotten overwhelmed with tourists, not yet. Sure, a few hours away, the college kids were running amok at some of the bigger beachside cities, but Hope was quieter.

Softer.

Nothing ever happened in Hope.

Except for the abduction of a sweet redheaded girl...

The man who'd taken Jill had never been caught. And Hayden... For years, he'd woken up from nightmares in a cold sweat because of that fact. He'd been so worried that someone would take Jill from him.

And in the end, I'm the one who lost her. I did that all on my own.

He marched toward her. The wind ruffled her T-shirt and her hair, but she didn't seem to care. She kept staring out at the waves, turbulent swells because a storm was coming.

When he was just a few feet away from her, Hayden stopped. "Hello, Jill."

She didn't whirl toward him in surprise. Didn't give any shocked explanation. That wasn't Jill's style. Instead, she slowly turned to him with a look in her guarded green gaze that said she'd known all along that she was being watched.

But her green eyes widened just the faintest bit, a small show of surprise that told him... Jill *had* expected someone else to be on that pier. She just hadn't expected that someone to be him.

"Hayden?" Her delicate brows arched as her gaze swept over him. "What are you doing here?"

He gave her a small smile even as he stalked a bit closer to her. That was the thing about Jill, she always made him want to get closer. Always pulled him in, even when he knew he should be staying away from her. Mingled with the scent of the ocean, he caught her fragrance. Sweet vanilla.

"I could ask you the same question," he murmured. Damn but she looked good. Better than good. Heart-shaped face, wide eyes, full lips. She had just the faintest hint of freckles across the top of her nose, a little bit of the girl she'd been still hanging on to the woman she'd become.

She took a step toward him and her hands lifted, as if she'd reach out and hug him. Once, she would have done that. Once, she would have run right into his arms and held him tight.

And she would have fit perfectly against him. The way she always had.

But she faltered. Her hands fell. Uncertainty flashed on her face. "I'm here for a vacation. Isn't that why most folks come to Hope?"

It wasn't why he was back in Hope, and he didn't believe for an instant that it was why she was back there, either.

His gaze swept over her. Jill was definitely grown-up now. She stood close to five foot six, and that meant his six-foot-three frame towered over her. When they'd been kids, she'd joked and asked him when he'd ever stop growing.

Every good memory I have is tied up in Jill West. So he didn't stop, he didn't falter. He closed the last bit of distance between them and wrapped her in a hug. Probably too tight, but he couldn't really help himself. It had been far too long since he'd seen Jill. Even longer since he'd held her.

She still fit him. Far too perfectly. His arms slid around her back and he pulled her close. Her scent wrapped around him and reminded him of all that he'd missed. Too many years away from Jill.

Too many mistakes. And—

She was hugging him back. A quick tightening of her arms around him as if she were just as glad to see him. His heart thudded in his chest. Maybe it wasn't too late. Maybe he hadn't screwed things to hell and back between them. Maybe—

She stopped hugging him. "Let me go," Jill said, her voice soft.

He did. The same way he'd let her go before, ten years ago. She'd been nineteen. He'd been twenty-one.

His hands slid away from her. "Still as beautiful as ever."

She frowned. Right, Jill never liked to be told she was beautiful. It made her uncomfortable.

"Am I supposed to say that you're still as handsome as ever?" Her head cocked and her gaze swept over him. "You are. But I'm sure plenty of women tell you that."

No other woman was Jill. *His* Jill.

"Mr. Navy SEAL." She smiled, but the smile was just a twist of her lips. No gleam appeared in her eyes and her expression didn't lighten. He'd always worked so hard to make her give him a grin—worked even harder to hear her laugh.

"Shouldn't you be out defending the world? Working those secret missions?"

Actually… "I'm not active duty any longer." He'd given ten years of his life to service. Now…now he knew exactly what he wanted to do with the years he had left. "I just bought a house here in Hope."

He heard her quick exhale. Ah, so he *had* surprised her.

"And here I thought you liked traveling the world. You

wanted to see everything, remember?" She turned away. "But now you're back here."

He reached for her hand. "And I thought you wanted to save the world." No, he knew she'd wanted to save children, kids who'd been just like her.

Taken.

Stolen.

"So what's a hotshot FBI agent like you doing in a small town like this?" His index finger slid along her inner wrist, a careless caress.

Or maybe a very careful one. Even he wasn't sure about that.

"Hiding." And this time, her smile broke what was left of his heart. "Because I'm really not so much of a hotshot." She looked down at their hands. "I've got too much blood on me."

Alarm pulsed through him. "Jill?"

"Let me go," she said once more.

Another caress, a gentle touch right over her rapid pulse point, and his hand slid away from her.

"I need to head home," she said, then seemed to catch herself. "Head to the cabin. I rented a place on the beach. The beach is supposed to be good for the soul, right?"

He wouldn't know. The only thing that had ever been good for his soul...well, that was Jill. She'd changed him, though he didn't think she realized just how much. He didn't think Jill even realized how influential she'd been in his life.

She'd always thought that he'd saved her.

Oh, baby, that could not be further from the truth.

She slipped by him and started walking toward the parking lot.

"Jillian West." Her name pulled from him.

She hesitated.

"We're not kids any longer."

Jill glanced over her shoulder. "I haven't been a child since I was thirteen years old."

No, she hadn't been. He knew that. One terrible act had changed her world.

"I came back to Hope for many reasons," Hayden said. Maybe she deserved that warning. "I didn't expect to see you so soon."

"So soon? Why expect to see me at all?"

Ah, now that was just cold. "Do you ever think about us?"

She faced the front again. "I try not to."

He took that hit straight on his heart. "Really? Because I pretty much think about you every single day." Though the nights were the worst. When he'd been fighting, when he'd been in one hell after another, memories of Jill had always come to him at night.

But a memory wasn't walking away from him right then. No memory, no ghost.

He'd watched her walk away before, but this time, things were going to be different. This time, he was fighting for Jill.

She just didn't realize it yet.

He wasn't the town troublemaker any longer. Wasn't the boy who'd never been good enough for Jillian West. Now he was back in Hope to prove himself to the person who mattered the most.

To you, Jill. For you. I'm back for you.

HE'D NEVER BELIEVED in coincidences. His life didn't work that way. Everything that happened was part of fate.

So when he saw the redheaded woman walking off the pier, the light glinting in her hair, the sunset hitting her just right…

He remembered another time.

A girl, not a woman. A girl who'd been walking alone. Who'd been coming right to him.

He'd had such plans for that girl. So many grand, wonderful plans.

But she'd left him. Ran away. Escaped before he could enjoy himself. Such a shame. In all of his years of hunting, she'd been the only one to escape.

His one failure. The failure that had changed everything for him.

THE REDHEADED WOMAN was coming closer to him, nearing the parking lot, so he cranked up his Jeep and drove away. As he left, he saw two young girls riding their bikes. So many kids enjoyed riding their bike in that area. There were many trails. Tons of paths.

So many places to vanish.

One of the girls had blond hair. The other had dark brown locks.

Pity one of them doesn't have red hair. Because, quite suddenly, he was seeing red in his mind. The red hair of a victim.

The red of blood.

He hadn't planned to ever hunt again in Hope. But... seeing that redheaded woman...

There are no coincidences. Maybe she was there, at that time, for a reason.

Maybe...

Chapter Two

She had a serious problem on her hands, Jill knew it. She was on Day Two of her vacation—*Day Two*—and she was heading toward the local sheriff's office. She should have been walking on a beach, riding a bike, reading a book, something…anything but…

Anything but looking for a case. She had so many issues. The plan had been to head home to Hope in order to relax, to get her mind off death.

Instead, she couldn't stop thinking about the missing.

She pushed open the door to the sheriff's office. A bell jingled over her head. It was quiet inside, she heard the hum of an air conditioner, the ticking of a clock and—

"Hello, there, Jill. Didn't expect to see you again so soon."

His voice. Dark and deep and rumbly. Jill had often thought that Hayden Black had a voice like whiskey—it just got better with age.

Sexier.

Her gaze slid to the right and she saw him. Hayden was smiling at her, that teasing half smile that too many women had admired. His dark eyes glinted at her as he stood in the doorway—the doorway that led directly into Sheriff Ronald Peek's inner sanctum. Only…

She didn't see Sheriff Peek. The big, rather bearlike older man was nowhere to be seen.

She *did* see Hayden…and his brown sheriff's uniform. The guy even had a gleaming, gold star pinned to his chest. *No way.* "You have got to be kidding me." Jill glanced around the little station again. No one else was there. Seriously?

"Kidding?" Hayden straightened. "Why? Don't you think I look good in this uniform?"

Her lips thinned. *Good* didn't even come close to describing the man and he knew it. Hayden's shoulders stretched far and wide, making the uniform shirt strain at the seams. He was tall and powerful, and he should *not* have been standing there.

Mostly because she wasn't quite up to handling Hayden. He'd always been able to see right through the mask that she tried to wear in order to hide her emotions. Considering how hollowed out she felt on the inside, the last thing Jill wanted was for Hayden to glimpse her weakness. She cleared her throat. "I'm here to see Sheriff Peek."

He winced and straightened away from the doorway. "Good luck with that, sweetheart—er, I mean, Jill."

She glowered at him.

"Peek retired about a month ago. Took off for Alaska. Apparently, facing the last great American frontier has always been a dream for him." Hayden's lips twitched. "And, it, uh, seems he'd been watching a lot of TV about building a cabin in the Alaskan wilderness. The call of the wild definitely got to old Ron." Hayden rolled back his shoulders. "You're looking at the new sheriff."

She shook her head.

He nodded. "Sheriff Hayden Black, at your service."

"You…you can't be sheriff. Was there a vote or—"

"Special appointment," he murmured. "Ron gave me

his highest recommendation, and, believe it or not, the folks in this town seemed happy to have me take the job."

Jill's breath heaved out. "Of course, they're happy to have you. I have no doubt that you'll be an asset here."

Surprise flashed on his face.

"What?" Now her lips pulled down. "You think because of our, uh, past, that I wouldn't support you? You're a good man, Hayden." And maybe she'd gotten a few glimpses of his case files from his overseas work. Some days, she'd wondered about him. She'd worried. When she'd first read his mission files and seen just how dangerous his SEAL work was, Jill had been terrified.

Knowing that he wasn't hers any longer...she'd tried to keep her emotional distance. That had been impossible.

He took a step toward her. "You know folks in this town didn't always think that way. I had to prove—"

She held up her hand. "Stop it, Hayden. You never had to prove anything to me. I hope you know that."

His mouth tightened.

The bell jingled behind her. Jill looked back and saw a young deputy saunter inside the station. He had black hair and blue eyes and when he saw her, he came to a quick stop—and he tightened his grip on the doughnut bag in his hand. "Uh, a visitor? A case?" His eyes seemed to light up. "Ma'am, do you need assistance?" He hurried toward the check-in desk and plunked down his bag. "I'm Deputy Finn Patrick, and I can—"

"She's not here for business, Finn," Hayden muttered. "It's personal."

A tingle snaked up Jill's spine. *Personal.* Once upon a time, things had been very, very personal between them. When she looked at Hayden, the memories slid through her mind. She figured all of the stories she'd heard over the years were true—a woman never forgot her first love.

Especially when that love happened to be a guy like Hayden Black.

But now Finn was looking at her with speculation in his eyes. Hope was a small town—very, very small. And the last thing she wanted was for gossip to start spreading about her hooking up with the new sheriff. Jill reached into her bag and pulled out her ID. "Actually, I'm here to talk about an old case."

Finn's eyes doubled in size. "You're FBI!"

"Yes."

Finn appeared absolutely thrilled.

"What case?" Hayden asked, his voice a low growl. "When I saw you yesterday, you didn't mention a case."

"And you didn't mention that you were the sheriff, either."

Hayden sauntered closer. He leaned in and said, voice soft, "That's because you ran before I had the chance to tell you."

She wanted to tell him that she didn't run—not from anything or anyone, but those words would have been a lie. After all, wasn't she in Hope because she was running? From all the death that seemed to stalk her? She stared into his eyes and said the name that she knew haunted them both, "Christy Anderson."

His jaw tightened.

"Christy who?" Finn asked.

Hayden curled his fingers around her arm. "FBI special agent Jillian West and I will be talking in my office, Finn." His voice had gone flat and cold as he steered her toward the open doorway.

"It was nice to meet you, Agent West!" Finn called out.

She glanced back and saw that he'd opened his bag of doughnuts. The scent of glaze drifted to her, but then she was inside of Hayden's office, and he shut the door with a very distinct click.

"What in the hell are you planning?" Hayden asked her.

She pulled her arm from his grip. "I'm planning on solving a cold case." Because maybe that case was one of the many demons that plagued her. Maybe if she could solve that case...maybe if she could give the family some closure...then every time she lost a victim with the FBI, she wouldn't feel so lost inside.

Maybe.

Maybe not.

"Did the FBI send you down here to research Christy Anderson's case?"

"No, I came down here because I knew it was time to face my own past. You can only hide from the truth for so long." Her smile felt bittersweet. "After all, you and I both know...we traded my life for Christy's."

He swore and advanced toward her.

Jill threw up her hands. "Don't! I don't want you touching me, okay, Hayden?"

He flinched, as if she'd hurt him, and Jill realized that she had. *Right. Like he never hurt me.* One night...ten years ago...he'd ripped her heart right out of her chest.

A woman could do a whole lot in this world without a heart.

"You used to like it when I touched you," Hayden said.

Oh, no, he had *not* just gone there. Jill's hands went to her hips. "And you used to not be a jerk who turned his back on the *one* person he swore mattered the most to him—"

Pain flashed on his face. "Jill—"

"No!" She squeezed her eyes shut. "This isn't what I want." It wasn't. And she wasn't just hurting Hayden. She was hurting herself. Jill forced her eyes to open. "I'm sorry." Time to be incredibly honest. "I didn't count on see-ing you again." Actually, she'd been sure he was an ocean away. So much for her contact at the CIA. Mr. Oh, Yes, I Know Where His SEAL Team Is. "I wasn't prepared for you, and I'm..." Her laughter held a rough edge. "I was already raw enough before I came to Hope."

"Believe me, Jill. The last thing I ever want is to hurt you."

He seemed so sincere. She wanted to believe him. "Maybe we can call a truce?"

His gaze drifted over her and turned wistful. "I didn't realize we were at war."

No? "I could use a friend right now." A stark admission. "I've... I've always thought you were my *best* friend." And that was why it had hurt her so much when he'd walked away. She hadn't just lost her lover. She'd lost her friend.

Did he have any clue...she'd used to imagine their wed-ding? She'd thought they would grow old together. That they would always be an unstoppable team. Because that was how she'd felt when they were together. Unstoppable.

Safe.

She'd always been safe with Hayden. Then he'd ripped away her safety net.

"I will be anything you want me to be," Hayden prom-ised, his voice a rumble.

Her stare lifted, held his. Did he know why she'd asked him not to touch her? Did he realize just what his touch did to her? Even the careless brush of his fingers over her arm had her tensing. His touch stirred her memories, stirred *her*. Her heartbeat raced, her breath hitched, and she ached...

For things that she couldn't have.

"Right now, I need you to be the sheriff who is coop-erating with an FBI agent." Though she had zero jurisdiction. She wasn't going to point out that fact, though. "I'm in town, you have a cold case, and I want to see if there's anything I can do to help solve it."

The faint lines on either side of his mouth deepened. Time had been kind to Hayden. Gone were the boyish looks he'd had years ago. Now, his face was ruggedly handsome, carved and hard.

Sexy.

Especially when he smiled. Hayden didn't have dimples, definitely not. But he did have hard slashes that appeared in his cheeks when he let himself really smile. Once upon a time, his real smiles had been reserved for her.

A lifetime ago.

"Christy Anderson has been dead a long time, Jill," he spoke carefully.

"I know exactly how long Christy's been dead." She paced toward the window and looked out. She figured this had to be the only sheriff's office in the country with a view of the ocean. Talk about a prime spot. And, most days, it was a plum job, too. There wasn't a whole lot of crime in Hope. The occasional bar fight, some drunk and disorderly conduct...nothing too bad.

The last *bad* thing...well, that had happened to Jill. And to Christy. Because one day—*one day*—after Hayden and Jill escaped from that little cabin on the edge of the marsh, Christy Anderson had gone missing. Only no one had been there to follow the girl when she was abducted. No one had been there to get her out of that sick jerk's clutches.

And...less than twenty hours later, Christy's body had been found on the beach. She'd been found completely dry, covered with a blanket. She'd never touched the water.

Her neck had been broken. Left behind in the dark.

I lived, but she died. And that truth would never leave Jill alone.

"I want to find the man who killed her," Jill said, nodding her head as she stared out at the waves. Last night's storm lingered on the surf. "Because if I find him..."

"You'll find the man who took you."

Yes. And she'd stop always looking over her shoulder, always wondering... *Is he watching? Is he coming back?* An FBI agent was supposed to be confident, supposed to fear nothing and no one, but Jill feared far too much.

"You of all people know..." The floor creaked beneath his heavy footsteps. "The odds of finding him—after all this time—it's going to be nearly impossible."

She rolled her shoulders back in a shrug. "So maybe I'll dig into the files. Maybe I'll spend a few days of vacation searching for evidence that won't lead anywhere. It's my time to waste."

He was behind her. She could feel him. Jill made herself look back. "I need this, Hayden."

He nodded once, grimly. His hand lifted as if he'd touch her cheek, but then his fingers curled closed as he seemed to catch himself. His fisted hand fell back to his side. "Jill, when are you going to realize that I'd pretty much do anything for you?"

Shock radiated through her. He stalked toward the wide, cherrywood desk that sat in the middle of the office. He pushed the chair back and opened the top drawer. A moment later, he was lifting a yellowed file and offering it to her. "Not a lot is in here, I'm afraid."

She felt rooted to the spot. "You...you'd already pulled the file?" She knew there was an old records room in the back of the station. As a teen, she'd trailed after Sheriff Peek many times once she'd realized that she'd wanted to go into law enforcement. He'd said she was interning with him...and he'd strode around with his chest puffed out.

The first time she'd met Peek, he'd been tearing into

Hayden. It was only later, much later, that she'd come to see the good heart hidden inside the hardened man. *And I came to learn just why he blamed Hayden that day.* Why so many in the town had.

"I pulled her file the day I took the job," Hayden answered.

Again, he'd surprised her. "Why?"

His lips twisted in his half smile, the smile that said he was holding back secrets. "Same reason you did. I want to catch the bastard."

Her heart thudded into her chest. Hayden wasn't the boy he'd been. Staring at him right then, she saw that his eyes had gone flat and cold, so hard and deadly with intent. This wasn't the boy she'd known or even the young man she'd loved.

This was the SEAL. Dangerous. Dark.

Almost…a stranger.

"He took you, Jill. *You.*" Hayden shook his head. "Do you think I have ever stopped wanting to catch him? I *won't* ever stop. I know he's still out there. He thinks he got away clean, but justice comes to everyone. Sooner or later."

She took the file from him. Her fingers brushed his and a spark seemed to slip though her at that soft touch. She pulled back—too fast—and held the thin file carefully.

"You want to hunt him?" Hayden asked. "Fine, we'll hunt him. We'll do it together. This time, we aren't kids running in the dark."

No, they weren't.

"But be warned…there's not a lot of information in that file." His words were grim. "The guy didn't leave a whole lot of evidence behind. He knew what he was doing. He was smart."

The smart, organized killers were the most dangerous. "I've worked cold cases before," Jill told him. The CARD team members were focused exclusively on child abduction cases. When there was not an active case for them to investigate, then they often turned their attention to older crimes, hoping that they could find a piece of evidence that had been overlooked or that new technology would lead them in a new direction on a particular case. "I know that it's often like searching for a needle in a very giant haystack."

His dark gaze dropped to the thin folder. "That's a small haystack. Peek is a good man, but he was in way over his head with her case. See for yourself. There's an empty office down the hall you can use. Once you've read over the file, we can talk. Compare our thoughts."

She liked that he wasn't trying to influence her by saying what he might already suspect. She'd found that it was always better to go into an investigation without another agent's expectations or suspicions already in the open, those just tended to cloud the situation for her. She liked to see things with fresh eyes. "Thanks." She turned for the door.

Her hand was reaching for the doorknob when he said, "I missed you."

Her breath seemed to chill her lungs. "Did you?"

"Yes, I did." His voice was flat. Stark. Not hiding anything from her. "It's damn good to see you."

I missed you, too. She opened the door.

"I won't make the same mistake again."

Now she did glance back at him. On this, they needed to be very clear. She'd survived a broken heart once, courtesy of Hayden Black. "Neither will I." Then she left him.

It was better this way. Far, far better to just stick to the case.

HE KNEW THE REDHEAD. And he'd been right. Seeing her on the pier yesterday, in that exact same spot, at nearly the exact same time of evening...it hadn't been coincidence.

It had been fate.

Sixteen years ago, Jillian West had come to Hope, Florida. Quiet, withdrawn, her parents dead. She'd seemed to be his perfect prey. A gift delivered right to his doorstep.

He'd been following her for days before he approached her at the pier. He always liked to watch before he made his move. He had to be smart. So he'd watched and he'd acted at just the right moment.

Jillian had fought him, but he'd gotten her away. He'd had such plans for her, but when he went back to his cabin, she'd been gone.

Long gone. And his rage had nearly blinded him.

Jillian West.

The victim who'd gotten away. She'd stayed in town. Stayed until her grandmother died. Then the gossip he'd heard said that she'd joined the FBI. She'd wanted to help find missing children.

The folks in the little town had admired her.

He'd hated her.

Because of her, he'd lost *everything.* He'd had to be careful and to watch his steps. Had to hold back his impulses. Had to *lose* himself.

But then his life had changed yesterday, when he'd seen her.

Now he knew the real reason he'd stayed in Hope all these long years.

I knew—one day—we'd finish what we started.

It was time to act. Time to catch the only prey to ever get away from him. And then…only then…would his work truly be finished. He wasn't weak any longer. Finally, finally, he was strong. Better than ever.

The timing was perfect. For him.

He paused for just a moment outside of the sheriff's office. She was in there and he knew she wasn't alone.

Hayden Black was close by, the way he always was when Jillian was near.

Tugging his baseball cap down, he turned away. As he headed toward the beach, he started to whistle. This was going to be different for him. Not as easy, more of a challenge. She was FBI. She'd had training.

But she wasn't better than him. Wasn't smarter. He'd been evading FBI agents for *years*. He had this down.

And Jillian...well, she was about to see what it was like to be prey again. *Only this time, you won't get away. I'll make sure there's no one there to save you, Jillian.*

He was getting his life back, and in order to do that, FBI agent Jillian West had to die.

Chapter Three

Hayden lifted his hand and rapped his knuckles against the door frame. At the sound, Jill's head whipped up and she blinked at him, a few dazed blinks, and he knew that she'd had herself fully immersed in the case file.

She'd made herself comfortable in the little office. She had a laptop open on the desk, positioned just to her right, and she'd started tacking some notes up on the bulletin board to her left. His eyebrows rose as he realized that she was certainly making the most of that slim file.

"Hayden?" She rose to her feet. "What's wrong?"

Not a damn thing. Finally, his world felt right. Because she was there. But he made a show of looking at his watch. "You've been in here for almost five hours. I thought you might want to take a lunch break with me."

"Five hours?" She seemed surprised and gave a little laugh. "Sorry, I, um, tend to get a bit lost in my work."

He thought that might be an understatement.

She snapped her laptop shut. "But I would like some lunch…and a chance to pick your brain, now that I've had a chance to form my own impressions of the case." She grabbed her bag. "How about we just pick up some sandwiches and eat on the beach?"

They'd done that so many times as kids. Tossed a blanket on the sand. Stared at the waves, talked and dreamed.

After Jill's abduction, her grandmother had gone through a phase where she was almost hypervigilant. She hadn't wanted to let Jill out of her sight. She hadn't let her granddaughter go anyplace but to school and right back home and...

Jill had turned reserved and quiet.

He'd gone to her grandmother and talked to her. He promised her that Jill would always be safe with him. And the lady...the lady had actually trusted *him*. She'd let Jill go on walks with him. Go to the beach with him.

Start to live again, with him.

They grabbed sandwiches from the deli next door, and then he snagged a blanket from the back of his SUV. Keeping a beach blanket handy was standard operating procedure for anyone who lived in Hope. The sunsets were not to be missed.

As they walked along the sand, Jill gave him a quick smile, a smile that actually reached her green eyes and made them gleam. "Just like old times, isn't it?"

Seagulls called overhead and the waves thundered as they hit the beach.

He stared at her a moment, and thought about the old times, the *best* times of his life. "Yes."

Her smile slipped. "Um, here, let me spread out the blanket." Jill eased it onto the sand, and then she sat down and he stared at her.

Jill was there, actually back with him. He was not going to mess this up. Hayden eased onto the blanket beside her and handed her one of the sandwiches. For a time, they ate in silence. He was far too conscious of her, beside him. The wind teased a lock of her hair and sent it dancing over her left cheek. He wanted to brush that hair back and tuck it behind her ear...but Jill had made it clear she didn't want him touching her.

Damn unfortunate, since touching her was the main thing he wanted.

"It doesn't make sense," Jill suddenly said. Her head turned and their eyes met. "Do you know how rare it is to have two girls taken within such a short period like that?"

Yeah, he did. He wasn't an expert on child abduction like she was, but because of her, he'd definitely done his share of research.

"The fact that the guy stayed here and took Christy after I escaped…it suggests that he was acting out a compulsion. That he *had* to kidnap and—"

"Murder?" Hayden cut in.

She nodded. "Yes." Her gaze fell to the sand.

"There were never any other cases in Hope that fit his MO." That had been the very first thing Hayden checked once he came back to town. "No abductions at all. After that one weekend, Hope went back to its normal 3.5 drunk and disorderly arrests a year." He blew out a hard breath. "No more murders. No more missing children."

"Just one hellish weekend." She put her empty sandwich wrapper back in the bag and took a sip of bottled water. "It doesn't fit. In all the cases I've studied, a one-and-done situation like this…it's too rare. If the perp were following a compulsion, he would have needed to act again. Sure, there would be a cooling-off period but—"

"Whoa, whoa, hold on." He balled up his own wrapper and tossed it in the bag. "A 'cooling-off' period?" Hayden repeated. "That sounds like we're dealing with some kind of…of serial killer or something."

"There are serial abductors," Jill murmured. "It's unfortunate, but it does occur. Most types of abductions are family abductions, but nonfamily abductions…well, there are different rules in place for those."

Rules? Okay, now this was just making him angrier.

"If this were a serial abductor we were looking at, there

would have been more victims," Jill said. Her delicate jaw hardened. "The perp wouldn't have just vanished, just— just totally disappeared off the grid."

"Let's back up," Hayden directed. The waves rolled onto the shore. "Tell me what you believe happened to Christy, based on the report."

"That tiny five-page report? The one that contained zero DNA evidence or crime scene analysis?"

A definite edge had entered her voice. "Yeah, that one." He'd felt the same frustration that she was showing when he'd reviewed the material.

"I think the killer had done those same actions before. He knew how to clean up after himself. He knew how to make sure there wasn't so much as a sliver of evidence left behind. This definitely wasn't amateur hour."

"That's why you think we're looking at a serial."

"Her neck was broken. A personal, intimate death. That type of kill suggests that the perp wanted to have power over his victim. He liked the control." She nodded. "That's probably why he picked two young teen girls as his victims here in Hope—he thought we were weaker than he was, that he could control us both."

"You're profiling him."

She rolled back her shoulders and finally caught that lock of hair that had been teasing her cheek. "I've taken some profile classes at Quantico, yes, but that's not exactly my strong suit. You want someone who can get into a killer's head?" Her lips lifted once again in a faint smile. "That would be my friend Samantha. When it comes to killers, she's an absolute genius."

Hayden found himself leaning closer to Jill. "You're the one who saw him, face-to-face." He'd just seen the back of the jerk's head, his baseball cap, his dark shirt, his jeans as the guy ran toward the front of that old SUV. An SUV that had later been found, stripped down and abandoned, two towns over.

Her smile flickered. "I saw him, and I'm the one who should have been able to identify him. I know that."

"Jill, that's not what I—"

Sadness was heavy in her voice as she said, "I know Christy's parents blamed me."

His hand fisted on the sand.

"Did you know…they came to my grandmother's house once?"

"What? You never said—"

"Her father had been drinking. Her mother was trying to keep him under control. He was yelling and saying that I could have stopped the killer. That I knew who he was. That it was my fault Christy was gone." Her lips turned down. "Kept saying I shouldn't be living when he was burying his daughter. That it wasn't right. That it was *my* fault."

"Why the hell didn't you tell me?" He jumped to his feet.

She tilted back her head and stared up at him. "Because I thought he was right. It was my fault. If I could have remembered more about the guy, if I could have described him better—"

"Jill," he cut in, growling her name, and then he reached for her—breaking that no-touching rule—and hauled her up beside him. "Nothing that happened was your fault. You were a victim. Just that. You didn't do anything wrong."

The wind blew against them.

"I remembered he was wearing big sunglasses, and a baseball hat. He had a square jaw, and I think I saw a little bit of blond hair on the side of his head, peeking from beneath the hat." He heard the faint click of her swallow. "He was tall, over six feet, I believe. And I remember thinking that he was far too strong."

Hayden hated that man. *Hated him.*

"Peek tried to get me to do a sketch," Jill said, "but that sketch could have been anyone. When the artist was done, I didn't even recognize the picture I was staring at." She gave a little laugh, one that sounded bitter and *wrong* coming from Jill. "Hell, right now, he could be you. You fit the description that I just gave. Blond, tall, strong, square jaw...is it any wonder that no one was able to find the guy?"

His hands tightened on her shoulders. "It *wasn't* your fault." He needed her to believe that.

"It wasn't until I started my criminal justice courses that I realized...eyewitness testimony is notoriously un- reliable."

He didn't let her go. Her voice had softened. He should back away. But he didn't.

"Just with my work at the FBI, I've talked to so many witnesses..." She gave a sad shake of her head. "Witnesses who saw the *exact* same perp, but who described him in completely different ways. It's just...unreliable. *I* was un- reliable. I could have described the man totally wrong. Even adult witnesses describe perps the wrong way...so, of course, a thirteen-year-old kid who'd been traumatized would make mistakes." She swallowed. "*I* made mistakes. To tell you the honest truth, I can't even swear to what I saw today. Maybe he wasn't blond. Maybe I *was* just thinking of you. You had such a big role in that day for me. Maybe *you* were all that I could see."

She'd been all that he could see. The first person who'd looked at him as if he weren't trash, as if he were someone who mattered. And then he'd seen her get taken.

I can't lose her.

Those had been his thoughts that day. He remembered them perfectly.

I won't lose her.

"It's the human memory," she whispered. "People think

it's like a video recorder or something but it's not. The way people think…my friend Samantha said it's more like putting puzzle pieces together. We have the bits and pieces there, but sometimes our mind makes jumps to fill in the rest for us. To close those gaps."

The wind caught a lock of her hair once more and blew it over her cheek. His hand rose and brushed back that hair, and then his fingers lingered on the silk of her skin. "It wasn't your fault. Nothing was."

She sucked in a sharp breath and seemed to become aware of just how close they were.

Aware that he was touching her.

I need to back away.

He started to ease away. His hand slid down her cheek and—

Jill caught his hand in hers. "It's because it hurts."

Hayden's eyes narrowed. "What hurts?" He *never* wanted Jill to feel pain. He would do anything necessary to see to it that she never suffered a single day of her life. Not—

"When you touch me, it hurts."

Her words pierced the heart she'd always owned.

"It makes me feel too much. *You* make me feel too much. You always did."

Was that good? Or bad?

"You make me want…" Jill said, giving a shake of her head. "You make me want things that I can't have."

Maybe they should be clear. She could have him anytime she wanted. Anytime, any way, any day. He was aroused for her right then. It was pretty much impossible for him to get close to Jill and *not* want her.

"That's dangerous," she continued, her voice husky. "*You're* dangerous to me."

No, he wasn't. She was the safest person in the world when he was near.

Her body brushed against his. It had been so long since he'd held her. Dreams weren't enough for him any longer. Memories could only get a man so far. She was close. He needed her.

A taste, just a taste to get him through...

"I never stopped wanting you," Hayden confessed. It was time to make sure there were no secrets between them.

Her lashes lowered. Such thick, dark lashes. The sunlight made her red hair gleam. "I tried to stop wanting you," she said.

He deserved that. Damn it. He sucked in a deep breath and made himself step back. "We shouldn't stay out too long. You always burned too easily." He should have brought her a hat. Or grabbed a beach umbrella. Her skin was so much paler than his own and—

Jill touched *him*. Her fingers curled around his wrist and Hayden stilled.

"I tried," she said, "but then I came face-to-face with you, and I realized the need is still there."

"Jill..."

"I'm not here to make the same mistakes. I'm here to get my life together. I'm here to end the past and to try and move on."

Was she saying he was the past?

"If I'd known you were here..." She licked her lips and didn't say another word.

"You wouldn't have come," Hayden finished. Damn, he hadn't realized just how much Jill hated him. He didn't want that. He *couldn't* deal with that. Not from her.

"No...I..." Her lashes lifted. "I would have been better prepared for you. I would have been able to hold myself back."

He didn't want her holding back.

"But maybe I'm making too much of this," Jill added, a faint furrow between her brows. "Maybe what I'm feel-

ing…it's just left over from our past." Her gaze dropped
to his mouth. "Why fear it…if I don't know what will
happen?"

"Jill?"

Her hand fisted on his uniform shirt. "Kiss me."

Wait. Had she just said—

"Maybe I won't feel anything and I can let our past go."

"Don't count on it," Hayden growled. He bent his head
and his lips took hers.

There was no uncertainty in his kiss, not with Jill. No
getting-to-know-you hesitation. He knew her intimately,
knew exactly what she liked and didn't like. All of those
memories were burned into his mind.

She'd said people's memories were like puzzle pieces.
His memories of her weren't. His memories of her were
complete in heartbreaking detail because she'd been the
one person who always mattered most to him.

Her lips parted beneath his. Hayden's tongue swept inside her mouth. She tasted so sweet, so good. He pulled
her closer and kissed her deeper. He longed for so much
more. A low moan built in her throat, a sexy sound that
just made the desire knife through him. He was hard and
aching for her.

But they were on a public beach.

People were around.

And she was…*running a test. Trying to see if she can
walk away from me.*

His head slowly lifted. He stared down at her, saw the
flush on her cheeks and the heat in her gaze. "Well?"

She let go of his uniform. "You always did know how
to kiss. But then, you *were* the boy who gave me my very
first kiss." She started to retreat.

Hayden caught her hand, held tight. *We are so past that
not-touching part.*

"That first kiss was on this very beach." Another memory that had gotten him through hell. When his life had become a battle, when the missions had been at their darkest, he'd pulled out those memories.

"What do you want me to say?" Jill asked, her breath hitching. "What do you want—"

You. Always you. "Time has passed. We've changed. But the desire hasn't, Jill. It hasn't lessened." Hell, no. For him, it had only gotten stronger. Right then, he wanted her naked and under him on a bed. Or over him. That would work, too. Any way with Jill would work. "But the choice is yours." It always would be. "You want us to stay only partners, just working the cold case? Fine, we can do that." He'd need a whole lot of very, very icy showers. "But if you want more…" He exhaled. "Then I'll give you everything I have."

Her gaze searched his. What did she see, Hayden wondered, when Jill looked at him?

He knew what others had seen…

Troublemaker.

Son of a criminal.

Trash.

Then…after Jill…

Hero.

Fighter.

SEAL.

Now…sheriff. Peacekeeper.

But what was he to her? *An ex she wants to forget?* "So how did the experiment go?" Hayden asked her, his voice gruff. "Are we to be just partners or—"

"Wanting you was never a problem, Hayden."

His brows lifted at her hushed words.

"Loving you? That was where I made my mistake." She gave him a brisk nod. "I'm going back to my rental house for a few hours. I want to call some contacts at the FBI. You and I—we can talk more later." She turned and began to walk away.

"Talk about the case?" Hayden called out to her. "Or about us?"

She looked back at him. The wind tousled her hair, fanning it across her face. "Both."

HE WATCHED JILL as she headed toward her car. He hadn't been certain which vehicle was hers—there were too many rentals in town right then. But she went to the small sedan with quick, determined strides and he smiled.

But then she stopped. Her gaze lifted and she turned, scanning the street.

He wasn't outside so she didn't see him. He was nestled, all safe and snug, in the little deli. The perfect place to watch. Because the sun could be so incredibly bright, the thoughtful deli owners had gotten the windows tinted. Their customers could see out and enjoy the million-dollar beach view, but folks outside couldn't peer into the deli.

Jill couldn't see him.

He rolled back his shoulders and let his grin stretch. Did she feel him? Somehow sense him? He'd heard that folks could do that, could tell—instinctively—when they were prey.

Jill was prey. Very, very long overdue prey.

She lingered a moment longer, and her gaze slid back to the beach. The sheriff was there, walking slowly toward her. He'd seen them on the beach, too. Talking, like old friends.

Kissing, like lovers.

Hayden Black was an interfering SOB. He'd make sure the guy didn't get in his way again. After all…how could Hayden prevent a threat…

When he never saw it coming?

Chapter Four

The cemetery was so small. A white, picket fence provided the border for the property, and the graves that waited there…they were marked only by the small, fading headstones.

Jill stared down at the stone near her feet, the grave for Christy Anderson. *Beloved daughter. Gone, but never forgotten.*

No, Christy had certainly not been forgotten. Not by her family. *Not by me.* Even though Jill and Christy had never met, the girl was forever burned in Jill's memory.

Jill had read over the facts of Christy's abduction. She'd accessed the FBI database remotely, she'd searched NamUs, looking for other victims who matched her and Christy's age at the time they were taken in the National Missing and Unidentified Persons System. She'd tried to figure out just who the perp was, what darkness had driven him, what motivations had possessed him.

Christy had not been sexually abused when she'd been kidnapped. She hadn't been tortured. She'd just been killed, quickly, and then she'd been dumped on the beach.

Not dumped. Her body was carefully arranged. Her face was even covered with a blanket. Normally, that would have been a sign of remorse but…

"I'm not sure he regretted what he did, not to either of

us," Jill whispered. The headstone was clean, gleaming in the fading light, while the other nearby markers were over-grown with weeds or covered in a layer of grime. Fresh daisies were near the grave. Someone was still looking after Christy. Someone was still taking care of her.

Never forgotten.

When she'd fled Georgia after that last case had gone to hell on her, Jill hadn't realized just why she was so des-perate to return back to Hope. Her grandmother had died just after Jill's eighteenth birthday. She didn't have any family left, and she'd sold her grandmother's home to pay for her college tuition.

But…

I needed closure. I needed to stop running. I needed to stop feeling like I was still looking over my shoulder, wait-ing for the man who took me to appear again.

She could relate so well to the victims she faced each day on her job. Mostly because she *had* been them.

Jill rubbed her chilled arms and headed back to her car. She had another stop that she wanted to make, another visit that was overdue. This time, she wanted to see Christy's parents. She needed to talk to them about the last day of their daughter's life.

Jill was sure that little talk was going to be a night-mare and that was why she was planning to have Hayden accompany her. It wasn't as if the Andersons could slam their door shut on the local sheriff.

They *shouldn't* slam it shut on an FBI agent, either, but when it came to her, Theodore Anderson had never been the most…reasonable man.

Why did she get to live but I'm burying my daughter? Why? The echo of his scream still haunted her. He'd been in her grandmother's living room, and she'd been on the stairs, desperately trying to cover her ears so she wouldn't hear all the terrible things he was saying.

And she'd been wishing, so desperately, that Hayden would appear. Bad things didn't happen when Hayden was close.

Until the day that Hayden *became* the bad thing in her life.

She headed for her rental car, she'd just taken a few steps when…

She heard the snap of a twig. Jill tensed and her gaze swung to the left, to the thick line of twisting pine trees and brush that covered the west side of the cemetery.

It wasn't uncommon for some wild animals to roam the area. Deer were often seen. Squirrels, rabbits—

Another twig snapped.

Every instinct Jill possessed told her that no squirrel was watching her. Her hand automatically went to her holster—only, she wasn't wearing the holster. She had her holster and her gun safely tucked away back in her room.

Her chin lifted. "Is someone there?"

No response. Not that she'd expected one. She glanced around the empty cemetery and felt a chill skirt down her spine. It wouldn't be the first time that a robber had waited near a cemetery, sure that a grieving—and distracted—family member would appear to be the perfect pickings. Time to make it clear—real clear—that she wasn't an easy target, gun or no gun. "I'm FBI Agent Jillian West!" she yelled. "Identify yourself, now!"

Instead of someone stepping forward, she heard the fast thud of footsteps, running away. *Definitely not a squirrel.* Jill hesitated for only a second and then she gave chase. She rushed toward the brush and slipped into the woods. Twigs and branches tugged at her shirt and jeans, but she pushed past them, determined to follow those retreating footsteps. Determined to figure out just who had been watching her.

But then she heard the quick growl of an engine. She surged forward, pushing herself to run even faster. She broke through the trees, breath heaving, and saw the front of an SUV. Her gaze jerked toward the windshield, toward the man behind the wheel—

The SUV surged toward her. She could feel the heat from the engine and she rushed to the side, but the vehicle turned after her, nearly clipping her hip, and Jill flew forward. Her hands scraped over the ground, her knees hit the earth, and the SUV whipped past her as the driver shot down the narrow road.

Jill pushed herself up, gazing after the vehicle as it fled.

So much for her vacation. Her few days away were starting to prove to be as dangerous as her job with the FBI.

"SHERIFF BLACK?"

Hayden glanced up to see Finn standing nervously in his doorway.

"Just…just got a call in to the station, sir," Finn said, pulling at his collar. "From the FBI agent—"

Hayden surged to his feet. "Jill?" Wait, okay, he needed to tone down, way down. He cleared his throat. "Does Agent West need more case files?"

Finn's eyes were wide. "No. She…she was nearly hit near the Jamison Cemetery."

Hit?

"Some SUV almost ran her down. She got the tag and she wants us to figure out who—"

In an instant, he was around the desk. He grabbed Finn by the shoulders. "She's all right?" A dull thudding filled his ears. It took Hayden a moment to realize that was his heartbeat.

Finn nodded quickly. "She said she was fine! She's on her way here…just wanted us to get the tag number and she said she wanted to go with you to confront the bast— um, I mean the driver."

Hayden would be confronting the guy, all right. "Run the tag, *now*."

Finn scrambled to obey. Hayden checked his weapon and grabbed his coat. He didn't put up with crap like this in *his* town, and to think that the guy had nearly hit Jill. *His* Jill.

Oh, the hell, no.

Hayden marched out of his office. Finn was tapping frantically on the computer near his desk.

"Uh, Sheriff?"

Hayden narrowed his eyes on the deputy.

"It's a stolen vehicle. It was taken from a parking garage in Jacksonville a few days ago."

"Report the sighting," Hayden ordered.

"It's an older model," Finn added. "No GPS tracking."

Of course not, that would have made things too easy.

The bell jingled over the front entrance. Hayden spun around. Jill was there—

Her clothes were rumpled, dirty, and…was that *blood* on her cheek? He rushed to her and his hand lifted to touch her cheek. It was blood *and* a bruise. "I thought you weren't hit," he gritted out, fury burning in his blood.

She gave a little wince. "Trust me, it could have been about a thousand times worse. I managed to jump out of the way just in time."

Jump? Had she just said that she'd *jumped* out of the way? His fingers feathered over the bruise. "Come with me," he ordered. Then, not waiting for her to obey, he caught her wrist in his hand and tugged her toward his office. "The vehicle was stolen from Jacksonville." He shot a quick glare toward Finn. "Get an APB out for that SUV! I've got some drunk jerk running loose and—"

"I don't think he was drunk," Jill said quietly. "I think he deliberately tried to hit me."

Every muscle in his body tensed.

"Definitely get out that APB," Jill told Finn. "Maybe another one of the deputies will spot the guy so we can bring him in for questioning."

Hayden wasn't interested in questioning the suspect. He was interested in making the guy pay for hurting Jill. He was still new to the sheriff business. In his mind, he was a SEAL. Battle ready and focused.

Get the enemy.

He shut the door of his office, then gently pushed Jill into his desk chair. It was the plushest chair in the room. "Be right back."

She blinked, her brow furrowing, but he just hurried toward the bathroom—the sheriff's private bathroom was a nice perk of the office—and he came back a moment later with a warm cloth in his hand. Carefully, he wiped at the blood on her cheek. "It's not too bad," he said, but he was still furious. *She shouldn't be hurt at all.*

Jill lifted her hands. "These took the brunt of my fall."

He cursed. Then he was pulling her up and hauling her into the bathroom with him. He cleaned the wounds, bandaged them, all the while wanting to drive his fist into the face of the jerk who'd hurt her. "Tell me what happened," he demanded as he held her hands in his. "Everything."

The bathroom was small, a tight space, so they were intimately close. Jill rolled one shoulder in a shrug and said, "I was at the Jamison Cemetery—"

"Why," Hayden cut in.

She blinked at the sharpness of his voice.

He should try to dial back his rage, he got that but...

this was Jill. Jill had always been his trigger. Something happened to her, and he freaked out.

That was just a general Hayden and Jill rule for life.

"Because I needed to pay my respects to Christy."

The guilt was there, sliding into her voice. "Jill..." Hayden began.

"Then I realized I wasn't alone."

His eyes narrowed.

"I heard someone in the woods right behind the cemetery. I called out to him and he ran."

His hand lifted to feather over her cheek. "So you followed him."

Her lips curled. "Of course. I'm an FBI agent. It's what I do."

You run into danger. Didn't he do the same thing? As a SEAL, he'd gotten addicted to the rush of adrenaline. To the thrill of the hunt. The blaze of battle.

"He had his vehicle stashed on Widow's Way."

He knew the old road that cut behind the cemetery. It had gotten the nickname because long ago, a widow who'd lost her husband at sea had traveled back and forth along that path every single day, desperate to see her husband.

"I tried to stop him but he...well, he had other plans." Her small nostrils flared. "The guy revved the engine and came right at me, even when I was trying to leap to safety. He *aimed* for me." Her gaze fell to her hands. Maybe he'd gone a little crazy with the bandages. "I was lucky to walk away with a few scrapes."

That driver wasn't going to be lucky when Hayden got hold of him.

"Probably some punk," she murmured, "looking to make some quick cash by robbing a visitor at the cemetery. And since you said the car was stolen."

"It was. A few days ago."

She nodded. "Obviously, we seem to have a guy who likes to steal. He's probably long gone, but the APB might give us a shot at catching him before he slips from town."

Maybe. If the guy's plan was to vanish. "You said he was watching you?" Alarm bells were going off in his head.

"Yes, probably trying to decide if I was worth robbing. His mistake. Robbing an FBI agent is never a good plan."

No, it wasn't but…

He stared into her eyes. The greenest eyes he'd ever seen.

"I forgot about the gold," Jill whispered.

What?

"Hidden in the darkness…" Her head tilted as she stared into his eyes. "You have a warm gold in your eyes."

His heart slammed into his chest. He became aware of just how close they were, of how intimate their position was. His lower body brushed against hers, his hands were on her. He—

A fist pounded against his office door, making the already wobbly door rattle. "Sheriff!" Finn called. "Sheriff, we got him!"

Jill's eyes widened. Hayden spun away and rushed out of the bathroom and toward his office door. He yanked open the door and found Finn beaming at him.

"Got the car," Finn said. "Deputy Hollow just spotted it near the West End Beach."

THE SUV WAS at the West End, all right, but there was no sign of the driver. Hayden put his hands on his hips as he surveyed the scene.

"Guess the guy up in Jacksonville will be real glad to get his ride back, huh?" Deputy Wendy Hollow murmured, her lips curling. The sun had set and the only light on them came from the bright moon over their heads. The West End Beach was the most remote beach in the area. Locals were the only ones who ever came down there because most of the tourists didn't even know it existed, a deliberate secret.

For the SUV to be abandoned there…

"The driver had to go someplace," Hayden said. He looked around, but there was no sign of another civilian vehicle, just Deputy Hollow's patrol car and his vehicle—Hayden had gotten Jill to drive over with him. "Not like the guy just vanished into thin air."

"We can check the car for prints," Jill said as she stood near him. "The suspect probably left plenty of evidence behind. He was looking to ditch the car and make a break for it. Our run-in at the cemetery probably scared him."

Hayden still wasn't so sure of that fact. During the past ten years, he'd learned to never ignore his instincts. When he was in the field, they always warned him when danger was coming. Right then, his instincts were screaming at him.

Jill was being watched at the cemetery. Now the vehicle her watcher used is abandoned and the driver is long gone. He turned toward her. "I think you should have protection tonight."

She laughed.

He didn't. "I'm serious, Jill. This scene…" He waved his hand. "It's not right. It's…off…and you know it."

"I'm an FBI agent, I think I can manage to look after myself tonight." She turned away.

He followed right on her heels. Hayden reached out and curled his hand around her shoulder.

She looked back at him, frowning. "Hayden…"

"Even FBI agents need protection."

"Look, I get that things are personal between us, but

I just have a few scratches. It wasn't anything life threatening."

"He tried to run you down!"

"Because he panicked." She looked over his shoulder, gazing at the abandoned SUV. "Prints are going to turn up in there. You'll find the guy, I have no doubt. The streets of Hope will be safe again."

But would *she* be safe?

Jill didn't seem worried.

Hayden sure as hell was. Because…

This is you, Jill. And I will always protect you.

HE'D MADE A mistake at the cemetery. He should have stayed farther back. Should have kept his distance.

But he'd wanted to get closer.

She'd looked so sad as she stood there, staring at the grave. She'd seemed such perfect prey. All alone. Prime for the taking. But…

Then he'd heard her voice, barking with authority, reminding him that she wasn't the girl he'd known before. She was an FBI agent now and he hadn't been able to tell if she was armed.

If she'd had her gun…if she'd shot at him…

I don't want to die. That was his truth. He wasn't anywhere near ready to die.

So he'd run. Fast. Hard. He'd fled and when she'd come rushing out of the woods, well, he'd taken that opportunity to end her. But he'd missed. She'd seen his car, and he'd had to dump it.

No big deal. He'd taken the vehicle when he'd been in Jacksonville. Taken it because…

Some habits die hard. I always liked to keep a throwaway vehicle close, in case I find a special girl.

Jill West was a very special girl to him. Very special,

indeed. The one that got away. The one that had changed so much for him.

He glanced up at her beachfront cabin. It was dark now because she was gone. Probably out hunting for him. *Never expected that I'd be waiting at home for you, did you, Jillian?* But here he was…

And he'd stay in the shadows. He'd wait until she came back. And then the real fun would begin. Because he'd carefully considered the situation with her. He didn't want to launch an attack straight at her, no, with her FBI training, that wasn't a fight he wanted.

He'd take the easy way. The better way.

He'd attack Jill when she was vulnerable. And the most vulnerable time for a woman? For *anyone*?

That would be during sleep. When Jill slipped away in her dreams, he'd go to her. He'd wait and bide his time and he'd watch. But the moment her guard was lowered, he would be there.

And, Jill, you will pay for everything that you took away from me.

Chapter Five

Her little rental cabin was dark when Jill pulled into the narrow drive. She'd stayed at the scene with Hayden, she'd helped search the area, but the driver had been long gone. Maybe he'd slipped away on some of the trails in the area. Maybe he'd had another ride waiting.

The maybes hadn't mattered. One fact was clear—he was gone, and it was highly doubtful they'd find the guy that night.

Hayden had taken her back to the station. She'd gotten her car, refused his protection one more time, and she'd pretended not to see the frustration that had filled his gaze. Spending the night with Hayden *wasn't* a good idea. She knew that.

Her feelings for him were too raw. When he'd been bandaging her hands in that little bathroom, she'd stared at him and just ached.

Too many memories were between them. Too much desire still remained.

When she climbed up the long flight of wooden steps that led to her cabin, Jill felt a bone-deep weariness. She unlocked the door. The wind blew off the ocean, bringing her the salty scent on the breeze. Jill looked back at that water. The waves gleamed beneath the moonlight.

The water had always soothed her, even when she'd been at her absolute worst.

The water...and Hayden. Her two constants in life.

Jill turned away from the ocean. She shut the door behind her and flipped the lock. There was no security system at the cabin, so she took a few moments to do a quick search and to double-check all of the locks on the windows and on the screen door that slipped away from the kitchen and led back to the big front deck. Side effect of the job...being hypervigilant. She'd seen too many horror stories, firsthand.

Jill headed into her bedroom. When she passed the TV, the floor gave a low groan. She couldn't help but tense at the sound. *This day has been too long.* Now she was nearly jumping at—quite literally—nothing. She'd shower and crash into bed. And maybe, if she was lucky, she wouldn't dream about two bright headlights coming toward her. She wouldn't remember the heat of the engine as it growled beside her.

If she was lucky.

HAYDEN SLOWED HIS vehicle as he slowly drove by Jill's cabin. One light glowed in her cabin. Jill was still awake. She'd refused his multiple offers of protection.

And he got it, he really did. She could take care of herself. Hell, yes, he'd read the stories about her work. Jill had often been in the headlines, particularly when she worked high-profile cases. She'd taken down some of the worst scum out there. He knew she was smart, tough and absolutely deadly with her gun but...

But this is Jill. If something happens to her, I worry I'll lose my damn sanity.

His hands tightened on the steering wheel.

And, as if on cue, the light in her cabin turned off.

Jill was in, safe and sound, for the night. Time for him to get the hell out of there. He accelerated but... Hayden couldn't help glancing back in his rearview mirror.

This is Jill. If something happens to her...

WAKEFULNESS CAME IN a sudden rush. One instant, Jill had been completely asleep, lost to her dreams, but in the next, her eyes were wide-open and a cold chill iced her blood.

She didn't move in that bed. Her heart galloped in her chest. She had an animal awareness crawling over her— *something is wrong*. Something had woken her, but she didn't know what. She didn't move so much as a finger as she tried to figure out what had brought her awake with such a sharpness.

Then...she heard the scraping. A small, faint sound. And...

She knew what caused that sound. When she'd opened the sliding glass door before—the door that led from the kitchen to the front deck, the screen had scraped when the door slid open. Wind and time had damaged the screen and when the door slid open a few inches, the screen scraped.

But she'd checked that door before bed. She *remembered* checking the lock. The door had been closed. There was no reason for it to scrape now.

Unless someone is out there.

Her fingers slowly moved toward the pillow on the other side of her bed. Before she'd gone to bed, she'd put her weapon there, wanting it to be close just in case. Her fingers touched the gun.

And she heard a groan.

This time, the sound was a little bit louder. As if the groan had come from the den. And again, she knew that sound...when she'd walked in front of the TV out there, the floor had groaned beneath her feet. There was a weak spot of wood. A spot that creaked when someone stepped on it.

Someone is out there. Someone is coming closer.

She'd shut her bedroom door. Locked it but...

Did she hear the soft click of that lock turning? Was it her imagination?

Jill took a deep breath. Her index finger slid off the safety of her gun. Her eyes had adjusted to the darkness and she was staring straight at her door.

It was opening.

"Freeze!" Jill yelled. "Freeze or I will shoot."

The door stilled. Each breath she took seemed far too loud.

Then...

Laughter. Cold. Mocking laughter. "You think you're the only one with a gun, Agent West?"

Oh, damn.

"You should have left Christy Anderson alone." The snarled words came from her doorway.

She dived for the side of the bed even as the thunder of a gunshot filled the room. *You missed!* She stayed low but Jill lifted up just enough to fire back.

But he was running. She could hear the thunder of her intruder's footsteps. Jill didn't hesitate. She jumped to her feet and rushed after him. "Stop!" she yelled.

He didn't. He *did* fire wildly back at her and Jill had to duck when the bullet sank into the wood a few inches away from her. The screen door scraped and his footsteps thudded over the wooden steps outside.

She should call for backup. Jill knew it, but she also knew if she stopped long enough to call the sheriff's office, her intruder would be long gone.

So she clutched her gun and she ran after him. When she got on the long line of wooden steps that led down to the beach, she saw him fleeing beneath the light of the moon. A man, tall, with broad shoulders. He was moving fast, too fast. Sand kicked up around his feet.

"Stop!" Jill yelled.

But he didn't.

And neither did she.

SO HE WAS OBSESSED. Hayden knew he had a problem. When it came to Jill, it was a very, very long-standing problem.

It was the middle of the night and he couldn't sleep. And he was driving by her cabin again because he obviously had issues.

But when his headlights cut across the beach, he caught a glimpse of a woman running—a woman wearing a T-shirt and shorts.

A woman with a gun clutched in her hand.

Jill.

He slammed on the brakes. Hayden grabbed his own gun from the glove box and took off after her. His heart pounded a double-time rhythm in his chest. Jill was zig-zagging in front of him, rushing frantically down the beach and kicking up sand in her wake. The moonlight shone down on her and—

And on the jerk she's chasing.

Because Hayden could see him. A dark, shadowy form about twenty feet in front of Jill. A shadow that was whirling back around and lifting his gun. *Firing.*

"Jill!" Hayden bellowed.

But she'd already ducked. The gunfire blasted and Hayden *thought* it had missed her. He prayed it had. The guy seemed to be shooting wildly now, panicking. Whoever the hell that man was, he'd better be afraid.

This was Hayden's town.

He drove himself faster, faster, determined to catch

the jerk up ahead. But the man had rushed off the beach, heading toward another dark cabin. A moment later, the growl of an engine reached Hayden's ears.

He saw a motorcycle hurtle from beneath that cabin. The motorcycle rushed into the darkness, flying away with its light off and the driver not even looking back.

Jill lifted her gun and aimed after him. Then she shook her head and Hayden heard her curse.

He ran to her, grabbed her arm and swung her toward him. "Jill!" His gaze flew frantically over her, but he didn't see any injures. "Baby, are you okay?"

"No, I'm not." She jerked away from him. "He got away!" She still had her gun gripped in her hand. "Should have known he had a getaway vehicle close by." Jill whirled on her heel—her bare heel because he realized she was shoeless—and glared into the night.

Hayden yanked out his phone. "Not gone yet." He connected with the sheriff's office. He started barking orders to Dispatch even as he grabbed Jill's arm. They ran back toward his vehicle and he pushed her into the passenger's side. "We're tailing the suspect now," Hayden said into his phone. "Get backup out here…this guy is armed and dangerous and I'm not having him run wild over *my* town."

He threw the SUV into reverse. The wheels squealed as he gave chase. "Tell me what in the hell happened."

Jill flattened her palm against the dashboard. "I woke up…and I heard him coming into the cabin."

What?

"He came to my bedroom."

The SOB was going to pay.

"I told him to stop, that I had a gun."

His foot had rammed the accelerator all the way to the floorboard.

"And he told me that he did, too. Then he fired."

His hands had fisted around the steering wheel. "You're not hurt." He needed to hear her say those words again.

"I'm not." She leaned forward. "I don't see him." Frustration hummed in her words.

He didn't see the guy, either. The road they were on was long and twisting, and it didn't connect with the highway for another six miles. He was hoping one of his deputies would cut off that highway entrance—that had been his order. The deputy would block the guy from the front and Hayden would get the guy from the back.

Provided, of course, that the guy on the motorcycle didn't go off road. If he did, if he slipped onto any of the trails around there…

We lose him.

HE HAD TO get off the bike. He risked a quick glance behind him and saw the glare of two headlights. He had a lead, a damn good one, but Jill would make sure everyone in Hope was looking for a man on a motorcycle. She'd get an APB out on him, and he'd be hunted.

I have to ditch this thing.

Where and when…hell, that was the question. It was dark, so that worked to his advantage. If he cut across the sand, his tracks wouldn't be spotted until the sun was up.

He could go through the woods. Follow a trail. Ditch the bike there or…

The scent of the ocean teased him.

Or he could try a different escape path.

He drove off the road. The bike spit up sand as the wheels churned. The beach was deserted, as it freakin' well should have been at that time of the night. He ditched the bike, tucked his gun into the back of his jeans and his gloved fingers fisted as he ran right toward the surf.

Jill could get every deputy in the area to search the roads for him, but he wasn't escaping via land.

He was heading for the water. The last place they'd expect to look. *Search the roads all night. Search every trail. I won't be there.*

The water lapped at his feet.

Good thing he was a strong swimmer.

THEY REACHED THE highway and Hayden braked when he saw the flash of patrol lights. Deputy Hollow stood beside her car, her hand on her holster. Hayden jumped out and ran toward her, aware that Jill was following close beside him. "Tell me you saw the guy," he said.

But Wendy shook her head. "Sorry...no one has come past me."

He whirled back around and stared at the darkness behind him.

"He diverted," Jill said. "He wanted to stay off the main road. He was planning this from the beginning, that's why he was on a motorcycle. Easier for him to slip into the woods."

To vanish.

"Get more units out here," Hayden ordered. "I want to search every trail. This guy is armed, he's been shooting, and I want him taken down."

Wendy nodded quickly and she slid into her car as she contacted Dispatch. Jill started to rush by Hayden, but he caught her arm. "What are you doing?"

"I'm going to help search. When backup arrives, we can coordinate into teams to divide the area and—"

"You don't even have shoes on your feet!" He pulled her closer. His voice dropped as he said, "I told you that you were in danger."

He heard the stutter of her breath. "Hayden, I'm fine."

"He shot at you." And that shook him, straight to his core. "I should have been with you. I should have—"

"We've covered this before." Now her voice was nearly a whisper. "How many times do I have to tell you, you can't protect me twenty-four hours a day?"

It was an old argument between them. Actually, it was one of the things that had driven them apart. When it came to Jill, he held on too tight.

He wanted too much.

Hayden glanced down at his hands. *Too tight.* He forced himself to let her go.

"He said something else."

Hayden shook his head, not following her.

"Before he fired at me, in my bedroom, he said…he said I should have left Christy Anderson alone."

Every muscle in his body locked down.

"I was at Christy's grave earlier…so I think…it must be the same man from the cemetery," Jill continued, her voice strained. "I thought he was there to rob me, but…"

"He came tonight to kill you." Brutal words, but if the man had broken into her home with a gun… Hayden's control snapped. He wrapped his hands around her shoulders again and yanked her close. *"I should have been there."*

"Hayden…"

"You just came back. And I could have lost you already." Hell, no. *No.* This wasn't happening. He wouldn't let it happen. "We're finding that sicko, and I'm going to make sure that he *never* hurts you again."

THE TRACKS WERE found near dawn, when the streaks of light crept across the sky and showed where the motorcycle had slipped off the road. The guy had been good, Jill would give him that much. He'd hidden the bike behind the dunes to make it harder to spot. The shifting sands had already blown over part of the line that had been left by the motorcycle's tires.

He must have walked away after he'd ditched the bike, but the sand was perfectly smooth as it led to the water. No sign of his footprints.

He knew those would be gone by dawn.

They'd been searching the area all night. Hayden had made sure she got shoes, and she'd made sure she was involved in the hunt. But despite their efforts, they hadn't come across the intruder. Maybe that was because he hadn't been on land. Her eyes narrowed as she stared at those waves.

Hayden was at her side, silent, angry. She could feel the frustration rolling off him.

"This man knows the town," Jill said. Not just the town…the whole area. He knew the private beaches, he knew the back roads. He knew the water.

They weren't looking for some drifter.

"The fact that he mentioned Christy, that he came for me…" Jill turned to stare at Hayden. "I think—"

"We're going to pay a visit to the Anderson family," he said.

Her stomach tightened. A trip to visit the Andersons had been on her agenda even before this madness had started. Christy's father had been so angry with her years ago, and when she'd been a teen and their paths had crossed in town, he'd always stared at her with such a cold, hard gaze.

She knew he hated her.

But…

Was he enraged enough to have come after her with a gun?

Chapter Six

The Andersons still lived at 1509 Sea Breeze Way. Jill climbed out of Hayden's car—his patrol car, not his SUV, he'd switched vehicles since he was on official business—and she slammed the door shut as she stared up at the house. It was clean, perfectly tidy with neatly trimmed hedges and a well-swept sidewalk. The house appeared to have been freshly painted white, and the shutters were a light blue to match the ocean.

From the outside, it looked like such a happy home. Such a normal place.

She knew just how deceiving appearances could truly be. She'd walked up to too many houses—ordinary houses just like the one at 1509 Sea Breeze Way—and found monsters living inside.

"Jill?"

She shook her head and glanced over at Hayden. He was wearing his sheriff's uniform. The badge shone in the light. They'd been up for most of the night and a line of dark stubble coated his jaw. He looked strong and…sexy.

And she really shouldn't be noticing that fact right then. She had enough to deal with as it was.

"You okay?" He moved to her side. His head cocked as he studied her. "For a minute there, I could have sworn that you were a million miles away."

Because she had been. "Sometimes, houses look perfect. Lives look perfect." She shook her head. "But they aren't."

He glanced back at the Andersons' house.

"In the case file, there were only minimal notes about her family. Peek never interrogated the father or mother. He just got general details from them about Christy, what she was wearing, what she'd done right before her disappearance…" Her words trailed away, and Jill pressed her hands to the top of her thighs. She wore dress pants and a crisp white shirt…what Jill thought of as her FBI gear. A light coat hid her holster. When working a case, it was standard protocol for agents to dress a certain way, and she'd gotten into the habit of almost arming herself with the clothing.

"You think they should have been interrogated?"

A curtain moved inside of the house. Someone was watching them. "Every case that CARD works…we *always* question the family." They were the starting point. And often, they were the very first suspects. "The first time I worked a case as an official CARD team member, I was looking for an eight-year-old boy who'd gone missing from his house in Birmingham, Alabama. His mother said that someone had come in during the night and taken him. There were signs of a struggle and his bedroom window was found open." Her hand lifted and, this time, her fingers pressed to her heart. It had started to ache. "Thirty minutes after we started to interview the mom, we noticed the inconsistencies in her story."

"Hell."

She pressed harder against her chest. "We found his body in the shed."

He caught her hand. Pulled her close. "I'm so sorry, Jill."

"Monsters," she whispered, blinking away the tears.

"They're everywhere. I thought I'd join the FBI and save people, but that isn't happening, and I don't know what I—" She broke off because the door to 1509 Sea Breeze Way had just opened. "This isn't the right time," she said, her voice as soft as the wind blowing against them. "They're watching."

Hayden slowly turned toward the house. He moved so that his body was in front of hers, a deliberate position, she knew. A protective one. *Some things never change.* Jill swiped her hands over her cheeks, but the skin was dry. She hadn't let the tears fall.

She couldn't remember the last time they'd fallen.

I didn't cry when we lost Jessica. I stared at the ambulance with dry eyes. I didn't cry when I talked to her family. I was just...too numb.

That was how she felt most days. Numb.

But...she didn't feel numb when Hayden was near her.

"You shouldn't be sheriff." The words were angry as they spewed from the man standing in that doorway.

Hayden gave a grim nod. "Hello, Mr. Anderson. Nice to see you, too."

A grunt came from Theodore Anderson.

Jill slipped to Hayden's side so that she could study the other man. Theodore Anderson was tall, still fit, but his blond hair had thinned. He was dressed in faded jeans and a loose sweatshirt. The lines on his face were deep, and his lips were pulled down in a frown as he gazed at Hayden.

"You aren't qualified for the job. I don't care what kind of war hero crap you pulled overseas," Theodore snapped. "Your father was a bum, a criminal who deserved exactly what he got, and you have no place—"

Hayden lifted his hand, stopping the guy's snarled words. "I *am* the sheriff here, and it would be wise to speak to me with a little more respect."

Theodore's face flashed red.

"I know you haven't had an easy time of things," Hayden said, voice curt, "but you need to calm yourself down, right now."

Theodore's chin jerked up. "What do you want?"

Hayden glanced at Jill, then he looked back at Theodore. "We have some questions for you."

"Questions? About what?" But Theodore's gaze had slid to Jill and he stared at her suspiciously. She didn't see recognition in his stare, not yet, his eyes were narrowed as they locked on her face.

"This FBI agent is following up on Christy's disappearance," Hayden said.

He hadn't told Theodore her name. Why? Did he think he was protecting her?

She wasn't going to hide. Jill cleared her throat and stepped forward. "I'm FBI Agent Jillian West."

And there it was. The recognition, flooding his face and turning his eyes cold and angry in a flash. His jaw locked and he glared at her with pure hate in his eyes. "Get *off* my property."

"Mr. Anderson, I'm investigating Christy's disappearance." The fact that the joker who'd taken a shot at her had mentioned Christy, well, that had just made her more determined than ever to find out the truth. "I'd like to ask you some questions about her last day with you."

"Why the hell are you digging that up now? Christy is gone!" His eyes glittered. "Dead and buried in the Jamison Cemetery."

"Yes, about that," Hayden murmured as he cocked his head and studied the other man. "When was the last time you were at that cemetery?"

"I go every week," Theodore fired back. "I make sure my daughter's grave is clean. That she is taken care of. I didn't take care of her while she was alive, but I will damn well do it while she's dead."

He doesn't just blame me for Christy's death. He blames himself, too. Jill could see that.

"And the date of your last visit was…?" Hayden asked.

"Yesterday. I go every Saturday, okay?"

So he'd just admitted to being there, the same day that someone had been watching her. *The same day someone tried to run me down.*

"Did you happen to see anyone while you were there?" Hayden's voice was mild.

"Why in the hell are you asking that?" Theodore shook his head. "No, I didn't see anyone. It was just me, got it? I swept her grave off, I put down fresh flowers and I left." Theodore took an aggressive step toward them. "FBI *special* agent," he said, lips twisting in distaste. "You think I haven't heard the stories about you, too? You go out there, you get your name in the papers and you—"

"And I try to bring home the children who were taken." She kept her voice calm with an effort. "I try to find children like Christy who were stolen from their families and I try to bring them back home, safe and sound so that their parents don't have to go and visit cemeteries every single week."

For an instant, his face crumpled.

"I'm in Hope for a little while, and I wanted to see if I could use my resources to bring closure to Christy's case."

His lips were trembling.

"I want to find the man who hurt her. I know you blame me for what happened to her—"

He turned away from Jill. "Hard to look at you," he rasped.

"Mr. Anderson—"

"Hard to look at you…because Christy would've been your age. I see you and I see everything I lost." He still wasn't looking at her. Maybe he couldn't, not any longer. "I see you…and I'm always reminded you came home, and she didn't."

His grief was heavy in the air.

His shoulders hunched. "My wife…she left me a few years back. Said she couldn't take it any longer. No more living with Christy's ghost, the pain was too much for her. She moved up to Washington. Took my son with her but he came back at least. Kurt's staying with me now. He's all I have left."

"I want to find her killer," Jill told him. "But I need your help."

Theodore still wasn't looking at her. "Peek said the guy was a drifter. In town probably just for the weekend. Took you, but you got away. So he took my Christy. Killed her and was long gone even before we found the body."

"That is one option." Jill shared a long glance with Hayden. "But there are others." Especially in light of her late-night visitor.

Theodore turned to frown at her. "What do you think happened?"

"I don't think a man like this would just kill one girl and never target anyone else again."

He backed up a step. His gaze fell.

"He took me, I got away, so he immediately acted again." Her lips pressed together. "I think it's fair to say he could have other victims out there, too. Back when he killed Christy, it was harder for authorities to connect the dots, especially when killers went across state lines or when they chose victims who had different ages or sexes. It was harder to piece together profiles because all of the information was so scattered."

Theodore swiped his hand over his face. She noticed that his fingers trembled.

"I want to help Christy. That's why I need to talk to you about the day she went missing. I want to know if you saw anything or anyone who was suspicious. If Christy mentioned *anyone* watching her. If she—"

"She was a good girl. She went to softball practice first thing that morning. She rode away on her bike." He glanced toward the garage. "And she never came back home. Her bike...it was found on the side of the road. Just left behind and she was gone. No one saw anything." His chin trembled as his stare jerked back to Hayden. "There was no one to race after my girl."

Hayden's hands had fisted.

"She died alone and that fact haunts me every single day of my life. I can hear her, in my mind." He tapped his temple. "I think she probably cried for me. And I wasn't there. I couldn't help her... *I wasn't there.*"

"Mr. Anderson—" Jill began.

He shook his head. "I need you to leave. I don't...I just can't talk to you any more now." His voice wasn't angry. He just suddenly seemed very, very tired.

She *needed* his help but she couldn't force his cooperation. Jill pulled a discrete white card from her pocket. She stepped toward him and held out the card. "This is my contact information. If you change your mind, please call me."

His gaze lingered on the card, but he made no move to take it.

"With or without your cooperation, I plan to continue my investigation." Because obviously, there was a lot for her to learn in that town. She didn't lower her hand. She kept that card extended.

The seconds ticked by. Then his hand reached up and he snatched the card from her. He turned, his movements angry and jerky and—he stilled. "I know you were there that day."

Jill looked back at Hayden. He was staring at Theodore Anderson, with his eyes narrowed and his face locked in tight lines.

"When I came to your grandmother's house, drunk, desperate, I know you were there." His hand had curled tightly around her card, crumpling it.

A car's engine rumbled and Jill saw a big, sleek vehicle pull to a stop near Hayden's patrol car. A tall man with sandy-blond hair and wide shoulders jumped from the fancy car. "Dad?" The man's voice rose. "Dad, what's happening? What's wrong?"

But Theodore didn't look at the man who was rushing toward him. "When I came to that house, I said you should have died in her place."

She didn't let herself flinch.

"It was wrong, and I knew it…"

"Dad?"

Jill knew the man staring at them in confusion was Christy's older brother, Kurt. He'd been in class with Hayden. A quiet, intense boy with bright blue eyes.

"What's happening here?" Kurt demanded once more.

"It's still wrong," Theodore whispered. "But I still…I feel the same way. I wish you were in the ground and my Christy was here with me." Then he shuffled up the steps that led back to his house.

Her heart was squeezing in her chest.

Kurt moved to follow his father, and then he stopped, glaring at Hayden. "Okay, Hayden, tell me what is going on."

Jill swallowed. "We're investigating Christy's death."

His eyes sharpened on her. "Jill?" Shock deepened his voice.

She gave him a tight smile. "Hello, Kurt. It's been a long time." As if following his father's lead, he'd never spoken to her much in school. In fact, he'd seemed to take deliberate pains to avoid her.

His focus jumped between her and Hayden. "You brought *her* to see my dad? 'Cause you thought that was a good idea?" His skepticism was clear.

"It was *my* idea," Jill said before Hayden could answer. "I wanted to talk to Mr. Anderson about the day Christy disappeared."

Kurt raked his hand through his hair. "Right. Let's just rub salt in that wound, why don't we?" He shook his head. "Christy is buried. Just let her rest in peace."

She was stunned by that answer. "Don't you *want* to find her killer?"

"My father is one year and seven months sober. *One year. Seven months.* I just got him back. I didn't plan on losing everyone in my family, but that's what happened when Christy was found on that beach. My whole world splintered apart." He heaved out a breath. "So just let it all go, got it? The past is dead and buried. Leave Christy alone."

You should have left Christy Anderson alone.

A chill skated down her spine.

Kurt hurried up the steps and followed his father inside of the house. She turned back to Hayden. His jaw had locked.

"They're not going to help, Jill," he said softly.

He was right but… "That doesn't mean I'm going to stop."

His lips hitched into that little half smile of his. The smile that always made her feel a bit warmer. "No, I didn't think that you would."

"Are they gone?" Theodore Anderson demanded.

Kurt peered through the window. He'd eased the curtains back just a bit so he could see outside. "They're getting into the patrol car now." Hayden had opened the passenger side door for Jill, and when she passed the sheriff, he noticed the guy's hand lingered just a moment on her arm.

Still as obsessed with her as ever. Everyone had known that truth in school. Hayden Black loved Jill West. The two had been inseparable. Until Hayden walked away from Jill. Most folks still didn't even know he'd left her. But Hayden had gone off to be all he could be, and Jill...

FBI special agent Jill West. "She just wants to help," he said, feeling sad for her. For them all.

"We don't need her help. Christy is at peace now. It's time to move the hell on."

Hayden was walking around the car, but his gaze lifted and, just for a moment, his stare seemed to lock on Kurt.

Kurt let go of the curtain and stepped back.

"Christy is dead and buried," his father muttered. "She deserves her peace. She doesn't need some FBI agent picking around at her...hell, this isn't some TV show. No one's going to go digging up my girl—"

Kurt's eyes widened as he spun to face his dad. "Is that what she wanted to do?"

His father was pacing, his movements tight and angry. "That's what they do on TV! They exhume the bodies, look for evidence and run all their tests."

Look for evidence. Kurt swallowed. "You don't want that to happen?"

Tears glittered in his father's eyes. "She's at peace now. I want her to stay that way. And I—I don't want to bury her again." His dad's face crumpled. "I need a drink."

"No," Kurt snapped out the denial. "That's the last thing you need." He closed the distance between them and put his hand on his dad's shoulder. "I'll take care of Jill West, okay? Don't worry about her. Christy can have her peace. I'll make sure of it."

JILL WAS DEAD on her feet. Not that she'd ever admit it, Hayden realized, but he could see the weariness pulling at her.

He eased his patrol car to a stop next to her cabin. The sun was dipping low over the ocean, striking the waves a dark red. It had been one hell of a day. They'd spent hours searching for her intruder, going over crime scene details, getting the motorcycle checked for prints.

Only there hadn't been any.

Just as there hadn't been any prints left on the stolen SUV that had been abandoned on the West End.

"Thanks for the ride back," Jill murmured.

Oh, she thought he'd just given her a ride? That was cute. Sweet.

She climbed from the car and her fingers moved in a little wave. "Guess we'll pick up tomorrow?"

Um, no.

"Good night." She slammed the door shut and headed for her cabin.

The same cabin some creep had broken into the night before. The same place that had meager locks and far too easy access.

He slid out of the vehicle and followed behind her.

Jill stopped and glanced over her shoulder. "Is there a problem?"

A very big one. "How long do you think it will take you to get your things?"

Her eyes widened. "My…things?"

"Yes, you know…fresh clothes. Your laptop, any other items that you feel you can't live without tonight."

"Why would I need my things?" She put her hands on her hips and faced him.

He stalked closer to her. All day long, he'd been walking on a tightrope. That rope was way too close to snapping.

He came after Jill. He'd shot at her. "You aren't staying here alone tonight."

Her eyes widened. "Uh, excuse me?"

"That intruder—"

"I think I did a pretty good job of defending myself."

She didn't get it. "Do you want me to stay sane?"

Her brow furrowed. "That would probably be a good plan."

He thought so, too. Hayden nodded. "Then you're staying with me tonight. I'll have a deputy keep watch on your place."

She crossed her arms over her chest. "Did you just tell me I was staying at your place?"

"I did." He inclined his head toward her.

"I'm not afraid, Hayden. If he comes back, I'll be ready for him. I'll be—"

"I know you're not scared." He got that. What she didn't get… "I am."

She laughed. "Right, the big, bad navy SEAL is afraid. You're—"

"Absolutely terrified that something will happen to you."

Her smile slipped away. His hand rose and his fingers slid into the thickness of her hair as he tilted her head back and stared into her eyes. "You just don't get that, do you, Jill? You don't see how important you are to me."

"So important that you walked away." There was pain in her words. Pain that he *hated*.

"I wasn't going to stand in your way. I cared about you too much for that."

Her lips parted.

"What was the *one* thing you always wanted to do?" Hayden pushed.

She licked her lips. "Join the FBI."

He nodded. "And you did. You're a great agent, I know that. I also know that you had to leave Hope to follow that dream." His thumb brushed over her cheek. "So you had to leave me."

Her eyes seemed to flash at him. "I didn't leave you. You're the one who walked away from *me*. The one who wanted adventure. The world...because I wasn't enough."

No, that wasn't what he'd thought. Not ever. "You were always enough." Then, because he wouldn't lie to her, Hayden confessed. "*I* wasn't."

Everyone in town had known that truth. Why hadn't she?

"Hayden..."

"You're the FBI agent," he murmured. "But I'm the town sheriff. Right now, my authority trumps yours. You're the crime victim in this case, not the investigator." He couldn't stop touching her. "So you have two choices. One, you come with me. You stay the night at my house."

"That's an interesting take on protective custody," she said, voice wry.

Oh, he'd make sure she was protected plenty. "Option two, we both stay at your cabin tonight." And if her late-night visitor came back, they'd both be ready.

"Option three," Jill added, "I stay by myself and you get back in your patrol car."

"It's not happening. You were nearly killed *twice* in the past twenty-four hours. My job is to keep the people of my town safe. *You're* one of those people, FBI badge or not. So you're either coming with me or I'll be bunking down with you."

He waited for more arguments. He waited...

"You know, when you're this close and when you touch like that...I keep expecting you to kiss me."

Okay, he hadn't expected *that* response. His heartbeat kicked up. "Do you *want* me to kiss you?"

"That's the problem, Hayden. I'm not sure what I want from you. Sometimes, I want you as far away from me as you can get."

Hell.

"And other times…" Her voice had gone so soft. "I feel like you're the one person in the world I need to hold close. Hold you close and tight."

And never let go. Because that was the way he felt about her. He wanted to grab Jill and hold her close, keep her safe and never, ever let her go again.

"You know what's better than one FBI agent waiting for a perp to attack?" Jill asked.

She was losing him. He wanted to get back to talking about her needing him close.

"An FBI agent *and* a sheriff waiting…that's what is better. So I'll take option two. You can bunk down on the couch." She stepped back.

His hand fell to his side.

"*Just* the couch, Hayden. I'm not offering anything else."

If only she was. She marched toward the cabin.

"Jill!" Hayden called.

She kept walking.

He smiled after her. "When you figure out what it is that you want from me, just let me know." *Hold you close. Never let go.* "After all, I'll be on your couch, so you just come out and tell me."

She gave a little snarl. His smile stretched. Maybe she didn't see it, but he was making progress with her. Real progress.

They just might have a real chance together.

If they could just put the past to rest.

Chapter Seven

"Do you still have nightmares?"

Hayden's quiet question caught Jill off guard. She'd just pulled an extra blanket from the hall closet, and she looked toward him, grasping that blanket close to her body.

"You used to have them a lot," he noted. "I was…just curious."

She hurried across the room and put the blanket on the sofa, right next to the extra pillows she'd already gotten out for him. "Worried I'll wake you up with my screams?" Jill backed away from the couch and turned—only to find him right in her path.

"No, that's not what I'm worried about. I'm worried about *you*."

Her breath whispered out.

"And you didn't answer my question. Do you still have nightmares?"

"Not the same ones I used to have." Terrible dreams about being back in that little cabin, only she'd been alone there. Hayden had never appeared. She'd been tied up, helpless and then the man in the baseball cap had opened the door. "Now I dream about my cases, about the victims that I don't get to find in time." They haunted her. "Excuse me." She stepped around him.

"You did find a lot of them in time, though," he said. "You've saved lives, Jill."

Her shoulders stiffened.

"The little boy in South Carolina, the one who was taken after he got off his school bus...you got to him in time."

She'd found the boy in the trunk of his abductor's car. The kid had been terrified, shaking and ice-cold because a sudden winter storm had swept into the area. "Another few hours," she said, remembering, "and I think Matt would have frozen to death."

"And what about the little girl in Mississippi? The one that was taken from her family's campsite?"

"Lula Jane."

He nodded.

"We got her right before the woman who'd abducted Lula..." Jill's lips pressed together. "We found Lula Jane before that woman had a chance to use her knife on the little girl."

"Those are just two of the kids you've saved. I read about your work in articles on the internet. I know there are dozens more."

Her gaze met his. "And dozens lost. You know what hits you worse? The ones that you find too late. They're the ones who wreck you, Hayden. They're the ones who haunt you." She paced toward her bedroom.

"So you *do* still have nightmares."

Her fingers pressed to the wall near her door. "Only some nights."

Silence. Then... "I still have them, too."

She glanced over her shoulder. "After all you've done, Mr. Navy SEAL, I don't—"

"The worst nightmares are about you. Not getting to you in time. Finding *you* dead on the beach."

Her breath chilled her lungs.

"But I have new nightmares, too. About my missions. About friends that fell in battle. About detonations going off right in front of me as I watch people I cared about get blown apart. Those dreams are always silent...weird, but... I think it's because when the explosions really happened, I couldn't hear anything for a few seconds after them. Usually about ten seconds. I counted once...it took ten full seconds before I could hear the screams."

She closed her eyes. How many times had she been awake late at night, wondering about him? Worrying? She'd gone to her contact at the CIA just so she could find out where he was. She'd bent rules because she'd needed to know he was safe.

Alive.

Her eyes slowly opened. "Those dreams sound like pure hell." She made herself face toward her bedroom again. But she didn't step inside. She didn't leave Hayden, not yet.

The floor groaned beneath his feet. She knew he was coming toward her, that he was just in front of that TV. She didn't move, and a moment later, she felt his fingers curl around her shoulder. Hayden turned her toward him. "Hell is not having found you. Being stuck in a nightmare where you're dead. Like I told you, Jill, those are the worst ones for me."

The way he talked, the way he looked at her...it was as if no time had passed between them. She was a nineteen-year-old kid. He was the twenty-one-year-old who'd grown up so fast. Right then, he still stared at her as if she were his entire world.

He'd certainly been hers.

The heat from his touch seeped into her. Her heart was drumming in a too-fast rhythm. Her breath was rushing from her lungs. She looked into his eyes, and Jill wanted.

Simple fact.

She wanted.

His touch. His kiss. His body, in hers. She wanted to get lost in the pleasure she'd known with him. Yes, she'd had other lovers since him. Ten years was a very long time. But...she'd always compared those men to Hayden.

Always, damn it, and she'd hated herself for doing that.

Hated herself for waking in the night and wishing that he were there beside her.

Jill wet her lips. His eyes seemed to heat as he followed the quick, nervous movement of her tongue. It was time for another true confession between them. "Sometimes, I feel like I'm just going through the motions. Doing my job, going to work, hanging with my friends...doing everything that I'm supposed to do because that's what a normal life is." She could hear the thunder of the waves outside. "But then I realize that I'm almost numb. Everything is happening, and I'm just...watching. Not feeling."

His fingers tightened on her shoulder.

"And then I came back to Hope and you were here. I looked at you, and feelings slammed into me." So many that she'd thought she would be crushed beneath them all. "I look at you, and I want you, Hayden."

His lips started to curl.

But Jill shook her head. "That's dangerous."

"I would never be dangerous to you."

He would be absolutely lethal to her. She'd survived one heartbreak from him. Was she up to another? *Don't give him the chance to touch your heart again. Keep it just business between the two of you. Focus on the case. Play it safe.* "I want you, but you terrify me."

Pain flashed on his face. "That's the last thing I want."

"You're one of the few people..." She swallowed and tried again. "You're one of the few people in this world that can hurt me." *Brutally. Completely.* "I promised my-self I wouldn't be hurt again, not by you."

She needed to get away from him. Needed to go in her bedroom. Shut the door and collapse. She was weaving on her feet, far too exhausted for this conversation. Actu-ally, her exhaustion was probably the reason *why* she was having this talk now. Because her barriers were broken. Gone. And she was baring her soul to him.

I shouldn't. I need to stop.

"I promise…I swear…" His head dipped toward her. "I will never hurt you again. You can count on me, Jill. Al-ways." His lips pressed to hers.

Back away. Back away. That little order whispered through her head, but Jill found herself leaning toward him, opening her lips and kissing him back.

Because when you live in numbness…well, is that re-ally living?

Her tongue slid out and traced over his lower lip. He gave a low growl in his throat, and that deep, sexy sound just urged her on. She found herself leaning up on her toes as her hands pressed to his chest. She could feel the hard expanse of muscles beneath her touch, could almost feel the drumming of his heartbeat.

The frantic rhythm matched her own.

The kiss deepened. The passion heated. The desire mounted. Her breasts were aching, her nipples tight. She wanted to rub her body against his. Wanted to just let go…

His hand slid down her side, curled fingers over her hip.

He nipped on her lower lip. A quick, hungry little bite that made her gasp.

His tongue thrust into her mouth. He tasted her. Seemed to savor her. The need she felt for him deepened. The de-sire burned hotter.

It would be so easy to give in…right then. Right there.

To keep kissing him. To strip away their clothes. To move into the bedroom.

There wouldn't be any numbness then. There would only be pleasure.

But…

What happened when the pleasure ended? When the sun rose?

When one of them had to walk away again?

Would the pleasure be worth the pain?

She didn't know. She—

He stepped back. His breath sawed out of his lungs and his glittering stare swept over her face. "I want to be clear on a few things."

She wanted his mouth back on hers.

"I will never hurt you again."

Her lips pressed together. She could still taste him.

"I will never let you down."

He'd only let her down once before. Unfortunately, that letdown had been epic.

"I *will* be the man you need."

She needed to step away. Before she crossed a line that went too far, for them both. She turned toward her bedroom, slipped across the threshold and started to shut that door. But then, Jill stopped. Something was wrong. Something about the way he'd said that last line.

"I will be good enough for you," Hayden promised.

She looked up at him. "You always were."

But his smile…it was a little cold. A little cruel. "You were the first person to look at me…*and see me*, Jill. Until that day on the pier, I was treated like trash by everyone in this town. Hell, even your grandmother thought I was trouble. They *all* thought that."

Her stomach was knotting.

"My father…"

She tensed. Hayden never talked about his father. *Never.* That was his one rule. She'd heard the stories growing up, but she'd never pressed him because every time she heard a whisper, she'd seen pain flash in Hayden's eyes.

"He was a killer. Before the kidnapper came to Hope, my father *was* the worst thing to ever happen to this town. He abused my mother, gave her more black eyes than I could count, and one drunken night, he robbed two tourists on the beach. Shot one guy in the chest…"

"Hayden—"

"I was always *his kid*. The killer's kid. The drunk's kid. The boy following in his father's footsteps. Because you know what I did?"

"Stop." He was hurting. He didn't need to tell her more. Not anything more. She just wanted Hayden's pain to stop.

"I stole when my mom and I had no food. I took things…from other kids when I didn't have clothes. Stole their gym equipment. Stole their fancy school supplies." His lips twisted. "I took what I wanted, and Sheriff Peek? He'd paid more than his share of visits to my house."

"That's in the past, Hayden. It's *always* been in the past for me."

"You know why I was on that pier?"

"Hayden—"

"I'd just gotten word that my dad had been killed in prison. My mother had drunk herself in a stupor after that, blaming herself. Like it was *her* fault the jerk had used his fists on her. I was on my own. I had nothing, *no one*. I was standing on that damn pier, looking into the water below and wondering…why the hell am I even trying?"

"Hayden—" She *hurt* for him. She'd tried to steel her heart against him, but this was Hayden. Beneath the anger she'd harbored for so long, the connection was still there.

She knew it always would be there. Some bonds went too deep to ever be erased.

He stalked toward her. His dark eyes seemed to burn. "Whispers followed me everywhere. I couldn't go into any store without clerks watching me, thinking I was about to steal from them. I was trouble. The punk kid. The guy who was going to turn out to be just like his father."

Her hand reached out and she grabbed on to his arm. Held tight. "You are nothing like him."

"Because of you."

Her lips parted.

"You came to me on that pier when I had nothing. When I was at my worst. A pretty girl with dark red hair, and you smiled at me. You stared at *me*. Not the piece of trash that everyone thought I was. You saw me."

She had to swallow the lump in her throat. *I always saw you, Hayden.*

"Then in a flash, you were gone. You'd wanted to be my friend, and I drove you away. I went after you and I saw him taking you." A muscle flexed in his jaw. "I knew right then, I would do cynthia to get you back. No one was going to take you from me. No one was going to hurt you. Not while I was around."

And he'd come for her. Later, she'd learned that he'd stolen a bike from the pier. That he'd ridden after the SUV, desperate to get to her. The bike's chain had broken, and he'd run until he found her. He'd stayed on her trail, he'd broken into that little cabin and… "He could have killed you, you know that, right? If he'd found you coming into that cabin."

He just stared down at her.

"Hayden?"

"You were worth the risk."

Her lips were trembling so she pressed them together.

She was still holding on to him. Far too tightly. She should let go.

"When we went back to town, people saw me differently then. Not trash. You turned me into a hero."

Anger had her shaking her head. "I didn't do anything. You did it. They just finally realized who you really were." Hayden had always been her hero.

That was why it had hurt so much when he turned away.

I'm leaving, Jill.

Those words had locked her heart in ice.

His hand lifted and curled under her chin. "You never got it, did you?"

"Got what?"

"They were right about me. I knew it, deep inside. I saved you because I'm a selfish bastard. You were mine, and I wasn't letting anyone take you away. Even back then, as young as I was, I looked at you, and I knew."

She shook her head.

His thumb feathered lightly over her jaw. "You deserved so much better. I knew it. I left. I joined the navy because I wanted to be the man you deserved."

Her eyes widened. "Hayden…that is such bull."

He blinked. "What?"

"You think I didn't know who you were?" Now her hand moved and pressed her fingers right over his heart. "In here? You think I didn't know you heart deep? Soul deep? You were my lover, Hayden. And I always knew exactly who you were." She paused, then said the truth she'd carried for so long. "You were mine."

Then you broke my heart.

His jaw hardened. "I wanted to be the man you needed. Holding you back from your dreams…that wasn't the way to go. I needed to prove myself."

He'd never had anything to prove to her.

"I was going to be more than just his kid. I became more."

A war hero. A man who'd battled mission after mission. An elite SEAL.

"The problem was..." Now his hand slid away from her cheek. "I learned I was far too good at a particular job."

Her heartbeat seemed too loud in her ears. "What job was that?"

His dark gaze held hers. "Killing."

LIGHTS WERE ON in Jillian West's rental cabin. A blaze of lights that glowed in the night. He drove past the cabin, barely slowing. Now wasn't the time. He had to think, had to plan. Jillian could *not* come back and wreck things. It just couldn't happen.

She had to be stopped. If she went prying into the past, she'd destroy far too much. Too many lives were on the line.

She has to be stopped.

His headlights blazed ahead as he accelerated. He'd think of something. He'd handle this. After all, it was his turn to do the job. His turn to protect the family.

Jillian wouldn't hurt anyone that he cared about. She wouldn't destroy the life he'd built.

He wouldn't let her.

Chapter Eight

I'm leaving.

Hayden stared up at the ceiling in Jill's cabin. The wind seemed to howl outside and the little cabin creaked a bit on its wooden stilts. The ocean waves roared outside and he just remembered…

I'm leaving.

They'd been on the beach when he told her his good-bye. She stared up at him, her green eyes stark, her face going slack with pain and shock.

He'd done that. He'd hurt her. The one person who mattered most in the world.

She'd buried her grandmother when she was eighteen. She'd spent months settling her grandmother's estate. She'd finally sold her grandmother's home, she'd gotten enough money to pay for her college. She had big plans for getting into the FBI. For starting her life, *their* life but…

I had nothing to offer her. He'd known the truth in his heart. She'd deserved so much better.

Two different paths. Two different lives. He'd seen it so clearly. She'd needed to follow her dreams, and he'd needed to prove that he could be more than his father's son. Needed to show that he was more than one act of courage on a desperate day.

He'd had to understand his own measure as a man. Had

to see for himself. When he was pushed to the limit, what would he do?

But that day, standing on the beach, seeing Jill's pain... it had broken something inside of him. Something that hadn't mended right in all of the years since then.

Did she know...did she have any clue...that when he got leave back to the States, he'd always gone to her? Just to get a glimpse. Just to see her. Just to make sure she was all right.

Sounded stalkerish as all hell, he knew that. But he'd just needed to make sure she was happy. The world was better when Jillian was in it, he knew that fact for certain.

Once, he'd planned to approach her. He'd even gotten flowers. Lilacs, her favorites. He'd been going to her apartment in Atlanta but then he'd seen another man heading to her door. Another guy carrying lilacs. He'd thought Jill had moved on.

I won't stand in her way.

So he'd slipped into the shadows. Gone on to another mission. But she'd always been there in his mind and in his heart. No matter where he went, she was there.

He'd discovered she was far more than just some boy's crush. Not just a man's obsession. She was everything.

And he'd lost her...all on his own. No one had needed to take her. He'd—

Her bedroom door opened with a soft click. Hayden surged upright, his body instantly on alert. "What's wrong?" He leaped to his feet and hurried—unerringly—toward her in the dark. He'd always had good night vision. His hands reached out and curled around her arms. "What is it?"

"I still have bad dreams." Her voice was soft, husky. "Sometimes, I just...I have trouble sleeping."

He should let her go. She'd probably just come out for

a glass of water or something and he'd practically jumped on her.

"You asked me before," she continued quietly. "And, yes, I still have those dreams."

So did he.

"But dreams didn't keep me up tonight."

Her skin was so smooth and soft beneath his touch.

"Fear kept me up."

Hayden shook his head. "Jill, you don't have to be afraid—"

But her soft laughter cut him off. "Everyone's afraid sometimes. Even FBI agents. Even big, bad navy SEALs."

He was still touching her. His fingers were lightly stroking her skin. *Get a grip, man. Let the woman go.*

"Do you know why I'm afraid tonight?"

Hayden cleared his throat. "I'm not going to let that guy get a second chance to—"

"I'm afraid that I've been numb for too long. Every case that I take—every victim I lose—the numbness grows more and more around me. I know I should feel more. I should be happy. Everyone should be happy, right? But I can't get that way. There's too much pain in the world. Too much darkness. I see it all around me, and I'm so tired of it." She moved her body closer to his. Her hand rose and curled around his neck. "I don't want to be numb any longer. For tonight, even if it's fleeting, I want to feel."

He was feeling plenty at that moment. Whenever she was close, the hunger he felt for her, the raw desire, was never far from the surface. But he needed her to be sure, because once they crossed this line...

There is no going back. Not for him.

Not for her.

Because he wouldn't give her up again.

"When I'm with you, the numbness fades away. I feel anger, I feel bitterness…"

That wasn't exactly sounding awesome.

"And I feel need. Desire." Her voice softened even more. "I want you, just as much now as I always did. That want burns past the numbness. You make me feel again." She rose onto her tiptoes and her body brushed against his. "Tonight, I want to be with you. Just tonight. A time to let everything else go and just…feel. Just be."

He'd give her tonight. He'd give her a thousand nights if that was what she wanted. His lips took hers, softly at first because part of him was afraid this was just a dream. He'd had plenty of dreams about Jill over the years. She'd come to him like this, soft skin, husky voice, sweet desire. He'd locked his arms around her in those dreams. His lips had pressed to hers…

And she'd vanished.

He'd woken on old cots, woken in darkened tents, safe houses on the edge of hell…woken without her.

She tasted sweet. Her lips were soft, her tongue tempting him.

She wasn't vanishing.

His hands slid down and locked around her hips. He brought Jill even closer to him, holding her tightly. The kiss deepened, hardened, and when she gave that faint moan in the back of her throat, the sexy sound that had always driven him wild, Hayden knew there was no turning back.

She wanted to feel? Wanted to lose the numbness around her? He'd make sure to give her more pleasure than she could stand. He'd give her every single thing that he had.

And it would just be the start for them.

Her breasts pressed against his chest. He'd ditched his shirt, and the soft cotton of her top was the only shield between them. Her nipples were tight, hard, and it had been far too long since he'd tasted them.

"Be sure," Hayden gritted out as he pulled his mouth from hers. But then he just started kissing a path along her throat. She'd always liked that. "No going back…" This wasn't a one-time thing for him. Jill would *never* be a one-night stand.

"Make love to me," Jill said.

Hayden was lost.

He picked her up, held her so easily and took her back to the bed. A faint light glowed from her bathroom, spilling onto the bed. He put her down there, right in the middle of the covers. She wore a little black T-shirt and a pair of tiny gray shorts. The long expanse of her legs was revealed to him. She'd always had truly killer legs. He stood by the edge of the bed, staring down at her, and then he had to touch. His fingers trailed up her leg. Starting at her knee, moving up higher, sliding over her silky thigh.

He heard the hitch of her breathing and then Jill was parting her thighs for him. Trusting him so completely.

His arousal shoved against the front of his pants. He wanted to ditch those pants and get naked on that bed. He wanted to be *in* her. But Hayden was going to make sure Jill had more pleasure than she could stand. That night, with him, she would feel every moment. His fingers slid between her legs, caressing her so carefully through the soft fabric of her shorts. She arched her hips toward him. No hesitation, just trust.

The way it had always been between them.

Hayden's gaze slid over her body. She was so perfect to him. Did she understand that? Every single inch of her had been burned into his brain. He remembered exactly what she liked, exactly how to touch her, where to touch her. How to drive her wild.

Jill wanted to feel? He'd make sure he gave her all that she needed.

His hand slid away from her.

"Hayden?"

"We're going slowly." Because he'd savor her. "It's been a long time, and I need to touch all of you." Every single inch. He reached down and caught the hem of her shirt. He pulled it over her head and tossed it into the corner of the room.

Her breasts were pebbled, hard peaks and thrust toward him. In the weak light, he couldn't see her nipples clearly, but he remembered the soft pink hue. Hayden slid onto the bed. He bent over her and he touched her nipple with his fingers, a careful caress. Then he put his mouth on her nipple. Licking her, tasting her.

Not so careful, not with the desire firing his blood and every instinct he possessed ordering him to *take*.

She gave a little gasp and her fingers flew to curl around his arms. He liked the faint bite of her nails. Loved the way she held so tight to him.

But they were only getting started.

Hayden took his time with Jill. Licking, kissing, caressing her. He worshipped her breasts. Couldn't get enough of her. She was whispering his name, her hips rocking against the long length of his arousal, but it wasn't enough for him. He needed her to go wild.

Then he'd follow her.

Hayden's hand slid down her body. He slipped down her shorts, moving so that she could kick them away. Her shorts and the thin scrap of underwear that she'd worn. Then he was touching her heated core. Soft, wet and ready. He nearly lost his damn mind.

"Hayden, I don't want to wait." Her voice was the purest temptation in the world. "It's already been too long."

Ten years too long. Ten years of memories and dreams. Ten years of being without her.

No more. He had her back in his arms next to him. He wasn't letting go.

He stroked her delicate sex. Pushed her to a fever pitch of desire. Her hands slid over him. Touching him and amping up the dark need that surged within him.

His mouth kissed a trail down her stomach. Down, down he went, driven to taste all of her. She smelled so good, felt so soft. Heaven in his arms. Heaven after too many years of hell.

He put his mouth on her, right on the center of her need, and Jill came apart for him. He felt her pleasure, heard it in her voice as her hips surged against him. There was no shyness, no restraint. Not between them. There was only pleasure.

And they were just getting started.

He kept stroking her, kept kissing her, as her climax crested. No one else was like Jill. No other woman had ever come close for him. She consumed him.

Was an addiction to him.

He eased back from her, still savoring her taste, and Hayden stared down at her. He wanted to sink deep into Jill, wanted to bury himself in her and erase the years of darkness that lay between them. "Don't move," he ordered, aware that his voice was gravel rough. His control was too thin. He was about to go over the edge any moment.

Have to protect her.

Always.

Hayden rose from the bed. He ditched his pants and underwear, then grabbed the wallet from his back pocket. He'd had an optimistic moment earlier and he had a condom with him. He put on the condom in pretty much record time and was back with her in an instant.

He positioned his length at the entrance to her body. His hands caught her hips and—

His gaze met hers. Her breath came in quick pants. Her body was open, waiting, his.

I need her to be mine again.

Because he'd never stopped belonging completely to Jill.

Hayden thrust into her, sinking deep, and his control shattered. Her legs wrapped around his hips, her nails scraped over his arms, and they drove toward completion. Faster, harder, she met him, thrust for thrust, her soft words urging him on. She licked his throat, kissing him just over the wild beat of his pulse point. She remembered what he liked. She—

Jill bit his earlobe. A quick, sexy nip. She whispered to him, dark and sexy promises, things they'd done, things they would do.

Her body was so tight and hot and he knew she could feel his release mounting, he couldn't hold back.

Jill, I need you to let go first. I need you to go wild. To feel—

Her body stiffened beneath him. "Hayden!" A quick, sharp cry and her delicate inner muscles squeezed him as her climax hit.

He followed her, pumping into her body and holding her tighter than he'd ever held anyone or anything. The pleasure ripped through him, making his heart pound too fast and hard, consuming him and reaching soul deep.

He bent forward and kissed Jill, tasting her pleasure, savoring the pure heaven of her and feeling—for the first time in ten years—peace.

Because he was right where he wanted to be. Right where he needed to be.

With Jill.

And he'd be damned if he'd ever let her go again.

SUNLIGHT TRICKLED ONTO the bed. Jill's eyes opened slowly, and then she blinked against that brightness. When the sun rose, it always came pouring right through that window and onto her bed.

Only I'm not in the bed alone. Not today.

Her head turned.

Hayden.

His eyes were still closed, his dark lashes looking incredibly long. His blond hair was tousled, courtesy of her fingers. They'd fallen asleep together, in each other's arms, as if it were completely natural.

His arm was still over her stomach, she was still cradled close to him. As if...as if he hadn't wanted to let her go, even in sleep.

Her breath slowly eased out as she stared at him. So handsome with such strong features. That hard jaw...she'd always loved to kiss it. Time had been kind to him. He was more rugged, harder and so incredibly sexy with that faint stubble.

Her gaze slid over his body. The broad shoulders and tan skin. The covers were pushed near his waist; the guy had always seemed to run a bit hot, she remembered that, and...

Scars.

Jill stiffened.

She knew Hayden's body—well. Knew just how to touch him. Knew just what he liked. Some things, a lover didn't forget. *Especially when the lover is your first.*

But the scars on Hayden, they were new.

Not just one scar. Not two.

She'd touched him last night. She'd felt the raised skin beneath her fingertips, but she'd been so far gone she hadn't stopped, hadn't realized—

"They look worse than they are." His voice was a deep, sleepy rumble.

"Bull." Now her hand reached out and traced those scars again. First the long, twisting scar that was near his heart. "Was this from a knife?"

"Machete."

Her heart stuttered.

"It didn't go in deep enough to do serious damage."

The damage looked pretty serious to her. "How many stitches did you get?"

"I was in the field, stitched it up myself...don't really remember how many...was just trying to stop all that blood."

Her eyes closed as she imagined that scene. "I...I didn't know." That little tidbit hadn't been in the files she received. Jill made her eyes open. Her hand drifted to another scar. Rounded, puckered. "Gunshot." She knew that one.

"Yeah."

"This one, too." Her hand rose to his shoulder.

His gaze held hers. "Barely a flesh wound."

"You are such a liar." She started to pull her fingers back, but his hand rose, catching hers and holding tight.

"They don't matter. I healed. They're in the past."

But seeing them *hurt* her because...*because he could have died, and I would have been an ocean away.* "You could have told me about them. Told me that you were hurt."

His jaw tightened. "I didn't want you to waste your worries on me."

Waste her—

Jill yanked her hand away from him and rolled from the bed. She didn't bother grabbing a sheet to cover herself. She just needed to get away from him before she *exploded* and—

"What in the *hell* happened to you?" His voice was lethally soft.

She stilled.

Then she realized...*my back*. It was such an old injury that she'd almost forgotten. Her first big case as an FBI agent and her first hit.

Her shoulders rolled back. "Don't 'waste your worries on me,' okay? It was nothing that a few stitches couldn't fix." She strode toward the bathroom.

She didn't make it. Hayden had leaped from that bed and closed the distance between them. His hand curled around her shoulder and he whirled her to face him. "You were shot." His eyes glittered down at her.

"Yes, well, it happens in the line of duty sometimes, but, apparently, you were hit more than I—"

"When."

Oh, now he was going to get all worried? He acted as if it were nothing for him to get injured, but she got one gunshot wound, and suddenly the world was ending. "My first case as an FBI agent. Back then, I made the mistake of thinking that a father couldn't hurt his own child, that there was no way the man sobbing so hysterically could be a killer... I was wrong." She'd turned her back on him at the wrong time. "It's a mistake I haven't repeated."

"You should have *called* me."

Did he even hear himself? Did Hayden see the craziness? She shouldn't be worried about him, but he was practically enraged over her injury. "I had my fellow agents at my side." Her lips twisted as she remembered. "And my partner back then, Steve Quick, he even brought lilacs to me when I got home."

Hayden let her go. Stumbled back as if he'd suddenly been burned.

"As much fun as this naked conversation is," Jill murmured. "Excuse me." Then she went into the bathroom and closed the door behind her with a very distinct snap.

She waited a moment, flipped the lock and her shoulders sagged.

He'd been hurt. She'd been hurt. Both so far apart.

When I was in that hospital, I wanted him with me.

When he'd been on the battlefield, had he—

"Jill?" He rapped against the door. "I'm…sorry."

For what? She didn't move.

"I never wanted you to worry about me. Never wanted to burden you."

Her back teeth clenched. *I never thought of you as any burden.* She grabbed her robe and yanked it on. She tied the belt with a nearly vicious twist of her hands.

"When I was shot…I lay in that medic unit, and I thought of you."

Her hands stilled, clenching the belt.

"When that guy came at me with the machete, when it sank into my chest, my one thought was… I don't want some guy in a government suit showing up at Jill's door, telling her about my death. I don't want Jill crying over me. I don't want her hurt."

She opened the door.

He stood there, wearing his pants, his face tight, and his eyes even darker than normal. "You were the one I listed as my emergency contact. Just you. I mean, my mom is dead. There is no other family. *You* were my family."

And he'd been hers.

"While I was overseas…" He gave a rough laugh. "I wrote about a hundred notes that I never mailed to you."

"Why not?"

"Because I thought you were moving on. That you'd gotten a great life, the life you always deserved and that you were free of the past."

Free of him?

"June 14."

She had no idea what that date meant. It wasn't some anniversary for them—

"That was the day I came to your apartment, wanting to ask you for another chance. Only there was this guy with dark hair, wearing a fancy suit, and he was at your door, with lilacs in his hand."

Jill sucked in a deep breath. *June 14.* She'd been shot in early June, she couldn't even remember the exact day but—

"Were you hurt then, baby?" His voice was so rough. Ragged. "Were you in there hurting, and I just walked away?"

She couldn't speak. Actually couldn't find the words to tell him that, yes, she'd been released from the hospital then and Steve had come to check on her.

Pain flashed on Hayden's face as he seemed to read the truth from her expression.

"Hayden…"

He swallowed and backed away. "I…I should go check in at the office. See if any of the deputies—"

"We should start over." The words just came out.

He stilled.

"Not look at the past. At what we did to each other. At what we didn't do." *I wish I'd been there when he needed me.* "Why don't we just see what happens?" One thing was certain—crystal clear after last night—she didn't just want to walk away. Not again.

"You…want me?"

Now she had to laugh. "Wanting you is always easy."

The way his expression changed…the way his eyes fixed on her mouth.

"I love your smile," he rasped.

Her smile faltered.

"Don't." His hand rose. His finger traced her lips. "It makes me feel good. I missed your smile."

Her breath whispered against his finger.

"I want to start over," he said, giving a hard nod. "Hell, yes."

A weight seemed to lift from her heart. She didn't want to wallow in their past or in the pain there. She was feeling again—and she liked that, but she didn't want to feel sorrow, not for either of them. Time to try something new. Time for something better.

His hand moved from her lips to her cheek. He was so warm and solid and strong before her. No ghost, no memory, no dream.

Hayden.

He bent his head and kissed her.

VANESSA GRAY HUNCHED her shoulders and pushed her hands into the pockets of her sweatshirt—or rather, into the pockets of her brother's borrowed sweatshirt. It was huge on her, dwarfing her small frame, but she loved to wear it anyway. NAVY was emblazoned on the front of the shirt, and it was so soft. Whenever she wore it, she always thought of her brother, Porter, and she felt better.

She really wanted to feel better that day.

The sun was slowly rising across the sky. Whenever possible, she liked to come down to the beach and watch the sunrise. It made her feel peaceful.

She could use some peace.

Her parents were fighting. Again. She knew all of the signs. Her mom was about to leave her stepdad. *Another one bites the dust.* Her mom fell in love fast. But the problem was that she also fell out of love fast. Four marriages in eight years was proof of that.

And Vanessa knew she'd soon find herself in another town. Maybe this time, there would be no ocean view. No view of the rising sun.

So she figured she'd better enjoy it while she could.

The sand rubbed against her bare legs. She was wearing shorts and a sweatshirt, and she didn't even care if she looked silly. Her legs spread in front of her and the cold water came to lap against her toes. Vanessa started to smile—

"You're out early."

Her breath sucked in on a sharp inhale. She turned her head, jerking it to the right, and she saw a man standing there. Tall, wearing a black coat. A baseball cap was perched on his head and his sunglasses tossed her reflection right back at her.

"I like to see the sun come up."

"So do I." He flashed her a reassuring smile. "Peaceful, isn't it?"

Her shoulders relaxed. He seemed friendly enough, and he didn't seem to be giving off any creepy vibes. She just hadn't heard him approach because of the surf, so he'd caught her off guard. "Yes, it's peaceful." She started to trace circles in the sand with her index finger.

"Do your parents know you're here?"

Her finger stilled. She glanced at him from the corner of her eye. Was he about to get her into trouble? "They know." They had no clue. They thought she was still sleeping. They *were* still sleeping, courtesy of their late-night fight. She'd slipped out, the way she often did, and they hadn't heard a sound. Sometimes, she just needed time alone. Time to think.

Time to...

Escape.

He smiled at her. "Enjoy your morning." He gave her a little salute and then he headed off down the beach.

She watched him for a few moments. No one else was out. What a waste of a perfectly good morning. Sure, it was early, but some views were worth crawling out of bed a few hours early.

She waited until the sun had turned the sky a pretty pink, and then Vanessa stood up. She brushed the sand off her legs and then reached for her flip-flops. She carried them with her as she headed toward the parking lot.

Wonder what's waiting at home? Would there be angry voices today? Or…maybe silence. Dead, cold silence. She never knew exactly what to expect.

I wish that Porter was home. If he were home, then she wouldn't have to leave with her mom. She could just stay with him. But she had no idea where he was. It had been so long since she'd gotten a letter from him.

She paused at the parking lot and slipped on her flip-flops. Her bike was locked to the rack. She just—

"I didn't know you were a liar, Vanessa."

Vanessa whirled around, a startled cry breaking from her mouth.

And he was there. The man in the ball cap. Smiling… a smile that chilled.

"Look, mister," Vanessa said as she backed away from him. "I don't know you and you don't know me, so—"

He took a step toward her. "I do know you. I've watched you for a long time. Just like I watch all of my girls."

OhmyGodohmyGod.

"I know your parents don't know where you are. I know you slipped away."

She turned and *ran* for her bike. But he moved fast, grabbing her by the hair and yanking her back. Vanessa opened her mouth to scream.

His hand slapped across her lips.

Chapter Nine

"So where do we go from here?" Hayden asked Jill as he stared down at her. He knew exactly where he wanted to go, back to bed, with her.

He was trying to take things carefully, trying not to screw up the tentative bond they were making. Jill was too important for a screwup.

"Where do you want to go?" she asked. Her lips were red from his kiss. She had such perfect lips. The sexiest mouth that he'd ever seen.

His fingers trailed over her arm. He *hated* that Jill had been hurt and that he hadn't been there. If he'd just walked to her door. If he'd shoved that other guy out of his way. "Life is all about the missed moments, isn't it?"

A faint furrow appeared between her brows.

"The things we don't do. The risks we don't take." The moments they didn't claim. "You ever think about that, Jill? How different life would be if one small thing changed?"

She swallowed. "Of course, I do. When I'm working a case…when I have to tell parents that their children won't be coming home…those moments are all I can think about."

The job was hurting her. He could see it.

"You're one of those moments for me," she continued.

Her lashes lowered. "If you hadn't come after me, if you hadn't gone into that parking lot at just the right time, I know I wouldn't be here."

"You *are* here." He tipped up her chin to make her look at him. "You are exactly where I need you to be."

With me. Always...with me.

"Hayden—"

Her phone started ringing.

Jill gave a little laugh. "Someone has really terrible timing."

He didn't look away from her. "Let it ring."

Her smile was bittersweet. "I can't. It could be one of my bosses at the FBI. I'm supposed to be on vacation, but if it's an emergency..."

If it's a child who was taken. He nodded and stepped back. "Right. Get the phone."

She brushed by him and grabbed her phone, catching it right in the middle of the ring. He saw her frown as she glanced at the screen. Then she put the phone to her ear. "Agent West," she answered. After a moment, her frown deepened. "Hello? Is someone there?"

Jill waited a beat. Hayden stared at her.

She shrugged and hung up the phone. "Guess it was a wrong number." But she bit her lower lip and stared at her phone. "Unknown number," she murmured. She rubbed her brow with her left hand.

"Jill?"

She shook her head. "Sometimes, I can't turn it off, you know? I get suspicious of everything. Of everyone."

"You don't need to be suspicious of me." He wanted her to understand this. "You can trust me."

He saw surprise flash on her beautiful face. "Trusting you was never an issue. Despite everything, you are the one person I trust completely."

When she said things like that, the woman came close to bringing him straight to his knees.

Her phone rang again.

He saw the flash of Unknown Caller on her screen and his instincts made him say, "Turn on Speaker when you answer it." She'd been attacked in that very house. Now two calls, from someone who was hiding his identity—*not good.*

Her fingers swiped over the screen and she turned on the speaker. "Hello?"

Silence. No, not just silence. Wind?

"Who is this?" Jill demanded. When no one spoke, her delicate jaw locked. "You're speaking to an FBI agent so don't play some joke with—"

"I know who you are." A man's voice. Low. Raspy. "The problem is...you never knew who I was."

Jillian sucked in a sharp breath.

"No one was there to follow her..." Again, the voice was raspy, as if the guy was trying to deliberately disguise himself. "Pity. If no one saw her vanish...guess no hero will come to save the day for her."

Jillian's gaze flew up to connect with Hayden's. He saw the flash of fear in her eyes. For just a moment, she was the girl she'd been so long ago. That girl...she'd had the same look.

He'd hated it then.

It enraged him now.

But, in a blink, the fear was gone from her eyes. Her chin notched up. "Listen, buddy, I don't know who you think you are, but I am not playing games with you. I'll get a trace on your call, I'll triangulate your signal, and you will *wish* you'd picked someone else to harass—"

"You know this is no game."

Jill's breath rushed out. "You're saying you've abducted some girl? You've taken someone? Prove it. Prove—"

"She can't talk right now. You remember, right, Jillian? You don't get to talk in the car ride. But maybe once she wakes up…"

His words trailed away and the call ended.

Sonofa— Hayden yanked out his phone. He called the station even as he heard Jill frantically making a call on her own phone. "This is Sheriff Black," he snapped when his call connected. "Have there been any reports of a missing girl in the area?"

"A missing girl?" Finn's voice rose sharply. "No, sir! I just came on duty but…no, nothing like that."

If she'd just been taken, there might not have been a chance for her parents to report her missing. He didn't think this was some prank call. Not with the attacks on Jill already. *No coincidence.* She was back in town and it sure looked like her abductor was, too.

And he'd taken someone else.

"I need to find that caller!" Jill's voice jerked his attention her way. She was pacing beside him, her phone at her ear. "Yes, jeez, yes, I did a reverse phone lookup immediately. The guy didn't answer—I don't know if his phone is shut off or what happened. That's why I need your help. Monitor his number. Triangulate the signal, track down the phone, do something! *Listen to me*…he just said a girl has been abducted!" She stopped and threw a frantic glance his way. "Do I have a confirmation on a missing person in the city?"

He shook his head. No, they didn't have confirmation, not yet.

"I think he called me right after he took her. No, I do *not* believe this is some joke! Can you tell me where the call came from or not? Can you find him?" She seemed to hold her breath and then...

She shook her head.

"Sheriff?" Finn said, jarring him, and Hayden realized he'd just been holding the phone while he watched Jill. "What's happening? What can I do?"

"Put all of the deputies on alert. We have a potential abduction in Hope. A girl." Because the caller had said *she*. "I want patrols going out. I want cars on the streets and our deputies looking for anything suspicious." He planned on getting out right away to start a search. *No one was there to follow her.* Oh, hell, yes, he would be there. He'd tear that town apart if he had to do it. Conduct a door-to-door search.

If that guy wasn't just scamming Jill, I will find that girl.

He hung up the phone and saw that Jill had done the same. "No trace," she said, "but I've got the FBI monitoring my phone." Her steps rushed toward him. "Hayden, he's doing it again."

"We don't know that, not yet." But deep inside, he thought she was right. The guy was striking again. After all of those years...

You won't get away again.

"He killed Christy Anderson within twenty-four hours of taking her." Jillian was dressing quickly, frantically, while she spoke. "That means we're working against the clock."

He yanked on his own shirt, then hurried into the den to grab his socks and boots. He pulled on his shoulder holster and checked his weapon.

Jillian rushed out behind him.

He turned toward her, hating the fear that he saw on her face. "We don't have a missing person yet, Jill. No reports have come in to the station. We don't have a victim, not yet."

"We will," she said with certainty, her expression stark, and her eyes so deep and sad. "We will."

IT WAS THE bike that caught Jill's attention. She'd gone with Hayden as he began a search of the city and the beaches. There were still no reports of any missing children but...

But the bike caught her attention.

Same place. She and Hayden had just pulled up at the parking lot near the big pier. A few fishermen were out now, an older couple walking hand in hand. And...

And there was a light blue cruiser locked to the bike rack.

The bike could have belonged to anyone at all.

Or...

She climbed from the patrol car and slammed her door. Her eyes wouldn't leave that bike.

"I see it," Hayden murmured as he came from the driver's side. "Come on." He marched toward the bike.

The handlebars were white and a light brown basket sat on the front of the bike. The lock was in place, securing the cruiser.

She turned, shielding her eyes from the sun. When she looked at the pier, she just saw the fishermen. The older couple. No kids. No girl.

When they'd left her cabin, they'd immediately come to this spot. Their first search point. She hadn't needed to tell Hayden to drive there, he'd gone instantly. *Because it all seems to be coming full circle.*

She'd come to Hope to get closure. She hadn't come so that another girl would become a victim. She'd never wanted—

Her gaze fell on the flip-flop. Just a dropped flip-flop on the concrete. It was about ten feet away from the bike.

"I'm going to talk to the men on the dock and see if they saw anything," Hayden said. Then he was gone, heading determinedly toward the men. She heard a few of them call out greetings to him.

The wind blew against her. It wasn't a cold day, not by a long shot, but a chill had settled bone deep for her. This was wrong. This *never* should have happened.

Her phone was ringing again.

She jerked when it vibrated in her pocket. Her fingers fumbled as she pulled it out and glanced at the screen. Unknown Caller. She waited a moment, one beat, two, just as she'd been instructed to do by her contact at the FBI. Then… "Hello?"

"She's awake now. Thought you might want that confirmation."

A girl screamed, a loud, desperate sound.

"Don't," Jill whispered. "Do *not* hurt her."

"I won't…"

She could see Hayden talking intently with one of the fishermen.

"In fact, Jillian, I won't do anything to her at all."

She took a step toward Hayden.

"Provided that you do *exactly* what I say."

She needed to keep him talking. She wasn't some terrified thirteen-year-old any longer. This wasn't her first, second or even third time to deal with a monster.

"Trade yourself for her, Jill. You give yourself to me, you take her place…and she can just walk away."

She was rushing toward Hayden. He looked up when her feet touched the pier and she saw the alarm in his dark eyes.

"Think about it," the caller said, and then he hung up.

She didn't have to think about anything. "We've got him," Jill nearly shouted to Hayden. *"We've got him!"* The FBI had been monitoring her phone. They should be able to find the jerk—they should have him.

IT WAS THE same cabin.

Jill let out a slow breath as she stared at the faded wood and the familiar, sloping roof. When she'd been a teen, she'd often snuck back to that place. The little cabin, nestled on the edge of the marsh. She hadn't actually gone inside during those days, though, because she'd been too afraid.

Since she'd come back to Hope, she'd thought about the cabin. She'd even intended to pay the scene of her crime a personal visit, but she just hadn't realized that she'd be returning *that* day.

"You're sure this is the spot?" Hayden asked softly. He was beside her, crouched down behind his patrol car. They'd gone in quietly, then parked behind the trees that surrounded the cabin.

"After he called me the first time, I got one of my buddies at the FBI to monitor my phone." Her heart was racing in a double-time rhythm, but her words came out calm, steady. "The call originated from *that* cabin."

A deliberate choice, she knew. The guy was sending her a message...

You're back. So am I.

And just where the hell had he been for all these years? Why start hunting again now? What had changed for him?

She had her weapon in her hand. Hayden had radioed in for backup during their drive over, but every moment that passed... *It's another moment that he could be hurting her.* "Are you ready?" Jill asked him.

Hayden's gun was at the ready. "Hell, yes."

"Then let's do this." Her breath whispered out. "I'll go in the front door, you take the back. The last thing we want is for him to slip away."

"Not again," Hayden gritted, his jaw locked tight. "He won't vanish again." He gave a grim nod. "Be careful."

Then he was gone, slipping away like a ghost as he kept to the line of trees. She wasn't surprised that he could move so stealthily. After all, that would have been part of his training. She knew he'd get to that back door and be ready. A perfect partner.

She kept covered as she made her way to the front door. She didn't want to present a target of herself. The guy in there—his phone calls had proved that he wanted vengeance against her. She wasn't about to give the perp a free shot.

If he wanted her, then he'd have to work for that hit.

She crept up the porch steps, moving slowly so that the old wood wouldn't creak beneath her feet. On the way over, Hayden had gotten Finn to pull up the property records on the cabin. It was currently listed for sale, a truth she'd noted when she glimpsed the slightly crooked for-sale sign near the front of the property.

The fact that the place was empty had probably made it even more appealing for the perp. *Was it like coming home for you, you sick jerk?*

The front door was ajar. A heavy lockbox—the type that Realtors always put on vacant homes—had been broken and lay smashed a few feet away. She eased out a slow breath. Jill couldn't hear any sounds from inside that cabin.

Not a single whisper.

She pushed open that door and slipped inside. No lights were on but sunlight streamed in through the windows. The front room was empty. The kitchen was covered with dust.

The hallway yawned before her, leading back to the

bedroom, the room she'd been held inside. It was a small cabin, tight, outdated.

A prison.

She crept down that hallway. The bedroom door was closed. Her grip on the gun never faltered as she approached the room. She had a sudden flash of waking in that small back room, of being on the floor. Of being tied, hand and foot.

She pushed open that door.

And Jill saw the phone that had been dropped onto the floor, dropped right in the spot she'd woken in years before.

"Step into my parlor," he whispered as he watched Jill vanish into the little cabin. She thought she was being so very clever. He'd figured she'd track his call. After all, she was the high-profile FBI agent now. Tracking him should have been easy for her.

He'd counted on that.

So he'd left a few...surprises for Jill. As soon as she went into the old house, he started to count. He figured it would take her a few moments to get inside. To get inside, then to find the phone.

He'd call her soon. And that call from him would be the last thing she'd ever hear.

When he'd been a kid, Hayden had tried to pick the lock at the back of the cabin. A flimsy lock, but he hadn't been able to get it open. He'd scouted around the cabin, found that broken window and slipped inside of it in order to get Jill.

A new lock had been put on the back door. Bigger, shiny. This time, he didn't try to pick the lock open. He just kicked in that door.

If you're inside, you won't get out.

He ran in with his gun up, sweeping around the rooms, looking for the man who'd thought to raise fresh hell in *his* town.

But the hallway was empty. The little cabin was too quiet. And when he went into the back bedroom, the bedroom that had haunted his dreams...

He saw Jill standing in the middle of the room. She was staring down at a cell phone. When he slipped into the room, she whirled, her gun aiming right at his heart.

"Easy." He inclined his head toward her. "No sign of him out back."

"The girl isn't here. *He* isn't here." Her gaze darted to the phone. "But he wanted us here. He left that..."

And even as her words faded away, the phone began to ring.

Jill reached for the cell phone.

But Hayden remembered another time, another place. A city where the sun blazed and sweat always seemed to slicken his skin. A cell phone had been left in a car near their safe house. It had started to ring. One of his team members had turned at the sound—

And hell had exploded around him.

Jill's hand had almost touched that phone. *"Jill!"* Hayden roared.

Her head whipped toward him. Her eyes had gone wide. He didn't say anything else—there was no time. He grabbed her hand and yanked her toward him. He was acting on pure, blind instinct, but the setup was too easy. An empty cabin, a phone waiting. Ringing.

"Hayden! What's happening?" Jill yelled, but she didn't fight his grip. She ran with him down the hallway.

He looked at her, his lips parted, and that was when he heard the explosion. A loud, reverberating blast that seemed to shake the entire cabin. He saw her face go slack with shock. She said his name once more, but he couldn't hear her voice. He couldn't hear anything but that terrible thunderous blast. Her lips were moving, though, and he knew clearly that in that last instant, Jill was calling out for him.

He grabbed her, locked his arms tightly around her, and they rushed toward the back door, even as a ball of flame seemed to roll through that house and come after them.

Smoke and flames raged as Hayden shoved open that back door. Jill was coughing, choking, clutching tightly to him. They were almost clear. Almost free of the fire and the bomb that had been set.

The phone was the trigger, I knew it, I—

The windows exploded. The roof groaned and that little cabin was swallowed by the flames.

He leaped out with Jill, holding her tightly, and they slammed onto the ground.

IT WAS ALL about proper placement.

He smiled as he watched the flames destroy the little cabin. When he'd realized that the place was for sale, that no one lived in the cabin near the marsh, he'd known it was going to be the perfect location for him.

It had been easy enough to set his explosives. Put them in the right spot, and *bam*. The whole cabin would come down. Once the ceiling collapsed, escape from that cabin would be impossible. The flames and the smoke would take care of his prey.

"Guess you didn't get away this time," he whispered as he kept his eyes on the front of that cabin. Jill had gone in…

But she hadn't come out.

Finally, he'd eliminated the threat she posed. A threat that had hung over him for far too many years. No more looking over his shoulder. No more wondering about the FBI agent.

He turned away from the cabin. The smoke and flames would attract attention soon. Deputies would race to the scene. The firefighters would swarm as they tried to battle the blaze. And, oh, wouldn't it be too sad when the remains were recovered? The town hero, the sheriff, gone down trying to save his precious Jillian again.

Should have never saved her the first time. Hayden Black should have just minded his own business. If he had, he wouldn't be burning right then.

He tracked back through the marsh and got to his car. Just to be safe—because if Jillian had taught him one thing, it was the importance of securing your prey—he headed toward the trunk. He lifted it up and stared down at the girl inside. Bound, gagged, she wasn't a threat to anyone. Her hair trailed over the black carpeting in the trunk and she barely seemed to breathe.

He smiled as he stared at her. He'd known he could get Jillian to appear if he dangled new bait in front of her.

The girl had been the perfect bait.

He slammed the trunk. It was good to be back on his game again. Back on top.

No one can catch me. No one can stop me. I have the power now.

He wasn't some weakling. Not anymore. He was the boss.

And he'd just proved it. He'd taken out an FBI agent *and* a navy SEAL. He was unstoppable.

Unstoppable.

Chapter Ten

"Jillian!" Hayden knew they'd hit the ground too hard. He'd tried to roll and protect Jill with his body, but he wasn't sure he'd done a good enough job. Jill was slack in his arms, her head sagging back. There'd been so much smoke around them at the end. *"Jill?"*

His heart barely seemed to beat as he stared at her. Her eyes were closed and she seemed far too still.

Not good, not good. "Jill, don't do this to me." He held her tighter and rushed farther away from the flames. When he was sure they were clear, he put her down on the grass and smoothed the hair away from her face. "Jill?" His fingers slid down to her throat and felt the pulse there, it was racing, too fast. Too—

Her hands flew up and shoved against him. A fast, defensive attack that probably would have sent anyone else sprawling, but Hayden's reflexes had been honed by years of training, and he caught her hands, holding them in a tight grip, but making absolutely sure not to hurt her. *Never her.* "Jill?"

"I blacked out." She seemed stunned.

"Only for a few seconds." And that scared the hell out of him. "Did you hit your head?" He let go of her hand and began to lightly search through the thickness of her hair for a lump.

She swatted his hands away. "Not now."

Not now?

Jillian lurched to her feet. She took a step, then swayed. Hayden surged up and caught her. "Jill, damn it, what are you doing?"

But she shoved away from him. "He set that place to explode."

Uh, yeah, he had.

"You knew…" Her breath came in quick pants. "When the phone rang, you…you realized what was happening."

He'd suspected and he was real glad they'd hauled butt getting out of there. Another few moments…

Jill slapped at his shirt. "You're smoking."

Hell. He yanked off the shirt and tossed it to the ground. Hayden stomped on it, putting out the flames. He looked up—and saw that Jill was stumbling away.

She must have hit her head. She's weaving.

He grabbed for her again.

She pushed his hands away. *"He's here."*

Blood trickled down her temple. He swore. "Baby, you're bleeding." He needed to get her to a doctor.

But once more, she pushed against him. "Don't you see? He had to be watching, to make the phone call, to detonate the bomb. *He had to be close.*"

The cabin was burning so fast and hard around them, he could feel the heat of the flames lancing against his skin.

"He *has* to be here," Jill said. "He's watching." Her eyes seemed far too dark as she said, "He's always watching."

Hayden started to shake his head but…but he thought he'd just heard the sound of a car cranking. An engine growling to life. Jill's head whipped to the left at the same time, and he knew she'd heard the sound, too.

When she broke from him and ran toward the marsh they'd crawled through one dark and long-ago night, he didn't try to stop her. Instead, he raced with her, his feet pounding over the earth, his whole focus locked on that growling engine.

Jill's right. He would need to be close so he could watch the cabin. He lured her out here, he'd want an up-close view of the action.

The action... Jill's death.

Tires squealed. The guy was getting away. Hayden pushed himself to run faster and Jill was right with him. They shoved their way through the marsh and he caught sight of the back of the car, a big, sleek ride and—

"Tag number," Jill gasped. "Get...it."

The car vanished, whipping around the corner. Hayden yanked out his phone, ready to call for backup and get patrols out to find that bastard but—

When he yanked his phone out of his pocket, he saw that the device had partially melted.

Jill stood as still as a statue, her gaze locked on the spot that the car had been in moments before.

"Jill?"

She didn't move.

His hand curled around her shoulder. "Jill!"

Her body jerked. She looked up at him, blinking. "I... I think I know that car."

She knew the car?

Jill rubbed her forehead. "Everything's...hazy."

And the blood was still pouring from her temple. "Baby..." He pulled her close. He thought of how fast that fire had spread, how it had come at them, rushing and destroying.

They'd walked into the killer's trap. They'd barely walked out.

In the distance, he heard the scream of sirens. Help, backup, rushing toward the black cloud of smoke that filled the air. But that help would get there too late. The perp was gone, only…

His eyes narrowed. He'd gotten a partial on the tag, and Jill was right…the vehicle did seem familiar.

"He made a fatal mistake," Hayden whispered as he stared into Jill's eyes.

Two fatal mistakes actually.

One, the SOB had dared to hurt Jill.

And two, *you didn't take me out, jerk. You left me alive and that means I will be coming after you. Coming after you with everything that I've got.*

JILL'S HEAD HURT, her clothes were covered in ash and they were more than a little singed, and she knew a new assortment of bruises marked her body.

She'd almost died that morning. She *would* have died if Hayden hadn't pulled her out of that cabin. A rookie mistake, going for that phone. She should have known better.

I'm too close to this case. I'm acting on impulse. On emotion. I'm not doing the job the way I should.

Or, at least, she hadn't been. But she'd gotten patched up by the paramedic on scene. She'd gotten her head clear. And—

I also got your tag number. When backup arrived at the cabin, Hayden had spouted off a description of the car they were after and he'd given the first three digits of the tag number. Even with her head feeling as if a sledgehammer had hit it, she'd been able to give the last four digits of that license plate.

She'd also been able to point the deputies in the direction of the owner because…

I know that car.

"Kurt Anderson," Jill whispered. "When he arrived at

his father's place yesterday…he pulled up in a car just like that one." A big, black, sleek ride.

Firefighters were battling the blaze, but she knew they weren't going to be able to save the cabin. It was long past the point of saving.

And I'm glad.

She'd never understood why anyone would want to leave that cabin standing. If she'd had her way, it would have been torn to the ground years before. Instead, it had nearly destroyed her, again.

"We need to talk to Kurt," Jill said.

A muscle jerked in Hayden's jaw. Someone had tossed him a T-shirt to wear, one that had Harris County Sheriff's Office emblazoned on the front. "Finn is running the tag number. Let's see what—"

"*Sheriff!*"

Finn was running toward them.

"Sheriff, Agent West is right! That tag—it's for Kurt Anderson's 2015—"

Jill didn't hear the rest of his response. *Agent West is right.* That was all she needed to know. She rushed toward the nearest patrol car. When the paramedic had bandaged her bleeding temple, he'd muttered a bit about her needing stitches, but she was fine. Definitely good to go.

She yanked open the driver's side door of that patrol car. She looked inside. Where the hell were the keys?

"Don't even think about it." Hayden's hand curled around her arm and he pulled her back. "The only place you're going is into the hospital for those stitches."

He had to be insane. "I'm going after Kurt Anderson." *Kurt Anderson.* He'd done this? Part of her was shocked but…*you know families are always the first suspects. No one ever looked hard at Kurt for the crime. Maybe he killed Christy. Maybe Christy had never been taken by the same man who abducted Jill. Maybe Kurt had been his sister's murderer all along...*

"No, you're getting looked after. You probably have a damn concussion, the last thing you need is to be driving." His face was locked in tight, angry lines. "I hate to do this, but you're not giving me a choice."

What was he even talking about? Do what?

"Finn, take Agent West back to the ambulance. Stay with her while she goes to the hospital."

Her jaw dropped. He *wasn't* serious.

"I'm pulling jurisdiction on you, baby," he whispered. "Because I won't risk you."

She wasn't his to risk. She was an FBI agent. She was—

My vision's blurry, my knees are shaky and I can feel blood trickling down my temple again.

"I will bring him in," Hayden promised her as a muscle jerked along his clenched jaw. "But I have to know that you're okay."

"I'm fine," Jill gritted out the words. "Just...go. Don't let him get away. He...took someone. I heard her scream."

"We both heard her." He nodded. "I swear to you, I will find her. I won't give up."

Finn rushed toward them. "Ma'am?"

She hated this. "Forget me, Finn. Go with Hayden. He needs backup." And she'd be calling in some backup of her own, just in case. This wasn't going to be some jurisdictional war, that wasn't the way she operated. CARD team members didn't take over, they didn't huff and puff and steamroll their way over a local investigative team.

They worked together. They saved the victims. The victims were what mattered. "Go get her," Jill whispered.

Hayden squeezed her hand.

Then he was gone.

The paramedic hurried toward her. "Agent West?"

"Stitch me up," she ordered him. "Or find me someone else who can." She thought of Kurt, of Christy, of the way monsters could lie in wait for so very long. And she knew that they needed extra help. "And give me your phone." Because there was one special person at the FBI that she wanted by her side.

RAGE BURNED INSIDE of Hayden's blood. His hands had a death grip on the steering wheel and the thunder of his heartbeat echoed in his ears.

"Uh, Sheriff? Should you...maybe slow down a bit?" Finn asked nervously.

Slow down a bit? They were after a man who'd just tried to *kill* Jill. Another few moments, and Jill would have burned. They *both* would have burned.

He took the corner fast, making Finn slam against the side of the door. In his mind, he kept seeing Jill, lying so still, blood trickling down her temple.

Too close. Too close. Jill had almost been taken from him, and the fool who thought he'd gotten away with murder...

He was about to be in for a very unfortunate surprise.

Hayden slammed on brakes in front of the Anderson house. His sirens were blaring, his lights flashing. He jumped from the car and ran up the sidewalk. The front door opened and Theodore Anderson stood there, blinking owlishly at him. "Hayden Black? What the hell do you want?"

Hayden grabbed him, fisting his hand in the guy's shirtfront and he pushed Theodore back against the side of the house. "Where's your son?"

Finn had run toward the garage. "The car isn't here!"

"What car?" Theodore's gaze darted toward Finn. "Why's he looking in my garage? What's going on here?"

The rage bubbled even hotter inside of Hayden, as hot as the fire that had destroyed the old cabin. "Where. Is. Your. Son?"

"He usually goes for a run in the mornings. At the beach…" Theodore's face mottled. "Now get your hands off me!"

Kurt wasn't there.

"Your son's car was at the scene of an arson this morning." He let Theodore go but didn't back away. "Two people were nearly killed in that fire."

Theodore's eyes bulged. "What? No." He shook his head once. Hard. "No way, my son is *not* involved—"

"We think another girl is missing." No parents had come forward yet. They'd had the morning from hell, and no one had reported the girl as missing so far. "I need to find your son, *right now.*"

It seemed to take a moment for Theodore to connect the dots. Arson. Kurt's car. The missing girl…

Then the man's face seemed to crumple. "What? What are you saying?" But the terrible, dark suspicion was there, wide in his eyes. So clear to see.

"I'm saying I want to talk to your son. He's a suspect right now and I *want*—"

"There, Sheriff!" Finn yelled. "I see him!"

Hayden's head jerked to the left. Finn was pointing, and, sure enough, he saw Kurt. The guy was in the middle of the street, wearing a sweat-soaked T-shirt, jogging shorts and running shoes. Kurt's gaze was on the patrol car in front of the Andersons' house, but then his stare swung toward Hayden and Theodore.

He's going to run from me. Hayden knew it even before the guy turned on his heel and rushed back down the street.

The innocent don't flee. Hayden took off after the guy, rushing fast and hard, adrenaline fueling him. Kurt wasn't getting away. He'd told Jill he'd bring in the guy, and that was exactly what Hayden intended to do.

His feet pounded over the pavement. Kurt was fast, he'd had a head start, but Hayden was faster. In moments, he was right behind Kurt, and Hayden launched himself into the air. His body hurtled toward Kurt's, and he tackled the other man, sending them both flying onto the pavement. The cement tore into Hayden's forearms and ripped through his pants, but he barely felt the sting. All of his focus was on Kurt Anderson.

He pinned the guy beneath him on the ground. "Where the hell is she?" Hayden snarled.

Kurt tried to kick him, tried to headbutt him. What did the guy think? It was amateur hour? Hayden spun Kurt onto his back, cuffed him in seconds, and then yanked the heaving man to his feet. "Where is the girl?"

"What girl?" Kurt shouted. "Get the hell off me! Let me go!"

Hayden swung Kurt around to face him. "Do you always run when you see a sheriff at your house?"

"I just— Let me go! I know my rights! You can't do this to me! I haven't done anything wrong!"

Finn pounded toward them. He had his gun out and pointed—a bit shakily—at Kurt.

"Don't hurt my son!" Theodore barreled after them.

Neighbors were peeking out, watching with wide eyes.

"Your rights?" Hayden laughed. "Fine, you have the right to remain silent, you have the right to an attorney, you—"

"Get these cuffs off me!"

Hayden stared into his eyes. "You should never have tried to hurt Jill." His voice was low, carrying just between them.

He saw it then—the flash of guilt. The nervous expression that told him he'd just hit pay dirt.

But then Kurt started sputtering. "I haven't done anything! I was just out for a run, I didn't—"

"Where's your car?" Hayden asked, cutting into his words.

Kurt blinked. "In the garage. I parked it there last night. I was out late, driving around. I came home and put it inside."

Hayden shook his head. "Try again."

"It's in the garage!" His frantic stare shifted to Theodore. "Dad, tell them—"

But Theodore wasn't saying anything.

"The car isn't in the garage," Hayden said as he locked his hand around Kurt's shoulder and pushed him toward the sidewalk. "But guess what? Jill and I saw you this morning. We saw your car right after you set that bomb. Couldn't get away fast enough, could you? Your mistake… you didn't take us out. *We saw you.*"

Kurt tried to wrench free and run.

Hayden just tightened his hand. "Where's the girl?"

"What girl?" Kurt was nearly yelling. "I didn't take anyone! I didn't do anything! Not to you or to your precious damn Jillian West! Let me go!"

"The only place you're going is to jail." Hayden stared at the man. "And all those secrets you've been keeping for so long? They're all about to be pulled out into the open."

Kurt blanched and he shot a guilty glance toward his father.

"You're done," Hayden said simply. "It's over."

Chapter Eleven

"I want to see him." Jill burst into the sheriff's station and flatly made her announcement. Finn jumped up when he saw her and rushed from behind the check-in counter. "*I want to see Kurt Anderson.*"

"Are you okay, Agent West?" Finn's gaze darted to the bandage on her forehead. "I heard the paramedics took you to the hospital. Did the doctors release you?"

She had a concussion, she was in a furious rage and she was very, very much *not* okay.

Before she could say anything else, though, the door opened behind her. She looked back, and saw a woman with pale blond hair standing in the doorway. The woman wore no makeup, and her hair had been pulled back into a tight ponytail.

"I need to fill out a report," the woman said, her voice was shaking. Her hands trembled as she lifted them into the air and waved vaguely toward the check-in desk. "My daughter… I can't find my daughter."

Oh, no. Jill spun toward her even as she heard the echo of a girl's scream in her ears. "Ma'am? I'm FBI Agent Jillian West. I can help you."

The woman blinked her light blue eyes. "You're… FBI?"

Jill pulled out her badge. The wallet had stuck together

a bit after the fire, but the badge was still good. "I specialize in missing persons cases. Children's abductions."

The lady backed up. "I think Vanessa just ran away. She wasn't abducted." Her smile was nervous. "I just need to see the sheriff, but…um, thank you, anyway." She started to walk around Jill.

Jill just moved, blocking her path. "How long has your daughter been missing?"

A crinkle appeared between the woman's brows. "I don't… I'm not really sure."

Jill didn't let her expression alter.

Red stained the woman's cheeks. "She was gone when I woke up this morning, but I figured she'd just slipped away for a bike ride. I mean… Vanessa does that. It's not like she's some little kid. She's a teenager—fourteen years old. I thought she'd be back but…"

But she wasn't.

The woman straightened her shoulders. "I had an argument with my husband last night. I know Vanessa heard it. She…she probably just got angry and is trying to punish me by disappearing for a while. I just need the sheriff to send out some patrols to find her and bring her back. Get her to stop this foolishness…" Her words trailed off as she stared at Jill. *Why are you looking at me that way?*

Jill released a slow breath. "What's your name?"

"Carol. Carol Wells, but my daughter is Vanessa Gray." She fumbled in her bag and pulled out a photo—it was one of those class photos with the overly springlike background. A girl with sandy-blond hair stared back at the camera, a small smile on her lips. "That's her. She's just—"

A door opened behind them. Jill heard the low creak and then the heavy thread of footsteps approaching.

"Sheriff Black!" Relief flashed on Carol's face. "I need your help! Vanessa's run away and I wanted to get a patrol to search the beaches for her."

Very slowly, Jill turned to face Hayden. The faint lines on his face seemed deeper, his expression dark. She knew that he'd taken Kurt into custody—Hayden had called her at the hospital and told her that much. But had he learned anything from Kurt yet? Anything like *where is the girl? What has he done with the girl?*

Carol rushed around Jill and grabbed Hayden's arm. "She's mad." She waved her hand in the air. "You know how teenagers get. I told her that I was thinking about moving. Maybe getting a fresh start somewhere else." Her voice dropped. "Ron and I aren't exactly getting along. We rushed into the marriage."

Jill stood there, her muscles tight, watching, waiting.

"Vanessa doesn't want to leave so she's acting out. But when you pick her up in your patrol car, that will scare some sense into her." She nodded decisively. "Yes, it will. So can you—"

Jill cleared her throat. "Carol doesn't know how long Vanessa has been missing." Then, because her suspicions were on high alert, Jill asked, "By any chance, does Vanessa own a blue cruiser? One with a brown basket?"

A wide smile spread across Carol's face. "She does! You—you've already found her?" Her gaze flew around the station. Finn watched the exchange, his face tense. "Where is she?" Carol blurted. "Is she in one of the offices?"

Where is she? That was the question they all wanted to know.

Hayden cleared his throat. "Mrs. Wells, I think we need to talk." He took the photo from her hand, and then Hayden nodded toward Finn. "Get this out to all the patrols. I want every man and woman we've got looking for Vanessa."

Carol backed up a step. "What am I missing?" She whirled backed to Jill. "Why is an FBI agent even here now? What's happening?"

There was no easy way to say this. "We believe a girl was abducted this morning."

"*My* Vanessa?" Carol staggered.

"We don't know who was taken yet," Jill said quickly. "But we are going to find out." She wanted to get one-on-one with Kurt Anderson. She'd make him talk.

"And…" Hayden added, his voice a low rumble. "We *will* find your daughter, no matter what."

Jill's gaze jerked toward him. In the FBI, the agents were always taught never to make promises like that to family members. Never, ever make a promise that you couldn't keep.

Because sometimes, the victims weren't found. Sometimes, they never made it back.

HAYDEN PULLED JILL into his office and shut the door behind her. "You should still be at the hospital." She looked too pale, far too fragile to him. The scent of ash still clung to her—hell, to them both.

But Jill shook her head. "I'm stitched up and the doctors weren't keeping me there."

"*Weren't?*" Hayden repeated. "Does that mean they wanted to and you wouldn't let them?"

Her lips thinned.

"Jill…" She was killing him.

"I want to see Kurt Anderson."

"The guy isn't talking, Jill. He clammed up the minute I mentioned a missing girl. He's back in holding, and the man is not cooperating." Every time Hayden looked at Kurt, rage filled him.

"I need to see him." Her voice was calm, her stare unflinching. "You think I haven't dealt with my share of uncooperative witnesses and suspects? I know how to handle them. I can handle *him*."

He knew she could. But…damn, it felt as if he were being ripped apart. He kept seeing the fire. Seeing *her*…

And I want to destroy the man who hurt her. But that wasn't what a sheriff was supposed to do. He was supposed to serve and protect. Deliver justice, not give in to his rage.

"Besides," she continued, tilting her head as she studied him, "Kurt wants to talk. The perp called me, remember?"

"Only so he could set you up to die." It had taken all of his self-control not to pound the hell out of Kurt. *You're the sheriff. You have the badge. It means something.*

It meant he couldn't give in to his fury. Not yet, anyway. Because somewhere out there, a victim needed them.

"How does this work?" Hayden asked her. "Your CARD team…what do you do? How do you—"

"There are certain investigative strategies that we always utilize. Normally, we immediately begin a search for any registered sexual predators in the area, we look for anomalies, we review video footage—" But she broke off, shaking her head. "This case is different. For this case, we begin with Kurt. He's our focus. You keep your men searching the streets for Vanessa, and you and I will make a run at him. We break him, and we find her."

He wanted it to be that simple.

"I've already contacted one of my most trusted friends at the FBI," Jill said. "She's on her way here now."

"Another CARD member?"

But her gaze turned shuttered. "No, not exactly. Samantha is…different. I think we need her talents here, not the other CARD members. Like I said, this case is different. We need different people to get the job done."

Okay. Well, he'd find out just how different the woman was soon enough. For the moment, they had a perp to interrogate.

VANESSA OPENED HER EYES. Her head hurt. A terrible pounding that had nausea rolling in her stomach. She tried to sit up but...something was wrong.

She couldn't move her arms, not fully. Or her legs.

Terror clawed at her.

She opened her mouth to scream, and she realized that a thick cloth had been stuffed between her lips. The cloth was pulling at her cheeks. *It's tied around my head.* A gag.

Rough hemp bit into her wrists. She twisted and jerked. Someone had tied her up. Bound her hands and ankles, then looped that rope together so that she was trapped in a small ball, hunched over.

This can't be happening.

Tears leaked down her cheeks. She...she wanted her mom.

She wanted her brother.

She wanted *help*.

HAYDEN LED THE WAY back to the holding cell. Kurt Anderson was the only occupant back there, and when the guy saw him coming, he shot to his feet and headed toward the bars. "Came to your senses?" Kurt demanded. "Good, now get me out—"

Hayden moved to the side so that Kurt could see Jill.

Kurt's words stopped completely and he just stared at her.

"Sorry," Jill murmured, not sounding the least bit apologetic. "Did I surprise you? After all, you worked so hard to kill me."

Kurt shook his head.

Hayden stayed silent. This was Jill's show. He wanted to see how far she could push the other man. *I'm betting damn far.*

"Hayden said that you haven't been cooperating with

the investigation." She moved closer to the bars. "Why is that? After all, you've gotten away with your crimes for years. Surely you want to talk about them now. You want to tell everyone *your* side of the story."

His hands curled around the bars. "I haven't done anything."

Jill shook her head. "We saw you. Saw your car at the scene of the arson. Rather full circle, wasn't it? To lure us back to that particular cabin. To set the bomb to explode right then and there."

"I didn't rig some bomb! I wouldn't even know how to do that!" He jerked his head toward Hayden. "He's the ex-military guy. Isn't that his department?"

The shock—or at least, the shocked act—appeared to have worn off because Kurt was sure saying plenty now.

"And look, I don't know what's up with the car." Kurt was sweating. "It must have been stolen or something because no way was I driving it—I was out on my run, I swear!"

"The sad fact is…" Jill offered him a tight smile. "Anyone with internet access can get bomb-making instructions. And for someone like you—someone who has committed murder before, I'd think a little bomb making might be right up your alley."

"I didn't do it!" Spittle flew from Kurt's mouth. "Look, this is all a mistake." His gaze jerked toward Hayden. "I mean, come on, I was a kid back then, too. When Jillian was taken, I was your age!"

Jill stared at Kurt. "You aren't the man who took me."

His shoulders sagged. "Damn straight. Now get me out of—"

"He was older. Bigger than you were back then. But…" She gave a small shake of her head. "But that doesn't mean you aren't the man who killed Christy. You didn't take me, but you may very well have killed your sister."

Hayden's gaze sharpened on Kurt. Once more, he saw the flash that could have been guilt appear in the guy's eyes.

"Everyone always assumed," Jill continued, her voice quiet, "that the man who took me also took Christy. But what if that wasn't the case?"

"I want a lawyer," Kurt snapped. "I want to see my father, too."

"What if…" Jill mused, watching him carefully. "There were two different attacks back then? My abduction…and Christy's death."

Hayden kept his expression locked. He didn't want to give anything away to Kurt, but what Jill was saying…

She thinks the guy may have killed his own sister. It took a special kind of sick mind to commit an act like that.

"Everything was fine for years in Hope, no abductions, no attacks, then I came back to town." Her lips curved down. "And one of my first stops was Christy's grave. Bet that made you angry, didn't it?"

Kurt was staring straight at her. "You should stay away from Christy," he whispered.

Jill nodded. "So I was told. But I didn't stay away. I showed up at your house. On your doorstep. I was talking to your father. You knew I was going to reopen the investigation, and you couldn't let that happen, could you?"

Kurt's hands fell away from the bars.

"So you had to stop me. You lured me to the cabin near the marsh and you set it to explode."

Kurt ran his hand over his face. "This isn't happening."

"You didn't want me finding out the truth about the past. You didn't want anyone to know the truth about Christy." Her voice had dropped, become sad.

Hayden realized she was manipulating Kurt, pushing at his emotions. She was good. Damn good. But Kurt hadn't broken, not yet.

Kurt's shoulders hunched. "I can't…"

"But Christy is gone," Jill continued, her voice still soft. Still sad. "There is nothing we can do for her now. The girl you took this morning…she isn't. There's still a chance to help her. To *save* her."

Kurt's hand fell. Once more, he looked over at Hayden. "You…you mentioned a girl."

Hayden gave a slow nod. *Yeah, I mentioned a girl, all right. Vanessa Gray. And her mother is currently sobbing in my office.*

"Where is the girl?" Jill asked Kurt. "I heard her scream when you called me on the phone. She was alive then." A pause. "Is she alive now?"

Kurt shook his head.

Hayden's heart seemed to stop. He couldn't stay silent any longer. "You killed her." The words were rough, guttural. He stepped forward, his hands fisted as—

"I didn't take anyone!" Kurt's eyes had flared wide. "I never took any girl today! I didn't set a bomb—*I didn't do this! It wasn't me!*"

Jill glanced at Hayden.

"I want a lawyer. Get me a lawyer!" Kurt pleaded. "I am not going down for this! I didn't take any girl today! I didn't do it!"

Jill turned away from him.

"Where are you going?" Kurt stuttered. "You're not leaving me here again?"

Hayden just stared at him. "You want a lawyer, then we'll get you one. But if that girl dies, if you've set her up to suffer while you're in here…" His teeth clenched. "I swear, you'll be sorry," he promised.

Then Hayden followed Jill out of the holding area, making sure to secure the doors shut behind them.

He took a few steps, then realized that Jill had stilled in that narrow hallway. He put his hand on her shoulder, and she turned to face him. "Something isn't right," she said.

There were a whole *lot* of somethings not right with that case.

"He's denying taking the girl today, denying the bomb..." She rubbed the back of her neck. "But did you notice that he never denied being responsible for Christy's death?"

Hayden realized she was right. The guy had flinched, he'd flushed when she mentioned Christy and the idea of two separate perps, but Kurt hadn't denied guilt for his sister's death.

Damn.

"We're missing something," she said. "I know it. I need to talk to Samantha. She can figure this out, she can help us."

And he needed to find out the damn status on the hunt for Vanessa. The girl was *his* priority. His citizen, his responsibility. And every moment that ticked away...

"Let's set up a base of operations here," Jill decided. "We need to retrace Vanessa's steps, figure out where the killer could have taken her. Any other empty houses that are close by—cabins, beach rentals—we need to search them all."

Hell, yes, they did.

His hand tightened on her shoulder. "Everything we have on Kurt is circumstantial at this point." The truth grated. "If he sticks to his story about his car being stolen, if he can produce witnesses who saw him on his run, then the guy will be walking right after his lawyer arrives."

She swallowed. "I know...just...keep him as long as

you can, okay? I'm telling you, he's holding back on us. I could see it."

So could Hayden.

She started to pull away, but he didn't let her. He brought her closer. They were alone right there, and he needed to—

I just need her.

His head lowered. His lips pressed to hers. Not a desperate, wild kiss. Soft. Careful.

Tender.

Emotion was in that kiss, all of the emotions he'd kept bottled up for far too long. When he thought of the danger around them, around *her,* he wanted to rage. "I can't let anyone take you from me." He bit off the words against her mouth.

Her hand pressed to his chest. "I am not going anywhere. I promise."

Promises were easy to make. But life was cold and hard and twisted, and fate could rip anyone's world apart.

She pressed another kiss to his lips. "Thank you, Hayden."

His brow furrowed. What was she thanking him for?

"You saved me today," Jill whispered. "I won't forget that."

He let her pull away. He *watched* her walk away, and Hayden shook his head. Jill just didn't get it. He wouldn't have left that cabin without her.

Not years ago.

Not that morning.

She'd saved him, long ago, and there was no way he'd ever let her suffer.

Chapter Twelve

Five hours later, Vanessa Gray was still missing. No one had seen her when she was on the beach. No one had seen her vanish from the parking lot.

No one had seen the girl at all.

Deputies were canvasing all of the vacant properties in the area. The news was running Vanessa's photo, and Jill feared they were running out of time.

Jill had established an on-site command post at the sheriff's office. She'd mapped out the locations of all registered sex offenders within a one-hundred-and-fifty-mile radius. Law enforcement personnel were en route to question all of those offenders. She was following standard CARD protocol but…

But this case is different. I don't think we're going to find some registered sex offender who has the girl. This case is deeper than that. Darker.

She looked at her phone. The guy had called her before. He'd lured her to the cabin, and then he'd rushed away.

If…*if* Kurt Anderson was telling the truth, then the perp had set him up. He'd deliberately taken Kurt's vehicle. Why?

So that if he was seen, the authorities would focus on Kurt? Did the guy *want* them looking at Kurt?

Tension was heavy and tight in the back of her neck.

This case was driving her crazy. She wanted to find Vanessa. Every time that she thought of that girl...

I see myself. Scared and alone in the cabin.

And it was just like the jerk on the phone had said. There was no one to rescue Vanessa. No one had seen her.

A knock sounded, a gentle rap against the side of her office door. The door was open, and Jill's head whipped up at the knock. She blinked, staring in surprise at the woman who stood in the doorway.

Samantha Dark gave her a slow smile. "You were expecting someone else?"

Jill jumped out of her chair. She was so glad to see the other woman that she almost hugged her, but protocol held her back. "I am so glad you're here."

Samantha Dark was *the* rising star when it came to profiling killers at the FBI. The woman's mind seemed to always be working, spinning, plotting, dissecting. Samantha took the darkest cases, the most gut-wrenching investigations, and the lady seemed to pull out the motives of the killers as if she were working magic.

Samantha's black hair was pulled back into a twist. Her golden eyes glinted as she shut the office door behind her. "You said you needed me, so that meant I got on the first plane available and got my butt down here."

Because Samantha was also a great friend. They'd first met at Quantico, and they'd bonded during training. Jill had known that she wanted to work the child abductions while Samantha had been bound for the behavior analysis unit. On day one, they'd clicked.

And, suddenly, Samantha was pulling Jill in for a tight hug. "I mean this in the nicest way," Samantha murmured into Jill's ear. "But you look like hell."

A shocked laugh escaped Jill's lips. "Thanks." She hugged Samantha, reassured to have the other woman there. Samantha had been there for Jill after she was shot on that very first case. She'd been there on the slightly drunk nights when Jill had broken down and spilled about Hayden.

She'd always been there, a true-blue friend.

Samantha eased back. Her gaze swept over Jill's face. Samantha was beautiful, but Jill had noticed that she always tried to downplay her looks. No makeup. No too-tight or low-cut clothes. Just business, that was Sam.

Most days, anyway. Jill had seen her friend cut loose a time or two.

"I read up on your abduction on the way here," Samantha said, giving a slight nod. Her lips pursed. "But to be honest, I have to confess...I dug up your case file years ago."

She'd done what?

"You carry a lot of pain, Jill," Samantha murmured. "I've wanted to help you for a long time."

"A girl is missing." She backed toward the desk and handed Samantha the file she'd composed on Vanessa Gray. "He called me—the bastard who took her. I heard her scream."

Samantha began to rifle through the file.

"We have a man in custody. Kurt Anderson."

Samantha looked up. "Christy Anderson's brother?"

Jill nodded. "You *did* do your research." It was a bit unnerving to realize that—all along—Samantha had known all of the secrets that Jill carried about Hope. Samantha had known those secrets, but hadn't said a word.

"Like I said—" Samantha inclined her head "—I wanted to help you. Sometimes, Jill, your pain was like a cloak around you. And there's always a reason..."

"A reason?"

"Why we choose the paths that we take. You wanted

to help children. That was your mission and burden. Your single focus. It only stood to reason there was a direct motivation for that desire."

Ah, there she went...*she's profiling me*. But two could play that game. "You only wanted to work with the serial killers, so what motivation do *you* have?"

Samantha's thick lashes lowered. "Maybe I understand them *too* much because I understand their darkness a bit too well." Then Samantha cleared her throat. "You think a serial is at work here, or you wouldn't have called me. You would have gotten some of your CARD teammates down here right away."

Jill bit her lower lip. "When I first talked to you, I did. Me, Christy Anderson...after the two of us, the killer seemed to just vanish. And that doesn't usually happen, not with serials."

"They have a cooling-off period," Samantha allowed as she thumbed through the documents. "But they don't usually go dormant for such an extended period."

"Then the girl taken now, Vanessa, we're all of similar ages at the times of our abductions. From the same town but..." This was driving her crazy. Jill started to pace. "But I searched the federal databases and no one else matches the victim profile. Just the three of us. There weren't any abductions in nearby areas. It doesn't make sense, not unless—" She broke off.

"Unless what?" Samantha prompted.

Jill turned to look at the map she'd tacked on the wall. Her eyes narrowed as she studied it. "Unless he went much farther away. Unless the killer left town and was hunting in another area all these years." And maybe...just maybe those other girls hadn't been labeled as victims. "Runaways," Jill whispered as everything finally made sense for her. "It was staring me in the face the whole time, and I never even saw it."

"Jill?"

She looked back at Samantha. "When Vanessa's mother came in today, she didn't report her daughter as missing. She said Vanessa was a runaway." Her heart was pounding, her heart racing. "What if…what if everyone thought the others were runaways, too? What if *that* is his victim type? He's picking girls that people—their own families—would think had run away. That would make the parents slower to report the crimes, especially if they thought the kids would be back." *Only they never came home.* "And when the authorities were finally notified, the investigation process for a runaway is different than for a suspected child abduction. Time would be lost, clues never found…"

Victims just…gone.

Samantha stared at her in silence a moment, and then she said, "Would they have thought you were a runaway, too?"

Her hands had clenched into fists. "Both of my parents were dead. I'd been moved to a new town, a place that was totally foreign to me. I had no friends. No one close to me at all. My grandmother and I…things were strained between us at first. I was distant. Reserved." She swallowed. "Yes, I could have gone down as a runaway."

"And Christy Anderson?"

"Her family can tell us that for sure." But her instincts screamed…*yes*.

"Her family," Samantha repeated, her lips giving a wry twist. "That would be the brother currently in holding, right?"

Unfortunately, yes.

"I want to have a go at him," Samantha said.

Jill nodded. "I knew you would." Because the perps

were Samantha's specialty. She never seemed to mind the darkness that cloaked the killers. Sometimes, Jill wondered if Samantha was drawn to that darkness.

"Will your sheriff give me the all clear to go in?" Samantha asked.

As if on cue, a light knock rapped against the office door. A moment later, the door opened, and Hayden slipped inside. "Jill, I need to talk to—" But he broke off when he glimpsed Samantha.

Jill realized her body was still too tense, her hands angry fists. She shook her head and tried to make herself relax. *I think I understand the perp now. I understand the victims.* "Hayden, this is my friend Agent Samantha Dark. And, Samantha, this is Sheriff Hayden Black."

Samantha offered Hayden her hand. "I have heard your name before…" she announced as her assessing gaze slid over him.

Hayden looked surprised. "You have?"

"Um." Samantha's face was expressionless, but her gaze had gone hard. "You're the man who—"

"I didn't save her," Hayden broke in quickly. "Look, if that's the story you heard. It's all wrong, okay? You want the truth? The truth is that Jill saved me that day. She pulled me back from a brink that no one else saw."

Samantha's head cocked to the right as her gaze slid over him, then slipped toward Jill. "Interesting. I was going to say…you were the man who broke Jill's heart."

Hayden's lips parted. His eyes jumped to Jill.

"But now…" Samantha nodded. "I see things are a lot more complex than I realized. Good. I like a nice mystery. Puzzles are my thing."

Hayden took a step toward Jill.

"I think I'll review these case files a bit." Samantha lifted the files. "I should also get a hotel room in town.

Maybe something with an ocean view. Love the water...
always reminds me of home." She headed for the door, and
then she paused, glancing back. "Will I be able to talk to
the prisoner?"

Hayden's gaze had narrowed as he glanced back her
way.

"Jill can vouch for me," Samantha added, voice soft. "I
assure you, I am very, very good at what I do. And if you
want me to discover Kurt Anderson's secrets, then you'll
let me have thirty minutes alone with him."

Then she was gone, easing from the room and shutting
the door softly behind her.

Jill released a low breath. *Way to keep a confidence,
Sam. I tell you one lousy truth during one drunken girls'
night and this is the thanks I get—*

"Is she right?"

Jill turned away and raked a hand through her hair,
being very, very careful not to touch her stitches. Her
head was still throbbing. "She's the best profiler I know."
Though to be honest, that wasn't Samantha's technical title
at the FBI. She was on the fast track to be the lead agent
in the Behavioral Analysis Unit. "Samantha knows how
to slip into anyone's mind. It's a talent she—"

"Did I break your heart, Jill?" He'd closed the distance
between them, and when he asked that question, his hand
lifted and his fingers stroked her shoulder.

She tensed at his touch, and Jill thought about lying.
But what would be the point? "Yes, but you knew that already." She turned to face him, tipping back her head as
she stared up at him. "You were the center of my world
back then. The person I loved far more than anyone else.
And you—"

"I wasn't good enough for you."

"That is such utter bull, Hayden."

"Whispers had followed me my whole life. Would I be like my old man? When would I get thrown in jail? I'd never amount to anything, then you met me on a pier. And after that day, everyone looked at me differently."

"Hayden…"

"People said I was a hero, but they were wrong."

No, he had—

"I followed that vehicle because I couldn't let you go. You looked at me in a way no one ever had before. You looked at me…" He swallowed. "And I changed. I liked the way I looked in your eyes. But I was holding you too tightly. I could see it. Hell, most people in the town did. You were becoming my obsession, and that wasn't right. You needed *more*."

"You dreamed of joining the FBI. Of making a difference. I wanted you to have that dream, Jill. I wanted to prove that I could be more than a selfish bastard with you. So I stepped back. I wasn't going to *hold* you back. I gave up the thing that was the most important in my life. Then I joined the military. I wanted to prove that I *could* be someone you'd be proud of. That I could protect and defend and that I could—"

"Stop." The word emerged, low, angry. "Just…*stop*."

He stared down at her. Jill's breath sawed from her lungs. "I was always proud of you. You should have seen that. I always wanted to be with you. You should have seen that, too." She pressed her lips together and felt the pain of the past once more. Only once…*because I don't want the past any longer.* "But we were two kids, Hayden. Two kids who'd clung too tightly to each other for so long. We were both making mistakes. Both stumbling along. That was then. We aren't those kids any longer."

"You're right." He nodded. "We're not. And I'll be damned if I make the same mistake again."

"Hayden?"

He pulled her even closer. "I love you."

Jill shook her head.

"I love you. If you hadn't come to Hope, I was coming to Atlanta to find you. I wanted another chance with you. I wanted to be with you. Taking the job as sheriff, joining the navy, damn it, don't you see? It was all for you. To show you that I could be the man you needed. That I am better. I am—"

Jill fisted her hand in his shirt and jerked him down toward her. She kissed him. Deep and wild and crazy. She didn't hold back her desire or the emotions that seemed to be ripping her apart. She just let go...the way she'd always wanted.

His arms closed around her. The heat of his body surrounded her. So close. So strong. So very Hayden.

His mouth lifted, just a bit and he growled, "When this case is over, I want another chance with you."

Her eyes were closed. She wanted to sink into him and escape the pain all around, but that wasn't an option. Christy needed them. "When this case is over..."

She made her eyes open. She stared at him.

His hard, determined face. So handsome.

"I want another chance with you, too," Jill whispered. Because she wouldn't be afraid. And she wouldn't let doubts hold her back. Hayden was the man she wanted.

Hayden was the man she'd have.

"THIRTY MINUTES."

Samantha nodded as she stared up at Hayden Black. He certainly wasn't the guy she'd anticipated. When Jill had talked about Hayden, well, Samantha had pictured a stuffy guy, reserved, strong but...controlled.

This man wasn't controlled. His emotions seemed to

spill from him, and, every single time that he glanced at Jill…

Jill wasn't the only one with a broken heart.

Hayden Black was strong, dangerous and, judging by the way he walked, that careful stride of his—

"You're profiling me, aren't you?" Hayden asked as he stilled in front of the heavy door that would take them back to the holding cell.

Samantha gave a quick, slightly nervous laugh. "Sorry. I tend to have trouble turning that off." And she knew it unnerved people. "My bad. Occupational hazard."

He faced her, crossed his arms over his chest and waited.

He was a sexy guy, she could see where Jill would have been attracted to the man but—

"Are you going to fill me in?" Hayden prompted.

"Excuse me?"

"I want to know what you think. Who am I?"

Uh… "Here? Now?" She wanted to get back into holding and take a go at Anderson. But, fine, if this was the price of admission. "I already knew you were ex-military, but I'm betting you were the leader of your team. You're too used to giving orders otherwise. You walk into a room and immediately access every threat, every weakness there. You thrive on risk, you love the rush of adrenaline. You're dangerous—"

His jaw hardened. "Dangerous?"

"Oh, yes." She believed that completely. She was staring into the eyes of a man who wouldn't hesitate to kill. Who probably *hadn't*. When you took a life, it left a mark on you, not outside, but deep within. Hayden carried that mark.

So did she.

"You think I'm dangerous to Jill?" His eyes had gone cold and hard.

But Samantha shook her head. "Not to her. I think she's probably the safest woman on the planet when you're near." Kind of like Lois Lane. "I think you'd do anything for her, but if some fool tries to take her from you again—"

"That *won't* happen."

She saw plenty when she looked at him. "Tried to live without her, huh? Tried to do the right thing?"

He lifted one blond brow.

"Bet that sucked." Samantha smiled. "Guess you won't be making that same mistake again."

"I'm surprised you're not telling me to stay the hell away from her."

"Why? Because you're so big and bad?" She laughed. "Jill can handle big and bad. What she *can't* handle is losing you again. Maybe you should ask her about her contacts at the CIA. Ask what she found so very fascinating about a certain SEAL team. Even when you weren't with her, trust me, she kept you close."

His eyes widened the faintest bit. Nice eyes. Dark. Deep. And the way he looked at Jill with those eyes...as if she were the center of his world.

Because she is.

For an instant, Samantha felt a brush of sadness. It would be nice to be looked at that way. To be cared about, in that way.

She cleared her throat. "So, look, as fun as profiling you is...you aren't the killer I'm after." And she chose her words with deliberate care. "So if you're still up to giving me that thirty minutes with Anderson..."

"I am." He motioned toward the door. "My deputy Finn Patrick will stay with you during the session. Jill and I are going to conduct some more sweeps of the beaches."

"Jill should call it a night," Samantha muttered. The

woman had looked dead on her feet. An up-close brush with a bomb would do that.

"She doesn't want to leave Vanessa out there alone. Jill thinks we're working against a clock. Twenty-four hours and then, well, that *then* part can't happen."

No, it couldn't.

He opened the door that led back to holding. She brushed by him and saw that a deputy was already back there, waiting on her. *Deputy Finn, I presume.* But she hesitated and glanced back at Hayden. "Stay close to Jill." Because while she'd been reading the files, alarm bells had gone off in her head. She was missing something with this case. They all were. She knew it...

What?

"Always." He gave her a little salute and turned away.

She marched deeper into the holding area. A man sat with hunched shoulders on a cot inside that cell. He glanced up at her. "My lawyer said for me not to speak with another soul here, so, lady, you should just turn around and keep walking right back out."

She did keep walking. Not out, though, but all the way up to his cell. Her high heels clicked on the floor.

His frown deepened. "Lady..."

"We can get your lawyer in here," Samantha said because she knew just how this game worked. "He can listen to my interview with you. He can tell you what to say or what not to say. We can do all of that."

His gaze slid over her. "Who are you?"

"Samantha Dark." The name would mean nothing to him. She had her FBI badge clipped to her hip but he wasn't looking away from her face. He was staring directly at her, gazing into her eyes as if he had nothing to hide.

Such a lie. We all have plenty to hide. Too much.

"We can certainly go that route," Samantha continued.

"But then, another girl will probably die. A girl just like Christy."

He flinched.

"Do you really want that to happen? Do you want another death on you?"

"I didn't kill my sister!"

And that was why he would talk to her. He couldn't talk to Jillian…when he looked at her, Samantha knew the past overwhelmed Kurt Anderson. Guilt tore at his insides. When he looked at Hayden Black, shame filled him. *Because Hayden saved Jill but you couldn't save your sister.*

This guy carried his grief like a cloak around him. Time to rip that cloak away. "You didn't kill her." She nodded. "So how about we find out who did?"

Chapter Thirteen

The full moon hung heavy in the sky as it shone down on the waves. The roar of the water was so loud, too loud, as it beat against the shore.

Searchers were sweeping the entire city. Deputies, volunteers, anyone and everyone. Jill knew that Hayden had already checked all the vacant and vacation rental properties in the area.

There had been no sign of Vanessa.

But, that morning... *It had all started on this beach.* Vanessa had been there. Her bike had been removed from the parking lot, taken in as evidence, but...

You were here, Vanessa. This is where everything started for you. Where would it end?

She looked to the left and saw Hayden patrolling. His flashlight swept over the beach. She knew what he feared, just as she knew why he'd wanted them to start beach searches immediately.

Christy Anderson's body had been left on the beach.

Hayden thought they'd find Vanessa's body discarded in the same way. Every minute that passed...*he thinks it is a minute that brings us closer to her death.*

Her grip tightened on the flashlight that she carried. There were no bodies to find, not yet. "He's still here." The words pulled from her.

Hayden was so far away, she didn't think he'd heard her, but he moved closer. He was a big, dark shadow in the night.

"He's still here," Jill said again, her voice stronger, harder. "There's something about this town. I think it's always pulled him back."

"Or maybe he just never left." Hayden's light pointed at the sand near her feet. "You and I did, but maybe he didn't. Maybe all of these years, he was right here."

A killer, hiding in their midst.

"Do you think Vanessa is still alive?" Hayden asked quietly.

She considered that for a moment. Not what she wanted to believe but the truth. *Was she still alive?* "Yes." And that was something they could use. "Because he doesn't have what he wants. Not yet."

"He wants you."

"No." Because that wasn't exactly the truth. "He wants me dead."

"Jillian West has a new theory about the victims," Samantha said. She stood a few inches away from the bars, her gaze on the man who'd risen to stare at her. "She thinks the perp picked girls who would have initially been labeled as runaways, not abduction victims. A smart move because that would have bought the perp more time to cover his tracks."

Kurt's brow furrowed.

"Would your sister have run away?"

"No, no, Christy *wouldn't*—"

"Your parents are divorced," Samantha interrupted. A deliberate tactic. *Never start with the question you really want answered. Trick, lead, catch your suspect off guard.*

"Yeah. My mom couldn't take it after—after Christy.

My dad was drinking all the time. Hardly the same man... she had to get away."

"And she took you with her."

His brows notched up, running toward his forehead. "Yeah, so?"

She just stared.

"You think I abandoned him? Is that it? Look, lady, I didn't have a choice. I didn't—"

"I don't think you abandoned him. But I do wonder, were there any problems between your parents *before* Christy's death?"

"My dad...he worked a lot, okay? He traveled all the time. He wasn't there much, that was my mom's complaint. That he was always on the road."

She blinked. "What kind of work did your father do back then?"

"Pharmaceutical sales."

Samantha didn't let her expression alter.

"He had a territory to cover. So he wasn't at home a lot. He was providing for us. Doing the best he could." He raked a hand through his hair. "He just...he lost it after my sister died. Drinking...drinking so much and yelling all the time. Always blaming—" But he broke off, clamping his lips shut.

"Always blaming you?" Samantha finished. "Your mom?"

He gave a bitter laugh. "No. Always blaming Jill. Always saying it was her fault." He turned on his heel. "Dad used to rage about her, over and over. Saying if she'd died, Christy would be alive. That it was always Jill's fault. Even when he got fired from his job—for all the damn drinking—that was still Jill's fault."

"But Jill was a victim," she said carefully. "You understand that, don't you? Jill didn't hurt your sister. Someone else did that. Someone else took her. Someone else broke her neck. Someone else put her on that beach. Covered her up…"

His head sagged. "Christy always liked the beach. She'd go out there for hours and just watch the waves. She loved that place."

Christy was covered. She was taken to a place she loved. Samantha thought of the crime scene photos that she'd glimpsed in the old file.

Christy's clothes had been perfectly arranged. No sexual assault. She cleared her throat. "Tell me about the last time you saw Christy."

He glanced back at her, frowning.

She'd deliberately switched her questions because Samantha was about to loop the knot.

So to speak.

"What was your sister doing, the last time you saw her?"

He rubbed his hand over the back of his neck. "She was looking for our dad. She came to my room right after she'd gotten home from her softball practice, asking where he was. She wanted to go out with some of her friends but she wanted money to spend, so she was looking for Dad." His shoulders rolled back. "I was leaving so I barely even said three words to her as I walked down the hall. I didn't have time for Christy. Too cool, you know? Too damn cool."

"What were those three words?"

He blinked at her.

"Do you remember those three words?" Samantha pushed.

He swallowed. "Yeah, yeah, I remember them."

Samantha waited.

"Dad's out back." He gave a grating laugh. "That's all I said. 'Dad's out back.' Hardly anything earth-shattering, right? Not like that is gonna break her case wide-open."

Before she could reply, the door to the holding room opened behind her. Deputy Finn Patrick rushed from his position to intercept the redheaded guy in the crisp gray suit who'd just stepped in as if he owned the place.

"Why is my client being interviewed?" The redheaded man pulled a folded white piece of paper from his suit pocket.

Another deputy was behind the lawyer—a woman with short-cropped brown hair. Samantha had met her earlier, Deputy Wendy Hollow. Wendy appeared none too pleased as she shared a fast glance with Finn. "Judge Eisen just called. We've got orders to release Anderson."

"Of course, you do," the lawyer retorted, voice saccharine sweet. "After all, at least one person in this town—a person in a position of power—realizes that the Anderson family has been through enough hell. My client is a victim here. Some twisted individual—the same individual who killed his sister—is tormenting him the same way that perpetrator is tormenting Special Agent West. A tragedy, all the way around." He nodded toward Finn. "My client needs to be processed so he can get the hell out of here. It's late. He needs to get home. After all, he has to take care of his father."

Samantha glanced back at Kurt. She wasn't done with him.

"I'm sorry," the lawyer murmured as he slipped closer to her. "But *who* are you? And why were you talking *alone* with my client?"

She turned her head and gave him her own saccharine smile. She was pretty good at that. "I'm not alone. Deputy Patrick was with us."

His gaze raked over her and lingered on the badge. "FBI? If my client's rights were violated—"

"I wanted to talk to her," Kurt suddenly called out.

His lawyer's eyes widened in surprise. Samantha made sure not to let her surprise show. Another trick she had—she only let her emotions out when she wanted others to see them. Most days, she knew it was better to *not* let anyone see her weakness.

Killers enjoyed weakness far too much. When they saw weakness, it was like a shark scenting blood in the water.

"I want to find Christy's killer. I want to stop him," Kurt stated flatly. "But I don't know anything that can help. I let my sister down years ago, and I'm still letting her down now."

HAYDEN'S PHONE RANG, a jarring cry in the dark. He swore and pulled the phone from his pocket, glancing at the screen. It was a new phone, one that he'd picked up just a few hours before. *Since his last one basically melted.* "It's Finn," he said. "Better take this." He turned from her, pacing a few feet away.

Her body stiffened as she watched him. *Don't let Vanessa's body have been discovered. Don't—*

"Judge Eisen did what?" Hayden exploded. "No, no, that guy is way overstepping his authority. Doesn't he realize the magnitude of this case? To let Kurt Anderson just walk—"

Her phone rang. She pulled it out, frowning. The screen had been smashed to hell and back at the bomb scene, and she was lucky the thing hadn't melted on her, like Hayden's had.

When Jill saw the name on the screen, her heart seemed to stop. Unknown Caller. She swiped her finger over that cracked screen, trying to make sure she didn't slice her skin and she slipped away from Hayden, hunching her shoulders. "Agent West."

"Were you afraid, when the fire came for you?"

"No, I was angry." She kept her voice low. Behind her, she could still hear Hayden blasting at Finn. "I thought we'd agreed to a trade."

"Um, but you cheated. You had a trace on the phone." He paused. "Bet you still have one going."

I bet I do. Uncovering an unknown caller's telephone number was actually an easy business. A simple reverse phone lookup revealed that information. But actually tracking the mystery caller's signal, *finding* that phone... it took more work. *And help from the FBI.*

"Here I went to all the trouble of getting a new burner phone..." He gave a rough laugh. "And you're still playing your same game."

"Sorry to put you out," she snapped.

His laughter had died away. "If you send all the deputies and your FBI buddies swarming on me, I promise you, Vanessa Gray will die."

That was the first official confirmation that he'd taken Vanessa. *Right from this beach. The same place, the same way.* "How do I know she isn't already dead?"

There was a beat of silence. "H-hello?" A girl's voice, weak and raspy.

"Vanessa?"

"I—I want my brother," the girl whispered. "Can I please get—" But her voice was abruptly cut off.

Each breath that Jill took seemed to chill her lungs.

"She's alive," the man rasped at her. "But how long she stays that way, well, it depends on you."

Jill looked over her shoulder. Hayden was pacing as he talked, but he was glancing her way. She started to signal to him—

"Don't." One word, growled.

And she knew the caller was close enough to watch her. *He's close and he has Vanessa with him.*

"I don't want Hayden Black getting involved. I don't want deputies. I don't want anyone but you."

She swallowed. "You still offering an exchange? Me for Vanessa?" She kept her voice as low as possible.

"Yes."

"Like I'm supposed to trust you?" Hell, no. "You just want to lead me into another cabin so that you can blow me to pieces."

"That is one option."

Her hold tightened on the phone.

"I could always kill Vanessa right now," he said. "Since you're so untrusting of me... I could snap her neck right—"

Vanessa was screaming in the background. Begging.

"Don't," Jill said. "Just...*don't*."

Silence.

"Give me the second option," she ordered.

But he didn't speak.

"Damn it—"

"It's your fault she's dead," he said, his voice different, aching. "I never meant...you did all this. You ruined everything. Destroyed the life I had. It was all so perfect before you."

He wasn't talking about Vanessa. She knew he meant Christy. *It's your fault she's dead.* "Another young girl doesn't have to die," Jill said softly. "We can end this. Tell me where to be and I'll come." With backup. With guns blazing. With enough strength to take him out and to save Vanessa.

"That's not how it works." Just like that, the emotion was gone from his raspy voice as if he'd just flipped a switch inside of himself. "Get rid of Hayden. Go back to your house on the beach. When I'm sure you're alone, I'll call you." A brief pause. "If you use the FBI to track this call, I'll know. I'll be watching. I'll see them come and she'll be dead before anyone breaches the door."

The line ended. Jill stared at her phone.

"No, no, Finn, just let the guy go, all right? But I want a tail on him. You make sure that a deputy is watching Anderson 24/7. Right. Yes, yes, I'm on my way."

She pushed her phone into her pocket and took a bracing breath. She turned to see Hayden end his call.

"Kurt Anderson is walking," he said, striding toward her. "Looks like we don't have enough evidence to hold him. All circumstantial. So he's leaving the station now."

So...if he was at the station, with eyes on him, then Kurt Anderson wasn't her twisted caller. His story had been real. Someone had taken his car to try and frame him. Someone who'd been able to get easy access to the Anderson house.

"I heard you talking, too," Hayden said. "What's happening? What's going on?"

Get rid of Hayden. She looked over his shoulder. In the distance, she saw a line of beach houses, with cheery lights glowing from their interiors. Beacons shining to her. The caller had been watching. He was *still* watching. Jill knew that.

She also knew...*if I follow his rules, Vanessa will live.*

The perp had made this a very, very personal battle. It wasn't about abducting victims to him. It was about getting back at Jill. Punishing her.

"I was getting the same news," she murmured, still looking off in the distance. "But I don't think Kurt Anderson is our guy. We need to be focusing elsewhere. I mean, he was too young to be the man who took me years ago."

"Yeah, but that doesn't mean he isn't the SOB who broke into your cabin or who set the bomb for you. He and his old man... Jill, they have a lot of fury in them. A lot of hate. And it seems to be directed right at you."

Just as the caller's fury was directed at her.

It's your fault she's dead.

"Yes," Jill said softly. "It is. It's all on me." Because she'd gotten away. She'd lived, but another had died in her place.

"I need to get back to the station."

Yes, that was exactly where she needed him to be.

His hand curled under her chin. "I know you want to keep searching, but there isn't anything out here for us."

Wrong. *He* was out there. The perp. The man who'd taken Vanessa. "She's so scared, Hayden." The words slipped from her. "She wants to come home. She wants her brother."

"I know her brother," he said, his thumb sliding tenderly along her jaw. "I served with him. Porter is a good man. I already put out a call through my contacts to get him back here. He's Black Ops right now, but I'm doing my best to get him home."

And she didn't want that man to return home only to bury his sister.

"We'll resume the search at first light. That's when the rest of your team is arriving, right?"

Yes, she'd called in the southeastern CARD team for backup.

"More boots on the ground," Hayden said. "We *will* find Vanessa."

She leaned up on her toes and pressed her lips to his. He seemed startled by her fast move, but she'd needed to kiss him once more. To taste him. To just remember what it was like to be safe and loved.

By him.

With him.

The wind blew against her and he was so strong and steady. Her haven.

His tongue slid against her lips, thrust into her mouth.

Desire flared hot in her blood. His kiss, his touch…that was all it took. She wanted him. Needed him.

But now wasn't the time to have him. She savored Hayden just a moment longer. Then she eased away from him. For a moment, she just stared at him in the darkness. Her Hayden. She swallowed and asked, "Take me back to my cabin?"

He gazed down at her, his eyes gleaming.

"My head…it's hurting a bit. I think I need to rest some so I can be sharp for the search in the morning."

Hayden nodded. "Of course." He took a step back but seemed to study her.

She exhaled slowly. "Thank you." She'd get him to leave her at the cabin and then…

Then the real fight will begin.

SAMANTHA TAPPED HER fingers on the check-in desk at the sheriff's office as she watched the lawyer hustle Kurt Anderson out of that place. Kurt looked tired, his shoulders slumped and…

His gaze darted back toward her.

That man looks guilty. Every time he glanced her way, she saw the taint of guilt in his stare.

"Sheriff said for me to send a tail with him," Finn murmured as he sidled up next to her. "I'm gonna be that tail."

Her gaze slid toward him.

"I'll make sure the guy doesn't hurt anyone. And if he does anything suspicious, if he can lead us to that missing girl, I'll be calling Sheriff Black right away."

She slipped him her card. "Make sure you keep me updated, too."

He blinked.

But before he could say more, Kurt's lawyer was opening the door and the guy was waltzing out with their number one suspect.

"Showtime for you, Deputy." Samantha inclined her head toward the door.

Finn waited a moment, probably trying not to look too obvious, and then he slipped out after the others.

Samantha exhaled. She didn't think Kurt was their perp, but things sure weren't adding up for her.

Dad's out back. She grabbed the file that Jill had prepared on Christy Anderson's disappearance, and she flipped back through the witness testimony. Theodore Anderson had been questioned about his whereabouts at the time of his daughter's disappearance. According to him, he'd been out on a solo fishing trip. He'd left late the night before and hadn't gotten back until midday…long after his daughter had been taken.

But why did Kurt say his dad was out back if the guy was actually out fishing?

Had Kurt been lying to her? Or had his father lied to the authorities years before?

Samantha nodded to Deputy Hollow—Wendy had taken over the check-in desk—and then she hurried outside. She needed to find Jill and talk to her more about that old case. Maybe Jill remembered details that could help her. She grabbed for her keys and hit the button to unlock her rental car. Her heels clicked on the pavement and the roar of the ocean filled her ears.

A sudden awareness had her tensing. A shiver slid down her spine and Samantha knew that she wasn't alone.

She looked to the left—the lawyer and Kurt Anderson were gone. Finn's patrol car was slipping from the lot.

Her gaze slid to the right—and to the man who was walking away from the shadows.

"There you are," he said, his voice deep and rumbling.

His stride was determined as he stalked toward her. "Want to tell me what the hell you are doing?"

Her brows lifted.

"Partners don't just cut out of town without any word," he added darkly. The light from the station fell on his face. And her new partner at the FBI—Blake Gamble— sure didn't look happy with her. "If you're working a case, *we're* working it. You don't get to leave me in the dust."

What in the hell is he doing here? "How did you know where I was? And *why* are you here?"

"The director sent me down. Said I should be with you, even if it isn't an 'official' investigation for us."

It was official as far as she was concerned. "I was called in as a favor," she said, turning to face him fully. Blake was a big guy, well over six feet, and built along the same hard, tough lines as Jill's Sheriff Black. "I'm here for a friend."

He stopped walking when he was less than a foot away from her. "And you didn't think I'd agree to help out your *friend*?"

She was still trying to feel out her new relationship with Blake. So far, the guy seemed to be a definite by-the-book type. But she had a feeling Blake had lots of layers hidden beneath his careful control. "I wasn't sure what you'd do."

"Well, let me tell you… I'd have your back."

The words were simple. Easy.

"That's what partners do, right?" Blake continued. "We watch out for each other?"

"Yes." That's what they were supposed to do.

"Besides, I know Jillian West, too. Not as well as you do, but I would never walk away from a case *or* from my partner. So tell me what I can do to help." He gave a decisive nod. "Because the boss said there was a missing kid in this town. What can we do to bring her home?"

Chapter Fourteen

"Seriously, Hayden, you don't have to walk me up." Jill had opened her door and the car's interior light spilled down on her. "I've got this."

He locked his jaw and forced a nod. He wanted to go up there, do a full search and make sure the place was safe... *because it's Jill.* But the woman was armed. She knew how to spot the signs of an intruder, and—

Hell, I just don't want to leave her.

"I'll check in at the station and be back," he assured her.

She climbed from the car. "You don't have to do that."

He jumped out and followed her, catching her arm before she could head for the stairs that would take her up to the main level of the cabin. "I want to do that." Didn't she get that? He wanted to spend his days and nights with her. They'd talked about a second chance, and he wasn't going to let that chance get away. For him, Jill was it. His everything. His one shot at happiness. He wouldn't lose her again. "I'll check in, then I'll be back." But as he stared at her, worry gnawed at him. "Hell, I'll just stay here." The woman had a concussion after all, damn it. "You might need me and I—"

"I need some time alone, Hayden." Her gaze was on the waves, not him. "Just...give me tonight, would you? I don't need you to keep guard over me. I can protect myself, and I need that time."

You're pushing her too hard. He looked down at his hand. "Right." Hayden made himself let her go. "I'll send a patrol by to—"

"Always the protector, aren't you? Even when I don't want protecting."

He was missing something. She wasn't looking at him and her voice seemed too calm. Too reserved.

"I need this night on my own. If it makes you feel better to send a patrol circling by later, then do it. But I'd rather every available unit you have...I'd rather your efforts be focused on Vanessa and not me." Now her gaze finally did come back to him. "She's what matters now. You understand that, don't you?"

"Jill—"

She backed away from him. "If I see any trouble, you'll be the first one I call."

This wasn't right. The scene was wrong. *She* was wrong.

"Good night, Hayden." Jill turned away. She hurried up the stairs and didn't glance back at him. He stood there a moment, watching until she disappeared inside. The lights flashed on in her cabin.

He still didn't leave. Something was wrong. Something was nagging at him. She'd kissed him so frantically on the beach...

And now she's sending me packing.

He lingered for a moment longer, then headed back to his patrol car. He slipped inside and a few moments later, he was heading away from Jill and her cabin by the shore.

He glanced in his rearview mirror, but Hayden only saw darkness.

I'll be back tonight, Jill. Whether you want me here or

not. I'll be back. Because finding Vanessa Gray was absolutely a priority for him. But keeping Jill safe?

That is always my first mission.

JILL HELD HER BREATH as she stared below and watched Hayden's car slowly pull away. He'd been suspicious at the end, and she hadn't been sure that he'd leave her alone.

She hadn't wanted him to go. She'd wanted to pull him in, to get him to help her stop the perp out there. *But he was watching.* And if Vanessa's abductor saw her rush in with Hayden at her side, then an innocent girl could die.

She put her phone down on the kitchen table. She stared at it a moment, willing the thing to ring. It didn't.

So she moved back. She went into her bedroom, and opened her suitcase. Jill took out her backup weapon and she strapped it to her ankle. Then she checked her service gun. Its weight was reassuring in her hand. She might be playing by the perp's rules, but she didn't intend to make herself easy prey.

No, when morning came, Jill intended to still be standing.

And Vanessa Gray would be at her side. *Alive.* Safe. She wouldn't lose another victim. She *couldn't* lose her.

Her phone rang, jerking her attention and Jill rushed back into the den. Her phone was shaking on the table, vibrating. She peered down at the broken screen.

Unknown Caller.

SHE JUST WANTS her brother.

Hayden slammed on the brakes. The car's tires screeched.

Jill's words had been replaying in his head as he tried to figure out why she'd withdrawn from him. Back at the beach, she'd been talking about Vanessa. About the girl being afraid.

And Jill had said that Vanessa wanted her brother.

Maybe she'd just been talking, piecing together parts of Vanessa's life and assuming that the girl would be afraid and wanting the security of having her brother close. After all, Jill had talked to Vanessa's mother. She'd known that Vanessa had an older brother who was currently out of the country.

Maybe she'd been making a victim profile.

He spun the car around and shoved his foot down on the gas.

Or maybe Jill had been repeating what she'd heard Vanessa say. Her voice had softened when she spoke on the beach. There'd been pain whispering in her words…

And then Jill had wanted to go home. Alone.

Sonofa—

He used his Bluetooth connection to call the sheriff's office. When his call was answered, he demanded, "I want to talk to Samantha Dark—is she still there?"

"No, Sheriff," Wendy answered. "She left a few moments ago."

Hell. "Do you know if she called Jill West before she left? Did Agent Dark make *any* phone calls while she was at the station?"

"I don't know, sir. Sorry."

"If you see her again, get her to call me. Right the hell away." He ended the connection and narrowed his eyes on the road up ahead. If Samantha hadn't been on the phone with Jill…then Jill could have been talking to the perp again. The guy had called her once, offering up a deal, maybe he'd called again.

But Jill would have told me. She would have—

He was near Jill's cabin. Close enough that he saw her car. Saw *her* heading to that car.

Hayden killed the lights on his own vehicle. Jill was

moving fast as she spun her car out and left the beach. She'd had her phone to her ear. She'd been talking frantically to someone.

To the perp?

Jill would lie to me...if it meant that she could help a victim.

The killer had offered Jill a trade once before. Hayden was very afraid that the guy had made her another deal.

Her voice slipped through his mind. *She's what matters now. You understand that, don't you?*

She'd been telling him, right then, and Hayden hadn't picked up on the truth. As her car headed down the narrow road, he didn't even hesitate. Hayden had followed Jill once before, followed her on a dark and desperate path, and he'd damn well do it again.

He'd follow Jill anywhere, even straight to hell, if that was what it took. He kept his lights off and he didn't go too fast. He didn't want Jill to see him. Jill...or the perp. *He could be watching.*

Whatever twisted plans that jerk had, they weren't going to happen.

You aren't getting her, bastard. I'll do whatever it takes, but I won't lose Jill again.

"It's the normal houses that hide the worst monsters," Samantha said as she slammed her car door and stared up at the house located at 1509 Sea Breeze Way. "They always look so innocent and then—too late—you see that facade was just a lie."

Blake hurried around the front of the car and came to her side. "So...we're going to interrogate the guy? Right now? In the middle of the night?"

"Not an interrogation. Just one follow-up question." She patted his chest and tried not to notice that the guy was seriously muscled. He was her partner. *Only* her partner. There was no mixing business with pleasure at the FBI, no matter how handsome she might find Blake to be. "And it's not as if the guy is asleep. He just got released a little while ago. His lawyer dropped him off and Kurt's in there, probably pacing the floors." She inclined her head toward the house that waited—with seemingly all of its interior lights turned on.

"As long as he doesn't go screaming to his lawyer about FBI harassment..." Blake muttered.

"He won't." She was sure of this. "Because something else is going on here." Something that Kurt knew but wasn't sharing, something that seemed to be tearing him apart. She glanced down the street, and, sure enough, sitting three houses back, underneath the heavy shelter of an oak tree's limbs, she saw Deputy Finn waiting in his patrol car.

It was good to know the sheriff's office was keeping watch on the Anderson house. Especially because that perfectly trimmed, perfectly normal house felt wrong to her.

Nothing is ever as perfect as it seems. Her friend Cameron Latham would have said that bit. Like her, Cameron had gotten his PhD in criminal psychology from Harvard. Cameron was her sounding board, whenever she had a particularly good—or bad—theory swirling in her head, she'd run her thoughts by him. Cameron would take one look at that little house and say, *Too perfect, Sam. Find the lies inside.*

That was just what she was there to do.

Samantha lifted her chin and led the way up the carefully trimmed lawn. She reached the door and rapped against the wood. She heard fumbling inside, the shuffle of footsteps, the hum of a TV and then—

The door opened soundlessly. No little creaks, no groans of the hinges. *Perfect.*

Kurt Anderson stood in the doorway, and he looked far, far from perfect. His hair stood on end, as if he'd been raking his fingers through it. His face was pale, his gaze desperate.

"Mr. Anderson?" Samantha tried a quick smile. "Our conversation was interrupted earlier…" *Conversation, interrogation—whatever you want to call it.* "I just had one question for you."

"He's not here."

Samantha frowned at that abrupt response. "Um, who isn't here?"

"My dad." Kurt's hand raked through his hair. "Knew this would happen… I was gone too long… He'd been so good…so good, but to mess up now…"

She didn't look back at Blake, but she could practically feel her partner's sudden tension. "Mess up what, exactly?"

Kurt's hand fell. "He's been sober for a year and seven months, ever since I came back to town. I *made* him get sober. But me being taken to the station… Jill pushing about Christy…opening up the past, I know it's pushed him over the edge. I found a whiskey bottle in the kitchen." He swallowed, his Adam's apple bobbing. "It's empty."

"May I come inside?" Samantha asked him, her voice soft.

Kurt stumbled back. "He's gone. I need…I need Hayden to put out an APB for him. My dad isn't the same when he drinks. He could get hurt." If possible, Kurt's skin turned even paler. "He could…hurt someone else."

The inside of the home was in shambles. The couch had been turned over, a lamp was smashed and a picture frame… Samantha bent to pick up the frame from the floor, and shards of glass dropped near her feet. She stared at the picture of the smiling girl with blond hair and dimples. The same girl who had been in the old file at the police station. A picture of Christy Anderson, standing with her father.

"Did you do this?" Blake's deep voice rumbled from behind her.

"This?" Kurt appeared confused, and then he glanced around the room. "No, no. Dad must have done it. I told you, when he drinks, he's not the same. He gets so angry, like a different person. But he was sober until Jill came back." His hands fisted. "She should have stayed away. He saw her the first day she was back in town, saw her and Hayden and everything came rushing back for him. Like a ticking bomb...I could see it happening."

A ticking bomb...pretty interesting description considering what had happened to Jill and Hayden.

"Wait. Who the hell are you?" Kurt suddenly demanded as his gaze sharpened on Blake.

Samantha kept her grip on the picture frame. "He's my partner, Blake Gamble. I told you, we had one more question for you."

"Forget your damn questions!" Kurt yelled. "Get Hayden on the line! Make him go look for my father! Get the guy out here, now!"

"I will," Samantha assured him. "I'll get a whole team to look for your father."

Kurt nodded, appearing a bit appeased.

"But I just need you to answer one question for me first. Just one."

"Lady," Kurt growled as he took an aggressive step toward her. "You aren't playing with my dad's life."

Blake was suddenly at her side. "Watch the tone, buddy. *Watch* it."

Her chin notched up as she met Kurt's blazing stare.

"I'm not playing any game. I'm just trying to find out the truth." *A very long overdue truth.* "The day your sister disappeared, your father said he was out fishing. But tonight at the station, you told me that he was home, that you'd told Christy your father was out back."

Kurt licked his lips.

"What's the truth, Kurt? Just tell me that. Where was your father when Christy vanished?"

JILL PARKED HER car near the pier. She sat behind the wheel for a moment, her hands gripping the steering wheel. And the phone beside her rang again.

Her hand flew out and her finger swept over that fractured screen.

"I can see you, Jill. And you came alone. Just as you said."

She was so tired of the grating voice. So tired of the games.

"Go to the end of the pier...and then jump in the water," he ordered her.

"Are you insane? Why would I—"

"Swim straight out, and you'll find my boat."

Jill sucked in a sharp breath. *He's on a boat. No wonder he was able to see me when I was on the beach with Hayden earlier. The guy was watching us from the water.* Probably using night vision binoculars.

And the man who'd broken into her cabin...they'd found his motorcycle but not him. *Why? Because he'd swum out to his boat?*

"I can see you perfectly, Jill. I'll watch you swim to me. Just you. If I spot another car coming with you, if I spot any deputies or the damn sheriff, then I'll break Vanessa's throat and throw her body in the water."

"I'm by myself. You don't have to worry."

"That's what I thought before, too. That I had you all alone, and *he* was there."

Jill checked her weapons. She hadn't counted on a dive in the water. The guns might not even shoot when she came out.

So I need another weapon. Something else I can use.

"Walk on the pier, Jill. Get in the water. *Now.* You have fifteen minutes to reach me. Fifteen minutes or Vanessa dies."

She hung up on him. Then she sent a text, fast and frantically. She opened her glove box and grabbed the screwdriver that was inside. Not much of a weapon, but it was one that water wouldn't destroy. She shoved the screwdriver inside the top of her jeans, hoping to keep it secured in place, and then Jill climbed out of the car. Her steps were quick as she headed out onto the pier. The moon shone down on her, giving Jill plenty of light as she hurried across the wood. She looked out at the water, but didn't see any lights from boats.

He's got his lights off because he doesn't want to be seen. He's out there, waiting. No cabin by the marsh needed for him this time.

How perfect was a boat for this type of crime? He could take his victims, kill them, dump the bodies. If he weighed them down, they might not be discovered at all.

The victims would just stay missing.

She reached the end of the pier and stared out into the darkness. For just a moment, she remembered a blond boy standing in that spot. Hair a little too long. Eyes so dark and deep.

Hayden. I love you.

She hoped he knew that. She'd never stopped loving him. She didn't think she could.

Jill exhaled slowly and climbed over the wooden railing

of the pier. She sat there a moment, staring at the waves. And then...

She jumped.

HE DIDN'T PULL into the pier's parking lot. When Hayden saw Jill turn up ahead of him, he braked his car, killed the engine and left it just off the road. Then he kept to the shadows as he hurried toward the pier. He arrived just as Jill started walking down that long wooden pier. She was looking straight ahead, staring out over the water.

His eyes narrowed as he scanned the area. There was no one else there. Jill couldn't possibly be meeting the perp...*he wasn't here.*

Or maybe, maybe the guy just hadn't arrived yet. Maybe Jill was supposed to meet the kidnapper. An exchange? Was that about to happen? Jill trading her life for Vanessa's? He could see her trying to do some move like that. Hell, he and Jill needed to have a serious damn talk. She couldn't keep risking herself like this.

He trailed behind her, but he never went into the moonlight. He stopped near the old souvenir shop. He could see Jill perfectly as she walked forward, never hesitating. And then...

His phone vibrated in his pocket. He pulled it out quickly but didn't look at the text he'd just received because—because Jill had climbed over the railing.

What in the hell was she doing?

Jill? He took a step toward her.

She jumped into the water. Just plunged straight into the waves.

Jill!

Chapter Fifteen

The water was colder than she'd expected. Ice-cold. It chilled her limbs, stole her breath and made every stroke that she took painful. Her wet clothes dragged at her, and Jill had to kick out of her shoes. She'd always been a good swimmer, thank goodness, so even the rough waves didn't stop her.

The salt water burned her nose, stung her face, had her coughing as the waves lapped at her face, but she could see the boat. Rising out of the darkness, hidden, because it was so far away from the beach. Anchored and waiting for her, it was at least a twenty-seven-foot sport yacht. She couldn't make out the name on the boat, not in the dark, but she saw the line of letters near the bow. Jill swam to the back of the boat, and her hand curled around the ladder there. She pulled herself up, her breath heaving out of her lungs. She stood there a moment, water pooling down her body and a bright light shone straight into her eyes.

"Hello, Jillian…"

His voice wasn't rasping any longer. Wasn't disguised. She knew his voice. She knew him. But then, Jill had known his identity even before she'd jumped into the water. She'd known when he called her on that beach. When he'd said…

It's your fault she's dead…you did all this. Destroyed the life I had.

Those had actually been words she'd heard before... from Theodore Anderson.

"Hello, Mr. Anderson," Jill said. She kept one hand behind her back. She didn't want him to see that she had the screwdriver tucked into her sleeve. When she'd pulled herself up the ladder, she'd pushed the screwdriver up her sleeve. Easy access. Perfect access.

But first I need to make sure Vanessa is here.

"Jillian West." He didn't take the light off her face. "Looking a bit worse for wear. Guess you didn't get out of that cabin unscathed, after all."

"No, I didn't." But she wasn't talking about the bomb. She was talking about a time long ago. "I came alone, just like you ordered. Now show me Vanessa."

"She's in the cabin below."

He had a gun in one hand. She could see its bulky shape just beyond the light.

"I need to see her," Jill snapped.

He laughed. "You aren't giving orders out here. You're not the big, bad FBI agent out here. You know what you are?" He took a gliding step toward her.

She shivered in the cold air.

"You're my victim," he told her, voice growling. "And tonight, you're going to die."

No, I'm not.

KURT RAN A trembling hand over his face. "My dad used to have an old fishing boat that he'd take out when he was in town. The weekend Christy went missing...the night that Jillian West was taken...he *was* out fishing. I'd seen him loading up his boat. He even told me where he was planning to go...skimming out in the Gulf, maybe heading toward Destin."

Samantha just stared at him. She felt her phone vibrate in her pocket, but she didn't pull it out. Not yet.

"But he came back," Kurt mumbled as he started to pace amid the chaos of the den. "I saw him that morning. He was in and he was...he was so mad. Drinking. I told you, he changed when he drank. He was yelling. Furious. So I went in my room and I stayed away from him."

"Your sister didn't stay away," Samantha said. "You sent her out to him."

Kurt stilled. "I asked him about her. Dad said he never saw Christy that day, that he went back down to his boat. See—it was just a mix-up, that's all. Dad *never* saw Christy."

Her gaze slid toward Blake. His jaw was locked, his eyes glinting.

Her phone vibrated again, reminding her that she'd received a text. "Excuse me a moment." She slipped back a few feet and pulled out her phone. She saw the text—a group text that had been sent to her and Hayden Blake.

A text from Jill.

Come to pier. Perp on boat. Has V.

She took in a long, slow breath. "Kurt, does your father still have that fishing boat?"

"No." He shook his head, but then he pressed his lips together.

"Kurt?" Blake prompted, voice tight.

"He...he has a sports yacht now. Bought it after he got sober. Said it was his present to himself." Kurt licked his lips. "The boat's called *Christy*."

"Thank you for your time," Samantha said. She turned on her heel. Strode for the door.

"That's it?" Kurt yelled after her. Then she heard the

fast rush of his footsteps. "No way, lady, you said you'd help me find my dad. You said— Ow! Let me the hell go!"

She whipped around to see Blake standing between her and Kurt. Blake had grabbed the other man's wrist.

"He was lunging for you," Blake said, shaking his head. "A bad mistake." He released Kurt, but his body was tense, as if he were ready to attack again.

Kurt's cheeks had flushed. "I just need to find my dad. Will you help me find him or not?"

Her gaze sharpened on him. "You're afraid of what he'll do, aren't you?"

She saw the answer in the sudden widening of Kurt's eyes.

"I'm afraid, too," she told him, her words nearly a whisper. "But don't worry. We're going to find him. And the *Christy*." She curled her fingers around Blake's shoulder. "Come on. We need to leave. *Now*." They hurried back into the night and she ran for the car. Blake was right on her heels.

"Samantha, slow down!" Blake urged.

They didn't have time to slow down. She yanked open her door.

He grabbed the door and held tight. "Tell me what the hell is going on."

"Jillian found the killer."

"What?"

"I think she's on the *Christy* with him—and Vanessa is there. We have to get out there, now." She shoved his hand off the door. "So come on, let's get moving! Jillian needs us, and I'm not about to let her down."

JILLIAN'S FINGERS CURLED around the screwdriver as she slid it into her palm. "I want you to bring Vanessa out to me."

Theodore didn't move. "It's your fault."

So he liked to keep saying.

"I had it all planned. You were going to be perfect. The new girl in town, the one that didn't fit in. I'd never taken a girl from Hope before, too close to home, if you know what I mean."

He'd been living in that town, for all those years...

"But you were perfect. Like a little bonus gift."

She edged closer to him. He had the gun in his right hand, but he wasn't aiming it at her. Just holding it by his side.

"Then you got away." Anger roughed his voice. The boat rocked in the water. "You weren't supposed to get away. What if you brought the police to me? I tried to be careful, tried to make sure that you didn't see me too clearly but I was afraid..."

"And people who are afraid make terrible mistakes." She slipped forward. "Is that what Christy was? A mistake?"

"She...she found me in the garage. I had...I had the rope and the drugs I'd used on you. Christy asked me what I was doing. Your story...it had just been on the news. My girl saw it. She stared at me and in her eyes, I knew she realized what I'd done."

Had she, though? Had Christy put the pieces together just based on a rope? Or had this twisted killer before her snapped and taken his own daughter's life?

He lifted his hand—the hand with the gun—and still didn't even seem to notice he held the weapon. He slammed the back of his hand against the side of his head hitting himself hard. *Punishing* himself? "The urge was so strong. I had to kill, but *you* were supposed to be the one. Only you got away. Christy was there. Staring at me. I saw the truth in her eyes...*I saw.* I lunged for her and she screamed."

He hit his head again. "Christy screamed. I couldn't let her scream."

And he'd killed his own daughter. But he'd actually felt remorse for her death. *Unlike the others.* "You took her body to the beach..."

"She loved the beach," he whispered. "Just like me. Always loved the water."

"You covered her up. Positioned her." All signs of remorse. Of care.

His hand fell away from his head. "It should have been you."

The gun was pointed at her now. *Great. Now he remembers the weapon.*

"If you'd died, Christy would have been safe. I would never have hurt her."

Like she believed that one. "How many girls have you hurt?"

He didn't speak. She couldn't see his face clearly but was he smiling?

"Hard to remember them all," he admitted. "After Christy, I stopped. Lost so much. Lost *me*. The drinking numbed everything. The days slid by. I let everything go. Then Kurt came back. Made me get clean. Everything started to focus again...and then, as if right on time, you came back. I knew what I had to do. Once I kill you, I can get back the life I had."

Jill shook her head. "That's not going to happen."

He put the light down on the seat near him, and that bright glow stayed locked on Jill. "No one is here to save you."

"*I'm* here to save Vanessa. That was part of the deal, remember? I come here and you let her go."

He advanced toward Jill. "Guess what, *Agent* West? I lied about the deal. I'm planning to kill you both. I told you...*I'm* getting my life back. My life. My power. My control."

Because that was what it had always been about. Control. Dominance. "Guess what?" She threw those words back at him as Jill tightened her grip on that screwdriver. She could have tried to use her gun, but if the water had jammed the weapon, she'd lose her chance to attack. "I lied, too."

His arm jerked and the gun's nozzle pointed down at the deck. "What?"

"I texted Hayden and one of my contacts at the FBI." She used her left hand to point toward the beach. "They're all out there now." Or, if they weren't, they'd be there soon. "They know about you and the boat, and you're not getting away this time. You're going to pay for everything that you've done."

"You damn—" He lifted that gun again.

But Jill was running forward. She lifted up her screwdriver and lunged for him. The gun exploded and she felt the bullet whip past her shoulder, burning into the skin as it grazed her arm.

She drove the screwdriver at him, sinking it into his shoulder. He roared his rage and lifted that gun again.

They were close, her head tipped back as she stared up at his eyes. The monster from the dark. The one who'd haunted her for so long.

She yanked the screwdriver out of him and prepared to hit him again.

He fired. This time, the bullet slammed into her side. She staggered back.

"Jill!" At that wild roar, her head whipped around. Hayden was there, pulling himself up the ladder, water pouring off him. His hands were fisted, the bright light

aimed in his direction and clearly showing the rage on his face.

Her feet slipped and she tumbled down, slamming into the back of the seat.

"Just had to follow her again, didn't you?" Theodore snarled. "Always messing things up for me...*always*..."

"Get away from her," Hayden shouted.

But Theodore lifted his gun. "Time to end you, too. Shouldn't have played hero. Not then, not now."

"Stop!" Jill yelled. She'd yanked out the gun from her ankle holster. She pointed it at Theodore. "Drop your weapon, *now*!"

He laughed. "You just swam through the damn Gulf of Mexico. That weapon isn't going to fire. You think I didn't realize you'd have a gun with you? It's useless. *Useless*. But mine isn't."

He was going to shoot Hayden. *Not Hayden. Not Hayden.* "No!" She squeezed the trigger and the damn thing didn't fire. It just clicked. The weapon didn't shoot—

But Theodore's did. His weapon fired even as Hayden slammed into him. The two men staggered at the impact and then—

They fell off the side of the boat, sinking into the waves with a splash.

"Hayden!" She grabbed the light and scrambled to the side, ignoring the pain from her wound.

Had the bullet hit him before they went over? She kept one hand at her side, trying to stop the blood from pumping out and her other hand gripped the light. She swept it over the waves, searching frantically for Hayden. She put her foot on the side of the boat, ready to jump in after him, ready to do anything, risk *anything* for him—

Hayden's head broke the surface.

Her breath left her in a frantic rush.

He swam toward the boat. Strong, powerful strokes. She ran to the back, dropping the light and she grabbed his arm to help pull him on board. Pain knifed through her, surging from her wound, and she bit back a ragged gasp.

Then Hayden was in front. Wet, strong, *alive*. Her pain didn't matter. *He's safe.*

"That bastard shot you." Hayden put his hand on her side. "Baby, I'm so sorry. I'm—"

She kissed him. Fast. Hard. Wild. *Wrong time, wrong place.* She knew that and didn't care. "You're okay." The words tumbled out, so frantic. "When you went over, I was so scared." More scared than she'd ever been in her life. "You're okay."

"Jill, you're the one who was shot." His fingers tested her wound and he swore. "Too much blood, baby, too much. You need help."

She needed him. And he was there. *Safe.* "He told me not to tell anyone. Said he'd kill Vanessa." *Vanessa.* Jill glanced back at the stairs that led belowdecks. "She's down there. We have to make sure she's—" Her body trembled.

Hayden scooped her in his arms and carried her to the seat behind the wheel. He sat her down with gentle care. "I'll check. You stay here." His gaze scanned the darkness around them. "I don't know where that jerk is. He could be at the bottom of the Gulf, he could be swimming away, or he could be coming back for us."

She grabbed his shirt. "Make sure Vanessa is okay."

He snatched up the radio and called in a quick Mayday, demanding help and, after a fast glance at the screen near the steering wheel, he rattled off their coordinates to the Coast Guard. Then he bent down and kissed her once more.

Hayden. Alive. We're both safe.

He picked up the gun that had fallen when he and Theodore had gone over the side of the boat. "If you see him—"

Jill's fingers curled around the gun. "Don't worry. I won't hesitate. He's destroyed enough lives."

Hayden nodded. Then he turned and rushed toward the stairs.

Jill gripped the gun and she stared into the darkness around the boat. Her heartbeat seemed to thunder in her ears. Her side burned, the blood soaking her shirt and making it cling to her skin. The moments ticked by. The boat bobbed, pulling against its anchor.

"She's all right." Hayden appeared, holding a girl tightly in his arms. "She's okay, Jill. You got to her in time."

He put Vanessa down on the deck, and he started yanking at the ropes that still bound her hands. Jill saw that a gag had been pulled away from the girl's mouth.

Tears stung Jill's eyes. *Safe.*

"I—I want to go home," Vanessa rasped.

"You will," Jill promised her. "We're going to take you home. Everything is going to be okay." *She's alive. We found her alive.*

But the man who'd taken her... Jill's gaze dipped to the waves...

Where are you, Theodore Anderson? Where did you go?

THE DOCK BLAZED with lights. Deputies, EMTs, hell, half of the town seemed to be there when they finally made it to shore.

Jill was immediately put on a stretcher. Hayden saw an EMT start to cut away the bloody shirt that clung to Jill's side. He stepped forward—

"Stay with Vanessa!" Jill cried out, her frantic gaze locking with his. "Make sure she's okay—her family—"

He had his arm around Vanessa's shoulder. She was trembling against him. Shaking. He'd checked her out on the boat and she seemed unharmed, thank Christ.

Theodore Anderson. Theodore damn Anderson. The killer had been right there, all along.

Samantha Dark pushed through the crowd and rushed to Jill's side. "What happened?"

A tall, dark-haired man was right behind her. His gaze swept the crowd, then locked on Hayden.

FBI. Hell, that truth pretty much rolled off that guy. Hayden pegged him with one glance.

"Come on, Vanessa," Hayden said softly. "We'll get you checked out." He motioned toward another EMT and the fellow hurried toward them. He caught sight of Finn, and Hayden jerked his hand at the deputy. Finn shot through the assembled group. "*Stay* with her, got me? In the ambulance, every single minute." Because he was afraid.

Hayden's gaze cut to the water.

The waves were rougher, hitting the dock harder. The boats bobbed in the water.

When they'd gone over the side of the boat, Hayden had heard a distinct *thunk.* They'd been fighting as they fell, and Theodore's head had hit the side of the boat. They'd gone into the water and the waves had ripped them apart.

Hayden had been frantic to get back on the boat, to get back to Jill.

He hadn't searched for Theodore. And the man hadn't come up.

Was he dead?

Or had the bastard gotten away?

"Vanessa!" The scream cut through the crowd. High, desperate. Afraid.

A mother's scream.

Hayden motioned to the deputies, and they immediately cleared a path for Carol Wells so that she could get to her daughter. When Carol appeared, tears were streaming down her cheeks. Her face was stark white and the terror in her eyes made his chest ache.

"She's okay," he said quietly. His hand patted her shoulder and he pushed Carol toward Vanessa as she sat on the edge of a nearby gurney. "She's safe."

Carol stumbled toward her daughter. "I'm so sorry, Vanessa," Carol sobbed. "I'm so sorry, I'm so sorry..."

"Mom." Vanessa was crying, too. She lifted her arms. "Mom!"

They hugged tight. Hayden stared at them a moment. Their family wasn't perfect. No family was. But Vanessa was safe. Alive. They could deal with the problems that came their way. They had a chance now.

A chance that Theodore wouldn't take away from them.

He grabbed Finn's arm. "You stay with them, every minute, got it?" Hayden ordered again, because fear gnawed at him. Theodore Anderson didn't let his victims go easily.

"I won't let you down," Finn promised.

Hayden slipped away from him. Jill was being loaded into the back of an ambulance. She was fighting the EMT—why the hell was the woman doing that? "Jill!" He ran to her.

"I need to stay here!" Jill snapped to the EMT. "He's still out there—I have to make sure they find him—I can't go!"

"Hell, yes, you can," Hayden growled.

Samantha and the dark-haired man with her were huddled near the back of the ambulance. At his words, they both looked his way.

So did Jill.

But when she stared at him, Hayden saw her gaze soften.

She still looks at me the same way. Only Jill had ever

looked at him like that. With eyes wide with hope and...
love. It was still there. He hadn't destroyed it years ago,
as he'd feared.

It was still there.

"You need to get to a hospital," he said, and he climbed
right into the back of the ambulance with her. "Baby, you
need stitches and you lost a whole lot of blood. You have
to let the EMTs and the docs take care of you."

She grabbed his hand and held tight. "But Theodore's
still out there."

"I'll keep the search going." He brought her hand to
his lips. Kissed her. For an instant, his eyes closed and
he remembered swimming desperately to that boat, grabbing the ladder, seeing her—and hearing the boom of the
gun. "Thought I lost you." The terror was still inside him,
twisting at his gut, hollowing his insides. "You've got to
stop doing this to me."

His eyes opened.

Jill was staring at him the same way—

"God, I love you so much, Jill," he told her.

Her lips parted.

"You're giving me that chance we talked about," he said
quickly. "You're going to get stitched up, you're going to
heal, and we'll start fresh."

But... Jill shook her head.

That twisting inside of him turned into ice-cold fear.
"What?"

"Don't need to start fresh..." She wet her lips. "Still...
love you."

He leaned over.

"Uh, excuse me, Sheriff," the EMT began.

Hayden's hands were careful as they brushed Jill's hair
away from her cheek. "I've loved you since I was fifteen
years old. You've always been my world." He needed her

to understand this. "I will *never* stop loving you." Just as he'd never stop fighting for her, for them.

He pressed a kiss to her lips. Gentle. Tender. "You saved her, Jill. You brought Vanessa home."

Her lips curved into a faint smile.

"And you saved me." She always had. "So do me a damn favor, okay?" Now his voice was rough. "Go to the hospital because I need you okay. You *have* to be okay." She was everything to him. And just seeing her in pain ripped him apart.

Jill nodded.

His breath expelled in a rush.

"Finish the search," Jill ordered quickly. "Stay here, Hayden. Make sure the crews look everywhere."

"Yes, ma'am." He squeezed her fingers once more, and then he slid from the back of the ambulance. His gaze jerked to Samantha. "Will you—"

She was already climbing into the vehicle. "Don't worry. I'll stay with her the whole time. I'll make sure she's a good patient and that she's safe."

Hell, yes.

That twisting inside eased as he backed away and the ambulance roared from the scene with a squeal of its sirens.

When she was clear, when Jill was gone, a long sigh eased from him.

"Must've been hard…"

Hayden glanced at the guy he'd pegged as an FBI agent.

The man pulled out his ID and flashed it at him. "Blake Gamble. I'm Samantha's new partner. Came down to assist her and Jillian. Though it looks like I was late to most of the party."

"Party's not over," Hayden denied grimly. "Theodore Anderson is still out there." But he'd just caught sight of a familiar face in the crowd. A face that was staring at the scene in shocked horror.

Kurt Anderson's face.

"I can't imagine what it was like," Blake murmured. "Swimming out there, knowing the woman you loved was in danger."

Hayden pulled his gaze off Kurt. *Hard* didn't even begin to describe what it had been like. Try *freaking nightmare.*

"Tell me how I can help," Blake said. "What can I do?"

"Get on a boat." Because search crews were mounting already. The Coast Guard was out, and Hayden was about to hit the water, too. "Let's go find the bastard." He wouldn't be satisfied, not until they'd locked Theodore Anderson in jail.

Or they'd pulled his lifeless body from the water.

Chapter Sixteen

Two weeks later...

The waves pounded against the beach. The sky was dark, clouds covering the stars, so Jill couldn't see the white-caps as they hit the shore. She stood on the deck of her cabin, her heart beating slowly, her gaze on the darkness.

Theodore Anderson hadn't been found. He hadn't come home. His body hadn't washed ashore.

Had he died out there? And his body had been pulled out to sea?

Or had he slipped away? Was he already planning another attack? Another abduction?

Warm hands slid down her arms, and she felt Hayden's strong body press to her back. "I still have patrols searching the town."

She knew he did. But the media circus that had hit the area when news broke about Theodore Anderson—that madness had died away. Thankfully. Life was starting to get back to normal for everyone in Hope.

Well...for most people.

Normal would be a long time coming for Vanessa. Her brother had returned to town, and Jill knew that Porter was staying close to his sister. Protecting her.

And as for Kurt...he'd already put his house up for sale.

When she'd talked to him after getting out of the hospital, he'd seemed to be a broken shell of himself.

"Do you think he's dead?" Jill asked. She turned in Hayden's arms, putting her back against the wooden balcony railing.

His gaze lifted and focused over her shoulder, on the darkness that was behind her. "I won't believe he's dead, not until I see a body. Until then, he's a threat. One that I won't ever forget."

That was how she felt, too. Like she just couldn't let go. "I looked over my shoulder for half of my life, always thinking the monster from the dark was out there." And he had been. "Now the monster has a face."

"He *won't* take you again." Fierce determination thickened his voice.

"No." She was certain of this, too. Because she wasn't a victim, not anymore. "He won't." Theodore Anderson was prey. Hunted by local authorities, by the FBI. His face had been on every newscast in the country. He was a wanted man.

He would be found.

"Jill, I have something to ask you." Hayden backed away from her. Exhaled slowly. He seemed…nervous. Odd, for Hayden. "I know that your job base is in Atlanta. Your team wants you back up there."

Yes, they did. But she'd been given extra leave in spite of…well, *everything*.

"Atlanta, Hope, wherever you want to be…I'd like to be with you." He bent down before her.

OhmyGod… He was on one knee. Hayden pulled a small, black box from his pocket. He opened it, and the ring sparkled in the dark. "I've loved you since I met you. Time just made that feeling even stronger. I want to spend my life with you. I want *you*, Jill. Always, you." And, once more, he gave a quick, nervous exhale. "Will you marry me?"

She stared at the ring, and then she looked at what really mattered... Hayden. Hayden's eyes. Her Hayden. And she smiled at him. "Yes."

He surged up to his feet. He put the ring on her finger and then he was kissing her. Wildly. Hotly. Happily.

There was so much emotion in his touch. So much joy. Jill felt that same joy. She wasn't going to let fear hold her back any longer. Yes, there were bad things in this world. So many bad things...

But there were good things, too. Kisses, smiles, love... hope.

Girls who were reunited with their families. People who fought to protect victims. People who cared.

The good beat the bad.

It won.

She curled her arms around Hayden's neck. He picked her up and carried her inside, stopping just long enough to lock the sliding glass door. Then he was walking through the cabin and taking her to the bedroom. He put her on the bed, his touch so very careful.

She smiled at him. "I'm not going to break."

"I know, baby. You proved that long ago." He tossed his shirt into the corner. Kicked off his shoes and socks and slid onto the edge of the bed. "But you're still healing and—"

She curled her fingers around his shoulder. "I'm all healed, Hayden. And I want you." Every bit of him. She kissed him, then bit his lower lip, a sexy tease that she knew he loved.

She toed out of her shoes and sent them flying. Then Hayden's hand was at the zipper of her jeans. The faint hiss seemed loud in the quiet room. He pushed down the jeans, shoved down her underwear, but when his fingers slid between her legs…he was so gentle.

Careful.

I told him I wouldn't break.

He stroked her, arousing her desire to a fever pitch, making her hips jerk against him. She still had on her shirt and her tight nipples thrust forward. "Hayden!"

His hand slid away from her. He jerked off her shirt, his touch a bit rougher now, but he didn't so much as brush her healing wound. The bullet wound that would always remind her of Theodore.

Hayden unhooked her bra. He put his mouth on her breast and she choked out his name as heated sensation poured through her. She loved Hayden's touch. Loved his mouth. Loved the way he made her feel.

But she hated it when the man made her wait.

Jill's fingers slid between their bodies. She found his heavy length—thick, hot, fully aroused. She pumped him, enjoying the feel of him in her hands. Then she pushed the head of his arousal between her legs. She needed this moment. She needed him. "Hayden." His name was a demand.

He kissed her neck, right over her pulse, in that spot that drove her crazy.

Then he thrust into her. For an instant, she could have sworn that time froze. Everything was perfect for her— love, need, desire…

Hayden.

Then he withdrew, only to drive deep into her once more. The bed squeaked beneath him. Her legs wrapped around his hips. Deeper, harder, he pistoned his hips against her. And Jill couldn't hold back her release. Her nails sank into his back and she called out his name as the pleasure broke over her.

Hayden was with her. He sank into her core once more,

and then he stiffened. He whispered her name as he came, a long shudder driving over him, and he held her tight. So tight.

As if he'd never let go. That was good, so good, because Jill never intended to let him go, either.

In the aftermath, Hayden pulled her close. Their fingers twined together. The diamond ring shined in the night.

And Jill closed her eyes.

IT WAS THE squeak that woke her later. The squeak that came from the sliding glass door that led out to her balcony. Her eyes flew open and she sucked in a quick breath.

"It's okay," Hayden whispered. His fingers squeezed hers.

But…it wasn't okay. Someone was breaking into her cabin.

"We were waiting for this," Hayden said. His hand slipped from hers. He opened the nightstand drawer and took out two guns.

Because, yes, they had known that if Theodore Anderson lived, he might try to attack again. That was the reason Jill had stayed in the same cabin on the beach. Why she'd been sure to go out on the deck every evening.

Bait.

She hadn't wanted Theodore to go after Vanessa. *I wanted him to come after me.*

She slid on a T-shirt and her shorts as Hayden jerked on his jeans. Then, armed, they both moved soundlessly toward her bedroom door.

She heard the groan from the outer room. Their intruder was near the TV. Hadn't he learned from last time? No, obviously not, he was making all of the same mistakes.

But I'm not.

She released a slow breath, and then Jill nodded toward Hayden. *Ready.* She mouthed the word at him.

He yanked open the door.

"Freeze!" Jill yelled.

Hayden hit the light. Illumination flooded onto Theodore Anderson as he stood in the middle of her den. Heavy stubble covered his jaw and in his hand, he held a long, glinting knife.

A knife wouldn't do much good against two guns. "You're under arrest," Jill said.

He screamed at her and he lifted his hand and charged right toward her. In that split second, she understood that he'd rather die than go to jail. For a man like him, prison would be a living hell. The girls he'd killed…his own daughter…

The other inmates would make him pay, every single day—and night.

Theodore Anderson wanted to die. He wanted to be taken out.

But on that boat, he'd boasted about other victims. Victims that the authorities hadn't identified. Those families deserved closure.

"Stop!" Jill yelled. She fired, just as Hayden fired.

Her bullet hit Theodore in the leg. Hayden's bullet slammed into the guy's shoulder. Theodore fell to the floor, injured, but not dead. *It won't be that easy for you.*

"No!" The anguished bellow had Jill's head jerking up and swinging to the left—toward her open screen door. Kurt Anderson stood there, his eyes wild, glittering. "You have to kill him! *You have to kill him!*"

And Kurt pulled out a gun.

"Was watching the house…waiting…knew he'd come back…" Kurt's words were slurred. *Drunk. Pain filled.*

"H-he hated you so much…knew he'd come back…have to stop him." His weapon pointed at his father.

Hayden had kicked Theodore's knife away from the injured man. "He is stopped, Kurt. Your father is *done*. He's going to prison, and he won't hurt anyone again."

The gun trembled in Kurt's hand. "Prison…won't bring Christy back."

Jill eased forward. "Killing him won't do that, either."

But Kurt smiled. "Killing him…will make me feel a whole lot better."

"Is that what Christy would have wanted?" Jill asked him, desperate. *I didn't think about Kurt…all the pain he felt…I should have realized he wouldn't let his father go.*

"Don't know what Christy wants," Kurt's breath heaved out. "She's dead. Can't ask her. He *took* her…and lied…lied for so long." He shook his head. She saw the tear tracks on his cheeks. "No more. No *more!*"

Kurt was going to fire. Jill knew it. She didn't want to shoot him but—

Hayden launched his body at Kurt's, tackling the other man. They fell against the couch. The bullet fired, but it went wild, blasting into the TV and shattering the screen.

"You aren't like him," Hayden said as he held the other man down. "You're stronger. *You aren't like him. We don't have to be like our fathers.*"

Kurt started crying—choking out hard sobs—as all of the fight went out of him. Hayden rose to his feet, tucking the gun he'd taken from Kurt into the back of his jeans and— "Jill!" Hayden roared her name, his eyes flaring wide.

She'd thought Theodore was beaten. Thought he was out. But at Hayden's frantic yell, her gaze flew to the fallen man.

Theodore had pulled a switchblade from his boot. He was struggling to get to her.

No, he's still trying to control me. "You don't have the control any longer." She kicked the backup knife out of his hand. "Jail is waiting for you. Punishment is waiting. There's no easy out."

At her words, something seemed to break in him. He screamed at her and staggered to his feet. He came at her with his fists clenched, his eyes bulging—

Hayden stepped in front of her before she could attack. "Been waiting years for this…" He drove his fist into Theodore's face. One punch. Another. Again and again and the older man stumbled back. Hayden was relentless, hitting, striking out with powerful blows and Theodore fell back against the wall. "You never should have taken her," Hayden's deep voice rumbled with his rage. "Never—"

Jill caught his hand before he could strike again. Theodore's eyes had rolled back into his head. The man was out cold, slumped on the floor. "Hayden," Jill said his name softly.

He looked at her. She saw the rage and pain in his eyes…and the fear.

But beneath it all, Jill saw his love for her.

"We're safe." She smiled at him. "And it's over." The nightmare that had started so long ago was over. Theodore wasn't getting away. He wouldn't take anyone else. There would be no more death left in his wake.

The end had come for the nightmare that had haunted them all for so long.

HAYDEN STOOD AT the end of the pier. His gaze was on the water below him, deep blue water.

He heard the soft pad of footsteps and glanced back to see Jill walking toward him. Beautiful Jill. Her red hair gleamed in the setting sun.

When she reached his side, Jill said, "Samantha is working on getting the names of his other victims. I...I asked her to handle the interrogation because I knew he'd just try to play me. It's too personal with him. With us." Her gaze slid toward the water. "But Samantha is the damn best there is at getting killers to talk. She'll find the truth for us. I know it."

Her hand curled over the railing. The diamond ring he'd given to her shined. He put his hand on top of hers. Squeezed.

Same pier. Same girl.

New life.

"I love you, Jill," he told her, aware that his voice had thickened. They'd had a plan in place, anticipating that Theodore might strike but when the guy had gone for her again, when he'd leaped at Jill, something had snapped inside of Hayden. He'd attacked. Fought back with the wild fury of the boy he'd been...and of the man who couldn't stand for another to ever threaten the woman he loved.

She leaned closer and pressed a kiss to his cheek. Surprised, he looked at her.

She was smiling. Such a beautiful, warm smile. No shadows were in her eyes. Just peace. Just...

Hope.

"I know," Jill told him softly. "And I love you, too. You're my partner, my lover...and my very best friend."

Her friend.

"You always have been," she said.

Just as she had been his...everything.

"Forever, Hayden?"

He pulled her into his arms and held her tight. "Hell, yes, baby. Hell, yes." As the waves pounded beneath him, Hayden kissed her.

* * * * *

She'd vowed never to get involved with a client. Not to trust any man.

Except. . .how could she resist this sexy, strong man who would give his life for a little boy?

"How about you?" she asked softly.

Cash's eyes darkened with pain, then flickered with something akin to desire. "I'll be all right when we find Tyler."

An image of her own son, pale and lifeless, taunted her. BJ looked down, battling tears. "Me, too. I just hope and pray. . ." She let the sentence trail off, unable to voice her worst fears out loud.

"Hey," Cash murmured. "Don't give up. I'm not."

He was talking about Tyler. And she hadn't given up on finding him.

But there was no bringing back her son. It was too late.

The grief she'd lived with since she'd lost him welled up and threatened to bring her to her knees again.

She looked up into Cash's eyes and was moved by his tenderness. Desperate for his touch, for comfort, she pressed her hand over his chest. His heart pounded, strong and alive, beneath her palm.

She leaned into him, and he brushed her hair from her cheek. "BJ?"

"Shh, just hold me for a minute."

He made a low sound in his throat as if he was struggling not to touch her. Then his eyes darkened, and he pulled her up against him.

THE MISSING MCCULLEN

BY
RITA HERRON

First Published in Great Britain 2017
By Mills & Boon, an imprint of HarperCollins*Publishers*
1 London Bridge Street, London, SE1 9GF

© 2017 Rita B. Herron

ISBN: 978-0-263-92868-6

46-0317

Our policy is to use papers that are natural, renewable and recyclable products and made from wood grown in sustainable forests. The logging and manufacturing processes conform to the legal environmental regulations of the country of origin.

Printed and bound in Spain
by CPI, Barcelona

Prologue

Ray McCullen faced his brothers, Maddox and Brett, with a knot in his stomach. For months they'd been searching for twin brothers who'd been kidnapped from their parents at birth.

They would be thirty this month.

He had good news and bad news. "I found one of the twins."

Maddox balled his hands into fists. "You don't sound happy about it."

"Where is he?" Brett asked.

"The babies were left at a church about an hour from Pistol Whip. Apparently, one of them was adopted, but the other was sickly and wound up being placed in foster care. A nurse took him in for a while, and named him Cash Koker."

"Where is he now?" Maddox asked.

Ray turned to the whiteboard where they'd listed clues regarding the boys' whereabouts. He tacked a photo on the board.

"I used age progression software and a special program I have to locate doppelgangers. This is him."

Maddox studied the photo. "He looks like a McCullen. Same stubborn jaw. Dark hair."

"He's got your high forehead and dark eyes, Maddox," Brett said.

Maddox cleared his throat. "The DNA matched?"

Ray nodded. "Yeah, his was in the system, but I still want another test done for verification."

"I agree," Maddox said.

"Does he know about us?" Brett asked.

"I don't think so."

Maddox crossed his arms. "You said his DNA was in the system. Does that mean what I think it means?"

Ray gave a quick nod. "He has a record. Got into some trouble as a juvenile, then a couple of bar brawls in his twenties."

"Hell, so did I. Is that it?" Brett asked.

Ray grunted. "Afraid not." He tacked another photo on the board. This picture was a mug shot. "Our long-lost brother has just been arrested for murder."

Chapter One

"I didn't kill anyone." Cash Koker flexed his hands on the scarred wooden table of the interrogation room, barely resisting the urge to punch Sheriff Jim Jasper in the jaw.

He'd answered these damn questions a dozen times already, but for some reason, the bastard thought he could browbeat Cash into admitting to murder.

There was no way in hell he'd confess to a crime he hadn't committed.

The bloodstains beneath his fingernails mocked him. Blood that belonged to Sondra, the woman he allegedly had killed.

"Just look at her picture," Sheriff Jasper said. "She was young and beautiful, but you took her life away from her."

Cash swallowed hard as he glanced at the image. Sondra was twenty-two, with pale skin and blond hair that fell to her shoulders.

That hair was tangled and bloody in the photograph. Her throat had been cut, her eyes wide in shock and horror. Blood soaked her thin white blouse, and her hands, which she'd obviously used to fight her attacker.

"I didn't kill her," Cash said again. "I cared about Sondra. We were friends."

"Friends?" Sheriff Jasper crossed his beefy arms and leaned back in his chair. Although he was only a few years older than Cash, the cocky man thought he owned the town. He also got around. Apparently women thought he was attractive.

Cash didn't like anything about him.

"Sondra's daddy said there was a lot more to it than friendship," Jasper said snidely.

Cash chewed the inside of his cheek. Mr. Elmore was a paranoid, pompous, demanding jerk who was rich as sin but barely paid his ranch hands minimum wage. He couldn't keep help because he was cheap and damn difficult to work for.

"In fact, Elmore claims that you knocked up his daughter, and that you denied paternity. He says you slit Sondra's throat to keep her from filing for child support."

Cash thumped his boot on the floor. "He's wrong. I'm not the little boy's father. You know as well as I do that a DNA test can prove it." Although, he had grown attached to the spunky three-year-old.

"Then who is the father?"

Cash sighed. "I don't know. Sondra never told me."

Jasper grabbed him by his shirt collar and practically yanked Cash across the table. "Listen to me, you good-for-nothing piece of trash. Lester Elmore is a respected rancher around here. He doesn't lie." He shoved another picture in front of Cash's face. "Neither does the evidence. We've got Sondra's blood under your nails, and a video cam clip from last night showing you entering the motel where she died."

Cash shifted, his mind racing for answers. The last thing he remembered was meeting her at the bar, because she'd been upset. He'd had a drink and they'd walked outside.

The rest of the night was a damn blank.

Hours later, he'd woken up in a motel room beside Sondra's dead body. He'd been in shock, panicked, and had called an ambulance. He'd also called Sondra's father.

It hadn't occurred to him that the man would accuse him of murder.

"You could ease your conscience by telling me what happened," the sheriff growled. "Or let me guess—you had a lover's quarrel, and she threatened to cut you out of the kid's life. Am I getting close?"

Cash went stone still. Nothing he could say would convince this man that he was innocent.

Worse, the evidence was damning. Given it, and the fact

that Elmore owned half the town, they could lock him away and he'd never see the light of day again.

"You are way off base," Cash said matter-of-factly. "I told you—we weren't lovers." In fact, he would never have gone to a motel with Sondra. They didn't have that kind of relationship. "Why aren't you looking at Elmore? He probably had enemies."

"Elmore is not the problem," Sheriff Jasper snapped.

"But I didn't do anything," Cash's mind raced. "You should be looking for someone else with a motive. Sondra said some guy named Ronnie was bothering her."

Sheriff Jasper raised a brow. "Stop trying to put the blame on someone else, and tell me what you did with Tyler. If Elmore gets his grandson back, he might go easier on you."

Cash's pulse jumped. "What the hell are you talking about? You don't know where Tyler is?"

The sheriff shoved him backward so hard the chair legs clacked on the floor. "Don't act dumb, Koker. If you took that kid, you're going down for kidnapping and murder."

Panic streaked through Cash. Someone had kidnapped Tyler?

Three days later

BJ ALEXANDER HAD made a lot of mistakes in her short career as an attorney. She just hoped coming to Cash Koker's defense wasn't one of them.

But her father and Joe McCullen had been friends, and now that Joe was dead, her father had asked her to help his sons find out more about their long-lost brother.

Possible long-lost brother, she amended.

She slipped from the safety of her small sedan, letting the warmth of the summer day chase away the chill inside her as she studied the sheriff's office.

The building was a one-story, ancient brick structure

with mud caking the brick. She'd called ahead and Sheriff Jasper had filled her in on the arrest.

Cash Koker had been locked up for murdering a young woman named Sondra Elmore. Apparently, Cash had once worked for Sondra's father on the Wagon Wheel Ranch.

Cash insisted he was innocent.

Like she hadn't heard that before.

A year ago, she'd represented a man named Davis Turner, who claimed he'd been framed for murder. After losing her ex-husband and son, she'd been in a bad place. Vulnerable.

Davis was charming, convincing, and seemed compassionate. She'd broken the cardinal rule of not getting involved with a client and had allowed their relationship to become personal.

She had gotten him acquitted in record time.

Two days later, she realized he'd played her. She'd overheard him talking to his mistress on the phone. He'd admitted he was guilty.

Worse, he was a free man because of her, and he couldn't be retried for killing his wife.

She'd hated herself for being so naive. Hated that she may have put another person in danger by helping a killer walk.

She wouldn't make that mistake with this case. *If* she took it.

Despite her father and Joe McCullen's friendship, that was a big if.

Cash Koker had to convince her he was innocent.

Resolved, she opened the door to the sheriff's office and entered. A tiny older woman with gray hair sat at a reception desk. Her name tag read Imogene.

BJ identified herself. "I'm here to meet with Cash Koker."

A tough-looking man in a sheriff's uniform, probably in his midthirties, appeared in the doorway. He might have been handsome if his scowl wasn't so off-putting.

He hitched his thumb toward the back. "You the attorney gonna represent that scumbag in there?"

BJ stiffened. It sounded as if the sheriff had already convicted Cash.

Did he have concrete evidence proving Cash was guilty?

CASH HAD TO get out of this cell.

He'd been here all weekend, shut off as if he was one of the most wanted people in Wyoming.

Dammit. He hated to be confined. Small spaces triggered bad memories of being locked in the closet when he was a kid in foster care.

He lurched up from the cot and paced the cell. He'd racked his brain all weekend, struggling to piece together what had happened Friday night. Had someone drugged him?

Was he with Sondra when she was murdered? How did he end up in a motel with her?

And what about Tyler? Where was that precious little guy?

Panic seized him at the scenarios that flashed through his head. He'd had his share of bad knocks in foster care and knew the dark side of the human mind. Knew the depravity that existed, and how difficult it was for a little kid to defend himself against those bigger than him.

He bit the inside of his cheek, battling despair. Maybe the sheriff had it wrong. Sondra had been upset when she'd called him to meet her. She could have dropped Tyler with a friend for safekeeping.

If so, wouldn't that person have come forward when news of her murder was revealed? Surely Elmore and the sheriff had posted an Amber Alert by now and had people searching.

If Sondra's killer had kidnapped Tyler, though, there was no telling what he'd do to the little boy.

Elmore had money. He'd probably made enemies. If someone wanted to get back at him, killing Sondra and kidnapping her child was the way to do it.

Cash dropped onto the cot and lowered his head into his hands. He'd called the lawyer in town, but got the message machine. So far no one had shown up.

Hell, for all he knew the man was in Elmore's pocket.

The door connecting the sheriff's front office and the cells screeched open. Cash braced himself for another interrogation.

The sheriff stomped toward him, but he wasn't alone this time.

A young woman with hair as black as coal and skin like ivory followed him. Cash couldn't help himself—his gaze swept over her, from those sexy black stilettos, to the curves hidden beneath her stuffy suit, to the wary look in her startling green eyes.

His body instantly hardened. After all, he was a man. And any man would appreciate her femininity.

Although whatever reason she was here, she didn't look happy about it.

He lurched up from the cot and raked a hand through his hair, well aware he looked scruffy and hadn't showered in days. Even though he'd washed his hands, the scent of Sondra's blood still lingered on his skin, and he wore drab prison clothes.

Jasper's boots shuffled on the concrete as he approached. When he reached Cash's cell, he halted, keys jangling in his beefy hand. The woman stood beside him, her dainty chin lifted high as if she was assessing Cash.

"Koker, this woman claims she's your lawyer." Sheriff Jasper looked at him as if Cash was an animal who needed to be put down, not have representation.

He narrowed his eyes. "My lawyer?"

The woman cleared her throat. "Mr. Patton had a stroke. My name is BJ Alexander."

Damn, her husky voice made Cash's body tighten even more.

"Sheriff Jasper, I need to talk to my client in private," she said. "Open the cell, please."

Jasper scowled at her, but jammed the key in the cell door and opened it. For a brief second, something akin to fear flickered in the woman's eyes.

She might be tough, but she was afraid of Cash.

That didn't sit well in his gut.

He would never lay a hand on a woman, at least not in violence.

But that damn sheriff had probably already convinced her he was guilty.

BJ SCRUTINIZED CASH. The man looked rough. Hair a little too long. Eyes deep, dark. Distrustful.

Body…well, hell, he was built. Broad shoulders. Tall. Muscles everywhere.

Which meant he was strong enough to overpower a woman.

The McCullens had just learned they had two brothers who'd been kidnapped at birth. They thought Cash was one of them.

Since she'd spoken to them, she'd done her research.

Cash had grown up in the foster care system. At twelve he'd been placed in a ranch home for troubled boys. He'd learned ranching skills, and as an adult had worked on several spreads across Wyoming. He'd moved half a dozen times, though, which made her wonder if he was searching for something, or if he'd been asked to leave.

The head of the ranch for boys had described him as sullen, brooding, angry. Said he needed guidance from a strong male.

Guidance he'd never received.

Two of his employers claimed he was an excellent rider, a natural cattleman and that he'd kept to himself but done a good job. After a season or two, he'd left of his own accord, saying it was time for him to move on.

He was a drifter. Probably had a new woman in every county he moved to.

All the more reason she should maintain her professional demeanor. She wouldn't fall prey to his charms like she had with Davis.

Although at the moment, Cash looked beaten—not like a womanizer. The disdain in his eyes was palpable.

"Sheriff, please show Mr. Koker to an interrogation room so we can talk." At least they would both be more comfortable. Sitting on that tiny cot beside Cash Koker was not an option. Sex appeal radiated from him in waves. There was also an air of danger about him that put her on edge.

The sheriff grunted in compliance, then gestured for Cash to hold out his hands so he could cuff them.

A muscle ticked in Cash's jaw, but he did as the man ordered. Jasper led him to a small room with a plain wooden table and two chairs. Cash's expression was grim as he sank into the chair. Handcuffs clanged as he spread his fingers on the table. Calluses and scars marked his hands and arms, a telltale sign that he did manual labor.

The sheriff cleared his throat. "You want me to stay?"

BJ shook her head. She couldn't show fear or any emotion. "No, I'm fine."

Jasper worked his mouth from side to side, one hand on his holster. "Yell if you need me." He squeezed Cash's shoulder so hard the prisoner's jaw tightened. "Touch her and you'll be sorry."

A frisson of nerves prickled BJ's spine as the sheriff left the room and Cash turned his rage toward her.

A jagged scar curled beneath his hairline on the right side, making him look frightening and sexy at the same time. She envisioned him riding a bull or galloping across rugged terrain, and her heart stuttered.

She gripped the edge of the table, silently cursing herself. She could not allow herself to think of him as attractive.

"All right, lady," he said gruffly. "What are you doing here?"

BJ forced herself to remember that he had no clue he was a McCullen. She'd expected the McCullen men would want to meet him, but they'd had trouble with a half brother named Bobby, and were cautious.

After all, Horseshoe Creek Ranch belonged to all of Joe McCullen's sons, which meant that Maddox, Brett and Ray would have to share land with the lost twins.

They intended to find the truth about Cash's character *before* they disclosed their relationship.

"I came to decide if I want to represent you," BJ said. "To do that, I need to hear your version of what happened the night Sondra Elmore died."

He arched a thick brow. "Why? You gonna believe me?"

BJ leaned forward, snagging his gaze with a cold look. "Sarcasm is not your friend right now, Mr. Koker. The truth might be, though, if you want to tell it."

Shoulders squared, she gathered the file, ready to leave. The last thing she intended to do was work for some ungrateful jerk who didn't want her help. "If not, I'll leave you alone and you can rot in that cell."

Chapter Two

BJ folded her arms across her chest. "You have ten seconds to decide how this will go before I walk out that door."

Anger flashed across Cash's face, along with distrust—and the realization that he did need help. That he might have to suck it up if he wanted to fight these charges.

"Just sit down," he growled.

BJ shook her head. "I don't take orders from you, Mr. Koker. If I accept your case, I expect respect. But first, you have to convince me that you're innocent."

Tension rippled between them. He shifted and stared at his fingers again, obviously torn. Or was he trying to concoct a convincing lie?

"All right, Miss Alexander," he said. "Please sit back down."

A tiny smile of victory twitched at her mouth, but she masked it, maintaining her neutral expression. He had said please, though, so she slipped into the chair facing him.

"Now tell me—has Tyler been found? Is he okay?"

"I'm afraid there hasn't been any word on the boy," she said quietly.

Cash pressed his knuckles over his eyes. "You have to find him."

"Do you know where he is?" she asked in a tight voice.

"No." His gaze met hers, suspicion flaring. "Are you working for Elmore?"

BJ frowned. "Why would you ask that?"

"Because Lester Elmore never thought I was good enough for his daughter." A muscle ticked in his jaw. "Did he pay you to get dirt on me so he could railroad me to prison for killing his daughter?"

BJ locked stubborn gazes with him. "For the record, I've never met the man, and he didn't pay me to do anything." She let that sentence sink in for a brief second. "In fact,

I can't be bought by anyone, so even if he had offered, I would have turned him down."

"Really?" Koker's mouth curled in a sardonic grin. "You mean I'm looking at a real-life *honest* lawyer?"

She gave him a flat look. "Believe it or not, yes."

She removed photos of the crime scene and spread them across the table. Cash zeroed in on a shot of Sondra Elmore drenched in blood, and his face paled.

"Did you kill Sondra?" BJ asked.

A tortured look darkened his eyes. "No."

BJ waited, hoping he'd elaborate, but he didn't.

She tapped a picture of a bloody hunting knife the sheriff had found at the scene. "This isn't your knife?"

Cash cursed. "Yes, it is, but I didn't kill Sondra with it."

"Then why was it lying on the floor beside her?"

"I have no idea." He leaned his head on his hands and inhaled several deep breaths. "Think about it. If I had killed her, you think I'd be dumb enough to leave a weapon behind with my fingerprints on it?"

No. But she had to ask.

Still, this man was a stranger to her. She wasn't certain she could trust her instincts, either, not after the mess she'd made with Davis.

THE PICTURE OF Sondra covered in blood made Cash's stomach roil.

The lawyer cleared her throat. "You knew Sondra well, didn't you, Cash? You were friendly?"

He gave her a scathing look. "We were friends. Period."

"According to the sheriff's notes and his interview with Mr. Elmore, you were more than that."

Cash shook his head. "Not true."

"You weren't lovers?" she asked bluntly.

Cash shifted. "I answered that already. We were just friends."

"They why did her father think you two were involved?"

He made a low sound in his throat. "Sondra may have implied that we were."

The lawyer tapped her manicured nails on the table. A reminder that his were ragged and had been bloodstained, that the cops had forensics that would work against him.

Even though he'd washed them, in his mind's eye, he could still see Sondra's blood.

"I see," she said wryly. "And you allowed her father to believe a lie?"

"I didn't like it. I told her that." Cash shrugged. "But I didn't dispute it."

"You two argued about the issue?"

"Not really. She begged me not to say anything and I agreed."

Cash rolled his fingers into fists. If he admitted that he and Sondra had argued the afternoon she died, he'd give this lawyer a motive.

"Why did Sondra allow her father to believe you were the boy's father? And why would you let her do that?"

"Elmore's a paranoid jerk who warned all of his employees, including me, to keep their hands off of his daughter. He wanted to keep her in some kind of bubble, but she was rebellious."

The woman raised a brow. "Rebellious as in she dated the hands to make him angry?"

"Sometimes."

"If she was so rebellious, why didn't she just move out?"

Cash shrugged. "First of all, Elmore controlled her trust fund. But I think she was secretly hoping her father would come around and accept Tyler."

"She dated you to get back at her father?"

"I told you, we never dated," he said firmly. "She was too young for me."

"But she got pregnant and told Elmore you were the father."

Cash heaved a weary breath. God, she was a professional interrogator. "Yes. But the boy wasn't mine. Do the DNA test and you'll see."

"We'll get to that." She glanced at her file, then back up at him. "So who was the child's father?"

He wished to hell he knew. "She never told me."

"Why not? You said you were close."

"I don't know why. She just didn't want to talk about him." Cash tensed. He was painting himself into a corner.

"Tell me more about your relationship then."

"She was like a kid sister to me," he said. "She used to come out to the barn and yammer on like a teenager. Mostly venting about her father and how overprotective he was. He pressured her to give up the baby after it was born so she wouldn't shame the family."

"But she kept the child?"

"Yeah, she was tenderhearted. Loved animals and kids." She'd cried on his shoulder about that decision. Cash had promised to provide emotional support if she kept the child and raised it on her own.

Yet he'd let her down and she was dead.

"Elmore allowed you to stay on after Tyler was born?"

Cash gritted his teeth. "No, he fired me, then bad-mouthed me to other ranchers. Finally, I found a job on a small spread not too far away."

"You still saw Sondra and Tyler?"

"Mostly Tyler. Sometimes she dropped him off so we could spend time together. Said he needed a male role model." Cash had been surprised she'd chosen him for the job. But hey, the kid didn't have a daddy and Cash related to that.

Images of the little boy tagging along behind him taunted Cash. Tyler loved horses and riding. He constantly talked about joining the rodeo.

"Cash?"

BJ's soft voice dragged him from the memories. God, what if something had happened to Tyler? "Tyler's three now. He's a pistol."

"Do you think Sondra intentionally got pregnant? Maybe she thought this man would marry her if they had a child."

"Sondra wouldn't have done that."

Disbelief tinged the lawyer's eyes. "Did she tell the father about the baby?"

Cash nodded. "He didn't want anything to do with Tyler."

"So Sondra never revealed the boy's father's name?"

"I told you she didn't," he said, his irritation mounting.

She fell silent for a moment. "If you didn't kill Sondra, it's possible that this other man did. Was Sondra afraid of him?"

Cash scrubbed his hand over his chin. "I don't know. Maybe."

"Tell me about the night she died," BJ said.

He'd been struggling to recall Friday evening, but the entire night was a fog. "She was upset when she called me, but she didn't explain. I assumed she and her daddy had had an argument, but I guess she could have fought with Tyler's father."

BJ pursed her lips. "She must have had a good reason to keep his identity a secret. He could be married or a prominent figure in the community. He had something to lose if word leaked he had a child."

"That's what I figured." Cash's heart hammered. The only way to clear himself was to find Sondra's killer. "What if she'd decided to come clean about him? Or maybe she needed money or help."

"Makes sense. If he didn't want his identity exposed, he could have killed her to keep her quiet." BJ crossed her legs, drawing his attention to their long slender shape. She must have noticed, because a second later she uncrossed them and leaned forward. "We need to know his name."

"If I knew his name, trust me, I'd tell you." Fear made his throat thick. "If your theory is right and he didn't want the boy, he could have killed him."

Her frown deepened. "It would be pretty coldhearted to kill a child."

Cash nodded. He couldn't allow himself to even think

about losing Tyler. But he didn't want to go to prison for a crime he hadn't committed. Offering another suspect could help his case.

"I'll try to get ahold of Tyler's birth certificate," she suggested.

Cash nodded again. "Look into Elmore, too. Maybe someone had a grudge against him and kidnapped Tyler for blackmail money."

BJ cleared her throat. "True."

"I tried to tell Sheriff Jasper this, but he didn't believe me." Cash didn't like any of the scenarios that flashed through his mind. "A few of the ranchers had squabbles with him, but I don't think they'd resort to kidnapping."

"I'll ask around," BJ agreed.

"Has Elmore received a ransom call?" Cash asked.

She shook her head. "Not that I know of, but I'll talk to him."

Emotions thickened his throat as he pictured the times he'd played horseshoe with the little guy. Then another time when Tyler had climbed a tree, but was too afraid to climb down, so Cash had rescued him.

That little boy had dug a hole in Cash's heart.

They had to find him and make sure he was safe.

BJ TAPPED HER fingernails on the table again. "There's another possibility, Cash. Do you have any enemies? Someone who would frame you for murder?"

Turmoil hardened Cash's face. "Elmore disliked me, but I haven't seen him in a while. Other than him, I can't think of anyone."

BJ's lungs squeezed. She'd come here skeptical about this man's innocence. But he couldn't fake the fear in his eyes or voice—he was sincerely worried about that child.

Still, she had to remain objective and consider every possibility.

"The sheriff thinks that you took Tyler and planned to blackmail Elmore."

"That's ridiculous. Besides, I didn't have to kill anyone to execute that plan, if that was really my intent."

"You must have hated him for firing you and blackballing you. You could use the money to buy your own place."

"I did want my own spread, I'll admit that." Anger sizzled in his eyes. "But not bad enough to hurt Sondra. I know what it's like to grow up without a family. I loved Tyler and would never have taken his mama away."

The pain in his voice was too raw to not be real.

"Tell me what happened then," BJ said. "How did you wind up in that motel room with Sondra's blood all over you?"

He released a frustrated sigh. "Like I told you, she called me, upset, and I met her at the tavern." He rubbed his chin. "I got there and ordered a drink. She came and...we walked outside for a minute. Then everything goes blank."

"Someone knocked you out?"

"I don't know." Confusion clouded his eyes. "Either that or I was drugged."

An excuse or the truth? "Unfortunately, it's too late to test your blood for drugs."

"I realize that, but it's the only explanation I can think of." His expression turned grim. "Seriously, one minute I was talking to her, the next I woke up in the room with Sondra, and she was dead."

BJ studied him. Shock and sorrow radiated from his eyes. If he was a liar, he was a damn good one.

But the security camera had captured his face outside that motel room. "You woke up and found her, then what?"

He lifted his shoulders in a defeated shrug. "I called 911, and then I phoned Sondra's father. I...thought I was doing the right thing."

He had done the right thing. That is, if he hadn't sliced Sondra's throat.

But BJ couldn't imagine him killing a woman in cold blood. Maybe a crime of passion?

She needed to question the ranch hands and find out if Cash was violent. If they thought he'd had an affair with Sondra.

If he wanted to get back at Elmore.

Another possibility hit her, one she didn't want to consider. But one the DA definitely would.

What if Cash was in love with Sondra, and wanted to marry her and adopt Tyler? She could have met with him to tell him to leave her alone. Maybe she'd even fallen for another man and planned to cut Cash out of the boy's life. He could have flown into a jealous rage.

Indecision warred with the instinct that Cash was telling the truth and needed help. That either Cash or Elmore had enemies.

That one of those enemies had killed Sondra and kidnapped Tyler to get revenge.

But what had they done with Tyler?

CASH COULD SEE the wheels turning in the lawyer's head. She was trying to decide whether he was innocent or guilty.

He wasn't sure which way she was leaning.

"Miss Alexander, even if you decide not to represent me, please make sure the police search for Tyler. If Jasper thinks I did something with him, he may be dragging his feet, thinking I'll confess. Tyler could be in danger."

"I'm sure he's doing everything he can to find him," she said. "An Amber Alert has been issued and NCMEC, the National Center for Missing and Exploited Children, has been notified."

Cash still didn't trust Jasper.

An image of the precocious three-year-old teased his mind. Tyler liked to trail ride with him. He could feel the little boy's arms locked around his waist, hear him giggling when the horse broke into a canter.

He even had a Western shirt like one of Cash's and wore it when they were together.

Miss Alexander gathered the photos of Sondra and stuffed them in her briefcase. She stood, her posture rigid, her lips pressed into a thin line.

"Don't take Jasper's word for it." Cash touched her arm.

She went stone still and stared at his fingers as if he'd burned her. He released her abruptly.

Just like Elmore, she'd put him in his place with a condescending look.

Hell, he'd never be good enough for a man like Elmore or a woman like her.

It didn't matter, though. All that mattered was making sure little Tyler was safe.

"Please," he said in a gruff voice. "Find Tyler. He needs your help more than I do."

Her gaze locked with his, and he swallowed hard. He could lose himself in those damn beautiful eyes.

But those eyes were cold and serious, assessing.

"Don't worry. I'll alert authorities to look for Tyler," she said, her voice cracking slightly. "We're meeting with the judge in an hour for a bail hearing."

Hope and despair crawled through Cash. He badly wanted out of this jail. But he was broke. All he had was a little bit of savings for the ranch he'd been dreaming about.

He was determined to have his own spread someday. Then he'd never have to bow down to bigwig ranchers like Elmore again.

"I appreciate you coming," he said, biting back his pride. "But I can't make bail."

She angled her head to look at him, her mouth forming a thin line. "Your bail money and my fee have been taken care of."

Without another word, she left, and closed the door behind her.

Cash's heart hammered as the lock clicked into place. Who the hell had paid her? And who was posting his bail?

His ranch hand buddies didn't have money. And he didn't have family to turn to.

He refused to take charity, too.

But what choice did he have? He needed to find out who'd set him up. He sure as hell couldn't do that from the inside of a cell.

And he trusted her a hell of a lot more than he would some court appointed attorney who might know Elmore or be in his pocket.

BJ LEFT CASH with unanswered questions. The sheriff frowned at her, but stepped into the room to escort Cash to the cell.

She needed to speak to Maddox before she revealed Cash's connection to the McCullens.

The pain in his eyes ripped at her. She was still straddling the fence about his innocence or guilt, although she was leaning on the innocent side.

One thing she knew for sure, though. He loved that little boy.

And he was seriously worried about him.

Which roused her own fear for Tyler.

She rushed into the restroom, grabbed a paper towel and wetted it just as the first wave of dizziness assaulted her.

Three-year-old Tyler Elmore was missing.

She'd had no idea when she took the case. All she was told was that Cash Koker had been arrested for murder.

Panic gnawed at her as she recalled Cash's last words. He wanted her to look for the little boy. He'd chosen that over his own release.

Even though he'd denied being the child's father, he was frightened for him.

Tears blurred her eyes, and she removed the rainbow drawing she kept with her. Her son had been obsessed with rainbows and had made this one for her for Mother's Day.

Time faded and she was back with her son.

"Mommy, tuck me in."

She wiped her hands on the dish towel, then went to Aaron's room. He was in his cartoon pj's, snuggled with his stuffed lion, holding his favorite book. She crawled on the bed and he nuzzled up against her as she began to read.

Seconds later, he fell asleep on her arm.

Two days later—the call that had shattered her heart. A highway patrol officer.

Her ex had taken Aaron on a camping trip, but they'd had a terrible accident.

Neither one of them had survived.

BJ wiped the tears from her eyes, folded the drawing and put it back in her pocket. It hurt too much to think about Aaron's little innocent face looking up at her as if she'd protect him from the world, when she'd failed.

If Tyler was in danger, she had to help.

She left the bathroom, then walked up front to talk to Sheriff Jasper. "Has Mr. Elmore located his grandson?"

A vein throbbed in the lawman's neck. "No, all the more reason you tell us what that Koker guy did with Tyler."

BJ bit the inside of her cheek. The sheriff definitely had made up his mind about Cash. He'd probably lynch him if he didn't think he'd get caught.

"My conversation with my client is confidential, although I don't believe he took the child or knows where he is. He seems genuinely concerned. If you haven't followed up on the Amber Alert, do so immediately."

"I know how to do my job." Jasper's sarcastic tone implied she didn't. "You just need to push Koker to talk."

Anger mushroomed inside BJ. "I told you he didn't take the boy. Have you spoken with Mr. Elmore to see if he received a ransom call?"

"He hasn't."

BJ tensed. That wasn't a good sign. "For a moment, let's just say I'm right, Sheriff. The first forty-eight hours are critical for a missing child case." She tapped her watch. "Every minute counts. So while you're sitting here on your butt, whoever abducted Tyler is getting farther and farther away."

Which meant they might not get the little boy back alive.

That terrified her more than anything.

Chapter Three

BJ stopped at the diner in town and ordered coffee and a muffin. Her stomach was too knotted to eat much, but she needed something before Cash's bail hearing.

She ran a search on her computer and found articles about Lester Elmore and his ranch, along with a story on his success. A photo of Sondra accompanying her father to a state fund-raiser when she was seventeen revealed the depth of the young woman's beauty. Her father was looking at her in adoration.

Her Facebook page revealed a photo of Sondra and Tyler. The kid had sandy-brown hair, was freckle-faced and so adorable that tears pricked her eyes. "Where are you, little guy?"

She quickly searched Sondra's friends and posts, hoping to find a clue as to someone Sondra may have left the boy with but came up empty. Although she had a close girlfriend named Diane who'd ridden with her when Sondra had been into showing horses. Those posts were dated two years before though.

She punched in Sheriff Maddox McCullen's phone number, sipping her coffee while she waited. The phone rang three times, then a male voice answered. "Sheriff McCullen speaking."

"Sheriff, it's BJ Alexander."

A heartbeat passed. "Call me Maddox. You met Cash Koker?"

"I did," BJ said.

"What do you think?" Maddox asked.

BJ hesitated. "I don't think he has a clue that he has brothers or any family."

Maddox heaved a sigh. "I figured as much. If he did, he would have probably called or shown up at Horseshoe Creek."

Cash didn't strike her as the type to ask for handouts.

"The bail hearing is soon." BJ fidgeted. "Have you read the sheriff's report?"

"No, but when I spoke to Sheriff Jasper, he was adamant that he had the right man."

"He's made up his mind," BJ said. "I don't think he's even considered that Cash might be innocent."

"So he's not investigating or looking for another suspect?" Maddox said with disgust.

"No."

"Do you think Cash is guilty?" Maddox asked.

BJ stared into her coffee, willing an answer to come to her. "I'm not sure," she said honestly. "He claims that he cared about Sondra, but denies that they were lovers. Sondra had a three-year-old little boy. That child is missing."

Maddox murmured something beneath his breath. "The sheriff thinks Cash did something with the kid?"

"Yes, but I don't."

Maddox's gruff voice jerked her from her thoughts. "What did Cash say about the boy?"

BJ massaged her temple where a headache pulsed. Kids were her soft spot. Sometimes she missed her own son so badly she could hardly breathe.

"Finding Tyler seems more important to Cash than his own defense."

"Hmm. Interesting." Maddox paused. "Who is the boy's father?"

"He claims he doesn't know." BJ sighed and recounted her conversation with Cash. Maddox was paying her, but she still had to be careful with client/attorney privilege.

"So Cash is either lying or someone drugged him and framed him," Maddox said matter-of-factly.

"Exactly."

Only to clear him, she'd have to prove it.

"Ray's still looking for the other twin. I'll have the DNA tests run on Cash and compare them to Tyler's. And I'll dig up what I can find on the Elmore family," Maddox offered. "Then I'll have that camera footage analyzed."

"Sounds like a plan." Meanwhile she'd talk to Elmore and get hold of Tyler's birth certificate.

After the bail hearing, she'd pay a visit to Cash's current boss and the place where he'd been living. There might be something in his room to tell her more about Cash.

Good or bad, she had to know before she committed to his defense.

CASH WISHED TO hell he'd had a shower and clean clothes before standing in front of the judge. But he'd had no choice. The sheriff had confiscated his clothing as evidence and given him a county jumpsuit.

Sheriff Jasper shot him a sinister glare as he shoved him in the back of the police car.

Cash had racked his brain to figure out who was bailing him out, and who'd paid for the lawyer, but he didn't dare ask Sheriff Jasper.

He kept his mouth shut on the short drive to the courthouse. Outside, dark clouds hovered as if a storm was gathering on the horizon.

"Judge'll go easier on you if you tell us where the kid is," Sheriff Jasper growled.

Cash choked back a curse. He had to remain calm or the bastard would make things worse for him. "If I knew where he was, I'd tell you."

The sheriff grunted. "If he turns up dead, we're gonna fry you."

Sweat trickled down the side of Cash's face. Outside, the trees swayed in the wind. Even with the breeze, it had to be a hundred degrees.

"Instead of blaming me, why don't you search for Tyler?" Cash said. "If he's with Sondra's killer, he could be in danger. Then that's on you, not me."

Jasper met his gaze in the rearview mirror. Anger

slashed the man's jaw. "I got the man who killed his mother right here."

Cash sent him a mutinous look, but remained silent. No use defending himself. Jasper had one mind-set—send him to prison.

They reached the courthouse, and the sheriff parked, then lumbered to the back door to let Cash out. The handcuffs and manacles around his ankles jangled as he walked, but he forced his head up high.

Still, humiliation washed over him as he entered the building. The pretty lawyer lady was waiting. She maintained that professional mask, every damn strand of hair tucked into place.

Did she really believe he was innocent, or was she just doing a job?

It didn't matter. As long as she cleared him, he'd find a way to repay her. Then he'd find Tyler and make sure the kid was safe.

Seconds later, Cash took a seat beside her, his nerves on edge as the bailiff announced the judge's entrance. Silence descended for a moment as the judge, a tall, imposing man with suspicious eyes, reviewed the case file.

Finally, he pounded his gavel and called the session to order. His gaze penetrated Cash like he was pond scum.

Cash's gut churned as the charges were read.

BJ gestured for Cash to stand and he inhaled a breath, willing his legs not to give way.

"Your honor, my name is BJ Alexander. I'm representing Cash Koker. Due to the fact that he has no priors, and that he's not a flight risk, we're requesting bail be set at ten thousand dollars."

A dark chuckle rumbled from the fiftysomething district attorney. "Your honor, Mr. Koker has been arrested for a brutal murder. Although Miss Alexander claims he's not a flight risk, Mr. Koker has no ties to the community and no family. According to his work history, he's traveled from town to town, even state to state, working odd jobs on different ranches."

Cash tapped his boot on the floor. He hadn't thought his nomadic lifestyle would come back to bite him in the butt.

"For all we know, he may have escape plans in place," the DA continued, "We are requesting bail be denied, and that Mr. Koker be remanded until trial."

The judge checked his notes, then removed his reading glasses and studied Cash.

Cash's breath stalled in his chest. The judge had obviously seen the bloody pictures of Sondra and was going to deny bail.

The door in the back burst open, jarring them. Cash turned to see three men enter, all dressed in Western attire, all big, broad shouldered and tough looking. One wore a sheriff's uniform.

"Your honor, my name is Sheriff Maddox McCullen of Pistol Whip," the tallest of the man said in a deep voice. "May I approach the bench?"

The judge arched his brows in question. "If it pertains to this case, yes."

Sheriff Jasper blustered a protest, but the judge silenced him with a single pound of the gavel. "Approach."

Sheriff McCullen strode toward the judge's galley, the other two men flanking him. As they passed Cash, each of them paused a second to scrutinize him.

Cash tightened his jaw. What the hell was going on?

Did this sheriff have some other trumped-up charges to make sure Cash stayed locked up?

BJ STOOD RAMROD straight in front of the judge beside the McCullens. "Your honor, I've spoken with my client and not only does he claim innocence, he's sincerely worried about the victim's son. The absence of the boy's birth father and his identity suggests that he is a possible suspect."

The judge waved his hand. "We are not trying the case today Miss Alexander. We're here to establish bail."

"Judge," Sheriff McCullen said. "May we speak in chambers?"

The judge rubbed the collar of his robe but nodded. "All right, but you'd better have good reason for this."

"Yes, sir, I do," Maddox said.

BJ and Maddox followed him into his private quarters, leaving Cash looking dumbfounded.

"Now someone explain what's going on?" the judge said as soon as the door was shut.

Maddox cleared his throat. "I realize that you're concerned about Mr. Koker being a flight risk, but I can assure you that he won't flee."

"Just how do you propose to do that?" the judge asked.

"By taking him into my custody," Sheriff McCullen said.

The judge leaned forward. "May I ask why you would do that? What is your involvement with Cash Koker? Has he committed a crime in your jurisdiction?"

"No." Maddox spoke in a low voice. "My brothers and I recently learned that we have twin brothers who were kidnapped at birth. We believe Cash Koker is one of those lost brothers."

The judge raised a brow with interest. "I see. And you plan to blindly take this stranger, who has been accused of murder, into your home? Are you sure that's a wise idea?"

Maddox glanced at BJ, then back to the judge. He was obviously considering her opinion on whether or not Cash was guilty or innocent.

"With all due respect, Judge, my brother Ray is a detective and I'm a lawman," Maddox said. "We'll get to the truth. I promise you that."

"And you'll keep Koker in your custody?"

"Yes, sir," Maddox agreed.

The judge made a clicking sound with his teeth. "All right."

BJ and Maddox followed the judge and bailiff back into the courtroom.

Brett and Ray had taken seats in the courtroom. Cash looked confused and anxious.

"Bail is set at fifty thousand dollars. Mr. Koker, you are released into the custody of Sheriff McCullen." He gave Cash a pointed look. "You are not allowed to leave the county or state. If you have a passport, you will turn it over to the court. If you attempt to flee, you will go back to prison, where you will reside until your trial. Do you understand?"

Cash nodded, his expression wary as he studied Maddox. "Yes, sir, Your Honor."

BJ's stomach knotted as Cash turned accusatory eyes toward her.

He didn't trust her or Maddox.

She certainly couldn't explain here in the courtroom.

The guard released Cash while Brett and Ray went to pay the bail.

"What the hell is your agenda, Sheriff?" Cash growled as the sheriff led him outside then to a police issued SUV. "Did Elmore hire you to get rid of me before the trial?"

Chapter Four

"Just shut up and get in," Sheriff McCullen ordered. "I'll explain later."

The two men who'd been with the sheriff walked down the steps of the courthouse, waved to the sheriff then climbed in a pick-up truck near the sheriff's vehicle.

Cash rubbed his wrists where the handcuffs had been, but he still felt the weight of the metal against his skin.

If they didn't find a way to prove his innocence, he'd go back to jail and stay there the rest of his life. The thought made his lungs squeeze for air.

For a man who liked the open wilderness, country air and the freedom to move around, being confined would kill him.

He tensed as the sheriff veered onto the highway. He had to be prepared in case he drove him into the boonies and tried to get rid of him.

Surely that lawyer lady wouldn't allow him to do something like that. She might not totally believe him, but he'd sensed that she cared about kids and would push the police to hunt for Tyler.

"Where are you taking me?" Cash asked.

Sheriff McCullen glanced at him in the rearview mirror. "To get some of your stuff."

"We're going to the Triple X?"

"Yes. I assumed you'd need clothes."

He did. The stench of blood and now his own body odor was getting to him.

The sheriff veered onto the road leading to the ranch where he'd been working, and Cash noticed the lawyer was following.

"Why did you bail me out?" Cash asked.

The sheriff released a heavy sigh. "We'll discuss that at Horseshoe Creek."

Cash had never been to Horseshoe Creek, but he'd heard about the McCullen spread. Hell, everyone within five states had heard about it. Apparently the patriarch of the family, Joe McCullen, had run a large cattle and horse operation. He'd died a year ago and left it to his three sons. Maddox was the sheriff. Brett, a big rodeo star. And the youngest, Ray, was a private investigator.

A few months ago, Cash had read an article saying that Joe hadn't died of natural causes as they'd originally thought, but that he'd been murdered.

Joe McCullen and Elmore, Sondra's father, had been rival ranchers, owning two of the largest spreads in this part of Wyoming. Was that why the McCullens were coming to his rescue now? To get back at an old rival?

A sign for the Triple X dangled from wooden posts. The sheriff turned down the drive. Spring had turned to early summer and everything was green. Cows grazed and horses roamed the pastureland. His boss, Wilson Donovan, owned a hundred acres, but that was small compared to the Wagon Wheel and Horseshoe Creek.

With no money for training and breeding, Donovan focused on his cattle.

Tires churned the gravel, bringing Cash closer to the main house and the man who'd taken a chance on him after Elmore had blackballed him in the ranching community.

The sheriff parked and climbed out, then opened Cash's door. Donovan strode down the wooden steps of the rickety porch toward them as BJ pulled her car next to them and got out. Somehow the fact that she'd been following them made Cash feel a bit safer.

A frown pulled Donovan's thick white eyebrows together as he glanced from the sheriff to Cash.

"I'm sorry, Mr. Donovan," Cash began.

Donovan held up a hand. "I'm sorry, too, Cash, but I think you'd better get your stuff and leave."

Cash gritted his teeth, but gave the man a clipped nod. Dammit. Donovan had taken a chance on him, and he'd failed him.

How the hell was he going to pay Sheriff McCullen back for his bail if he had no job or income?

BJ WANTED TO question Donovan without Cash present.

"I'll accompany Cash to his quarters so he can retrieve his clothes," Maddox offered.

Cash glared at him. "You think I'm going to run?"

Maddox crossed his arms. "Are you?"

Anger flashed across Cash's face. "No."

BJ traded a knowing look with Maddox. "Mr. Donovan and I will join you at his cabin."

"Bunkhouses are about a mile from the main house," Donovan said. "Sheriff Jasper already come out and searched Cash's room."

Cash heaved a weary breath. "Of course he did."

BJ made a mental note to ask Jasper about the search.

Maddox motioned for Cash to get back in the car, and he did so. But he looked irritated and worried. Did he have something to hide?

Donovan tipped his hat. "You think Cash killed the woman?"

BJ shrugged slightly "He claims he didn't, that he and Sondra were only friends." She paused to see if he reacted, but he didn't, so she continued. "The woman's three-year-old son is missing. Cash is afraid someone kidnapped him. What do you think about Cash?"

"I know what Elmore said, but I liked Cash. He was a hard worker and seemed honest." Donovan worked his mouth from side to side. "Elmore's cutthroat to us smaller ranchers. He was also protective of his daughter. Hell, I figured he'd kill anyone who touched her."

Interesting. His opinion backed up Cash's story.

"Did Sondra visit Cash here at the ranch?"

"She dropped her kid off a few times," Donovan said. "But I don't know what happened between them. What the hands do on their time off is their business, long as they don't bring trouble here." He hesitated. "You might ask Hanks, Cash's bunkmate."

"I will. And if you don't mind, I'd like to talk to some of your other ranch hands."

Donovan scratched his chin. "Feel free. I'd like to see Cash catch a break. But unfortunately, I can't keep him on here. The negative publicity is bad for business, and business is bad enough as it is."

"Thanks." Donovan sounded like a fair man. "Is there anything else you can tell me about Cash?"

"I never seen anyone ride like him. He has a knack for herding, too." He removed his hat and ran a hand through his thinning hair. "Cash is ambitious. I think it's always bugged him that he's not in charge. Was saving up to buy his own land someday."

His earlier comment replayed in her head. "You said you figured Elmore would kill any man who touched his daughter. Do you think Elmore was dangerous?"

"I can't say." Donovan shrugged. "Elmore was ruthless in business, and he ran some guys off. Two of my hands before Cash used to work there. Said he fired them for flirting with his daughter."

"What about Elmore's grandson, Tyler?"

"Cash adored that kid and took him riding. But Elmore didn't talk about Tyler." The rancher adjusted his hat on his head. "Thought that was odd. Most grandparents gush over their young 'uns."

"Did you see Elmore often?"

Donovan shook his head. "Just at the Cattleman's Club. He kept to business, though."

"Elmore thought Cash was Tyler's father, but he claims he's not. Do you have any idea who the boy's father is?"

Confusion clouded the man's eyes. "No. Like I said, Elmore stuck to work."

Did Elmore have any real friends?

And how about enemies?

If Elmore gave his rivals a difficult time, one of them could have cozied up to Sondra to get back at Elmore. If so, and Sondra found out she'd been used, she wouldn't have wanted her father to know.

That would explain the reason she'd lied about Tyler's father being Cash.

CASH CLIMBED FROM the police car at the bunkhouse, his instincts alert. He should be grateful this sheriff had stopped to let him pack his things.

He wished he could get his truck. But Jasper had had it impounded and searched for forensic evidence.

Maddox grunted as he walked toward the bunkhouse. Dammit, he still had no idea what the man's agenda was. Strangers in these parts didn't just up and pay fifty thousand dollars to help murder suspects, much less take one into their home. Did Maddox McCullen want to help him or find the evidence to lock him away for life?

Each bunkhouse held two rooms, with a common bathroom. His bunkmate, Will Hanks, was out working the herd, so the place was empty.

The sheriff entered first. A muscle ticked in his jaw as he glanced at Cash. "Looks like Sheriff Jasper did more than search the room."

Rage mushroomed inside Cash. The room looked as if it had been tossed. The dresser drawers holding his clothes were open, his clothing spilling out. The few books he had were dumped on the floor, some of the pages bent and torn as if someone had searched between them. His ranching magazines were scattered everywhere, as well.

The sheriff strode through the room, skimming the surfaces. Cash had no idea what he expected to find. He had no personal photographs. No mementos of his past.

Nothing in his past was worth holding on to.

If there had been anything of interest, Jasper had already removed it.

The closet was just as big a mess. The shoebox on the top shelf that held his personal papers had been pilfered through. His checkbook and the envelope with cash in it were there, but his business plan was gone.

Why would the sheriff take that? It had nothing to do with Sondra.

Thankfully, his guitar was standing against the wall in the closet. His heart hammered, though, as he knelt to check beneath his bed for his guns. Both missing.

"What is it?" the sheriff asked.

Cash swallowed hard. "My guns are missing."

The man narrowed his eyes. "What kind and how many?"

"A rifle and a pistol."

"I'll ask Sheriff Jasper if he confiscated them. Have they been used lately?"

Cash rubbed his forehead, grateful he had backups. "I fired the rifle a few days ago at a snake when we were herding."

A quick nod of his head was the man's only reaction. "Pack some clothes while I make the call."

Phone in hand, the sheriff stepped outside.

Cash yanked his duffel bag from the closet, then retrieved the extra pistol he kept in the storage compartment beneath the floor. Thankfully Jasper hadn't noticed the rug covering the spot. Granted he'd get in trouble for having it since he was out on bail, but he might need it for protection.

He couldn't rely on anyone else.

He piled his clothes on top. Jeans, work shirts, a couple dressy Western shirts, an extra pair of work boots. Even though it was summer and he didn't need it, he grabbed his long duster. Basically, it was everything he owned.

Because he wouldn't be coming back.

His toiletries went into a toiletry bag and he was ready to go.

He took one last look at the bunkhouse room and wondered what the sheriff had thought he would find under the mattress.

Jasper had probably been disappointed that Cash didn't have incriminating pictures of himself and Sondra or a damn journal describing how he planned to kill her. Instead, he'd found Cash's business plan, not a blueprint for murder or kidnapping.

Still, he had that damn video of Cash entering the motel where Sondra had died. And his knife with his bloody fingerprints on it.

Frustration blended with fear.

That might be enough to put him away for life.

BJ STUDIED DONOVAN. "We think the little boy's birth father might have something to do with his mother's murder. Finding him could be key to proving Cash's innocence."

Donovan leaned heavily on his left leg as if his other was hurting. "I told you, I got no idea."

"Did something happen between you and Elmore?" BJ asked. "Did he try to sabotage your business?"

Donovan shook his head. "I'm small potatoes. He offered to buy me out once, but I turned him down." He gazed across the ranch. "I love this place. It's home."

"Did he pressure you?"

"No. No need to. I certainly wasn't any competition for him." He gestured toward his truck. "The hands should be at the dining hall for lunch. I'll drive you over so you can talk to 'em."

BJ studied his face. He seemed genuine, as if he held no grudge against Elmore.

BJ climbed in the passenger side. The truck was old but clean, the motor humming as he drove the half mile to the dining hall. The rustic building boasted a big cowbell in front. The ranch hands were lining up on the porch and trickling inside.

The scent of barbecue drifted to her as soon as she climbed from the truck.

As they entered, she counted ten men in line, and a cook and two helpers were setting out trays of buns, barbecue, coleslaw and baked beans. Another station held water, milk, coffee, tea and lemonade.

"There's Will Hanks," Donovan said. "He shares the bunkhouse with Cash."

BJ scrutinized the tall, lean cowboy. Probably in his twenties. Good-looking with an air of confidence. A flirtatious gleam lit his eyes as his gaze met hers.

"This is BJ Alexander. She's Cash's attorney," Donovan said.

Hanks's smile wilted slightly. "They think he killed Sondra Elmore, right?"

"Those are the charges," BJ said. "Why? Do you have information regarding the case?"

He shifted from foot to foot, then looked away. "I don't think Cash is a killer. But he liked that woman and her kid."

"Was Cash violent?" BJ asked.

He grabbed a tray. "I don't know. He had a rough childhood," Hanks said. "One of his foster fathers beat him a lot. That'd make a man angry."

BJ's heart squeezed. She'd heard horror stories of foster care. "Did he talk about Elmore?"

The man added extra barbecue sauce to his bun. "He said Elmore reminded him of that foster father."

Hmm, that comment could work against Cash in court.

"Do you know who fathered Sondra Elmore's child?"

He shook his head. "No, ma'am."

They talked for another minute as he filled his tray, but

he had nothing bad to say about Cash. Just as she was about to join Donovan again, another cowboy approached her.

This man was shorter and introduced himself as Hyatt Spillman. "You asking about Cash Koker?"

She nodded. "What can you tell me?" she said as they stepped onto the porch.

He shuffled a toothpick in the corner of his mouth. "I heard a phone conversation between Koker and that woman Sondra the morning of the day she died. They were arguing."

BJ's pulse jumped. "What did they argue about?"

He made a clicking sound with his teeth. "I couldn't hear what she said, but he told her he loved her and promised to take care of her and her kid."

BJ crossed her arms in front of her chest. "Go on."

"She must have turned him down, 'cause he got mad. Told her he'd never let her go."

Anger seeped through BJ.

Cash had lied about being in love with Sondra. And they'd argued the day she died.

What if he'd flown into a rage because she wanted him out of her and Tyler's life, and he killed her in a fit of passion?

Spillman's story brought up all sorts of doubts. She couldn't automatically rely on the man, because it was clear someone could be trying to frame Cash.

But if not...

She was going to have to be extra thorough on this one to get to the truth. And not let Cash's attachment to Tyler cause her to free another guilty murderer.

Chapter Five

BJ texted Maddox and asked him to meet her at the dining hall.

"Thank you for your cooperation, Mr. Spillman." She handed him a business card. "If you think of anything that can shed light on Sondra Elmore's death, please call me."

He tapped the card against his hand. "You be careful, Miss Alexander. I'd hate to see the same thing that happened to Sondra happen to you."

The hair on the back of her neck prickled. Was that a threat? Or a warning about Cash?

Maddox pulled up with a grim-looking Cash in the back.

"Did you find anything?" she asked when he rolled down his window.

"Jasper already thoroughly searched the place. If there was anything there, he confiscated it."

"If he says he found something, he planted it," Cash said in a voice laced with anger. "I told you I didn't kill Sondra."

"I'll call Jasper." BJ entered the sheriff's number into her phone, her own temper close to the surface. "This is BJ Alexander. I need to know everything you found when you searched Cash Koker's bunkhouse."

"I don't have to tell you anything," Sheriff Jasper barked.

"Yes, you do. Before the trial, you're required to disclose all evidence to the defense attorney. That's me. So why don't you make both our lives easier and do it now?"

Jasper cursed. "All right, lady. We found pictures of Mr. Koker and Sondra. Looks like they were all lovey-dovey."

She twisted to look at Cash, her pulse clamoring. "Explain."

"They were wrapped up in each other's arms."

Cash had denied being romantically involved with Sondra. "Text me a copy. I need to see them myself. What else?"

"Ask him about my business plan," Cash said from the backseat. "And my guns."

BJ gripped the phone tighter. "Did you find a business plan?"

"Sure did," Jasper said. "Koker needed finances to make that happen. My guess is he hated Elmore for firing him and decided to use that kid for blackmail money to buy his own spread."

BJ bit her bottom lip. She and Cash had discussed a blackmail accusation back at the jail, but he hadn't disclosed his plans to start his own business. Unfortunately, jurors might see that as a motive.

"What about Koker's guns?"

"Took them for analysis," Jasper said. "Besides, a dangerous man like him doesn't need firearms in his possession."

BJ gritted her teeth. "What about other suspects?"

"Listen, Ms. Alexander, we have motive and physical evidence. We got the right man."

"We'll see." BJ ended the call, irritated.

Jasper did have a case. No doubt he'd twist the fact that Cash claimed he had amnesia to suggest he was lying. The ranch hand's testimony about that phone call between Cash and Sondra would also be incriminating.

Damn. With motive and physical evidence, Jasper might get a conviction.

CASH WAS SHOCKED that Sheriff McCullen went by the impound lot and allowed him to retrieve his pickup truck.

"Just follow me to the ranch," Sheriff McCullen said. "You can stay at Horseshoe Creek until the case is over. Miss Alexander is already staying in a cabin on the ranch."

Suspicion once again flared inside Cash. Nobody helped

a stranger for nothing. He'd just have to bide his time until he figured out what the sheriff wanted.

Questions nagged at him as he followed the police SUV. Farm and ranch lands spread for miles and miles, the open space beckoning.

He could not give up his freedom. He'd rather die than be locked away for the rest of his life.

All the more reason he find out who'd framed him and killed Sondra. Poor little Tyler—he must be scared out of his mind.

Sweat beaded on Cash's neck. The cards were stacked against him, though. How hard would BJ Alexander fight to get him acquitted?

And what the hell did any of this have to do with the McCullens?

A sign for Horseshoe Creek Ranch mocked him as the sheriff veered down a long drive. The lawyer lady followed in her fancy car.

Cattle grazed in a pasture to the north and barns and horses were scattered throughout the beautiful farmland. An article a few months ago had featured Brett McCullen, former rodeo star, and his awards. He'd also expanded the ranch to include horse training and breeding. His popularity and skills definitely drew customers, and his contacts across the states aided in him securing the best horses.

Elmore had an impressive spread, but he'd talked about Joe McCullen with both admiration and resentment. McCullen had built a legacy for his sons—a fact Elmore envied. Sondra hadn't cared about the ranch business, and Elmore had never had a son.

The sheriff drove toward the main ranch house, an impressive farmhouse with wraparound porches that sat on a hill overlooking the massive acreage. He bypassed the house, though, and veered onto a lane that weaved through the property. A half mile from the house, several smaller cabins had been built for employees or guests. Sheriff

McCullen pulled in front of one and parked. Cash swung his truck in beside him, then the lawyer parked on the other side.

"This is where you'll be staying, Cash," Sheriff McCullen said.

Cash straightened. "I don't understand why you're doing this, Sheriff."

The sheriff and lawyer exchanged a look. "Get cleaned up, then we'll meet in the main house to discuss the situation."

"You mean you trust me to stay here alone, or do you have a guard dog on me?" Cash asked.

The sheriff folded his arms. "Are you going to jump bail?"

Cash bit the inside of his cheek. His flight reflex was strong. How many times had he moved when things became sticky or uncomfortable where he was?

Too many to count.

But if he ran from this, the law would hunt him down. And he needed help finding Tyler.

"No." He swallowed hard. "I intend to clear my name." It was the only way he'd be free. "Tyler needs me, too. That kid has to be scared."

The sheriff's gaze met his, some kind of emotion flickering in his eyes that Cash couldn't read. "All right then." He gestured toward Miss Alexander. "Let's meet in half an hour at the house."

She agreed and Cash nodded. Then maybe he'd finally learn what the McCullens wanted with him.

BJ BATTLED HER uneasiness at sleeping in a cabin in close proximity to Cash. He thought she was afraid of him because she believed him guilty of murder.

But that wasn't the problem. Cash Koker was too sexy. Sexy men were dangerous.

She stepped onto the porch of the cabin where she'd

been staying, phoned her father and left a message updating him. A breeze ruffled the leaves on the trees, bringing her the scent of wildflowers and freshly cut grass. Rays of sunshine slanted across the ranch, the sky so beautiful that it nearly robbed her breath.

And reminded her of Aaron's rainbows.

She allowed herself a second to imagine him running across the field, then forced the image at bay. Work always helped take her mind off her grief.

Work was all she had.

The McCullens had lived here for decades, but they'd suffered their share of loss, both with the murder of their mother, and then the loss of their father to questionable circumstances. Yet they'd found a way to stay together as a family.

She wasn't sure she could say the same about her own father. All her life, she'd craved his love. She'd tried to please him and make him proud, but nothing she did brought them any closer.

Sometimes, she thought he blamed her for her mother's death, that he wished she'd never been born.

And although he hadn't said much about her mistake with the Davis case, she had disappointed him.

She slipped into the cabin and surveyed the interior, admiring the space for its hominess. Painted wood-paneled walls. A kitchen and an adjoining living area with a stone fireplace. Bathroom and bedroom complete with a queen four-poster bed draped in a country blue quilt.

Feeling overdressed, she considered a change of clothes.

But she hadn't brought anything casual enough to wear on a ranch. No jeans or flannel shirts or cowboy boots.

She went to freshen up and stared at herself in the mirror. It didn't matter if she had ranch clothes. Or if she wore her hair pulled back in a tight bun.

Or if Cash Koker thought she was a stuffy bitch.

She was here to do a job and nothing more.

Her phone dinged, alerting her that she had a text, and she rushed to see it. Anger hit her as a photo of Cash and Sondra hugging appeared on her screen.

Sheriff Jasper was right. The two of them looked close in the picture, a lot closer than Cash had led her to believe.

But pictures could be deceiving.

Still, she was more confused than ever by the man in the cabin next to her.

CASH THREW THE prison clothes into the trash and strode naked to the shower, anxious to rid himself of the scent of Sondra's blood.

How in the hell could he have gotten her blood on his clothes and hands and not remember it?

He closed his eyes as he scrubbed his body and hair, trying to force the memory to return, but his mind was a big black hole.

So was his heart. Sondra had been his friend, Innocent. Young. Vibrant. In love with life. She had a bright future ahead of her.

And she'd loved Tyler so much.

He would miss her smile and chatter.

An image of little Tyler laughing as he pushed him in the tire swing Cash had made for him taunted him.

Emotions churned through him. He'd kill anyone who hurt that kid.

Heart hammering, he dried off and dressed in clean jeans and a denim shirt.

Anxious to hear the sheriff's explanation, he snatched his wallet and stepped outside.

The fresh air and scents of summer hit him, then the door to the cabin where the lawyer was staying opened. Sun slanted off her pale skin, giving her a radiant glow.

She was still wearing that tight-assed suit, but even though it was modest, it didn't disguise her curves. Nice sized breasts, a thin waist, hips a man could hold on to.

Dammit, his body twitched with desire.

Not a good thing.

She held the key to his freedom. He couldn't screw it up by screwing her.

Squaring his shoulders, he strode toward her.

Her eyes flickered with wariness as she met him on the path between their cabins. "Ready?"

He nodded, willing his libido under control. If he made a wrong move toward her, she might drop his case.

At the moment, he needed her brains more than he needed her body.

But could he trust that she wasn't working for the enemy?

"We can take my car," she offered.

"I'd just as soon walk." He needed the fresh air.

"Sure."

She fell into step beside him although she was wearing heels, which slowed her pace, so he slowed his own so she could keep up.

He'd like to see her in a pair of tight jeans, but he refrained from comment.

An awkward silence stretched between them as they followed the drive to the main house. By the time they reached it, she was wobbly on those heels. She stumbled, and he caught her arm. She felt small and delicate next to him, and she smelled so damn feminine, like jasmine, that it stirred images of making love to her in a bed of wildflowers.

Her gaze met his, a warning in those eyes, and he dropped his hand.

Idiot. A woman like her wouldn't be caught dead in his bed, much less naked in a field of wildflowers with him.

The thought made his anger rise again. "Sorry, Miss Alexander. I was just trying to help."

She paused, lips forming a thin line as she stared him down. "It's BJ."

"BJ?"

"Yes, that's my name," she said, with a bite to her voice. "If we're going to work together, you can't keep calling me Miss Alexander like it's a dirty word."

A smile tugged at his lips. "All right, BJ." He liked the way it rolled off his tongue. "So why the initials? What does BJ stand for?"

"None of your business." She tossed him a withering smile, dispelling any semblance that she planned to get friendly, then walked ahead and climbed the porch steps. He followed like a damn dog in heat.

A chubby lady with a warm smile greeted them, and introduced herself as Mama Mary, the housekeeper and cook. She studied Cash for a moment as if she was dissecting him, then her eyes twinkled. "Nice to meet you, Mr. Cash. Y'all come on in and make yourselves at home." She shook the lawyer's hand, then Cash's, her gaze lingering on him, welcoming. Friendly.

An odd reaction, since she must be aware he'd been arrested for murder.

Remembering his manners, he tipped his Stetson. He'd felt naked without it in jail.

She directed them toward a closed door. "I'll get some coffee for everyone and sandwiches, and I just made a cobbler."

Cash didn't think his arrest warranted cobbler, but he was starving so he kept his mouth shut.

Voices from inside the room echoed through the wall. "You think he's innocent?"

"I don't know, but we'll find out." That voice belonged to the sheriff.

"I don't think we should tell him who we are, not yet," a third man said.

Anger gripped Cash, and he stormed through the door. He didn't intend to be in the dark another minute.

Chapter Six

Tension vibrated through the room as Cash faced the McCullen men. If these men were his enemies, he had a right to know.

Sheriff McCullen and his brothers exchanged odd looks, an awkwardness heating the air.

"Why did you bail me out and bring me here?" Cash demanded. "What do you want from me?"

The sheriff cleared his throat. "I'm Maddox, and this is Brett and Ray."

"I know who you are," Cash said between gritted teeth.

"You do?" Ray said, brows raised.

"Of course." Cash frowned. "Everyone in this part of Wyoming knows the McCullens own Horseshoe Creek."

The men traded looks again.

"What else do you know about us?" Maddox asked.

Another inquisition? "The story about your father's murder was all over the news." He folded his arms. "Now, answer my question. Why did you bring me here? Are you in cahoots with Elmore?"

Surprise flared on the men's faces. "Why would you ask that?" Ray said.

"Because you don't know me and I don't know you," Cash said. "Yet you posted my bail. Maybe you're working with him or whoever's framing me."

"Good God," Ray said. "You can't be serious."

"I work for the people of Pistol Whip and this county," Maddox said stiffly. "My job is to uphold the law. I can't be bought."

The lawyer touched Cash's arm. "Cash, trust me, they aren't here to hurt you. They want the truth, the same as you and I do."

He whirled around, his pent-up rage exploding. "Look,

lady, in my experience, no one comes out of the woodwork to help someone, especially not someone like me. Not without his or her own agenda."

A heartbeat of silence passed. A knock sounded, and Mama Mary appeared with a tray. Her bubbly smile seemed at odds with the tension in the air.

"Hey, boys. I have food and coffee."

Cash crossed the room to the window and stared out at the horses galloping on a hill in the distance, while Mama Mary set the food on a bar by the wall.

"Thanks, Mama Mary." Brett gave her a hug. "You're the best."

Heat flushed Cash's neck. Everything he'd read about the McCullens indicated they were honest folks. So why all the secrecy?

Mama Mary closed the door of the study as she left, and Maddox gestured toward the sitting area. "Sit down, Cash, and we'll explain."

He jammed his hands into the pockets of his jeans as the McCullens seated themselves.

Still on edge, Cash hesitated, but the lawyer gestured to two wing chairs. She sank into one, and he finally relented and took the other.

"Coffee?" Maddox asked.

"Not until you give me some answers."

Maddox's gaze skated over him. "All right. We paid your bail and brought you here because we wanted to get to know you, to find out if you killed Sondra Elmore."

Cash swallowed hard. "I didn't. But why do you care? I thought you and Elmore were rivals."

Maddox shrugged. "He and my dad were, but we've made peace between the families."

"So you're trying to help him by wringing a confession out of me?"

"No." Maddox glanced at his brothers, then leaned back in his chair. "Last year, when we learned our father was murdered, we also discovered that our mother's death wasn't an accident."

He had no idea where they were going with this. "I had nothing to do with that."

"Man, you are paranoid," Ray said.

"We aren't implying that you did," Brett added.

Cash studied them, confused.

"Just listen," Sheriff McCullen said gruffly. "Our mother was murdered because of twin boys she gave birth to."

"Her doctor told my parents that the babies died at birth, and that he cremated them," Brett said. "But they didn't die."

"They were kidnapped," Ray said. "Once we realized they'd survived, we started searching for them. They were left at a church. One of the babies was adopted, although I haven't tracked his adopted parents down yet." He hesitated. "The other baby was sickly and ended up in foster care."

Cash's head spun as he tried to keep up. *He'd* grown up in foster care...

The sheriff folded his hands and leaned forward, pinning Cash with his dark gaze. "Cash, we believe you may be one of the twins."

WHATEVER DOUBTS BJ had that Cash knew about his relationship to the McCullens faded. The shock on his face was so real that compassion flooded her.

In the past three days he'd been accused of murdering his friend and kidnapping her son, had been locked in a cell, crucified by Sheriff Jasper and bailed out by virtual strangers.

It was no surprise that, after a lifetime of injustices, he was suspicious of their motives. He'd been raised in foster care, shuffled from one place to another, then fired by Elmore for fathering Tyler, when he wasn't the father.

"I don't believe it." Cash's voice cracked. "Is this some kind of sick joke?"

"We wouldn't kid about something this serious," Ray said curtly.

"Of course, we want to run DNA to confirm," Maddox said matter-of-factly.

"We can also use that test to prove you didn't father Tyler," BJ said.

Cash scrutinized each brother, one at a time, as if searching for the lies in their eyes. Then he turned to BJ, as if in the midst of the madness, she was the one he trusted.

An awkward silence filled the room while Cash absorbed what they'd told him.

"I don't know what to say," he finally muttered.

Ray cleared his throat. "What did the social workers or your foster parents tell you about your past?"

Cash shrugged. "Nothing. Just that someone abandoned me on the steps of a church."

"Did they mention that you had a twin?" Brett asked.

Cash shook his head, his face strained with shock. "No, nothing about any siblings or family."

"Like Maddox said, we'll check DNA," Ray said, "but if you are a McCullen, you have a twin."

Cash dropped his head into his hands and rubbed his forehead. When he looked up at them, pain darkened his eyes. "That's the reason you posted my bail? Because you think I'm a Mc... Cullen?"

Maddox exhaled. "Yes. And if DNA proves you are, we'll do everything we can to help you." Maddox hesitated, his voice hard when he continued. "Although, brother or not, if you killed that woman, we won't cover for you."

Cash stood, his pulse pounding. "I didn't kill her. And I sure as hell didn't take Tyler. I don't care what happens to me, but I want you to find that little boy."

Maddox and his brothers traded another conspiratorial look. Then Maddox went to his desk. "Then let's take that

DNA sample and send it to the lab. It sounds like we've got our work cut out for us."

CASH'S HEAD WAS reeling as Maddox swabbed the inside of his cheek. The last thing in the world he'd expected to hear was that these men thought he was related to them.

Or that he had a twin.

Shock mixed with bitterness. All these years he'd been alone, had no family, no one who gave a damn about him. But he might have three brothers and another one out there somewhere who, like him, had no idea who he was.

Had his twin found a home with a family? Maybe his life had been better than Cash's.

Or maybe he wasn't a McCullen at all and this conversation was a big mistake.

He wouldn't get his hopes up.

Still, he needed help to clear himself.

Maddox bagged the swab. "We'll have that run ASAP. Now, we need to address the charges and the evidence against you."

BJ lifted a finger. "I phoned Sheriff Jasper. He forwarded a photo he found of you and Sondra together, Cash." She removed her phone from her pocket and showed him the text. "It looks like the two of you are cozy."

Cash's eyes widened. "I don't know who took that, but it's not what it seems."

"You and Sondra are in each other's arms," BJ said.

Cash studied the photograph again. "She was upset that day," he said. "Her father sent her away for a while to hide the pregnancy, but she came back and announced that she was keeping the baby. Elmore pressured her to give Tyler up for adoption, said he'd make arrangements to keep it quiet so she could resume her place in society by his side."

He made a sound of disgust. "She didn't give a flip about society. She came crying to me because she knew I grew up in foster care, and that I'd be sympathetic."

"And you were?" Brett said quietly.

"Damn right I was." Anger gripped him. "I always figured my mother gave me up because she was a teenager or didn't have money to raise me. Lester Elmore had plenty of money and a big house and could have hired a damned nanny for Sondra if he wanted. There was no reason to give that little boy to strangers when Sondra wanted to keep him."

"You didn't sleep with her?" Maddox asked bluntly.

"No," Cash said just as bluntly. "Never."

Maddox set a laptop on the table in the middle of the seating area. "I asked for copies of the evidence Sheriff Jasper had against you, and received a copy of the video camera footage. It showed you entering the motel where Sondra's body was found."

Cash's stomach roiled. How could he possibly disprove all this physical evidence?

Maddox pointed to the screen. "Look at it, Cash. Tell me what you see and what you remember."

Cash scooted his chair closer to the computer, and the others gathered around to look. A sick feeling churned in his gut.

Shadows hovered around the outside of the room, the moon barely a sliver in the sky, making it appear eerily dark.

The camera time indicated it was after midnight, twelve fifteen to be exact.

But there he was. Standing at the edge of the bushes by the motel room, a Stetson pulled low on his head, his face cast downward as if avoiding the camera.

The sheriff had been sure it was him, but how could he be when his face was in the shadows?

He mentally retraced what he remembered from that night. He was wearing jeans and the shirt he'd been arrested it. In the photo, it looked like the same shirt, but something was different.

"Is there any way you can enhance the picture?" Cash asked.

Maddox shrugged as if to say no, but Ray tapped some keys and enlarged the shot.

"The time on the photo says twelve fifteen." Cash drummed his fingers on his thigh. "Sondra called me about ten. She was upset and asked me to meet her. I got to the tavern around ten thirty."

"What happened next?" BJ asked.

"I ordered a whiskey and drank it."

"Did you talk to anyone?" Maddox asked.

Cash strained to remember. "The bartender. I think his name was Henry."

"Anyone else?" Ray asked.

He struggled to recall, but the details were fuzzy. "Not anyone in particular. The bar was packed. Sondra rushed in and was frantic. We ordered drinks, then she wanted to go outside to talk." He rubbed his forehead, his fingers tracing the jagged scar, a reminder of where he'd come from. He'd let his hair grow a little shaggy, but nothing could hide it. "I remember heading into the alley and then…everything goes black."

Ray clicked a few more keys, and zoomed in on his head in the camera shot.

Cash's heart hammered. It was difficult to see his face with the Stetson on, a hat exactly like his, but…his scar… where was it?

"Do you see what I see?" he asked.

Maddox grunted. "What?"

"That's not me," Cash said.

"It sure as hell looks like you," Brett said.

Cash removed his hat, laid it on his lap and pushed the hair away from his forehead. His scar ran from the top of his skull in a jagged, curvy line and wrapped around behind his right ear.

"By God, you're right," Ray said. "The man in this video footage has no scar."

"He looks shorter, too," Maddox pointed out.

For the first time since his arrest, hope shot through Cash. The picture proved he wasn't at the door of the motel during the time frame of Sondra's death.

Which meant that someone had framed him for murder.

Chapter Seven

Questions bombarded Cash.

The idea that he had a twin struck him like a fist in the gut. Did his twin know about him? Could he have been at the motel?

Or was another man pretending to be him?

Who hated him enough to set him up for murder?

And how had he ended up in that room next to Sondra's dead body? Had someone knocked him out or drugged him and put him there?

"I'm going to find our other brother," Ray said. "And I'll figure out who this is in the picture."

"It's time we talk to Elmore," Maddox said. "If he received a ransom demand, maybe it'll lead us to Sondra's killer."

Emotions ping-ponged inside Cash. He didn't know how to respond. All his life he'd been on his own.

Did these men really believe him? Were they actually going to help him?

Brett walked over to the bar where Mama Mary had left the food and coffee. "I say we chow down before you go. Mama Mary went to a lot of trouble for us."

"You know she loves it," Ray said with a twinkle in his eye.

"She's been with us since we were kids," Maddox said to Cash. "She took care of us when Mama died."

Envy stirred inside Cash. These men looked slightly different but had similar features—strong jaws and high cheekbones, tanned skin, dark hair—just like his own. Yet they'd grown up together, had wrestled as boys, had shared memories with their parents. Had bonded.

If he was their brother, he'd lost years of being with them.

How would his life have been different if he'd grown up on Horseshoe Creek? If he'd had family? Someone who gave a damn.

If he was their brother. That was still the operative word. He still couldn't believe it.

Maddox motioned to BJ and him. "Come on and grab a plate."

BJ stepped to the bar, poured a cup of coffee and choose a sandwich from the tray. Cash's stomach growled. He'd hardly eaten since the arrest. The grub Sheriff Jasper had shoved in the cell could hardly be called food.

Cash poured himself a cup of coffee, then chose a hearty roast beef sandwich.

"Take all you want," Brett said. "Mama Mary will be offended if we don't clean this tray."

The men's affection for the older woman was obvious.

He grabbed a second sandwich, then scooped potato salad into a bowl and carried his plate and coffee over to the long table at the far end of the study. He sat awkwardly, waiting on the McCullens to fill their plates.

The scene was almost surreal. He'd come here suspicious of their motives, but as far as he could tell, they'd been honest. And now they were sharing a meal like…a real family.

Cash's throat closed. He'd never had a real family.

What if he wasn't one of them?

Or what if he was and he let them down? Would they claim him as blood kin if he ended up in prison for the rest of his life?

BJ SIPPED HER COFFEE, well aware of Cash's discomfort. She felt slightly awkward herself.

This family was nothing like her own. Her father was stiff and formal. She'd been raised by nannies and house-keepers who were stuffy and rigid, not loving and friendly like Mama Mary, who felt more like a family member than an employee.

Maddox folded his hands prayer-style. "Let's say grace."

Following the men's lead, she folded her hands and bowed her head. Cash took a second longer, his posture stiff, as if saying a blessing was a foreign concept to him.

Maddox blessed the food, then the men dug in with gusto. Cash finally relaxed, and judging from how quickly he scarfed down his food, he hadn't eaten in days.

He'd been locked up by Jasper, who had made no bones about his dislike for Cash.

"Did Sondra say anything to you about Tyler when she met you at the bar?"

Cash wiped his mouth with a napkin. "No, we barely talked. It was loud in the bar so she pulled me outside."

"Then you blacked out?" Ray asked.

Cash exhaled, then rubbed the back of his head. "Yeah. I thought someone might have hit me in the back of the head, but there's no bump."

"You could have been drugged," BJ pointed out. Maddox cursed. "Jasper should have had your blood tested, but he didn't."

"What about Sondra's friends? Did she have a close girl-friend she might have left Tyler with?" BJ asked.

"She had more guy friends than girlfriends," Cash said. "But she kept in touch with some girl named Diane."

"You know her last name?" Maddox asked.

Cash shook his head.

"I saw a post with her on Facebook," BJ said.

"Jasper probably talked to her, but we'll follow up." Maddox polished off his food.

"He won't like your interference," BJ said.

"I don't care," Maddox said. "I don't trust him. I know a judge who will agree with me, too." He stood, shifting back and forth, obviously antsy. "Besides, the murder occurred in Sheriff Jasper's jurisdiction but technically the Elmore's live in mine so I have to investigate the kidnapping."

So he could justify his involvement.

"I'm going to question Elmore myself." BJ turned to Cash. "I think you should go, too. I want to see Elmore's reaction."

"I need to check on Rose and the baby first." Maddox pushed back from the table.

"We have some new quarter horses coming in. I have to be here," Brett said.

Ray set down his fork. "I'll work on identifying this guy in the camera. We find him, he can fill us in on what really happened that night."

BJ's mind raced. What if that man was his twin and he'd set him up? Although why would he do that?

Maddox folded his napkin and placed it on his plate. "If you get an address, call me and I'll pick him up."

"Thank you for lunch," BJ said.

"Yes, thanks," Cash said. "And please thank Mama Mary for me. That's the best meal I've had in a long time."

"Hell, if you think that was good, you should taste Mama Mary's chicken 'n dumplings," Brett said.

Maddox rubbed his belly and Ray muttered an *Amen*.

BJ's heart melted at the uncertainty in Cash's eyes. For a man who'd never had a family, becoming part of this close-knit group could be something special.

But they needed the DNA test first. And they had to prove Cash's innocence and find Tyler.

She didn't know the child, but she was worried sick about him.

With Jasper's stubbornness about Cash's guilt, they'd already lost precious time tracking down the child.

She only hoped Tyler didn't end up like Sondra.

CASH TAMPED DOWN any smidgen of hope that he belonged to this family. Things like that didn't happen to people like him.

Loser. That's what his foster father used to call him.

Not that he cared about that bastard's opinion. But he had believed it as a kid.

Then he'd met this social worker named Darma who'd told him he could wallow in pity or be the man he wanted to be.

He'd taken her advice and learned ranching skills. He'd

even enrolled in business classes to help him if he ever could afford his own spread.

Mama Mary bustled in to get the dirty dishes, and he thanked her for the food.

She looked him up and down for a moment, as if trying to decide if he was who they thought he was, then her plump cheeks turned rosy with her smile. "You're certainly welcome, Mr. Cash. It's nice to meet you."

Nice to meet him? He was under arrest.

He tipped his hat. "You, too, ma'am. You're a fine cook."

Her smile widened, the dimples in her cheeks deepening. "I don't have to wait on DNA. You've got more of your mama in you than the other boys." She pressed a hand to his cheek. "She was a good woman and loved the other three boys. But when that doctor told her she lost those twins, it tore her up something bad."

Cash had always wondered if his mother regretted giving him up. If she'd thought about him over the years, or missed him, or even remembered him on his birthday.

If he'd been kidnapped at birth and was part of this family, it meant his mother had loved him. That she'd grieved when he'd been taken.

Sadness welled in his chest.

BJ stepped back. "We'll meet Maddox at Elmore's," she said. "It'll take time to get those warrants. I'm anxious to see if Elmore has received any word about Tyler."

She led the way through the house and outside.

Maddox had taken him off guard with that blessing. Cash didn't pray often.

But he said a silent prayer that Tyler was still alive, and that he'd been found as they headed to her car.

BJ CALLED SHERIFF Jasper as she slid into the driver's seat. The phone rang four times, then his voice mail picked up. "Sheriff Jasper, it's BJ Alexander. Call me with an update on the Amber Alert."

She ended the call and drove from the ranch toward El-more's, grateful Maddox was on top of the search for Tyler. Horseshoe Creek was a huge operation, but the wide-open spaces, land and animals created a homey feeling.

Her father's city estate was large and had never felt like home, whereas the McCullen farmhouse felt warm and welcoming.

Cash looked grim. His mind must be churning with dozens of questions about the case and Tyler, and about the Mc-Cullens and the possibility that he was part of that family.

Finding Tyler had to take precedence, though. "Did Sondra mention someplace she'd go if she moved from her father's?"

Cash swung his gaze her way. "She used to talk about the beach, but that was a long time ago."

She changed tactics. "Let's talk about Elmore. Did he have any enemies that you know of?"

Cash removed his hat and ran one hand through his hair. Another scar—this one a cigarette burn on his hand.

She dragged her gaze from it, knowing what it meant. He'd been abused.

An image of a little boy who looked like Cash taunted her. Then an image of a big man pressing a lit cigarette to him to punish him...

"He ticked some other ranchers and employees off, but no one who'd kidnap Tyler, at least not that I can think of," Cash said. "Although, a while back, Sondra mentioned that her father and another rancher had a falling out."

"Did she tell you any details?"

"Just that the man accused her father of cheating him out of a small fortune." He hesitated. "I tried to tell Jasper to look for Elmore's enemies but he blew me off."

"Just tell me what you remember," BJ said softly.

"Not that much. I didn't work for Elmore long at all. In fact, I'd forgotten about that conversation until just now."

"Maybe you forgot, but the rancher didn't." BJ's pulse clamored. "What was his name?"

Cash twisted his mouth to the side as if he was thinking. "Something like Hicks. No, maybe Nix."

"I'll look into it. Anyone else have a beef with him?"

"He fired me, but I wasn't the first he let go."

Another leap of her pulse. "A hand who got involved with Sondra?"

"Yeah. A dude named Ronnie made a pass at her a few months back. He was gone the next day."

"What was his last name?"

"Thacker."

She made a mental note of his name. "Go on."

"He accused one of the ranch hands of stealing cattle from him. Threatened to press charges if he didn't hightail it out of town."

"So why didn't he press charges?"

Cash shrugged. "Said he just wanted the trouble to go away."

"Did you see either man around the ranch after that?"

"No. Although Sondra mentioned that Thacker kept calling her. But that was months ago."

A possible suspect. "You said Sondra was upset when she called you. Maybe they had a confrontation? He could have followed her, saw you and flew into a rage." Stalkers were obsessive personality types. Their obsessions could become dangerous.

"I suppose. But that seems a stretch."

She sighed. "Cash, work with me here. We have to come up with an alternative suspect if we're going to clear you."

"All right. So the guy drugs me, then kills her and makes me look like the guilty one," Cash said.

It made sense. There was just one problem—the video camera footage of the man who looked like Cash. If he'd been part of a scheme to frame Cash, the killer had planned ahead.

Which meant he hadn't simply flown into a rage and lost control. His anger had built up over time and festered.

That the murder was premeditated.

Chapter Eight

Cash's blood pressure soared as he and BJ walked up the stone drive to Elmore's humongous Georgian home. The man not only had money, but he liked to boast about his good fortune, and showcase it in the details of his home and the furnishings.

Marble floors, custom woodwork, high-end leather couches, custom paintings, and decorated by a designer—there wasn't a space inside that Cash had felt comfortable.

Having grown up in foster care with nothing, at first he'd been irritated at Sondra's comments about growing up in a glass house where she'd been afraid to move or touch anything. But after meeting Elmore and his staff, he'd understood. Sondra had been young, vibrant, and craved love. But she'd felt like a visitor in her own home.

No wonder she hadn't wanted to give up her baby. She was trying to create the family she wanted, not the one she had.

"Should we wait on Maddox?" Cash asked.

BJ shook her head. "Let's talk to Elmore first. If he and Jasper are tight, he may not like idea of another sheriff working the case."

He might even hold back in front of McCullen.

BJ rang the doorbell, and the housekeeper, Ms. Wood, answered with a stiff expression on her gaunt face.

BJ introduced herself. "Mr. Koker and I would like to speak to Mr. Elmore, please."

Disapproval radiated from her pores. "I don't think he wants to see you."

Cash tamped down his anger. He hadn't expected Elmore to welcome him.

"Sheriff McCullen is on his way," BJ said. "You can either let us in now or when he arrives."

The woman cut BJ a sharp look. "Have a seat in the parlor. I'll inform Mr. Elmore that you're here."

She escorted them to a small room situated off the two-story foyer. BJ rubbed her arms as Ms. Woods disappeared down the hall. "Is it just me or is this place cold?"

Cash grunted. "It's not you. Elmore likes power and social status. He wants everyone to know he has money."

BJ raised her brows, but he quickly clarified his statement. "And no, I didn't resent him for it. I felt sorry for Sondra. Maybe that's why I befriended her. She might have grown up wealthy, but—"

"She grew up poor in other ways," BJ finished.

Cash gave a quick nod. "She never could please her father."

Pain flickered in BJ's eyes for a second. "I can understand that."

"Your father?" Cash asked, surprised.

"My mother died giving birth to me. He shut off his feelings after that."

"You mean he didn't have room to love you?" Cash asked gruffly.

Footsteps echoed from the hallway, and BJ clamped her lips together as Elmore entered the room. He wore a three-piece designer suit and Italian loafers that probably cost a fortune.

Elmore gave Cash a condemning look. "You have nerve showing up at my house, Koker."

"I didn't kill your daughter, Mr. Elmore," Cash said bluntly. "And I certainly didn't kidnap or hurt Tyler. I'm here to help."

"Help?" Elmore said sharply. "I heard my daughter arguing with you on the phone that morning. She said she didn't want to be with you, and you got mad and killed her. Then you took Tyler to get back at me."

"I don't know what you heard, but you have it all wrong." Although they had argued. "That morning when Sondra called me she was upset, but she didn't tell me the reason."

"You're lying to cover for yourself."

"I'm not lying," Cash said. "And for the record, I'm not Tyler's father. Sondra let you believe I was because she didn't want you to know the real father's name."

Elmore's thin face went stone cold. "Of course you'd deny being his parent."

"Listen to me, Elmore, I love that kid. If he was mine, I'd gladly take responsibility for him. Unfortunately, he's not," Cash said.

"We're running Cash's DNA," BJ stated, cutting in. "We'll know soon enough."

"It will prove what I'm saying," Cash said. "Someone set me up, Mr. Elmore. If we work together, maybe we can discover who killed Sondra, and find Tyler."

"Have you heard anything about Tyler?" BJ asked.

Worry creased the man's forehead. "No." He looked at Cash again, his voice earnest. "Listen to me. Just tell me what you want and I'll give it to you. I may not have been the best father, but I want my grandson back."

Cash's chest clenched. "I didn't take him, Mr. Elmore. I swear I didn't."

Elmore paled as if he finally believed him. "Then who the hell did? And why haven't they contacted me with a ransom demand?"

No one voiced the fear that was hanging over them.

Because Tyler is dead, too.

BJ STUDIED ELMORE.

In the case of murder or a child kidnapping, the first place the police usually looked was at the home situation. Family issues or financial problems drove people to do things they might never do. Elmore might appear wealthy on paper, but oftentimes people hid their debts.

The fact that Elmore's relationship with his daughter wasn't perfect raised her suspicions. Had something happened between father and daughter?

"Mr. Elmore, Sheriff McCullen and I reviewed the camera surveillance that allegedly showed Mr. Koker entering the motel where your daughter was killed. The man in the camera footage is not Mr. Koker."

"It sure as hell looked like him!" he said with disbelief. "So what makes you think it wasn't?"

"This," Cash said, pointing to his scar. "The man in the footage didn't have it."

Elmore jerked his head toward Cash, then her. "Then who was it?"

"I was hoping you might have an idea," BJ said.

Anger slashed his features. "How the hell would I know?"

"You might have enemies who want to hurt you. Think about it."

He rubbed his chin with a shaky hand, then poured himself a finger of Scotch and downed it.

"First, though, let's talk about your daughter," BJ continued. "Is there anyone she might have left Tyler with?"

Elmore poured another drink, then swirled it in his highball glass. "Her best friend was from childhood. Diane Stuckey. But Tyler's not with her. I've already checked and Sheriff Jasper checked with her as well."

"Did she talk to Sondra the day Sondra was killed?" BJ asked.

"Diane said she called Sondra, but Sondra didn't answer."

"I'd like to speak to her." BJ would follow up. If Sondra had confided having problems with her father, Diane wouldn't have divulged that to Elmore.

"I'll have my secretary text you her number."

"Thank you." BJ shifted. "We'd also like to look at Sondra's phone and her computer."

"Sheriff Jasper has her phone. He examined her computer and returned it already. It's in her quarters."

The doorbell dinged, and a minute later, the housekeeper escorted Sheriff McCullen and Deputy Whitefeather inside.

Maddox introduced himself and his deputy.

"You're Joe McCullen's oldest, aren't you?" Elmore said.

"Yes, sir."

Elmore shook Maddox's hand. "I'm sorry about your daddy. He was a good man."

Maddox's mouth tightened. "Thank you. I'm also sorry for your loss. I intend to find the person who killed your daughter." He removed an envelope from his pocket. "I have search warrants for your house and for your daughter's living quarters, her phone, car and computer."

A vein pulsed in Elmore's forehead. "You want to search my house? Just what are you looking for?"

Maddox squared his shoulders. "Anything that will lead us to her killer." He gestured toward Cash. "It's possible that Tyler's birth father had motive to take the boy. It's important we find out who he is if you want to bring your grandson home alive."

CASH BRIEFLY ENTERTAINED the idea that Elmore had fought with Sondra and killed her in a fit of rage. But so far the evidence they had uncovered suggested her murder had been premeditated.

Unless Elmore had killed her in the moment, then hired people to frame Cash afterward. He could have paid someone to alter the camera timing and make it appear that "Cash" had been conscious when he'd entered the motel. He could also have paid someone to stage the scene.

Cash tried to envision a scenario of what had happened. If Elmore had argued with Sondra, he would have probably pushed her, not slit her throat with a knife. That type of crime was more violent, implied anger and a cold viciousness.

It just didn't seem likely, any way Cash tried to justify it. Elmore was a rich, snotty son of a bitch who hated Cash, but in spite of their differences, the man had loved his daughter. Slashing his Sondra's throat was too damn bloody for a man like him.

Elmore's hand shook as he gestured to Maddox. "Go ahead and search. More than anything, I want to know who took my daughter and grandson from me."

Cash frowned. Did he know more about Tyler's disappearance than he was letting on? Was he suggesting that Tyler was...dead?

"Is there something you aren't telling us?" Maddox asked. "Do you have any idea who did this, Mr. Elmore?"

Elmore rubbed his forehead with two fingers. "No." He glanced at Cash. "When Sondra's friend Diane didn't have him, I assumed you took Tyler."

"Mr. Elmore," Maddox said. "Consider for a second that Cash had nothing to do with this. Think hard about who'd want to hurt Sondra or you."

Elmore sank into his desk chair. "I've had trouble with a few ranchers over the years." He gave Maddox a pointed look. "Your father and I had our differences, too. But we went by the Cattleman's code of ethics and were civil enough not to stoop to sabotage. We certainly would never go after each other's family."

"Sondra said you accused one of your ranch hands of stealing cattle," Cash said.

Perspiration beaded on Elmore's forehead. "Yes, a man named Biff Lenox. It was after your father discovered the cattle-rustling ring. I thought Biff was working with them," he said to Maddox.

"Did you have proof?" Maddox asked.

"No, or I would have come to you, Sheriff."

"What happened when you confronted him?" Maddox asked.

"He denied it. But he disappeared the next day and never came back." He sighed. "Frankly, I was happy to see him go."

"You put out the word that he was a thief?" Cash asked, remembering the way he'd felt when Elmore had black-balled him.

"I didn't want any of my friends to be taken advantage of," Elmore stated.

"Did you mention this to Jasper?" Maddox asked.

Elmore shrugged. "No, it happened a while back. I didn't think it was connected to Sondra or Tyler."

"I'll look into him," Maddox said. "He might have gotten pissed and come back for revenge."

Elmore stroked one finger over his gold tie clip. "If he hurt Sondra or Tyler, that bastard is going to pay."

"Let me handle it," Maddox said. "My deputy is going to look around your house. I'd like to see Sondra's living quarters."

"Jasper already went through the house and Sondra's things," Elmore said defensively.

"Just humor me," Maddox said. "He might have missed something."

Elmore motioned toward the hallway. "The guesthouse is out back past the pool."

Deputy Whitefeather headed upstairs to check Sondra's old room and Cash followed Maddox and BJ to the guesthouse.

As soon as they entered and Cash saw Tyler's toys scattered across the den, a pang caught in his chest. Tyler had loved the wooden animals he'd carved for him, especially the horses.

It was hard enough losing Sondra. What if he never got to see Tyler again?

BJ PRESSED A hand to Cash's arm as they stood in the entrance to the guesthouse. "You should stay outside, Cash."

"She's right." Maddox gestured to the patio. "Since you're a suspect, I can't have you inside the victim's home. The DA could argue that you influenced the search. Plus we don't want your fingerprints or DNA on anything here."

Cash's jaw tightened. "I won't touch anything."

"I'm sorry," BJ said. "But Maddox is right. If we find

evidence, we don't want the DA or a judge to throw it out because you compromised the scene."

Cash's chiseled jaw went rigid, but he stepped back onto the patio beside the pool.

Maddox moved through the room to search it while BJ did the same. She checked the kitchen while he examined the desk in the den. Two used wineglasses sat on the counter, suggesting that someone had joined Sondra for a drink the day she died. Unless she made a habit of leaving dirty dishes for days?

"If Jasper searched in here why didn't he send those to the lab?"

"Good question." Maddox bagged them. "I'll check with Jasper to see if his people found prints or DNA."

BJ peeked inside the dishwasher. Half-full. The cabinets were neat and orderly, the pantry filled with kid's cereal, a box of macaroni and cheese, Goldfish, pudding cups, and a stack of energy bars that she assumed were Sondra's.

The fridge held a carton of milk, yogurt, various cheeses, orange juice, salad fixings, condiments, hot dogs and a leftover pizza box with two slices of cheese pizza.

Silverware and kitchen utensils were in the drawers. A box of matches from a honky-tonk named Cowgirls. Receipts for clothing at a women's boutique. A bill from a martial arts studio for lessons for Tyler.

BJ hoped to find a day calendar or journal, something to provide information about what Sondra had been doing the day she died, or about Tyler's father. No luck.

Maddox looked up from the desk. "Nothing in here. I'll search the bedroom."

A cookie jar shaped like a bear stood on top of the refrigerator. If Sondra wanted to hide something, it was the perfect spot.

BJ grabbed a paper towel so as not to contaminate it with her fingerprints, rose on her tiptoes and pulled it down, then dug inside. Disappointment filled her when she found chocolate chip cookies, but nothing else.

Frustrated, she stepped into the bedroom. Maddox had donned plastic gloves and was searching the dresser, so she went to the closet, a walk-in that held more clothes than BJ had owned in her entire lifetime.

Although she expected expensive ball gowns, designer shoes and purses—and there were a few of them—most of the items were casual clothes, jeans, sweaters and T-shirts she probably wore to play with her son. BJ dug in the pockets of the woman's coats. A pair of gloves and lip gloss.

"I found her computer," Maddox said as he booted it up. "Now I need her password."

"I'll ask Cash and see if he knows." She stepped outside. "Cash, do you have any idea what Sondra's password is?"

He frowned. "Her birthday? No, wait, try Tyler's birthday."

That made sense. "What is the date?"

"June 5."

BJ rushed back to Maddox and gave him the information. Maddox typed the date. "That's it. Thanks."

"I'll look in Tyler's room." BJ crossed the hall. Her heart melted at the sight of the little boy's sports-themed comforter and the assortment of trucks, cars and building blocks.

A set of what looked like hand-carved horses and farm animals stood on a shelf as if they were special.

She pressed her hand to her chest, her heart aching as an image of her son flashed back. She could see him building a castle with those blocks. Drawing a picture of the horse he wanted one day.

Tears blurred her vision, but she swiped at them and forced her feet to move forward. Sometimes the painful memories brought her to her knees.

But she had work to do. Tyler's life might depend on them getting answers fast.

Using a small towel to cover her hands, she searched the

little boy's toy chest and dresser, then opened his closet. On the top shelf, several shoeboxes filled with toys were lined up.

She discovered another box in the corner, and she pulled it down and opened it.

Her pulse picked up. Two envelopes were tucked inside. She opened the first one and found Tyler's birth certificate. Hope spiked. Surely Sondra had listed the boy's father on the paper.

BJ flipped it open and gaped at the name listed as Tyler's father.

Cash Koker.

Chapter Nine

Cash paced outside the guesthouse. He felt helpless and useless and he damn well didn't like it.

If someone had planted evidence against him, no telling what BJ and Maddox might find in Sondra's place.

He racked his brain to remember if Sondra had mentioned any particular man other than Ronnie who'd expressed an interest in her. But no one came to mind. Although she was young and attractive. There *had* to be somebody.

He should have pushed her to tell him what was wrong over the phone that night.

But he thought they'd have time.

BJ stepped from the guesthouse, her expression solemn. Suspicious again. Maddox followed, his jaw set.

Cash's stomach clenched. "Did you find something?"

Maddox cleared his throat. "Sondra's computer. But someone erased content. I'll talk to Jasper and see if he found anything, then I'll see if the lab can recover what was deleted."

BJ was holding an envelope. "I found Tyler's birth certificate tucked in a shoebox in Tyler's closet."

"So she listed Tyler's father," Cash said with a burst of hope.

BJ met his gaze with troubled eyes, then gestured toward the paper. "She listed you as Tyler's father, Cash."

His breath stalled in his chest. Dammit to hell. She'd been serious about keeping the father's identity a secret.

BJ WANTED TO believe Cash, but this birth certificate made it difficult. "You said you weren't Tyler's father."

"I'm not," Cash said.

Maddox examined the document. "Then why did Sondra Elmore list you as the baby's daddy?"

Cash rubbed the back of his neck. "I honestly don't

know. I figured she left the father's name blank. Maybe she wanted me to have ties to Tyler in some way, but the DNA will prove the truth of the matter.

"That would explain why everyone is so adamant that Tyler is your child," Maddox observed. "I don't think I need to guess Elmore's reaction to the whole thing."

Cash stretched his hands in front of him and stared at his blunt nails. Scars crisscrossed his skin and one finger was completely crooked, as if it had been broken and never been treated. More burn marks stood out, cigarette burns that revealed more about his past.

"I wasn't good enough for Sondra," Cash said. "It's not like I have a pedigree. I was a ranch hand. I had no idea who my parents were." He grunted. "Not exactly what Elmore wanted in a son-in-law. He wanted someone who fit into society, someone to show off to his friends."

"Sounds like the way Dad described Elmore," Maddox said.

Was Cash Joe McCullen's son, as well?

Maddox stowed Sondra's computer in his SUV. "Cash, tell me about the argument you and Sondra had the day she died."

BJ stiffened, hoping Cash had a good answer. So far, things kept stacking up against him.

Cash lifted his chin, his jaw hard. "Yes, we argued, but it's not what you think. I suggested she ask Jasper to issue a restraining order against this guy Ronnie, but she said she couldn't talk to Jasper."

"Did she say why?" Maddox asked.

Cash shook his head. "Apparently Jasper's father and Elmore were friends. She didn't want her father to worry."

"It seems odd that Jasper and Elmore are friends," Maddox said. "The age difference is significant. Plus Jasper isn't a rancher."

"Apparently, back in the day, Jasper's father and Elmore were roommates at some elitist boarding school," Cash said.

Maddox made a low sound beneath his breath. "I see. So Elmore could have the sheriff in his pocket."

"That would explain a lot," BJ said. "Did Elmore have financial problems?" she asked Cash.

Cash rolled his eyes. "If he had money trouble, he certainly didn't tell me about it."

"What about Sondra?" Maddox asked. "I assume he supported her and Tyler financially?"

"Yes. She received a monthly allowance."

"If she was rebellious and her father was controlling, why didn't she try to get a job and move out on her own?"

Cash shifted. "I wondered that, too. When I first met her, she was in college, said she wanted to study journalism. But when she got pregnant, she changed."

"How so?" Maddox asked.

"She dropped out of school. Started staying home more. At first she even seemed withdrawn." He worked his mouth from side to side. "I asked her if something was wrong, but she claimed she was just tired."

BJ raised a brow. "You said she and her father argued—maybe he told her he was cutting back that allowance."

"I guess it's possible," Cash said. "Sondra depended on that money for her and Tyler to live."

"Did the baby's father contribute financially?" Maddox asked with a frown.

Cash shook his head. "She said she didn't want anything from him."

BJ made a disapproving sound. "She could have been frightened of him."

Maddox removed his hat and scraped a hand through his dark hair, then settled his Stetson back on his head. "Do you think it's possible that this guy took advantage of her, Cash? That they weren't romantically involved?"

Cash jerked his head up, his eyes cold. "You mean do I think he raped her?"

CASH HAD NEVER considered that possibility. But it would explain the reason she seemed afraid to talk about Tyler's father. And also the reason she didn't want to disclose his identity or care that he wasn't in her and Tyler's life.

If Elmore thought a man had forced himself on Sondra, he would kill him.

Cash would kill him, too.

But surely Sondra would have told him if she'd been attacked.

Wouldn't she?

Unless…she'd been a victim of date rape. She'd always said it was her fault she'd gotten pregnant, that she'd been stupid and irresponsible…

He'd assumed she meant that she simply hadn't used birth control.

Maybe Whitefeather would find something inside Elmore's house.

"Cash?" BJ said with an eyebrow raise.

"I…don't know," he said honestly. "It would explain why she refused to talk about him. And the reason she was so upset when she first discovered the pregnancy."

"Also the reason she didn't move out," BJ added. "Perhaps she didn't feel safe."

"Did you ever see bruises on her?" Maddox asked.

Cash struggled to recall the past three years. "A couple of times, maybe. Once I touched her shoulder and she reacted in pain, but she said she'd taken a fall off a horse."

"You think her father hit her?" BJ asked.

Cash's mind raced to comments between the father and daughter. He'd heard raised voices, and Sondra had been in tears a few times. "Elmore threatened to disown her when he learned about the pregnancy. But I don't think he hit her. And in the end, he gave her the guesthouse and supported her, although he spent very little time with Tyler."

"So if she wasn't afraid of her father, she was afraid of Tyler's daddy," BJ said.

Cash balled his hands into fists. He'd tried to respect her privacy by not pushing her too much for the man's name.

She might still be alive if he had.

BJ HATED THE train of thought her mind had taken. But they had to consider all the possibilities.

Elmore was a proud, astute man who valued his place in society, just like her own father.

How would her dad react if she'd turned up pregnant and decided to stay single?

He would be livid. He would have suggested a quiet abortion. He might have even cut her out of his life.

Just telling him would have made BJ ill.

Had Sondra felt that way?

Still, Tyler was an innocent little boy. How could Elmore not have loved that child?

Deputy Whitefeather appeared from the house, carrying a box.

"Did you find something?" Maddox asked.

The deputy gave a quick nod. "A few pictures of Sondra with a couple of different men. Thought one of them might be Tyler's father."

"Their names?" BJ asked.

"Not on the pics, but the lab can run them through facial recognition."

"Good idea," Maddox said. "Anything else?"

"Some notebooks, journals that belong to Sondra. I haven't gone through them, but they seem personal."

"Let me examine them," BJ said. "Maybe she talks about the baby's daddy in there."

Maddox and the deputy agreed, and they walked to their vehicles together. Maddox's phone buzzed and he stepped aside to answer it. Worry knitted his brow as he hung up. "Elmore agreed to let me put a trace on his phone in case of a ransom call."

Whitefeather stepped up. "I'll take the computer and pictures to the lab. I'll also check Elmore's bank accounts and financials. If he's in trouble, and had an insurance policy on his daughter and/or grandson, that would be motive."

"Keep me informed," BJ said. "Just put the box in my car."

"Could I see the pictures?" Cash asked. "Maybe I'll recognize one of the men."

"Sure," Maddox said. "But let's do it at the sheriff's office. I don't want any question over proper procedure or chain of custody."

Whitefeather stowed the box in the backseat of BJ's sedan.

BJ and Cash followed Deputy Whitefeather to the sheriff's office, where he left the box in an interrogation room. Cash shifted as if he was growing antsier by the minute.

BJ spread the pictures across the table before they tackled the notebooks.

There were several candids of Sondra and Tyler at the park. Others depicted them riding horses, celebrating the little boy's birthday and Christmases. Sondra was smiling and obviously doted on her son.

Oddly, there were no pictures of Tyler and his grandfather.

She shuffled further and found photos of Sondra and two different men. One was a tall, fair-haired cowboy who was standing close to her in one of the stables.

"Do you recognize him?" BJ asked.

Cash studied the photograph. "Mike Cranford. He works for Elmore."

"Were he and Sondra involved?"

"No. The man's gay."

Hmm. Another picture revealed a shorter, stockier guy with reddish hair leaning in for a kiss. "How about him?"

"No clue," Cash said.

BJ listened for jealousy in his voice but detected none.

Cash thumped his boot on the floor. "I wonder who took these pictures."

BJ drummed her fingers on the table. "Good point."

"What if Ronnie Thacker was following her and he took them?"

"That's a possibility," BJ said, her mind racing. "If she was romantic with one of these men, Ronnie could have been jealous. But if he took them, why did Sondra have them?"

"Maybe he sent them to her. And that's the reason she thought he was stalking her?"

"Another good point." A possible scenario flashed in BJ's mind's eye—of Sondra confronting Ronnie. Ronnie became upset, lost control and killed her.

Then in desperation, he'd come up with a plan to frame Cash.

CASH FELT LIKE he was invading Sondra's privacy as he and BJ combed through his friend's notebooks.

"Look for dates, references to men, to Ronnie, to any arguments with her father or anyone else," BJ said. "If this is about Elmore, she may have heard something, an altercation between him and another rancher or person who wanted to hurt him."

The lab tech texted with an address for Thacker. Biff Lenox, the man Elmore accused of working with the cattle-rustling ring, had disappeared.

"Let's go," BJ said.

Cash checked his watch as they drove to Thacker's. Dammit, he wanted to find Tyler before nightfall.

"You should wait in the car," BJ said as they approached the farm.

"No way." Cash folded his arms. "I want Thacker to look into my eyes and tell me he didn't hurt Sondra or Tyler."

A debate settled in BJ's eyes, but finally she conceded. "All right, but if you don't control yourself, Cash, it'll be the last time I allow you to go with me. If it's necessary, I'll have Maddox lock you back up."

A dozen curse words rattled in Cash's head, but he bit them back. He didn't play by the rules. He never had. But at least BJ was on his side. He couldn't afford to lose that help.

Farm and ranch lands spread for miles, signs of summer evident in the blazing sun, and how the lack of rain was frying the grass. Her SUV bounced over the uneven terrain.

A second later, BJ made a turn onto a long dirt road, but just as she did, a gunshot rang out. BJ screamed and swerved to the left. Cash jerked his head around to see where the shot was coming from and spotted a black pickup barreling on their tail.

Another gunshot pierced the back window. "Duck!" Cash yelled.

BJ dropped her head as low as possible and cut to the right, but another gunshot sounded. The bullet must have hit the tire because it blew, the sedan swerved out of control and they careened toward a boulder at the edge of the ridge.

Cash saw the drop off approaching and realized they weren't going to stop in time. "Jump, BJ!"

Her eyes widened in panic. She was clearly too frightened to propel herself from the moving vehicle. He whipped his seat belt off, then hers, grabbed her hand and threw open the door.

He dragged her across the seat and yanked her out of the car with him. He wrapped his arms around her to protect her and took the brunt of the fall. Gravel, pavement and dirt clawed at him, and he rolled them toward the grassy roadside.

A second later, BJ's car slid over the edge.

Chapter Ten

Terror streaked through BJ as Cash dragged her from the car, wrapped his body around hers and rolled away from the ravine. The impact jarred her shoulder; gravel scraped her cheek and hands. A bullet zinged by her head.

"Stay down!" Cash shouted.

The weight of his body felt warm and comforting, yet whoever was shooting at them was still firing.

Cash's breath gushed out as he lifted his head and scanned the area. BJ's car had skidded to the edge and was hanging by a thread over the side.

"Crawl behind that bush," Cash whispered next to her ear.

Footsteps crunched gravel. Terrified, BJ scooted toward the bushes. Cash slid his hand inside his jacket, removed a pistol and fired back at the man. Shock bolted through BJ. When had Cash gotten hold of a gun?

She didn't have time to analyze the fact that he was violating the law because the shooter fired again. She hid in the bushes and tried to get a look at his face, but his hat sat so low on his head that it was impossible to see his eyes or even his hair color.

Cash released a round, and a curse rent the air as the bullet pinged on the ground near the man's foot.

Their assailant fired into the bushes, and she scampered to the right and crouched behind a tree.

Cash moved quietly, sneaking up on the man. More noise suggested the shooter had pivoted and was stalking toward them.

A grunt followed. Cash attacking the man.

He grabbed the guys' legs and dragged him down to the ground. They rolled and fought for the gun. It went off again, this bullet hitting a tree branch and sending leaves raining down.

Cash punched the shooter with his fist. Blood spurted from his nose and the gun flew out of his hand. BJ eyed the distance to it, but the man kicked Cash in the face and scampered toward it. His fingers touched the handle just as Cash reached him. Cash launched himself on top of him, flipped him over and slammed his fist into the man's face once more.

The shooter bellowed, but managed to lift the gun and shove it in Cash's chest.

BJ lost her breath. Cash grappled for the weapon and rolled, fighting and punching.

Just as they neared the edge, the gun went off again.

CASH HEAVED A breath as the gunman fell over the edge. The man clawed the embankment, struggling to keep from falling below. A bullet had grazed Cash's shoulder, and he tasted dirt as he looked into the man's eyes.

An expression of cold evil glinted back. "You gonna kill me by pushing me over?"

Cash was tempted. But he wanted answers instead.

A dead man couldn't talk.

The sound of BJ's car crashing to the bottom of the ravine rent the air. Dammit. They would have been in that car.

Cash grabbed the gunman's hand and tried to pull him back up.

The man's hat flew off, sailing to the bottom of the ravine just as BJ's car had. He felt like dead weight as Cash hauled him to safety. The man groaned and fell onto the grass, his breath rasping.

A second later, he punched Cash and grabbed the gun again.

Cash cursed and rolled sideways to avoid the bullet. The man lunged toward him again. Cash kicked him hard in the chest and sent him careening backward. His attacker's foot hit a loose rock, more rocks skittered down the embankment and the man flailed his arms to keep upright.

He failed, bellowing as he plunged below.

Cash crawled to the edge, his breathing ragged, and stared into the ravine. BJ jumped up from her hiding place, raced to him and dropped to her knees. The man's body lay twisted and mangled on the jagged rocks.

She gently laid a hand on Cash's back. "Are you hurt?"

Anger shot through him. "No, but dammit, he's dead."

Her gaze searched his. "Do you recognize him?"

"Never seen the bastard before."

"So that isn't Ronnie?"

Cash shook his head. "No. But I intend to find out who he is."

And why he wanted them dead. Or at least why he wanted *him* dead.

Things had just gone from bad to worse. If Sheriff Jasper got hold of this news, he'd use it as an excuse to lock Cash's butt back up and throw away the key. Even if BJ backed up his story, Jasper would do everything he could to make Cash's life hell until the truth came out.

If the truth came out. Someone was clearly trying to frame him for murder. There was no telling what lengths they'd go to. And he didn't want BJ hurt.

"My purse was in the car, but I've got my phone," BJ said. "I'll call for help."

"I'll check out his vehicle," Cash said. "Maybe his ID is inside. We can also try to run his plates."

BJ caught his arm. "Don't touch anything, Cash. Remember you're the primary suspect in a murder investigation."

Cash cursed beneath his breath. How could he help himself if he had to sit back and twiddle his damn thumbs?

"Maddox will help us," BJ said softly.

His stomach somersaulted at the concern in her eyes. How long had it been since a woman had cared about him?

She doesn't care, Cash. She's your lawyer. Hell, if she decides you're guilty, she'll call the cops on you herself.

"Are you sure you don't need a doctor?" she asked.

Cash swallowed hard. "Trust me, I've had worse." From foster fathers with a hard hand.

Sympathy filled her eyes as if she'd read his mind.

By God, the last thing in the world he wanted from her was pity.

He yanked a handkerchief from his pocket and dabbed at the blood to prove the wound wasn't serious. "See, it just grazed the skin."

Her hand trembled as she punched in Maddox's number. She obviously didn't get shot at every day. He'd had enough scrapes and beatings in his life to blow this one off without a second thought.

Despair threatened to choke Cash. What if he'd killed the only person who knew Tyler's whereabouts, and Tyler was someplace alone, hungry and cold? And so far off the grid no one would ever find him?

That thought made Cash want to double over in rage.

But he couldn't waste time. He needed answers.

Desperate, he picked himself up, retrieved his gun and stowed it in his jacket. Then he rushed to the dead man's car. Hopefully, he'd find something inside that would lead him to the truth.

BJ READ THE frustration on Cash's face. He'd hidden his gun in his jacket, but she decided not to mention it.
The only way to help him was to get answers.

She phoned Maddox and explained the situation.

"My deputy will be there ASAP," Maddox said, then he hung up.

She raced to the shooter's truck. Cash had the door open and was searching the interior.

She looked over his shoulder. A box of ammunition on the seat. A rifle lay on the floorboard—the weapon the gunman had used to shoot at her car. He'd also had a pistol. He'd pulled it from his back pocket and used it to fire at Cash.

She snapped pictures with her phone, then opened the dash and found more shells. No wallet. He probably had it on him.

"I'll look in the truck bed," Cash said.

She started to argue, but if this man had stashed Tyler somewhere, the little boy's life depended on them acting quickly.

Cash rushed to the back while she checked the vehicle registration. She found proof of insurance, a hunting and fishing license, and a burner phone.

The truck was registered to a man named Taft Rumkin. The other documents were registered under the same name.

"Anything in the truck bed?" she asked.

Cash lifted his head, a weary look in his eyes. "No. No sign of Tyler."

A siren wailed, and Deputy Whitefeather sped up in his police-issued SUV. A tow truck and crew, along with a crime scene unit from the county, careened to a stop behind him.

A flurry of motion ensued as the workers exited their vehicles and joined the deputy.

She'd done her homework on the deputy sheriff. Apparently Joe McCullen had been romantically involved with Whitefeather's mother before he married the woman who'd given birth to the McCullen brothers—and possibly Cash. That made Whitefeather a half brother.

He'd also spearheaded the investigation into Joe's death and had uncovered the fact that Joe McCullen's wife had been murdered and the twins kidnapped.

The head of the towing company and his men began to assess the situation and develop a plan to extricate her car. Two of the CSI team members harnessed up to climb down, photograph and process the body, and bring it up.

BJ carried Rumkin's documents to the deputy. "The man

driving that pickup shot at us and tried to kill Cash. According to the vehicle registration, his name is Taft Rumkin."

The sun glinted off Deputy Whitefeather's dark skin as he turned to Cash. "Did you know him?"

"No, never heard of him." Cash swiped at a bead of sweat on his forehead. "We had to jump from the car or we'd have gone over that ridge with BJ's sedan."

Deputy Whitefeather scowled, then glanced down at BJ's demolished car. He whistled at the distance. "Looks like he ended up there, too. What happened?"

"I lost control," BJ said. "Cash pulled me from the car and saved my life."

The deputy's eyes focused on Cash. "That true?"

Cash simply shrugged, then jammed his hands in his back pockets.

"The man kept shooting," BJ continued. "We rolled into the bushes, and I hid behind a tree while Cash snuck up on him." She paused, her breath heaving as her adrenaline waned. "Cash and the man fought. The man lost his balance and fell over the edge."

"You push him?" Deputy Whitefeather asked Cash.

BJ cleared her throat. "That's not the way it happened. Cash actually dragged him up over the edge to save him, but he attacked Cash again. If Cash hadn't defended us, we'd both be dead."

The wind swirled the smoke still rising from BJ's vehicle below as the gravity of the situation sank in.

Cash was innocent. Tyler was still missing.

And someone didn't want them asking questions or poking around. Someone who'd kill to keep them from finding the truth.

Chapter Eleven

BJ shivered at the sight of her crushed vehicle as Deputy Whitefeather and the crime team worked.

If Cash hadn't dragged her from the car, she'd be dead. "Someone is nervous that we're asking questions about Sondra's death and about Tyler."

Cash murmured agreement, his face a solemn mask. She could almost feel the anger building inside him. He was a tough, huge man, with muscles strong enough to tear up a rock.

What would happen if he unleashed his frustration? According to his rap sheet, he had a couple arrests for bar brawls.

"I'm sorry about your car," he said quietly.

BJ's jittery nerves settled slightly. "It's insured. I'll get a rental until I replace it."

"We can use my truck," Cash offered. "It's not as nice as your car, but it runs."

The realization that he had little money and Elmore had treated him as if he was lesser because of it roused BJ's temper. "Cash, we need transportation. It doesn't matter what kind of vehicle it is. I'll call the McCullens and ask one of them to bring your truck."

He nodded, but the uncertainty in his eyes endeared him to her even more. What would it take for Cash to learn to trust someone?

"The McCullens are good people," Deputy Whitefeather said. "You can trust them. They accepted me."

Cash narrowed his eyes. "You're related to them?"

Deputy Whitefeather nodded. "Half brother."

Which meant that if Cash was a McCullen, the deputy was his half brother, as well.

Late afternoon shadows painted the skies a murky gray

as the crew finished hauling BJ's car from the ravine. The medical examiner arrived along with an ambulance, and he examined Rumkin's body.

Cash studied the dead man's face for recognition, but nothing clicked.

The ME looked up from Rumkin's body. "Cause of death was head trauma from the fall."

Deputy Whitefeather knelt beside the ME and checked the man's hands. "Powder burns confirm that he fired the weapon."

The crime team collected bullet casings and retrieved the gun he'd fired at Cash. Another investigator dug two bullets from BJ's car. So far everything supported his and BJ's statements.

Brett arrived in Cash's pickup truck, with one of the ranch hands following. "Gosh, you guys were lucky," he said as he peered over the ridge.

"Cash's quick thinking saved us," BJ said.

Brett met his gaze, making Cash fidget. The McCullens were dissecting every movement and word he said. Even if he was related to them, which was still a big if, they didn't have to call him a McCullen.

Elmore had talked about how close-knit the family was, that although they'd had problems, they stuck together.

He couldn't imagine that kind of loyalty.

"Thanks for bringing my truck." He turned to BJ. "Maybe you should let me look into this on my own. Being with me is putting you in danger."

"There's no way I'm walking away," BJ said. "Besides, you're the one who shouldn't be involved in the investigation."

The sound of BJ's scream as he'd jerked her from the car taunted Cash. "I just don't want you to be hurt because of me."

"Don't worry about me. This is not the first case I've worked that got rough." She took her purse from one of the

CSIs and thanked him for retrieving it. "I want to talk to Ronnie Thacker tonight."

Deputy Whitefeather made a clicking sound with his teeth. "I'll go with you two. The judge or DA can't argue with that."

The deputy stowed the box of Sondra's notebooks in Cash's truck, then Cash and BJ followed Whitefeather along the farm road to Thacker's. The deputy eased into the drive and Cash parked behind him.

The property was run-down, the pastures overgrown, farm equipment rusty and broken. A dilapidated barn tilted at an odd angle, as if it was sinking into the ground. Vultures soared near a dried-up creek.

They climbed from their vehicles and strode up the graveled drive. Whitefeather knocked on the door, but the hair on the back of Cash's neck bristled.

He pivoted, braced for trouble. Ronnie Thacker stood by a giant oak near the barn with a rifle pointed at them.

BJ FROZE AT the sight of the rifle. Cash instantly pushed her behind him. "Don't move, BJ."

Deputy Whitefeather's hand slid to his gun. "Listen, Mr. Thacker, put down the rifle. We only want to talk. No one needs to get hurt."

"You're the law. That mean I'm in trouble?" Thacker shouted.

"Not if you haven't done anything wrong," Whitefeather said calmly.

BJ pressed one hand to Cash's back. She could practically feel his heart pounding. She and Cash had escaped death once today. She didn't intend to push their luck.

Thacker aimed the rifle toward Cash. "What are you doing on my land?"

"We need to talk to you about Sondra and Tyler Elmore," BJ said.

Thacker tilted his hat backward, revealing bushy eyebrows and sweat streaking his face. But he kept the gun trained on Cash. "You here to gloat and tell me the two of you are getting hitched?"

Cash glanced at the deputy, then BJ. Was Thacker pretending innocence or did he really not know about Sondra and Tyler?

BJ gave a little shrug, silently urging Cash to play along. If the man was lying, they'd find out soon enough.

"Sondra and I were just friends," Cash said.

Whitefeather gestured toward the rifle. "Nothing can come of shooting anyone," he said. "So put the gun down."

Thacker spewed a litany of curse words, then slowly lowered the weapon. "All right. But someone better start talking or else get the hell off of my property."

"You liked Sondra," BJ said, taking the lead. Hopefully, Thacker would open up more to a female. The man had been eyeing her with appreciation. "Were you dating?"

Thacker shrugged. "We were. At least I thought so, then she got all weird and stopped answering my calls."

"When did you last see her or talk to her?" Deputy Whitefeather asked.

Thacker grunted. "Last week. Why?"

Cash tensed, but BJ gently placed a hand on his arm. "Did you see her or talk on the phone?" she asked.

The man glanced down at his boots with a sour expression. "She was in town at the honky-tonk."

"Really?" BJ asked. "Were you two hanging out?"

Thacker cut his eyes toward the pasture. "No, she took out this stupid restraining order, so I stayed on the other side of the room. She was flirting with some cowboy."

"You didn't talk to her?" BJ asked.

He shook his head. "No. I...didn't want to bother them."

"You mean you didn't want to violate the restraining order," Deputy Whitefeather said.

Thacker's shoulders drew back defensively.

"Who was Sondra talking to?" Cash asked.

Thacker hissed. "I don't know the jerk's name, but he wasn't good enough for her."

"But you were?" BJ said.

Thacker shuffled onto the balls of his feet. "I love her. Now, why you asking me all these questions?"

BJ traded looks with Cash and the deputy. "Because Sondra Elmore was murdered Friday night."

Thacker's face paled, and he staggered sideways. "No… Sondra can't be dead…she can't be."

He dropped his head into his hands and moaned. "She and I were going to get married one day. Have a family." He waved his hand, gesturing to the farm. "I was going to fix this place up, show her I could be somebody."

"Maybe you told her that, and she said she could never love you, so you killed her," BJ suggested.

"No!" Thacker lunged toward her and grabbed her arm.

BJ gripped his hands with her fingers to loosen his hold.

A second later, Cash grabbed Thacker by the collar and slammed him against the wall of the house.

CASH SHOOK THE BASTARD. "Sondra called me to meet her. She was upset, but she wouldn't tell me the reason. Said she had to see me in person. It was because she was afraid of you." His voice cracked. "You were stalking her," Cash continued. "You couldn't stand that she didn't want you, so you finally lost it and got revenge."

The man trembled. "That's not the way it happened."

Cash tightened his grip. BJ murmured something in the background, urging him to release Thacker.

Whitefeather moved up behind him. "Cash, take it easy."

"Then how did it happen?" Cash barked.

"I didn't hurt Sondra," Thacker cried. "I loved her. I would never have done anything to harm her." Tears leaked from his eyes. "I had a plan. After she filed that damned restraining order, the judge talked to me and I signed up for anger management classes."

Cash kept his fingers clenched around the man's collar. "So you went to tell her, but it wasn't enough. You realized nothing you did would ever be enough. Maybe she threatened to call the police."

"No." Thacker pried Cash's fingers from his neck. "I did see her at that bar, but I didn't talk to her. I wanted to prove to her I was changing, so I left."

"Anybody leave with you?" BJ asked.

Thacker cursed. "No."

"Then what did you do?" Cash growled.

Thacker scraped a shaky hand over his face. "I went driving around and then went skeet shooting to blow off some steam."

"Is that all you were shooting?" Cash asked.

"Y-yes," Thacker stammered.

"Where did you go shooting?" Deputy Whitefeather asked.

Thacker wiped sweat from his neck. "To the pond on the north side of my property. My daddy set up a little fishing camp there years ago. That's always where we went to shoot."

"Can anyone corroborate your story?"

Fear streaked Thacker's face. "No. I…I was alone."

Cash couldn't stand the tension another minute. Tyler's life might be hanging in the balance, and Whitefeather was beating around the bush, probably worried about violating the bastard's rights.

No one had given a damn about his rights when Jasper threw him in a holding cell and refused to let him call anyone for two days. "Is Tyler out at that fishing camp?"

Thacker stumbled backward, his mouth agape. "What do you mean? Why would Tyler be here?"

"Whoever murdered Sondra took Tyler." Cash's agitation mounted. "You'd better not have hurt him, Thacker. Now take us to him."

"I didn't take the kid." Thacker looked panicked. "That's the God-honest truth."

"Then you won't mind if we search your property?" Deputy Whitefeather said.

Thacker sucked in a sharp breath, then glanced from one of them to the other, worry darkening his eyes. "You're serious? Sondra's little boy is missing?"

"Yes," BJ said. "He may be in danger. So if you know where he is, tell us. The DA will go a lot easier on you if we find Tyler alive."

Chapter Twelve

BJ studied Thacker. He was shaking in his shoes.

Because he was innocent or guilty?

He seemed sincerely shocked that Sondra was dead and that Tyler was missing.

You've been wrong before.

"You can look around all you want," Thacker said. "Sondra's son isn't here."

"Did you take him somewhere else?" Cash asked.

"I told you, I didn't kidnap that kid." Ronnie scraped a hand through his shaggy, unkempt hair. "Why would I take the boy? I wanted Sondra, not him."

Cash gave him a cold look. "Maybe you killed Sondra in a fit of passion, but the boy was there and you had to do something, get rid of him."

"You're crazy," Thacker said.

Cash ignored the man's barb. "Then you had the boy and decided to use him to extract some cash out of Elmore." Cash gestured at the run-down farm equipment parked by the dilapidated barn. "Looks like you need some updates around here."

Ronnie shook his head vehemently. "I wanted to fix the place up to impress Sondra. If she's gone, I've got no incentive."

"IF YOU'RE INNOCENT, let us look around inside," BJ said.

Thacker scowled "Don't you need a warrant?"

"You want me to get a warrant," the deputy said. "Makes it sound like you're hiding something."

Ronnie gripped his hands together. "I ain't hiding nothing."

Deputy Whitefeather tossed BJ a pair of latex gloves. "Koker, wait outside and don't touch anything, you hear me?"

Cash silently cursed. He wanted to do something, dammit. He'd never in his life left his fate to strangers.

BJ is defending you, he reminded himself. *And the deputy may be your half brother.*

If he couldn't trust them, he couldn't trust anyone.

Still, he didn't like depending on anyone else. Or owing them.

Whitefeather hooked a thumb toward his SUV. "Take me to the pond where you went skeet shooting."

BJ disappeared inside the house, and Cash leaned against his truck, images of Tyler haunting him as the deputy drove across the farm with Thacker.

"Where are you, Tyler?" Was he safe? Hurt? Terrified? Did he know that his mother was gone?

A sick feeling welled in Cash's gut as another possibility occurred to him.

Tyler had been with Sondra the night she'd called him in a panic. He'd heard the little boy's voice in the background.

He hadn't come into the bar with her, but what if she'd locked him in the car? That would explain why she'd been in such a hurry to go outside to talk.

Cash's anxiety mounted. What if Tyler hadn't been kidnapped for a ransom? What if he'd witnessed his mother's murder and the killer took him to prevent Tyler from talking?

BJ KEPT HER senses alert as she entered Thacker's house. She didn't know exactly what she was looking for, a toy or kid's blanket—anything, that might indicate a child had been in the house.

Or that Thacker had kept something of Sondra's—a souvenir of some sort.

His history of stalking, the restraining order against him, plus the fact that he was at the bar the night Sondra was killed and had no alibi all made him a viable alternative suspect to Cash, at least enough to cast reasonable doubt on Cash's guilt.

She scanned the entryway. A coat rack with a denim jacket draped over it. Muddy work boots on the floor. She had a clear sight into the den, which held a faded brown plaid couch and a leather recliner. A deer head hung over the mantel. Dark hues and paneling made the place feel masculine, but the threadbare curtains and pillows gave it a dated feel.

No signs a female had been inside. BJ dug through the desk looking for motel receipts indicating that he'd booked a room at the motel where Sondra had been murdered, but the only paperwork she found were past-due bills.

She moved to the kitchen next. The outdated linoleum was ripped, and the cabinets desperately needed painting. A chipped pine table held empty coffee cups and dirty dishes along with takeout bags. The refrigerator held a carton of milk, eggs, stale bread and leftovers. No kids' cereal or juice or any sign that Tyler had been here.

She examined the pantry and coat closet, then moved to the extra bedroom. An ancient iron bed with a faded throw and tattered carpet. Nothing suspicious.

Next she scoped out Thacker's bedroom. An oak bed with a rustic quilt, brown armchair, curtains hanging askew. Again, no signs of a female or a child.

Thacker had supposedly stalked Sondra, though.

Stalkers were obsessive; they fed their fantasies by keeping photographs or objects belonging to the people they were infatuated with.

She searched Thacker's dresser drawers. Nothing female inside.

Still not satisfied, she dropped to her knees and peered under Thacker's bed.

A boot box.

Her interest spiked, she pulled it out and lifted the top. There were dozens of pictures of Sondra inside.

Candid shots of Sondra in town, exiting a restaurant, entering a store, at the park with Tyler, riding on the ranch with Tyler.

A cold chill rippled up BJ's spine.

In the pictures, Sondra looked beautiful with the sun glinting off her sun-kissed skin and hair. The love and adoration for her son brought tears to BJ's eyes.

A mother and son's bond was special.

If Tyler was alive and they found him, he would grow up without his mother.

That fact alone hardened her resolve to find the truth.

CASH SCANNED THE property for a place Thacker could hide Tyler. He strode around the outside of the house in search of a crawl space, root cellar or emergency underground fallout shelter, but found nothing.

Damn.

A dilapidated barn that looked as if it was sinking into the ground sat to the right. He started toward it, but BJ shouted his name just as he reached for the wooden door.

"Cash, I told you not to touch anything."

He kicked the dirt at his feet, but stepped to the side. "I haven't touched anything. But we should give this place a look."

She blew out a breath that sent her bangs flying upward as she walked toward him. She looked so damn sexy, he wanted to feather his fingers through the strands.

Good grief. How long had it been since he'd been laid?

He couldn't remember. He'd been so damned focused on working and saving money for his own spread that his personal life had been put on the back burner. That was the only reason he was attracted to this uppity lawyer lady.

Only she didn't seem quite as uppity as he'd first thought. With her hair tangled around her cheeks, she looked downright earthy. He wondered what she'd look like if she ever let go.

She paused at the door, her gaze dark and intense. "I found pictures of Sondra inside. Thacker definitely had an unhealthy obsession with her."

Cash clenched his jaw. "You find anything else?"

She shook her head. "No signs of Tyler or that he'd been in the house."

"You know if he was watching Sondra, even if he didn't kill her, he could have seen the person who did."

"I'll ask him.' BJ said.

"Check the pictures. Maybe he caught someone else watching her in one of the pictures he took."

"Good point." BJ examined each one, scrutinizing the backgrounds. "I don't see anything here."

Cash sucked in a breath. "I searched the exterior. No root cellar or emergency fallout shelter where he could have hidden Tyler."

BJ reached for the wooden door to the barn. "Then let's look in here." She jiggled the latch, but it was locked. Cash scanned the area, then spotted some tools in a corner of the makeshift carport. He found a pair of bolt cutters, then broke the lock.

Cash held his breath and paused to listen as she opened the door.

BJ PULLED A small flashlight from her pocket and waved it around the interior of the barn. With the two windows boarded up, the space was dark, and a stench permeated the air.

A low sound, like scratching, drifted to her, and she paused. Tyler? Was he locked inside something in here?

She scanned the floor and walls. Shelves had been built on the far side, and farm tools hung nearby. A wooden door to the left probably led to a tack room. She crossed to it, then jiggled the knob, but the door wouldn't open.

It had been nailed shut.

"Something's inside." Cash grabbed a tool from the wall,

rushed back to her and used the tool to rip out the nails. Wood cracked and splintered. Cash jerked the door open and BJ shone the flashlight across the space. Dirt and straw on the floor. An old saddle and ratty blanket on the wall.

"I don't see anything," BJ murmured.

Cash gestured toward the corner. The wood in the corner was rotting, and several boards were cracked. He yanked one away. "Looks like raccoons got in."

BJ covered her nose as the stench grew heavier.

"Two dead inside the wall," Cash pointed out. Animal droppings. "Looks like there might have been a whole family, but the others got out."

Relieved it wasn't Tyler, BJ sighed and backed from the room. Cash followed, his own relief palpable in the breath he exhaled.

"There's nothing here," BJ said.

Cash lifted the flashlight and aimed it toward the back of the barn. "There's another door."

BJ followed him past the tools, weaving between a rusted wheelbarrow and a bundle of hay. Cash pushed the door open, and they stepped into a pen that led to two stalls.

Hay bales were stacked in one corner. Cash headed toward them. Was Tyler behind the bales?

Cash lifted one and threw it to the side, and BJ jumped in to help. One by one, they moved the bales until they could see behind the stack.

Nothing.

Relief blended with disappointment. Where was Tyler? Was he on this ranch or were they wasting precious time?

THE BARN WAS EMPTY.

If Tyler was on the ranch, where was he?

Cash's gut tightened. What if the boy was here but he wasn't alive? There were acres of land where Thacker could have hidden—or buried—him.

Nausea rose to his throat. Surely to God Thacker wouldn't have been so cruel.

Cash stepped outside into the pen and searched the ground for freshly turned earth. The soil was dry, flat, with hay scattered around as if the wind had blown it into the pen.

He opened the gate and scanned the area, then noticed footprints in the dirt. Following the path the footprints made, he walked up the hill, where they ended by a cottonwood.

He sucked in a breath. The grass beneath the tree was patchy, the dirt disturbed. It also created a small mound.

Fear shot through him. The mound was small—the perfect size for a child's grave.

Chapter Thirteen

BJ sensed something was wrong.

Cash had rushed up the hill as if he'd found something. Now he stood ramrod straight, his head bowed, his face strained.

She took a deep breath and hurried to join him, her heels digging into the dirt. When she reached the cottonwood, she gently touched his shoulder. "Cash, what is it?"

He pivoted, the grim expression in his eyes tearing at her heart. Then he gestured toward the ground.

BJ's chest clenched at the sight of the mound of dirt. Denial screamed in her head as the memory of her own son's grave flashed before her. Her pulse quickened. A dizzy spell overcame her, and she staggered sideways.

"I'm going to get a shovel," Cash said gruffly.

A fine sheen of perspiration coated BJ's neck, and she leaned against the tree and forced calming breaths just as her therapist had taught her. For months after she'd lost her husband and son, she hadn't wanted to go on. She'd wanted to join the two of them in heaven.

Her therapist assured her those feelings were normal, that she just needed time to heal. Everyone told her the grief would lessen over time.

It hadn't. Sometimes a picture or a song or seeing another child brought it all back, pain so raw that she felt as if she was drowning in it.

The wind kicked up, shaking the leaves and adding a chill to her already trembling body. Her vision blurred.

Her little boy's face appeared. *It's okay, Mommy. I love you.*

Tears burned her eyes, and she blinked, willing them not to fall until she was back at the cabin, alone.

One slipped down her cheek, anyway.

Reality returned as Cash appeared with a shovel. His hand brushed her cheek. "BJ?"

She sighed, stifling emotions that had a will of their own.

"Are you okay?" Cash asked, his voice low. Concerned.

She brushed the tear away. "He can't be in there, Cash. He just can't."

His mouth tightened, then he gave her arm a quick, soft squeeze. "Go back to the car. I'll let you know when I finish."

She shook her head. She had to be here. If Tyler was in the ground and Cash dug him up, the police would have dozens of questions. Why was Cash at the grave? How did he know where the boy's body was?

Because he'd buried him...

CASH CLENCHED THE shovel with a white-knuckled grip. BJ looked as if she was going to faint. Was she just worried about Tyler, or was something else wrong?

He touched her hand and her skin felt clammy. "At least sit down, BJ. You don't look well."

She nodded weakly, then stumbled a few feet away from the mound, sank onto the grass and leaned her head back against the tree. "You should wait on Deputy Whitefeather."

"If he's searching the farm, he may be a while." And Cash had to know if Tyler was buried here. He sensed BJ did, too.

"We still need to wait, Cash. If there's a body and you contaminate it with your prints, it'll be hard to prove that you didn't put it there."

Cash jammed the shovel into the ground. Anger, worry for Tyler and anxiety fueled his adrenaline, and he paced back and forth. "You can't think I'd put a little boy in the ground."

BJ shook her head. "I don't, but believing you and proving your innocence are two different things. If I'm going to clear you, you have to take my advice."

"Of course I want you to clear me, but Tyler is more important." Although if Tyler was buried by the tree, it was too late to save him.

That fear made his knees give way. He caught himself and stiffened his spine. Dead or alive, he'd find Tyler, and he'd make whoever took him pay.

An engine rumbled, and Deputy Whitefeather's SUV chugged down the graveled drive. Hope spiked that Whitefeather had found Tyler safe. Cash rushed down the hill toward the SUV.

Whitefeather slid from the driver's side and Thacker from the passenger seat. Cash gave the deputy a questioning look.

"No sign of Tyler," Deputy Whitefeather said in a low voice.

"I told you, I didn't take the boy," Thacker said. "You're wasting time talking to me when you should be looking for him."

Cash cleared his throat. "There's a grave at the top of the hill, Thacker."

Whitefeather pivoted, leveling Thacker with a suspicious look. "You buried someone on your property?"

Thacker bounced his leg up and down. "No, it's my dog. He died a couple of months ago."

Whitefeather crooked his head toward the hill. "Let's see."

"You've got to be kidding," Thacker said in a childish whine.

"Kidnapping and murder are not anything to joke about," Whitefeather said.

"I...didn't mean it like that," Thacker argued.

"I found a shovel." Cash pointed to BJ. "We were waiting on you." BJ *had* insisted, but the deputy didn't have to know that.

Whitefeather jerked his thumb at Thacker. "Come on, let's see if you're telling the truth."

Thacker glared at Cash, but led the way. Cash followed behind Whitefeather, his pulse hammering.

If Thacker was lying and they found Tyler in that grave, he'd kill the son of a bitch with his bare hands.

BJ STRUGGLED TO pull herself together. For a year after her son's death, she'd dropped out of work and life. Slowly, she'd made a comeback, and then taken the job at her father's firm.

Although they disagreed ethically about certain cases, she'd needed a safe place to heal.

But the missing little boy resurrected the grief she'd struggled to bury.

Cash's love for the child was obvious, too. The terror in his eyes when he'd shown her that grave reeked of pain and fear. The kind of fear a parent felt for a child.

Deputy Whitefeather approached with Thacker and Cash. His brows furrowed as he glanced at her. "You okay?"

She nodded.

"The kid's not in there," Thacker said. "My bloodhound Clyde is."

BJ twisted her hands together but said nothing. Cash walked over and stood beside her, his hands jammed in his pockets as the deputy began to dig.

Gray clouds moved across the sky, shrouding the sun and casting a gloominess to the land. The wind shook the trees again, sending a shiver through BJ. The sound of the shovel hitting dirt and rock echoed in the quiet.

Thacker shifted on the balls of his feet, his breath rattling. The deputy dug deeper, slinging dirt and gravel and grass to the side of the mound.

A half foot down, the shovel hit something hard. Cash peered into the hole, a low sound erupting in his throat.

"Bones."

BJ's lungs squeezed for air.

"I told you, my dog is buried there," Thacker said, his voice warbling.

Deputy Whitefeather knelt and raked dirt away with his

hands, gently scooping more out. BJ watched him carefully working away at the grave so as not to disturb the remains.

Tense seconds passed. The sun slipped away for the night. The air turned chilly, a gust of wind picking up twigs and scattering them about. Somewhere an animal howled, and a dog barked.

Whitefeather shone a light into the hole, then raked another section of dirt from the bones. He murmured something in his native dialect, then gestured toward the lower part of the skeleton.

"It is a dog," he said, relief in his voice.

"How can you be sure?" Cash asked.

"I worked with a vet on the reservation." Deputy Whitefeather pointed to a section of remains. "There are four canine femurs. This jaw structure supports Thacker's statement about his bloodhound."

Relief flooded BJ. If Tyler wasn't buried here, there was a chance he was still alive.

CASH RELEASED THE breath he'd been holding. Thank God Tyler wasn't in the ground.

Knowing that meant that they might still be able to save him. If they could find out where the hell he was and who'd taken him.

"I told you," Thacker snarled.

Cash started toward him, but Whitefeather laid a hand on his back. "It's not worth it, Cash. Let's go."

The deputy was big and tall, but Cash rivaled him in size. Still, his gruff, quiet control forced Cash to reach for his own and reel in his temper. He didn't want to go back to jail.

He wanted to find that little boy.

BJ stood, regaining her composure. "Mr. Thacker, you've been watching Sondra. Maybe you saw something that could help us. Was anyone else following her?"

Thacker shook his head. "Not that I saw."

Judging from the pictures, he'd been too focused on Sondra to have noticed anything else.

The deputy handed the shovel to Thacker so he could cover the dog's skeleton with dirt. "Mr. Thacker, we may need to talk to you again. Don't leave town."

Thacker spewed curse words, but Whitefeather held his head high as he strode toward the SUV. Cash couldn't shake the feeling that something was seriously wrong with BJ as they followed the deputy.

He would find out. But he wouldn't press her in front of the deputy.

"Where to now?" BJ asked Whitefeather.

"I'm going to talk to Sondra's girlfriend. Diane Stuckey."

"We'll follow you. I'd like to speak to her, too," BJ said. "Cash can wait in the truck."

"Like he did at Thacker's," Whitefeather said wryly.

"I didn't interfere," Cash said.

"You pointed out that grave. If Tyler had been buried there, the DA would have argued that you led us to his body because you put him in the ground."

"That's ridiculous," Cash muttered.

"He's right," BJ said.

Cash clenched his hands into fists. "I swear I won't interfere. But I need to hear what Diane has to say."

He just hoped to hell she knew something helpful.

BJ STUDIED THE condominium complex where Diane Stuckey lived. It was a new development on the outskirts of Pistol Whip that catered to the thirtysomething crowd. Residents enjoyed views of the countryside, but also had the amenities of a big city development.

Deputy Whitefeather identified himself to security at the gate, parked, then slid from the SUV. BJ parked behind him.

Each condo had its own single-car garage, yet several expensive cars were parked in the driveways.

"Koker, you've met this lady before?" Deputy White-feather asked Cash as they headed up the sidewalk.

Cash nodded. "She visited Sondra when I worked at the Wagon Wheel. They met in high school and were best friends. I think they showed horses together."

"Is she married?" BJ asked.

"Not that I know of, but I didn't talk to Sondra very much the past few months. I took all the work I could get." He rubbed the back of his neck. "Besides, Elmore didn't want me on his land, so I didn't push it."

Whitefeather gestured toward Diane's unit, a light gray, two-story stucco that faced the east, offering beautiful views of the sunrise. Colorful wind chimes dangled from a horse figure carved out of metal.

The deputy punched the doorbell, which delivered a musical sound. Seconds later, the door opened and a striking brunette dressed in a designer suit and stilettos greeted them. "Hello."

Deputy Whitefeather introduced himself and BJ, then Cash threw up a hand. "Hey, Diane."

She folded her arms across her chest, making her ample bosom protrude even more. "I can't believe you'd show up here, Cash. I thought you were in jail."

"He's out on bail," BJ said. "I'm representing Mr. Koker. We need to ask you some questions."

"I've already talked to Sheriff Jasper."

"It'll just take a moment," BJ said quietly.

A wary look settled on Diane's face, but she invited them inside. The woman's condo reminded BJ of her father's house—everything was decorator perfect. White furniture, expensive vases, artwork that should have been in a museum, not a home. The place felt cold and empty.

She'd thought Diane and Sondra were best friends, but judging from their lifestyles and the photos she'd seen of Sondra and Tyler, Sondra was definitely more down to earth.

Diane escorted them to the living room and offered sparkling water, tea or coffee, but they declined. She poured herself a glass of mineral water, then sank into a plush white chair. "Deputy Whitefeather, Mr. Elmore called me when he first heard about Sondra. I...can't believe she's gone." The woman shot an accusatory look toward Cash. "She and I have been friends since grade school. We competed in dressage competitions together, were both cheerleaders and in the homecoming court. Then we roomed together our first year in college."

"You must be devastated over losing her," BJ said, although the woman didn't look devastated. She looked as if she was about to go out on the town.

Diane plucked a tissue from the end table and dabbed at her eyes. "I am. I...can't believe she's gone. That someone murdered her."

"I didn't kill her," Cash said gruffly. "Do you have any idea who did, Diane?"

She sniffed and shook her head.

"Was she dating anyone?" BJ asked.

Diane wadded the tissue in her hand. "Not that I know of. But after Tyler was born, she dropped out of the dating scene. Although she did mention that some guy was bothering her."

"Ronnie Thacker?" BJ asked.

She nodded.

"We've already spoken to him," the deputy said.

"Excuse me, Diane," Cash said. "Could I use your restroom?"

Diane frowned, but gave a slight nod. "It's down the hall on the left."

"Thanks."

BJ glanced at Cash, but he gave nothing away. What was he up to?

He slipped into the hallway.

"Do you really think he's innocent?" Diane asked.

"I do," BJ said. "Why? Do you have reason to believe Cash was dangerous?"

Diane shrugged, then picked at a piece of invisible lint on her suit jacket. "I guess not. I always thought he was in love with Sondra, but she said they were only friends."

"Do you know who fathered Tyler?" Deputy White-feather asked bluntly.

Diane shook her head. "She told everyone it was Cash, but she told me she hadn't slept with Cash. She swore me to secrecy though."

"So she didn't tell you his name?"

"No. She said no one needed to know."

"Do you think she was afraid of Tyler's father?" the deputy asked.

Diane's eyes widened. "You think Tyler's father killed Sondra and took Tyler?"

"I don't know," BJ said. "But Cash is innocent, so that means that Sondra's killer is still out there, and Tyler may be in danger now."

Diane looked down at her manicured nails. "I'm sure Tyler is fine."

"Why do you say that?" Deputy Whitefeather asked.

Panic flashed in Diane's eyes. "I…just hope he is, that's all. I mean, why would anyone hurt him?"

"Maybe he saw the person who killed his mother," BJ suggested.

Panic flared again, and Diane walked over to the window.

BJ wanted to push her more, but the deputy's cell phone trilled. He removed it from his pocket and connected the call. "Yeah? Okay, I'll be right there."

When he disconnected, he stood abruptly. "I need to go, Miss Alexander."

Footsteps echoed in the hallway and Cash appeared. "What's going on?" he asked.

Deputy Whitefeather clenched his jaw. "That was Maddox. Elmore just received a ransom call."

Chapter Fourteen

Cash's heart raced. A ransom demand was a good sign.

Deputy Whitefeather turned to Diane. "Thank you for your time, Miss Stuckey. If you think of someone who had a grudge against Sondra or her father, or anything she said about the baby's father, give me a call." He placed a business card in her hand. "Sometimes even the smallest detail can break a case."

Diane studied the number for a moment, then laid the card on the side table. "I will." She bit her lower lip. "I... hope you find Tyler and that he's all right. Sondra...loved that little boy more than her own life."

Cash agreed. Had she died trying to protect him from something? Or somebody?

BJ left her card on the table beside the deputy's. "Cash, let's go." She brushed his arm with her fingertips, and Cash followed her and the deputy outside.

"What were the ransom demands?" Cash asked.

"A million," Deputy Whitefeather replied. "Kidnapper said he'd call back later with instructions."

"Did they trace the call?" BJ asked.

The deputy shook his head. "Call was too short to trace and the voice sounded altered. Probably used a computer. The lab is going to see if they can work their magic."

They separated to go to their vehicles. Just as they were leaving, Diane rushed out and jumped in her BMW.

"Did you find anything in Diane's house?" BJ asked.

Cash tensed. "What do you mean? I just went to the—"

"Come on, Cash," BJ said. "We all know that was an excuse for you to look around. Did you see anything suspicious?"

He grunted a no. "There's no sign that Tyler has been at Diane's house. No kids' clothes. No toys. Every room is immaculate. Like a damn glass house."

"Hmm. Sondra's place was homey. Makes me wonder if Sondra and Diane were really that close lately." BJ looked pensive. "Sondra seemed like a loving mother, like she'd settled down, and Diane is still into the party scene."

Cash's heart squeezed. "True." If Sondra hadn't been too young for him, and Elmore's daughter, he might have fallen for her.

But he hadn't.

He *had* admired the way she loved her son, though. Every little boy needed a devoted mother like her. Cash sure as hell hadn't had one.

His breath caught. Or had he?

If he was a McCullen, his mother and father had wanted him. What if whoever had taken Tyler dumped him with strangers or on some church doorstep? What if whoever found him didn't report it?

No telling where the kid might be now.

BJ's PHONE BUZZED with a text. From Diane.

Remembered the name of a rancher Elmore drove into bankruptcy. Sondra said she was afraid of him. His name is Dale Nix.

"I'm going to do rounds in town, then head to Elmore's," Deputy Whitefeather said. "I'll see you guys back at the ranch."

"We'll meet you at Elmore's," Cash said.

"No," Whitefeather said. "Maddox said he'd call you when he knew something."

Frustration creased Cash's face. BJ wanted to go to Elmore's, too, but she trusted Maddox.

"He's right, Cash," BJ said. "Maddox is on our side."

Cash looked grim-faced, but gave a quick nod. The deputy started the engine and drove away from the condominium complex. Night had set in, gloomy shadows darkening the landscape as he pulled onto the highway.

BJ gently touched his hand. "Cash, Diane texted me with the name of a man Elmore drove into bankruptcy."

Cash sucked in a breath. "He could be after money to get back at Elmore."

BJ nodded. "Let's go see him."

"BJ, someone almost killed us earlier. I think you should stay out of it and let me handle it."

Fear gnawed at BJ as an image of her car going over that ridge flashed behind her eyes. She had been terrified.

But a little boy's life was at stake and she refused to let the kidnapper intimidate her. "I appreciate your concern, Cash, but I'm not giving into a threat. Tyler needs us."

Cash's gaze met hers, tension seeping between them.

"Just tell me where to go," Cash said.

BJ used her phone to research Nix. "Nix lives in public housing about thirty miles from Pistol Whip. His wife had a heart attack and died a month after they lost the ranch."

"If he blames Elmore for his bankruptcy, he may also blame him for his wife's death."

"That would be motive," BJ agreed.

BJ gave him directions to the housing development where Nix had moved. Storm clouds rolled in, the wind kicking up and stirring dust and blowing it across the highway as the truck chugged toward town.

The rumbling of the engine echoed through the cab. BJ's silence stood between them, a bridge he didn't know how to cross. He wanted to ask about her personal life. Why the grave at the tree had upset her so much.

He would find out.

But first they had to talk to Nix. He could have killed Sondra. He could have Tyler.

They had to hurry.

Chapter Fifteen

BJ winced as night shadows plagued the roads. She couldn't imagine the terror little Tyler was feeling. He needed to be home in his own bed with his mama reading him a story and tucking him in.

That would never happen again. Just as she would never tuck her own son into his bed.

Grief threatened to overwhelm her, but she tamped it back.

Cash parked in front of the low-income housing development, and they climbed out. Knowing Nix had moved from a hundred-acre spread to this tiny, tired-looking concrete block building roused her sympathy. On top of that, he'd lost his wife.

The units were connected, the only grassy area a small shared space in front of the building. No kids' toys or bikes. A black, beat-up pickup was parked in front of Nix's unit.

Cash strode to the door and knocked.

"Let me handle this, Cash," BJ said.

He shot her an irritated look. She understood his frustration, but she didn't want to see him locked up again. "Please, Cash. I'm not trying to clip your wings—I'm trying to keep you out of jail. Help me do my job."

He nodded solemnly.

Footsteps echoed from the other side. A short, chubby man with a gray beard and wire-rimmed glasses answered the door. He reeked of whiskey.

BJ introduced herself and Cash, earning a deep-set frown from Nix. "What the hell do you want?" he asked.

"We need to talk to you about Lester Elmore," BJ said. "You accused him of driving you into bankruptcy."

Nix scratched his beard. "You here to help me get my farm back?"

BJ bit the inside of her cheek. She hated deceiving the man, but Tyler's life depended on them finding the truth. "We'll see if you have a case. Right now we need you to tell us about Elmore. When did you last see or talk to him?"

"Been months," Nix said. "The day the bank foreclosed on me. He and the damn banker were buddies. Both damn vultures. Elmore was just waiting the days out. Picked up my place for next to nothing."

"That must have made you angry," BJ said.

"Damn right it did," Nix said. "Wife was devastated over losing our house. We lived there for forty years. Raised our boys on that land."

BJ's heart squeezed. "I'm sorry. I'm sure that was difficult."

"Broke her spirit. She had a heart attack the week we moved."

"You hated Elmore, didn't you?" Cash cut in. "You blamed him for her death."

Nix narrowed his eyes at Cash. "Sure did. Elmore refused me water rights, made it impossible for me to keep up my land and herd. That's why I couldn't pay the bills."

"Did you know his daughter, Sondra?" BJ asked.

Nix scowled. "I knew he had one, but I never met her. Heard in town he was mighty protective of her."

"He was," Cash said.

Suspicion flared in Nix's eyes. "What is this really about?"

BJ debated on how to approach him, then decided to be direct. "Mr. Elmore's daughter, Sondra, was murdered."

Nix pulled a hand down his chin. "I heard about that. That was too bad."

"Whoever killed her kidnapped her son, Tyler," Cash said bluntly.

Nix's eyes widened in alarm, then with the realization that he was a suspect.

"I hated Elmore," the man said. "But ain't no way I'd

kill a woman or kidnap no kid." He jerked his thumb toward the parking lot. "Now leave, and don't come back."

A second later, he slammed the door in their faces.

BJ's phone buzzed with a text.

Ransom drop tonight. Midnight. Stone Gap.

She angled the phone so Cash could read the text.

"I want to be there," Cash said.

BJ shook her head. "Cash, let Maddox handle this."

A muscle jumped in his cheek. "If the kidnapper brings Tyler, he'll be scared. He needs a friendly face."

He was right. But convincing Maddox would be a challenge. She punched in his number.

"What exactly did the kidnapper say? Is he bringing Tyler to the drop site?" she asked.

"He didn't give details," Maddox said. "Instructions were for Elmore to come alone."

"Could be a setup," BJ said. "He takes the money and kills Elmore."

"I know."

Cash grabbed the phone from her. "If you think this is a setup, let me go as Elmore," Cash said. "I'll wear his hat and clothes and make the drop."

BJ clenched his arm. "That's too dangerous, Cash."

"I don't give a damn. All that matters is saving Tyler."

CASH MET MADDOX at Elmore's door, braced for an argument.

Maddox led him and BJ into the study, where Elmore was pacing, his cell phone gripped in his hand. "I don't give a damn if I'm penalized by pulling money from that account," he bellowed. "I need cash and I need it tonight."

Sheriff Jasper was standing close by, his arms folded. He looked up at Maddox and Cash with a scowl. "What are you doing here?" Jasper bellowed.

"Working a kidnapping case," Maddox said bluntly.

Jasper cursed. "I can handle it."

"No way," Maddox said. "This is my jurisdiction."

Rage flared in Jasper's eyes, rage directed toward Cash. "And what are you doing here?"

Cash cleared his throat as Elmore hung up and faced them. "Trying to find a missing little boy."

"Or trying to make sure Elmore pays," Jasper said.

Cash barely held back from slugging the bastard. "I want to deliver the ransom," Cash said. "I'll do whatever it takes to bring Tyler home safely."

Elmore hung up the phone, his nostrils flaring. "Maybe you're offering 'cause you set this whole thing up and you know who has my grandson."

Cash whirled on him. "That's ridiculous, Elmore. You know I cared about Tyler. I spent a hell of a lot more time with him than you did."

Elmore went ashen-faced. "Is that why you did this? So you could be the hero? You thought if you saved him, I'd let you see him whenever you wanted."

Cash balled his hands into fists. "I would never have hurt Sondra or scared Tyler. We were friends." Fear clogged his throat. "If you let me help you get him back, I'll walk away and you'll never see me again."

An undercurrent of anxiety and distrust charged the air as Elmore studied him.

Maddox cleared his throat. "Cash didn't take the boy or kill your daughter."

"He's been with me ever since he was released from jail," BJ stated, backing up Maddox.

"Let me do this for you," Cash said. "If it's a trap, you could get hurt, Mr. Elmore. Then Tyler would have lost all his family. He's going to need you when he comes home and learns his mother's gone. If he doesn't already know."

Jasper put his hand on Elmore's shoulder. "Don't listen to him."

Elmore scrubbed a shaky hand over his face, then sank

onto the leather sofa in the seating area. "What if the kidnapper recognizes it's not me?"

"I'll wear your clothes, your hat, your glasses," Cash said.

"No, Cash, I'll do it," Maddox said.

Cash shook his head. "That won't work, Maddox. You're too tall. I'm more Elmore's height."

Maddox seemed to stew over that for a second.

"Besides, you need to be there to make the arrest," Cash pointed out.

Maddox sighed heavily. He couldn't argue with that.

Cash's pulse jumped. "Now, let's make a plan."

Maddox shifted and crossed his arms again. "The instructions said to leave the duffel bag of money at Stone Gap. When they confirm it's there, the kidnapper will send Tyler to you," Maddox said. "That means he'll probably be watching from a distance. He won't be close enough to tell that it's Cash instead of you."

"I don't think this is a good idea," Jasper said.

Elmore threw up a warning hand. "Stay out of it, Jasper. Right now I just want Tyler back."

Jasper muttered an oath, shot Cash and Maddox and BJ a dark look, then stormed out the door.

Elmore pressed his knuckles to his eyes and rubbed them. He looked weak. Frail. Broken.

Nothing like the astute arrogant bastard who'd fired Cash and pressured his daughter to give away her child.

"You'll bring the boy back to me," Elmore said.

Cash nodded. "Yes, sir." He'd bring him back or die trying.

BJ DIDN'T LIKE the situation. Although, if Elmore paid the ransom, hopefully they'd get his grandson back. They might even get lucky and catch the kidnapper.

Elmore's phone buzzed again. He glanced at the number. "My accountant. I have to take this. He's working on securing the ransom money."

He stepped over to his desk, and BJ motioned to Maddox

that she wanted to talk. Cash joined them in the hallway. "Did you check out Elmore's financials?" she murmured.

"Of course I did, but he appears clean," Maddox said. "Why? Do you have information?"

BJ tucked a strand of hair behind one ear. "No. He seems truly upset and worried about the little boy. But he might have taken out an insurance policy on Sondra and Tyler. If he was in financial trouble, he could have agreed to a kidnapping. But things went south. Sondra might have been killed trying to keep that kidnapping from happening."

"No kidnapping insurance on the child," Maddox said. "He did have a life insurance policy on Sondra, but Tyler was the recipient."

BJ arched a brow. "And if Tyler's gone?"

"Money goes to Elmore," Maddox said.

Cash made a low sound in his throat. "If that man killed his own daughter and put Tyler through this, he's a monster."

"If he did, he'll pay," Maddox said. "But we have to go by the book. Elmore agreed to having his phones tapped so we can monitor all communication between him and anyone else. So far, there's nothing to indicate that Elmore set this up."

"He'd better not have," Cash muttered.

Maddox adjusted his Stetson, worry creasing his face. "You're going to make the drop, Cash, but I'll be close by, watching your back. Whitefeather is staying with Elmore, and Brett agreed to keep an eye on Nix."

Elmore appeared in the doorway, wiping sweat from his forehead with a monogrammed handkerchief. "My accountant got the cash. He'll be here in half an hour."

"Let's go over the plan," Maddox said. "Mr. Elmore, please get some of your clothes, one of your hats, something recognizable so we can pull this switch off."

Elmore gave Cash a sharp look, but removed his signet ring. "This was specially made for me by the Cattleman's

Club in honor of my achievements and leadership. I never go anywhere without it."

Cash's jaw snapped tight as he accepted the ring. It was snug but he managed to get it on. "I'll bring it back, sir."

"Don't worry about the ring. Just bring my grandson home."

BJ bit her lower lip. She had to consider Elmore as a suspect, but the fear and anguish in his voice sounded real.

Cash's eyes darkened with worry, too.

Her heart stuttered. God, he was just the kind of man she admired. He loved the land, the outdoors, and even though he'd never had a break in his life, he still fought for what was right.

Admiration for him stirred along with concern. What if this meet was a setup and he got hurt?

Fear seized her. She'd vowed not to care about another man. Not to fall for Cash's sexy, bad-boy looks.

But how could she not fall for Cash? He was the sexiest and bravest man she'd ever met.

He'd risked his life to save hers. She couldn't ignore the importance of that.

And he was willing to give up his life for this child, a child who wasn't even his son.

THE EVENING DRAGGED by as they finalized the plans for the drop. Elmore's accountant showed up with the money, marked bills tucked between unmarked ones, to enable them to eventually trace the kidnapper—if he escaped.

Elmore shocked Cash by venturing into the guesthouse and retrieving pictures of Tyler—a scrapbook of memories Sondra had put together. Elmore's hand shook as he flipped the pages.

It seemed the fear of losing Tyler was sinking in, and he was probably regretting not being part of the boy's life while he had the chance.

Cash disappeared into one of the guest rooms and

dressed in Elmore's clothing: a pair of expensive jeans that Cash wouldn't be caught dead in and a custom-tailored Western shirt that bore a symbol for the ranch. Both fit snugly, especially with the bullet proof vest Maddox insisted he wear, but he could make it work.

Maddox attached a wire to Cash's chest before he buttoned the shirt, then gave him a tiny earphone so Maddox could communicate with him.

Elmore's Stetson and a pair of sunglasses helped camouflage his face. Elmore's boots, slightly too tight, were trimmed with gold spurs that sparkled, and probably cost a small fortune.

Cash and Maddox descended the steps and joined BJ, Elmore and Whitefeather in the study. BJ fidgeted, her expression anxious, but Whitefeather gave him a small smile of approval as if he thought the disguise might work.

Elmore lifted a tumbler of Scotch and took a sip, his eyes assessing. "Square your shoulders and act like you're somebody," he grunted.

Cash glared at the man, but stiffened and stood more erect.

"The money's in that bag," Elmore said. "Go get my grandson."

"I will." Cash grabbed the keys to his truck, but Elmore shook his head. Then he pulled a set of keys from his pocket. "Show up in that piece of junk and whoever has Tyler will know it's not me." He shoved the keys at Cash. "Take mine."

Cash sucked in a breath. Elmore's Cadillac was pricey. What if he wrecked the damn thing?

BJ approached, her eyes dark with concern. "Maddox and I are going with you."

Cash shook his head. "The instructions said for Elmore to come alone. If the kidnapper's watching, he'll see you."

"I'll be hunched in the backseat," BJ said.

"No way," Cash said. "I won't put you in danger."

"He's right," Maddox said to BJ. "I'll park a safe distance away in some bushes, then hike in on foot and cover you, Cash."

Nervous tension knotted Cash's stomach. Tyler's life might lie in his hands. What if he messed this up?

BJ squeezed his arm. "You can do this, Cash. Tyler needs you."

Cash swallowed hard. Her faith in him made his chest ache. No one had ever believed in him before.

Maddox checked his watch. "It's time. Are you ready, Cash?"

Cash nodded. "Let's do it."

Elmore started to follow them outside, but Maddox pressed a hand to his chest. "Stay inside until you hear from me. If this perp is watching your house, we don't want him to see that we made a switch."

Elmore hesitated but agreed. "Just don't let Tyler get hurt."

Maddox offered a tentative smile. "We'll do our best."

Cash and Maddox stepped aside for a moment to check the mike before he got into the car.

"Don't try to be a hero, Cash," Maddox said. "Just park, get out and drop the money where the kidnapper instructed you to, then sit tight in the car. Hopefully, the kidnapper will send Tyler in on foot. If not, he should send us word where to find him."

"I understand."

Cash started the engine, eased from Elmore's drive, then followed the GPS directions to the drop spot. As he maneuvered the rocky road to Stone Gap, a desolate stretch of Wyoming with a natural ravine and giant boulders and trails that led through the scrub, a dozen possible scenarios traipsed through his mind.

So many things could go wrong.

No. Nothing could go wrong.

Cash steered the Cadillac around a curve, then passed the sign for Stone Gap and drove along the graveled road to the drop-off spot. He scanned the area in search of a car or someone hovering in the bushes.

Someone who planned to kill Elmore, take his money and run.

A noise jarred him. Was someone out there? Maybe they were coming up behind him?

He glanced in the rearview mirror, then cursed. Dammit, BJ had stowed away in the back floor.

"What are you doing?" he barked. "I told you to stay at Elmore's."

BJ released a breath. "I wanted to be with you in case you get Tyler."

"It's too dangerous, BJ." He checked his watch. Dammit. He didn't have time to take her back to Elmore's.

"I'll stay in the car," BJ whispered. "But if Tyler's scared and upset, I can help."

That was true. But he didn't like it one bit.

And now he had to worry about keeping BJ safe.

Sweat beaded on his lower lip as he parked. The sky was gloomy, the wind picking up, stirring dust and sending tumbleweed across the desolate terrain. An animal's howl echoed from the deep cluster of bushes on the hill. He narrowed his eyes, scrutinizing the trees and rocks.

"What's going on?" Maddox said into his ear piece.

Cash gritted his teeth. "BJ stowed away in the back seat."

A litany of profanity spewed from Maddox. "That was stupid."

Cash bit back a comment of agreement. "She thinks she can help if we get Tyler and he's frightened."

"Tell her to stay in the damn car," Maddox said. "This kidnapper is not playing games."

"I know that," BJ snapped from the back seat.

"I'll make sure she stays put," Cash said.

Maddox heaved a sigh of frustration. "All right, it's too late to turn back now. We might create suspicion. Go ahead and make the drop."

Cash tugged the hat low on his head to shadow his face, grabbed the bag, opened the car door and slowly climbed out. Elmore's ring felt heavy on his hand as he gripped the duffel bag.

With every breath he took, he visually searched for an ambush.

The animal howled again—a mountain lion?

He went still, afraid to move too quickly in case it was waiting to attack. Seconds passed. The bushes parted and a streak of orange flashed past, quickly gliding from one rock to another.

Pulse pounding, he slowly inched up the small hill to the rock formation.

Elmore's boots dug into the dirt, the wind swirling dust at his feet as he lowered the bag to the ground. Just as he descended the small hill, a shot rang out.

The bullet skimmed past his head, then another one sailed at him. He ducked to avoid it, his gaze scanning the bushes.

The bullet zinged by his head and nearly clipped him.

Chapter Sixteen

Cash braced his gun at the ready, then peered above the rocks where he'd hidden, searching for the shooter.

The shots had come from his left. Higher. On the hill, he spotted a giant boulder where the shooter could be hiding.

He fired his weapon toward it. A bullet pinged off the rock and hit the ground.

He watched, waiting on the shooter to move or fire back.

Instead, tree branches swayed above. The bastard was getting away!

He swung a glance at the duffel bag. It was gone.

"Cash?" Maddox bellowed in his ear. "Are you hit, man?"

"No, I'm good," he said, as he continued to peruse the area. "Where is the son of a bitch?"

"Headed toward the top of the ridge. Must have a car there."

"The money's gone."

"I know. There are two of them. I saw a figure in black snatch it and run." Maddox's breath heaved out. "I'm going after the shooter."

A dark figure caught Cash's eye. To his left. On a path that led to a scenic overhang.

"I'll follow the money." Cash kept his eyes trained on the figure as he darted down the hill and jogged toward the Cadillac.

BJ was running toward him. "Cash!"

"I told you to stay in the car," he growled.

She caught his arm. "Are you hurt?"

"No." He ushered her back to the car, ignoring the fear in her eyes. "Now get in," he rasped. "We need to go."

BJ slid into the seat, and he jogged around the front of the car and jumped in. A quick flick of the switch and the car sputtered to life.

He threw the car into Drive, swung it around and raced over the graveled road to a parking area. Just as they reached it, a dark green SUV tore from the lot.

Cash stomped on the gas and sped after it. The SUV's tires screeched as it roared down the incline. The Cadillac's tires churned over gravel as he followed.

"Did you see the shooter?" BJ asked.

"No, he was up higher." He swung a right, desperate to keep up with the SUV as they careened around a curve. "Did you see anything?"

"No." She gripped the dash as he made the turn on two wheels.

"Is Tyler in the car?"

BJ leaned forward, eyes narrowing as she searched. "I can't see anything. The windows are tinted."

Cash cursed. "Tyler had better be in there."

"You said there were two," BJ's voice cracked. "The shooter might have him."

Cash swallowed hard to control his panic. The fact that they had been ambushed was a bad sign.

Tyler might not be with either one of them. He might be dead, just like Sondra, and this was a setup to extract enough money for the kidnappers to escape.

TERROR SHOT THROUGH BJ.

If Tyler wasn't in the car, the kidnappers could have left him somewhere safe. Maybe they'd planned to get the money, then go back, pick up Tyler, drop him somewhere, then call Elmore and tell him where he was.

Or they might not have planned to give him back at all.

Cash hit a pothole and the vehicle bounced, jarring her even more. She clawed at the seat to keep upright as he swung to the left and sped up on the SUV. Seconds turned into minutes as he chased it onto the highway. A truck pulled out, nearly cutting them off, and Cash rode the shoulder to keep from hitting it.

The river loomed ahead. Cash picked up speed. The SUV did the same, but it suddenly swerved as an oncoming car crossed the line. The car zoomed past. The driver of the SUV tried to straighten its course, but it was going too fast and he lost control.

The vehicle skidded, careened to the right, then went into a spin. Instead of coming to a stop, it flipped, then rolled.

Cash muttered a curse, slowed the Cadillac, then threw it into Park on the side of the road.

The SUV dived nose first under the water, the rest of the vehicle slowly sinking.

If Tyler was in there, he might drown.

Déjà vu of losing her son made BJ's head spin. For a moment the world blurred. She was standing on the embankment, watching rescue workers haul her ex-husband's car from the lake.

Panic, fear and sorrow gripped her, and tears blurred her eyes. If she'd been with them, maybe she could have saved her son.

Dammit, BJ. Get a grip.

It might not be too late for Tyler.

She threw open the door, yanked off her shoes, ran toward the river and dived in.

The current was strong and immediately swept her downstream, but she took a deep breath, swam below and fought it as she searched for the vehicle. The water was muddy and cold, and a chill invaded her as she spotted Cash yanking at the door to the driver's side.

She kicked hard and swam deeper, pushing forward until she reached the other side of the SUV. The murky water blurred her vision, and loose strands of her hair drifted in a tangle around her face. She pushed them away, leaned toward the window and peered inside. No one in the passenger seat.

Heart pounding, she swam to the back window, then

pressed her face against it. A child's blanket lay on the seat, a bulge beneath it.

Fear choked her. Was Tyler under that blanket?

CASH PULLED AND yanked at the car door, but it wouldn't budge. One look inside and he'd seen the driver, a dark-clad figure slumped over the wheel. Blood gushing.

No seat belt.

Muddy river water seeped into the car, slowly filling it and making it impossible to see if anyone else was inside. He spotted a blanket in the back and prayed that if Tyler was under it, he was alive.

He had to get the damn door open. But it wouldn't budge.

The window was his best bet. He ripped off his shirt, wrapped it around his fist, then punched the glass. Nothing happened and he tried again.

The force of the current was too strong.

And his lungs were about to explode.

Suddenly, BJ appeared beside him with a rock in one hand. Hair swirled around her face, and terror widened her eyes. But she shoved the rock toward him.

Adrenaline fueled his strength, and he swung the rock against the glass. It took three tries, but it finally shattered. Water gushed into the SUV, and he fought the current to reach inside and open the car door.

The force of the water threw him backward. BJ was struggling. He motioned for her to surface for air, but she shook her head.

He didn't have time to argue.

He grabbed the car door, swam to the driver, then yanked the body from the car. The hooded sweatshirt had shrouded the person's face. The body was lighter than he'd expected.

A woman?

He didn't take the time to look. He tucked the body under one arm, desperate to see if Tyler was in the backseat.

BJ must have been thinking the same thing. She fumbled with the seat, trying to move it forward so she could reach in back.

The current tried to sweep her away. He caught her and pushed her forward. She clutched the edge of the door, and he guided her inside.

His heart pounded as she grabbed the blanket.

BJ's LUNGS STRAINED for air as she dragged the blanket from the seat. Thank God...

Tyler wasn't there.

Relief flooded her but her lungs were about to explode. She frantically searched the floor, but found nothing.

Cash pulled her from the vehicle and held on to her as they swam upward. As soon as they broke the surface, she gasped for a breath. Cash did the same.

He clutched the driver's body under one arm and motioned for her to swim to shore. She took another breath to get a second wind, then gathered her strength and pumped her legs and arms to propel her to the river's edge. When she reached the embankment, she crawled onto it and collapsed, the soggy blanket clutched in one hand.

Tears blinded her vision, and a sob broke loose. She pressed the blanket to her cheeks, inhaled the little boy's odor blended with the smell of the murky water, and emotions overwhelmed her.

An image of Tyler hugging this blanket for comfort taunted her. Her son had loved his blanket, too. A ratty yellow one that he'd worn thin by rubbing one section of ribbon with his fingers.

Her heart had broken at the thought of him being without it. But she hadn't wanted to part with it, either.

So she'd cut it in half, kept a piece of it under her pillow and buried the remainder with him. She remembered tucking it under his arm the way he'd held it at night, then kissing his cheek as she'd been forced to say goodbye.

Behind her, Cash's grunt brought her back to reality.

Her son was gone, but they still might be able to save Tyler. She prayed the driver of that car was alive and could tell them where he'd left the little boy.

Cash's muscles were straining as he shoved the body onto the dirt. She crawled to them, and he flipped the body over.

All black clothing, black hoodie.

Long strands of hair peeking out. Tangled and wet.

Cash pushed the hood back. BJ gasped again.

Diane.

Sondra's best friend.

Diane had acted so concerned and worried. Elmore had trusted her. Had believed she didn't know where Tyler was.

Sondra would have trusted her, as well.

Which would have made it easy for Diane to get close enough to kill Sondra. Diane would also have known Sondra's routine. Her schedule.

But why would Diane kill her best friend?

Cash checked the woman's pulse. "We need an ambulance."

BJ pushed to her feet, then staggered back toward the Cadillac. She dug her phone from her purse, then punched 911. "We need an ambulance at Stone Gap. A woman ran her car into the river. She's unconscious."

She hung up and rushed back to Cash.

He was on his knees, patting Diane's cheeks in an attempt to rouse her to consciousness. Diane's face looked sickly white. Her clothing was soaked and covered in murk from the river.

A siren wailed.

"Come on, dammit," Cash said. "Wake up and tell us what you did with the boy."

It did no good. Diane didn't move.

She lay stone still, the slight rise and fall of her chest the only indication she was alive.

The ambulance screeched to a stop, lights twirling in the darkness falling over the land.

Land as desolate as BJ felt.

Medics jumped out and ran toward them, then took her vitals. Seconds later they retrieved a stretcher and loaded her onto it.

"Do you know her name?" one of them asked Cash.

"Diane Stuckey," he replied. "I have no idea if she has family."

The medics carried her to the ambulance.

"I'd like to ride with her," Cash said.

"I'm sorry, sir, but that's against the rules. You can follow us."

Irritation darkened Cash's eyes, but he didn't argue. BJ was trembling as she followed him to the Cadillac. His jaw hardened as he started the car and followed the ambulance.

BJ turned to look out the window. Emotions racked her, and she swiped at tears she couldn't stop.

Cash reached out and laid his hand over hers. His palm felt warm and strong, comforting. She held on to it for dear life.

Traffic and night noises blurred into the background. Storm clouds rolled in, making it seem dark and eerie.

She kept seeing her son in that wreck. His face battered and bruised. His still chest... The soul-deep ache that never went away stirred to full force.

Cash's phone buzzed. He snatched it up. "The kidnapper crashed into the river. I'm following the ambulance. Did you catch the shooter?" A pause. "Hell. Just meet us at the hospital."

Cash veered into the hospital parking lot, and they both jumped out and ran toward the ambulance.

But the medic shook his head, his expression grave.

Diane was dead. The shooter had escaped.

And they had no idea if Tyler was dead or alive.

Chapter Seventeen

Frustration built inside Cash.

Diane Stuckey was dead.

Sondra's friend had kidnapped her son and now they had no idea where he was.

Had she hurt Tyler?

And why would she steal her best friend's little boy? Was she jealous of Sondra? Did she want the child for herself?

Or was it all about the money?

"I issued a BOLO for the truck," Maddox said. "White-feather is examining the woman's car and searching for a phone. We'll look for a computer at her home. Somewhere in there, we'll find this son of a bitch."

"You got the license plate of the truck?" Cash asked.

Maddox frowned. "Afraid not. We need to know more about Diane."

BJ had excused herself to go to the ladies' room to clean up. She was obviously shaken over the death of Sondra's friend, and they were both still wet from the river. But something else seemed to be bothering her.

She'd looked almost despondent when they'd emerged from the river.

Maddox's phone buzzed. "It's Elmore."

Maddox stepped aside to talk to Elmore and Cash went to the Cadillac to retrieve his shirt. The damn thing was wet but he couldn't do anything about that until they returned to the cabin.

By the time he made it back to the waiting room, BJ had emerged from the ladies' room. She'd combed her hair and wrung some of the water from her clothes, but her face was splotched. She'd been crying.

Cash's gut clenched. "BJ, are you okay?"

She averted her gaze but nodded. "Any word on the shooter?"

"Not yet. Maddox issued a BOLO." He gestured toward Maddox. "He's talking to Elmore now."

"That can't be a pleasant phone call."

"No." Cash touched her elbow gently. "BJ?"

She lifted her chin. "I'm fine, Cash. Let's just focus on finding where Diane might have taken Tyler."

Cash hissed between his teeth. "Right."

Finding Tyler was all that mattered.

Maddox walked toward them, his expression worried. "Brett said Nix has been home all evening, so we can rule him out. Whitefeather's searching Diane's vehicle. Elmore said Diane has no family. I have her address. I'm going to search her house."

"We'll go with you," BJ said.

Maddox shook his head. "This is police business. Besides, you two were almost killed tonight. BJ, you probably have enough now to get the charges dropped against Cash. Focus on that. Go back to the cabin and I'll keep you posted."

"Look, Maddox, we'll be safer with you," Cash said. "If we find Tyler, he's going to need me. I'm not going to let him down again."

BJ FOCUSED ON finding out all she could about Diane Stuckey from the internet as they swung by Horseshoe Creek so she and Cash could change.

Maddox's wife Rose loaned her some jeans and a shirt along with a pair of cowboy boots. Meanwhile, Maddox secured a warrant for Diane's condo, car, computer, phone and her personal belongings. Cash retrieved his truck, and they followed Maddox to Diane's condo.

"Her parents weren't well-off like Elmore, but they tried to give her a good life. She and Sondra became friends when they met at a horseback riding class. Both girls excelled, and went on to show. Diane had to work mucking stalls to help pay for her trainer." She skimmed for more information. "Both girls did well in competition, although Sondra always placed first and Diane second."

"Friends and rivals." Cash made a low sound in his throat. "So Diane could have been jealous of Sondra. She got tired of coming in second."

"It's possible." BJ found some photos Diane had posted of her and Sondra on the first day of college and at dressage award ceremonies. Sondra's father stood beside her, looking regal and important, while one photo caught Diane watching them with envy.

"YOU MIGHT BE RIGHT. Diane may have wanted the life Sondra had." BJ found a photo of Diane holding Tyler at his first birthday party. "Sondra always came in first in everything. She had her father's love, and then her own child."

"But Diane has that expensive condo. Where did she get the money?"

"There are pictures of her with several different men, a couple of them older. She may have had a sugar daddy."

"Then why ask for ransom money?"

"To throw police off of the real motive?" BJ searched Diane's Facebook posts "There are some comments here about Diane having health issues a couple of years ago. I don't think she could get pregnant."

BJ drummed her fingers on her thigh. "If she wanted Sondra's family and loved Tyler, at least she would have taken care of him. She would've left him somewhere safe."

Cash nodded. "What if Tyler was with the shooter, though? Just because Diane wanted Tyler doesn't mean her cohort does."

Cash veered into the complex and parked. They climbed out and met Maddox at the door.

"Cash, you have to stay outside again," Maddox said.

"I don't want any evidence thrown out because of your presence."

"Maddox, the fact that you're related to Cash could raise doubts," BJ said.

"Maybe. But you can testify that Cash didn't take part in the search, and that I didn't plant evidence."

Cash hissed in frustration but stepped back. Maddox picked the lock, then pushed the door open.

"Sheriff McCullen here. I have a warrant. Is anyone home?" Maddox called out.

"I think she lived alone," BJ said.

"Let's look around," Maddox said as he went inside.

"What are we searching for?" BJ asked.

Maddox tossed her a pair of latex gloves. "Phone records, personal notes, a calendar, journal, anything to indicate who she was working with."

BJ yanked on the gloves. "I'll check the kitchen."

"I'll take the desk in the den," Maddox said. "BJ, search Diane's bedroom first."

BJ veered down the hallway, once again struck by the plush furnishings. As Cash had said after his initial search earlier that day, there was nothing visible to indicate a child had been here. No toys, children's books, kid's blanket or bedding.

The master held a canopied bed draped in white with a white satin comforter.

She searched the dresser drawers. T-shirts and yoga pants, sexy lingerie.

The pictures on her Facebook page were months old. Did Diane have a recent lover? If so, who was he? Was he involved with this kidnapping plan?

BJ moved to the closet, and found jeans, T-shirts, Western attire, boots and belts. According to her social media sites, Diane gave horseback riding lessons to children at the stable where she'd taken lessons herself.

Maybe someone there knew who Diane was involved with—or someone that could have been her accomplice.

She dug deeper in the closet and found two boxes with designer stilettos, and several cocktail dresses. One side also held a man's pair of work boots and a man's denim duster.

The coat was size 40, the shoes size 11. No business card or ID inside, though.

She ran her fingers along the top of the closet shelf in search of a journal or calendar, but found nothing. Same with the nightstand drawers. She even checked beneath the mattress. Nothing.

She moved to the master bath and checked the drawers. Basic cosmetics and toiletries.

One toothbrush in the ceramic holder but there was an extra one in the drawer.

A blue one.

The blue one could belong to Diane's male friend.

She plucked it from the holder and carried it to Maddox.

"A man's coat and boots are in the closet. And this toothbrush might belong to Diane's male friend."

Maddox bagged the toothbrush. "I'll send this and her laptop to the lab."

Maddox pushed a sticky-note pad toward BJ. "I found this in the desk. Phone number. No name. I called it and got the voice mail for Hyatt Spillman."

"He worked with Cash at the Triple X," BJ said. "He claimed Cash was in love with Sondra and that he argued with her the morning she died."

Maddox shifted, his jaw tight. "And he's connected to Diane. He could have been the one who framed Cash."

DISBELIEF CHURNED INSIDE CASH.

Sondra's best friend had betrayed her. And now she might have taken Tyler?

God, he'd never suspected her. She'd acted innocent

when they'd questioned her about the little boy's where-abouts.

BJ joined him outside and explained about finding Spillman's number in Diane's condo. Had that bastard set him up?

Maddox clenched his phone in his hand as he stepped out of the condo. "Whitefeather just called. He found some discrepancies in Elmore's financials. He also had a life insurance policy on Tyler. I'm going to question Elmore again."

The possibility that Sondra's father might have been part of this mess made Cash curse. "We'll find Spillman."

Maddox gave him a warning look. "Wait, Cash, I'm running this show."

BJ cleared her throat. "Maddox, if he has Tyler, he might be panicking. We need to get to him before he disappears completely."

Maddox looked torn, but finally agreed. "Just don't do anything rash. If he's at home, just watch him. Let me know and I'll be right there."

Cash wrangled his temper under control, then lifted his fingers in a Scout's pledge. "Yes, sir."

The clouds darkened, hovering above, threatening rain. A stiff wind picked up, swirling dried tumbleweed and dust, a reminder of Wyoming's dust storms as Cash drove toward the Triple X.

BJ checked her watch. "Tyler should be home in his bed right now."

The pain in her voice twisted Cash's insides. "So should you, BJ. Let me take you back to the cabin. You've done enough for me already."

"No," BJ said. "I'm not giving up until we bring Tyler home safe."

BJ bit down on her lip and turned to look out the window. A second later, a tear seeped from her eye and trickled down her cheek.

He wanted to comfort her, ask her why this case was

getting to her. But hell, she probably just had a soft spot for kids, like he did.

That alone made him worry about her.

God, he'd already lost one friend this week. He didn't want to care about BJ, but he was starting to. And he couldn't live with the guilt if something bad happened to her.

Nerves on edge, he turned onto the road that led to the Triple X. A sliver of moonlight glowed across the pasture. Horses galloped and cattle grazed on the hill. Donovan's truck was parked in front of the farmhouse, but they passed it and parked at the bunkhouses.

At this time of night, most of the ranch hands had turned in. Work started at first light. Spillman's rusted truck was parked sideways by the bunkhouse.

BJ touched his arm before he climbed out. "Remember what Maddox said, Cash. We just need to see if he's here."

An engine rumbled in the quiet as he slid from the truck. Cash scanned the surrounding area in search of trouble. Car lights flickered across the terrain in the distance and disappeared over a hill.

BJ started toward the bunkhouse, but Cash had a bad feeling. The bunkhouse door was ajar.

He caught BJ's arm and motioned for her to stay behind him. If Spillman was involved in this mess, that meant he'd tried to kill them.

He was damned tired of sitting on the sidelines and letting Maddox and BJ put themselves in the line of fire for him.

The hair on the back of his neck prickled as he inched forward. Wind whistled through the wood slats. He hesitated, pausing to listen for someone inside.

Nothing.

Still, Spillman could have seen them coming and be hiding, waiting to ambush him.

BJ followed on his heels, but he held his arm out to keep

her from entering, then glanced through the door. His chest clenched at the sight of blood on the floor.

"Wait," he mouthed to BJ.

He crept inside, then came to an abrupt halt. More blood. Dammit. Spillman couldn't help them. He was dead.

Chapter Eighteen

"Is he in there?" BJ whispered from the doorway.

"Stay there," Cash growled. He quickly scanned the adjoining bath, but no one was inside. It appeared that no one was using the second bedroom, either.

The room and Spillman's body needed to be searched, but he couldn't contaminate the scene or Maddox would be furious.

He urged BJ away from the bunkhouse. "Spillman's dead. I have to call Maddox."

BJ's eyes widened, but she nodded and straightened, then began scouring the area. Cash pressed Maddox's number. The phone rang three times before he answered.

"Sheriff McCullen."

"It's Cash. We're at Spillman's bunk. He's dead. Gunshot to the chest."

Maddox muttered a sound of frustration. "Don't touch anything. I'll be there ASAP and I'll call a crime unit."

"How's Elmore?" Cash asked.

"Distraught, but Jasper was there for support. He says he can explain the financial discrepancies. Says his accountant's assistant skimmed money from him. He fired both of them six months ago.

"Whitefeather verified his story. The accountant moved to Texas and took the assistant with him. Apparently they were an item."

"What about the life insurance on Tyler?"

"His lawyer advised him to do that for Sondra's sake. I asked the lab to put a rush on the DNA on the toothbrush and compare it to Spillman's." He paused. "I'm on my way. Jasper was going to hang around and make sure Elmore was safe in case the kidnapper came after him. We'll need to talk to everyone on the Triple X."

Maddox hung up, and Cash surveyed the hill where the car lights had been. Could the person driving that vehicle be their shooter?

"Were there any signs Tyler had been in that bunk?" BJ asked.

Cash shook his head, then headed toward Spillman's rusty truck. He wanted to search it himself.

But he forced himself not to touch it. Instead, he paced the yard and waited on Maddox.

FATIGUE PULLED AT BJ as Maddox and the crime unit arrived. She and Cash were once again delegated to watching. She sensed it was hardest for Cash—he'd grown up depending on himself, not on others.

One of the team found an envelope of cash inside Spillman's truck.

"Fifteen thousand," Maddox said as he counted the bills.

"Could be payment for his part in the kidnapping," Cash suggested.

"Or it could be savings from his job," Maddox said. "We need more proof."

The ranch owner, Wilson Donovan, showed up looking harried and upset. "I can't believe he died here on the ranch." The man removed his hat and slapped it against his thigh. "Nothing like this has ever happened to me." He shot Cash a questioning look. "You know what's going on, Koker, you better fess up."

"I'm sorry, sir." Cash squared his shoulders. "It looks like Spillman was involved in Sondra Elmore's death and with her son's disappearance."

"We need to speak to all the ranch hands and employees," Maddox said. "Ask them to meet me in the dining hall in half an hour."

Donovan checked his watch. "It's ten o'clock at night, Sheriff. Can't it wait till tomorrow?"

"No," Maddox replied. "A man was murdered here this

evening. Questioning everyone on the ranch as soon as possible is imperative. Whoever shot Spillman could still be on the property."

Donovan's eyes widened in alarm. "All right, I'll make some phone calls."

"Mr. Donovan," Cash said. "I saw a vehicle driving in the distance on the property when I arrived. I think it might have been a Jeep."

Donovan grunted. "Several of the hands drive Jeeps. What color was it?"

Cash jammed his hands in the pockets of his jeans. "Couldn't tell. It was too far away."

Donovan grunted again, then gripped his cell phone and stepped back to his truck to make the call.

"He blames me for bringing trouble to his place," Cash said, his voice full of regret.

"This isn't your fault, Cash." BJ squeezed his arm. "Hang in there. We'll find out who framed you and bring Tyler home safely."

"What if we don't?" The agony in Cash's voice tugged at her heartstrings.

She couldn't resist. She took both his hands in hers and cradled them against her chest. "We will, Cash. You have my word."

CASH DESPERATELY WANTED to believe BJ, but anxiety knotted every muscle in his body. He felt helpless as he watched Maddox and Deputy Whitefeather question the ranch hands and other employees.

"Listen, guys, one of your ranch hands, Hyatt Spillman, was murdered in his room," Maddox said. "We believe Diane Stuckey and Spillman conspired to kill Sondra Elmore and kidnap her son."

Shocked gasps and murmurs followed.

"We found a large sum of cash in Spillman's truck,"

Maddox continued. "If you know where he got the money, please come forward. Any information will be helpful."

A hand Cash recognized as a new hire named Jordan stepped up and approached Whitefeather. Cash stood a safe distance away, but the condemning looks from the other men suggested they thought he was behind the trouble on the ranch.

BJ coaxed him outside, and he paced the porch as the interrogations continued.

"Maddox is looking for gun residue on the workers' hands," BJ said.

Meanwhile, the sun had faded hours ago, and the clock was ticking, precious time slipping by.

Midnight struck as Maddox and Whitefeather finished and joined them on the porch. One by one, the men headed back to their bunks to get some shut-eye before the sun signaled another day on the ranch.

Across the way, the ambulance was pulling away, transporting Spillman's body to the morgue for an autopsy.

Maddox approached him and BJ. "One of the hands said Spillman was a gambler, that he might have been in debt."

"So he needed money," Cash said.

Maddox nodded. "We'll verify the information. Unfortunately, no one saw anyone hanging around tonight."

Whitefeather cleared his throat. "One guy said he'd seen Diane with Spillman. Said they looked as if they were arguing. Later, he asked Spillman, but he said it was nothing. That Diane was just moody."

Cash balled his hands into fists. Dammit, they needed more. Something concrete to lead them to where Tyler was being held.

"There's not much we can do tonight," Maddox said, his voice tired. "Maybe DNA, phone records or financials will turn up something in the morning. Jasper said he asked the media to keep running Tyler's picture on the news. Maybe someone will spot him and call in."

The hope he tried to inject into his voice fell flat. Maddox looked as frustrated as Cash was.

"Everyone get some rest. I'll keep you posted."

Cash hesitated. He didn't want to give up tonight.

How could he sleep, knowing Tyler was still missing and that two people associated with his kidnapping were dead?

BJ'S HEART FELT heavy as Cash dropped her at the cabin on Horseshoe Creek. The day had been a nightmare. Memories of almost being killed and diving into that river in search of Tyler would probably keep her awake all night.

Cash looked tortured, too—which made her even more determined to clear his name. She had a basis now to get the charges dropped.

But all he cared about was Tyler.

Cash insisted on searching the cabin to make sure the shooter wasn't hiding inside, waiting to attack. When he cleared the space, he returned to her in the living room. She stood by the window, looking out at the night. A few lone stars glittered through the clouds, the moon barely a sliver. The sky looked gray and just as gloomy as BJ felt.

"You all right?" Cash asked gruffly.

"Yes, are you?" She lifted her hand and brushed it across his cheek. He sucked in a sharp breath.

She'd vowed never to get involved with a client. Not to trust any man.

Except…how could she resist this sexy, strong man?

She looked up into Cash's eyes and was moved by his tenderness. Desperate for his touch, for comfort, she pressed her hand over his chest. Beneath her palm, his heart pounded, strong and alive.

He sucked in a sharp breath, the hunger radiating from him stirring her own. How long had it been since she'd slept with a man? Since someone strong and caring had held her?

He brushed her hair from her cheek. "BJ?"

"Shh, just hold me for a minute."

He made a low sound in his throat as if he was struggling not to touch her. Then his eyes darkened, and he pulled her up against him.

BJ leaned into him, savoring the strength and safety in his big, powerful muscles. He rubbed her back gently, soothing her, stroking away her anxiety and arousing a part of her she thought was dead.

The need to be with a man, to be intimate. To feel his love erasing the heartache that would never leave her.

"Talk to me," Cash murmured. "Today was rough. But something else is wrong. I can feel it."

She swallowed hard. She couldn't make her voice work.

Instead she lifted her head and gazed into his eyes. Dark, soulful, tinged with the pain of his past and his worry over Tyler.

And his need to prove himself innocent. Maybe to prove he was worthy of being a McCullen.

"I don't want to talk," she whispered.

She cradled his face between her hands, rose on tiptoes and pressed her mouth to his.

He stiffened, his hands gripping her arms as if to set her away from him. She refused to let him.

She needed him.

Her emotions mingling with desire, she traced her tongue along the seam of his lips until he opened for her. She teased his mouth and drove her hands through his thick hair, deepening the kiss.

With a low growl in his throat, he finally gave in and plunged his tongue into her mouth. Their tongues met, thrust for thrust, a dance of need and hunger and a longing so strong that she lowered her hands to stroke the hard planes of his back.

His hands moved, as well, dragging her into the V of his thighs, settling her against his thick, hard sex. Erotic sensations spiraled inside her, creating a slow burn that made her tear at the buttons of his shirt.

One button popped open, then another, and she raked the fabric back to press a kiss to his bare chest. He gripped her arms, threw his head back and moaned.

"God, BJ..."

Emboldened by the depth of his desire, she spread kisses all along his chest, touching scars from injuries that must have been traumatic, scars that aroused protective feelings for the man.

His fingers tangled in her hair and he tilted her head back, then planted kisses along her neck and throat.

She wanted more.

So did he.

They frantically kissed again, whispered longing in each stroke, and he walked her backward toward the sofa. She allowed him to push her onto it, but she refused to release him.

Instead she teased him again by stroking his chest and lowering her hands to his hips. He grunted and reached for the bottom of her shirt. Then he climbed on top of her, straddling her hips as he lifted the shirt over her head. He tossed it to the side, but it hit a picture frame, and the frame fell onto the table.

Cash reached sideways to right it, then went very still.

BJ held her breath, need mingling with the realization that the picture he was looking at was of her lost son.

"BJ?" His eyes searched hers. "You're married? You have a family?"

Sadness choked her. She didn't want to talk about her loss. She wanted to feel his hands on her, making her forget.

He angled his head in question and set the picture back on the table. Questions darkened his expressive eyes. "Answer me."

"I was divorced," she said. "I...lost my son."

He muttered a low curse. "How?"

"A car accident." In spite of her resolve to control her emotions, tears choked her voice.

His posture stiffened, anger and frustration twisting his expression, and he lifted his body from hers.

She reached for him again. "Cash, please."

He cleared his throat. "I've done a lot of things I'm not proud of in my day, BJ." He lowered his mouth and dropped a tender kiss on her forehead. "But I don't want making love to you to be one of them."

Without another word, he walked toward the door. When it closed behind him, the tears she'd been fighting spilled over.

Chapter Nineteen

BJ wanted to run after Cash.

But his words echoed in her head. He didn't want to regret making love to her. Which meant he would regret it.

So would she.

At least he'd had the good sense to put a stop to their frenzied behavior.

She picked up her son's photo, stared at his sweet little face and then hugged it to her chest.

Making love with Cash might have temporarily assuaged the anguish, but it would always be there.

She couldn't allow herself to feel anything for Cash. Loving someone meant agony when they were gone. Cash wasn't even a free man. He was a cowboy struggling to find his place and clear his name.

Worse, he was her client.

She swiped at her tears, walked to the bathroom and washed her face, then slipped into pajamas. Exhausted, she crawled into bed and tried to banish the memory of Cash's hands touching her.

But when she closed her eyes, she felt his arms wrap around her. She savored that comforting feeling.

For one moment in time, she'd felt wanted. Almost loved, as if she deserved it, when for the last two years she'd known she didn't. That she was broken after her son died, and she'd never be whole again.

But the sound of the wind beating a tree branch against the windowpane made her jerk her eyes open and face reality.

She glanced at the window to make sure the shooter hadn't found her.

Then she reminded herself that Cash was next door, plus Maddox had security on the ranch. Sondra's murderer and

Tyler's kidnapper would have to be pretty ballsy to come after her or Cash on the sheriff's property.

She was safe here tonight. But she was alone.

And she worried she always would be.

PERSPIRATION BEADED CASH'S neck as he climbed the steps to the porch of his cabin. Before he entered, he stared at the sprawling ranch land. Horseshoe Creek.

He'd never imagined staying here, much less being a part of it and the family it belonged to.

The light in BJ's cabin went out, and he realized she was probably going to bed.

Dammit, it had taken every ounce of his strength to walk away from her. He wanted her more than he'd ever wanted any woman in his life.

The anguish in her eyes tore him up inside. She'd had a child.

A little boy. But she'd lost him.

He wanted to know the story, yet he'd left before she could explain because...because why?

He didn't want to know. Didn't want to hear the despair in her voice or her sad story. Didn't want to get close to her or care.

You already do, fool.

All the more reason to keep his distance—at least emotionally. Which meant he wouldn't touch her again.

Hopefully, they'd find Tyler and end this case soon. Then she'd go back to her life. Her father was a well-known attorney, prestigious.

She was completely out of Cash's league.

He didn't fit here on Horseshoe Creek, and he sure as hell didn't fit with BJ Alexander.

The wind rustled the trees, the dark clouds hovering. Exhausted, but too antsy to sleep, he stepped inside the cabin and turned on the television. A news segment was airing.

Tyler's picture appeared on the screen, with a plea for

anyone who had information regarding his disappearance to call the tip line at the sheriff's department. NCMEC, the National Center for Missing and Exploited Children, had been looped in and a nationwide Amber Alert issued.

Elmore had agreed to pay the ransom.

He had made the drop. But it had been a setup. The kidnapper had never intended to return Tyler.

It made sense that Diane might want the little boy, but whoever had him now might hurt him or get rid of him.

Cash studied the photograph of Tyler with a pang in his chest. That afternoon, he'd taught Tyler how to play T-ball in the yard, while Sondra went riding with a friend. Tyler's laugh still echoed in his ears, then his shout of joy when he'd hit the ball.

The picture of BJ's son flashed in his mind's eye. He didn't know how old he would have been if he'd lived, but in the picture she kept on the end table, he looked to be about three. Tyler's age.

No wonder it had hit her so hard when she'd seen that car fly into the river.

Cash flipped off the television, found a beer in the fridge and popped the top. One sip and he stretched out on the sofa with his phone in his hand. He needed sleep, but he needed answers worse.

And he needed to know BJ was safe.

With one ear cocked for sounds of trouble, he closed his eyes. "I'm going to bring you home, Tyler," he promised.

BJ's sweet scent lingered on his skin, tormenting him.

But he would keep his hands off BJ.

THE SOUND OF her phone buzzing with a text woke BJ. She'd tossed and turned and dreamed about her son most of the night.

Her heart ached this morning.

She had had the same dream over and over. She and Aaron were playing or singing or hiking, then she tucked him in bed, only to wake up the next morning and find he was gone. That his little bed would never hold him again, and she would never see his little smile again or hear his precious voice.

She brushed at more tears, then her phone buzzed with a text.

DNA tests on the toothbrush found at Diane's matches Cash's. We need to talk.

BJ bolted out of bed. Cash had said he'd met Diane, but he hadn't mentioned they were involved.

Had he lied about their relationship?

He'd seemed shocked to find out she was driving that car and that she was involved in the kidnapping.

Because he'd slept with her?

A SECOND TEXT came in seconds later. Also from Maddox.

Get Cash and meet me at the house for breakfast. Will drive to the lab from there. The analyst has more information on DNA and Tyler's father. She wants to deliver the news face-to-face.

BJ texted Okay, then texted Cash to be ready in half an hour to meet Maddox. Then she jumped in the shower. She needed to be fresh and alert when she saw Cash. Needed to wipe the scent of his kisses off her.

And forget that she'd almost made love with him.

Had he played her for a fool so she wouldn't see his playboy side?

Irritated that she'd lost her objectivity, she rinsed and dried off, then pulled her hair back into a low bun at the nape of her neck.

A minute later, a knock sounded. She hurried to answer

and found Cash standing on the porch. In spite of her resolve to remain detached, her breath caught as his big masculine body filled the doorway.

His gaze raked over her, then he set his jaw with a scowl. He must regret the night before as much as she did. "Maddox has something?" he asked in a deep voice.

"DNA results. We're having breakfast at the house, then going to the lab. The analyst wants to talk to us."

Cash climbed in his truck and drove to the farmhouse. As they entered, the homey scents of maple syrup, pancakes and bacon filled the air, making BJ's stomach growl.

Mama Mary greeted them with hot coffee and ushered them to the dining room, where she'd set out the food buffet-style.

Cash hung back, obviously still uncomfortable with the McCullens.

"Help yourself," Maddox said. "Rose is feeding the baby or she'd be down."

She took a plate and filled it, then Maddox and Cash did the same. An awkward quiet settled over the room.

"What's the news?" Cash asked.

"The analyst has DNA results that she needs to talk to us about." Maddox stabbed a piece of bacon and munched on it.

"What's wrong?" Cash asked. "I saw that look between you two. Do you know something you're not telling me?"

Maddox worked his mouth from side to side. "DNA on the toothbrush we found at Diane's belongs to you, Cash."

Cash dropped his fork with a clatter. "What?"

"I thought you weren't involved with Diane," BJ said.

Cash straightened in the chair. "I wasn't. I mean, I met her a couple of times when she was with Sondra, but we never spent any time together."

Maddox pinned him with a questioning stare. "Then how do you explain your DNA on a toothbrush in her bathroom?"

CASH FORCED HIMSELF not to react, when he wanted to punch a wall.

He had no explanation for the toothbrush. "I have no idea. Someone must have placed it there to frame me."

"Just like they put you in that motel with Sondra's body?" Maddox asked.

Cash ground his teeth at the doubt in BJ's eyes. That hurt the most. He thought he'd finally convinced her of his innocence. "I know it sounds crazy, but until we went there, I'd never been in Diane's condo, much less her bathroom."

BJ set her coffee cup on the table. "Setting you up like that took planning."

Cash scraped a hand through his hair in frustration. "Damn right it did. And I want to know who did it."

"Let's find out what Devon has to say. She's our lead analyst." Maddox polished off his coffee, then stood.

Cash pushed aside his plate. "Then what are we waiting for?"

Mama Mary popped her head in. "Y'all want seconds?"

"No, thanks, we have to go," Maddox said.

"Thanks for breakfast," Cash said with a tentative smile.

BJ wiped her mouth, then placed the gingham napkin on the table. "It was delicious. We appreciate the meal."

Mama Mary gushed, "Anytime! I love cooking for my boys."

Cash swallowed hard. She meant Maddox, Brett and Ray. Or was she including him?

Sun slanted through the trees as they veered onto the highway. The memory of the night before tormented Cash.

Whatever trust he'd gained with BJ had evaporated.

"I'm sorry about your son," he said, remembering the anguish in her eyes when he'd found that photo. "What happened, BJ?"

Her sharp intake of breath vibrated with raw grief. "I don't want to talk about it."

Cash had a dozen questions about her and the man she'd

married and lost, and about her child, but her statement made him clamp his mouth shut. She had her right to privacy. After all, she was his lawyer, not his friend.

Or…lover.

He had to remember it.

Although seeing her in those tight jeans and cowboy boots stirred his hunger for her.

He parked next to Maddox, and the three of them entered the county lab together. Maddox led them down a corridor to a small office with windows that overlooked one of the labs.

An attractive brunette named Devon Squires introduced herself.

"You have news?" Maddox asked, cutting to the chase.

Devon tapped a set of papers on her desk, then nodded. "First of all, I told you the DNA on the toothbrush belongs to Mr. Koker."

"Yes," Maddox said.

The need to defend himself hit Cash. He opened his mouth to argue, but Devon held up a warning finger. "Let me finish. There's more."

"Were there fingerprints?" Maddox asked.

Devon consulted another file. "Actually, we found Diane's prints and a partial print but it didn't belong to Mr. Koker."

"Whose were they?" Maddox asked.

"I haven't identified them yet, but if we find a suspect, I can compare."

Cash knotted his hands in his lap. Not finding his prints was a good sign.

"You sounded excited, as if you had a lead," Maddox said.

"I do," Devon said. "After analyzing Mr. Koker's DNA, I determined he is not Tyler Elmore's father."

"I told you I wasn't," Cash said.

"There's something else," Devon said. "We ran Tyler's DNA in search of his father, and got a hit."

Cash's pulse jumped. "You know who his father is?"

"No, the hit wasn't for the father."

"I don't understand," Maddox said.

"That's the kicker," Devon replied. "Tyler's DNA was a familial match to another child in the system."

"That's impossible," Cash said. "Sondra only had one child."

"That's true. The match didn't belong to Sondra," Devon said. "Actually, the common genetic markers point to the fact that both children share the same father. I looked at an electronic version of the child's birth certificate and, just like Tyler's, you're listed as this child's father."

"You have a child?" BJ asked, her voice cracking.

Cash shook his head in confusion. "No. That's a mistake."

"Yes, it is," Devon said. "Neither Tyler nor this child shares your DNA, Mr. Koker."

"Then someone *is* framing Cash," Maddox said.

Devon smiled. "It certainly appears that way."

"Where is this child?" BJ asked. "Why was his or her DNA in the system?"

A frown tugged at Devon's eyes. "It's a little boy. He's five years old," she said. "His DNA is in the system because he's on a list for a kidney transplant."

Cash took a deep breath. "The child's condition must be serious."

"It is," Devon said. "He needs a donor match ASAP. A family member would be best."

"But Tyler's too little," BJ said.

"What about the little boy's mother?" Maddox asked.

Devon breathed deeply. "His mother was murdered."

Shock waves rolled through Cash. Tyler and the boy were half brothers. Both boys' mothers were murdered.

Were the two cases connected?

Chapter Twenty

BJ's mind spun with questions.

When she'd first heard the boy's birth certificate listed Cash as his father, doubt had filled her.

But DNA didn't lie. Cash wasn't Tyler's father or this other child's. But someone had intentionally listed his name on the other child's birth certificate.

Who? And why lie?

To set up Cash and protect the boy's real father.

"Who was the little boy's mother?" Maddox asked.

Devon read from the file. "A woman named Frannie Cooper. She used to live in Cheyenne and worked as a hair-stylist. She died when her son, Drew, was two. She had no family, so Drew went into the foster system."

"God," Cash said. "Poor kid."

Just like Cash had. Only he had family—he just hadn't known it. Tyler didn't know about Drew, either.

"He was never adopted?" BJ asked.

"No." Devon shook her head. "He got sick about a year ago. He needs that kidney transplant."

"What about his foster family?" Cash asked.

"They turned him back into the system, said they couldn't take care of an ill child, not with a handful of others in their house. So far they haven't found a match," Devon answered.

"Did the police arrest anyone for Frannie's murder?" Maddox asked.

Devon shook her head. "No."

"That was three years ago," BJ said. "Do you think her murder is connected to Sondra's?"

"It seems coincidental that both boys' mothers were mur-dered." Cash drummed his fingers on his thigh. "Maybe

Drew's father didn't want his name revealed, just like he didn't want it disclosed that Tyler was his son."

"We have to consider the possibility that Drew's father may not even know about him," Devon said.

"True," BJ said. "But I don't buy it. It makes more sense that he's the one who put Cash's name on the birth certificate."

Maddox snapped his fingers. "Devon, get an official copy of Drew's birth certificate and analyze it to make sure it wasn't altered."

"I'm on it," Devon agreed. "If the father does know about Drew and he knows Drew is sick, maybe he thought he could use the ransom money to pay for the treatment, maybe even pay to get Drew bumped up on the transplant list."

"Let's go to the hospital," BJ said. "If the father has visited or made inquiries about the transplant, one of the nurses or a staff member might be able to ID him."

"Why don't you and Cash pursue that angle," Maddox suggested. "I'll consult with the sheriff who investigated Frannie's death."

Devon nodded. "Meanwhile I'll get hold of that birth certificate and tackle Sondra's computer."

Maddox stood. "Keep me posted."

BJ made to follow Cash out to the truck. She was anxious to talk to the nurses at the hospital and meet this little boy, Drew.

The poor little guy was sick and must feel all alone.

"THERE'S ONE MORE THING," Devon said before everyone could leave.

Cash frowned, bracing himself for more bad news.

Maddox shifted, his expression solemn. "What?"

"The DNA from Cash—was positive." She smiled at Cash. "You're a McCullen. You share the same mother and father as Maddox."

His breath left Cash in a rush. A dozen emotions flickered across Maddox's face. He turned to Cash with an odd look.

Cash didn't know what to expect, but the tough-as-nails sheriff jerked him into a bear hug.

"Good God, all these years we didn't know you even existed." Maddox's voice thickened. "I'm sorry, man. We would have looked for you, found you sooner."

Cash's chest swelled with unexpected pleasure, a feeling he'd never felt before. He had a family. A real family.

Brothers. Sisters-in-law. Nephews.

He even had a surrogate mother in Mama Mary.

"I'm just sorry as hell that Mama and Daddy died without knowing we found you," Maddox said.

Cash slapped Maddox on the back. "I can't believe it. I... never thought I had any family." At least none that wanted him.

But he choked back those words.

Getting close, expecting things from family, not disappointing them—it all came with the territory.

He'd lived his life not having to please anyone.

Sure, it had been lonely as hell, but he'd survived.

Maddox wiped at his eyes. "I have to let Ray and Brett know."

"Let's clear my name first," he said. He couldn't face the disappointment or disapproval in their eyes if somehow he wound up going back to jail.

Maddox studied him for a long minute. "All right. But we are going to clear you, Cash. And we're going to find your twin. He's one of us, too."

One of us? Cash had never been one of anything before. Not a family or a couple.

Dammit, he wanted both. To be a McCullen and to have BJ by his side.

The thought terrified him to the core, and he headed to the door. They had people to talk to about this other kid.

Drew, a little boy who'd been in foster care like him. A child who had a brother he knew nothing about.

They would fix that. They'd find that little boy a kidney.

Once he was well and Tyler was home, maybe Elmore would take them both in.

COMPASSION FILLED BJ. Cash was a McCullen.

In the midst of being framed for murder, he'd found a family. *His* family.

One he'd been torn from years ago.

And not just a family, but a respected one with a successful working ranch and a reputation for being fair and honorable.

Cash parked at the hospital, then cut the engine and rubbed a hand over his face.

"Are you all right?" BJ asked softly.

When he glanced at her, he looked torn.

"I don't know what to do," he said in a gruff voice.

"What do you mean?" she asked softly. "The McCullens are good people. They want you."

His brow wrinkled. "What if I disappoint them?"

BJ couldn't resist; she brushed his cheek with her fingers. "You won't, Cash. All you have to do is be yourself."

A heartbeat passed. "How do you know that? I told you, I've done things I'm not proud of."

She smiled slowly. "You willingly put your life in danger to save Tyler and me," BJ said. "You're tough and strong, and you're fighting to find a lost little boy. That's admirable."

He leaned into her hand. "I'm nobody's hero, BJ."

"You're Tyler's," she whispered. "Now, let's see if the hospital staff knows anything about Drew's father." She and Cash climbed out and walked up the sidewalk together. "What if Spillman was Tyler's father?" BJ asked. "Did you ever see the two of them together?"

"No," Cash answered. "Like I said, she dropped Tyler

off a few times, but we didn't spend much time together the last couple of years."

They stopped at the front desk to inquire about Drew. "Where is he?" BJ asked.

"He's on the third floor in the children's wing," the receptionist said.

"How's he doing?" Cash asked.

The woman's face fell. "He's hanging in there. But I'm not at liberty to discuss his condition."

Frustration knotted BJ's insides. "I understand. Maybe we could talk to the social worker in charge of Drew's case."

She raised a brow. "How did you find out about Drew?"

BJ leaned over the counter separating them from the woman. "We've been working with Sheriff Maddox McCullen on a case that may involve him."

The woman's eyes widened. "I know Sheriff McCullen. He's a good man."

"Yes, he is," BJ said. "Has Drew had any visitors since he was admitted?"

The woman looked down at her computer for a moment.

"It's important," BJ said. "We're trying to find this missing child—"

"Are you talking about Tyler Elmore, the little boy on the news?" she asked.

BJ nodded.

The woman inhaled sharply. "Let me get the director." She paged Dr. Ingles, then made a quick phone call.

Heels clicked on the hard floor, then a middle-aged woman with a dark bob appeared. She spoke to the receptionist, then joined them. "I'm Dr. Ingles. You're inquiring about one of our patients?"

"Yes, the child named Drew. Can we go somewhere private to talk?" BJ said.

Dr. Ingles nodded. "Let me tell the social worker to meet us." She sent a text, then led them to her office.

When the social worker arrived, Dr. Ingles introduced

the twentysomething young woman, whose name was Candace Winterbottom.

"Why do you want to know about Drew?" Dr. Ingles asked.

BJ explained the situation. "Tests confirm that Tyler Elmore and Drew are half brothers. With both boys' mothers being murdered, we're working the theory that the two murders are related."

Dr. Ingles and Candace exchanged concerned looks. "Is Drew in danger?" Dr. Ingles asked.

BJ hesitated. "I don't think so," she said. "But the father is a common denominator. We need to know his identity."

"Did you check the birth certificate?" Dr. Ingles asked.

"Yes, but DNA proves the man listed is not Drew's father," BJ said. "We thought he might have visited Drew."

Candace shook her head. "Drew hasn't had any company."

BJ's heart swelled with sympathy for Drew. "How about inquiries into his condition?"

Sadness tinged the woman's eyes. "No inquiries. No relatives or friends of the mother's. No offers to be tested for a DNA match."

"Perhaps his father doesn't know about him," Dr. Ingles suggested. "That happens more than you'd think."

"That's possible," BJ said. Although she had a bad feeling Drew's father did know about him.

And that he'd killed Drew's mother because he didn't want to be exposed.

BJ and Cash followed Candace to Drew's room. The little boy's face looked pale against his dark brown hair. IVs and other tubes helped provide medicine and fluids, but it was clear he wasn't well.

Candace padded across the room to his hospital bed and gently raked his hair from his forehead. Cash stood ramrod straight in the doorway as if his feet were frozen in place.

BJ's heart melted. She crossed the room and stood beside Candace. Slowly, Drew opened his eyes. They were as green as the grass in the pastures on Horseshoe Creek. Did his mother or father have green eyes?

"Drew, you have a visitor," Candace said in a low voice.

Drew's eyes widened. "Someone came to see me?"

"Yes." Candace gave BJ a warning smile. BJ understood the silent message. She couldn't give the child false hope.

Still, she squeezed his limp little hand in hers.

Who in the world could be so cold to take a mother away from a child?

She would have done anything to save her son.

Worse, what kind of a man wouldn't help his own little boy when he needed a kidney to live?

CASH'S HEART ACHED for the kid. Drew reminded him of himself.

He'd been sickly the first three years of his life, and no one had wanted him.

At least his illness hadn't been life-threatening. He'd suffered from asthma and an underdeveloped lung, but he'd outgrown both.

Drew had nobody.

Cash didn't know what he could do, but he would see about changing that once they found the child's damn father.

BJ leaned close to the boy, talking in a low voice. That fancy lawyer he'd thought was stuffy was full of surprises.

She'd shocked him with her passion the night before.

And now…the tenderness in her eyes told him exactly what kind of mother she'd been.

And would be in the future.

Don't go there.

You don't have your life together enough to even think about a relationship with BJ Alexander.

What did he have to offer a woman like her, anyway?

Cash's phone buzzed. Maddox. "It's Cash," he said as he punched Connect.

"Where are you?" Maddox asked without preamble.

"At the hospital. We met Drew and spoke to the social worker. No one has inquired about him."

"Damn," Maddox said. "Listen, Deputy Whitefeather just called. Elmore somehow slipped out but we've got a trace on his phone. He received another ransom call, Cash. He's on his way to meet the kidnapper."

"I thought Jasper was with him," Cash said.

"He had to leave," Maddox replied.

"How did Elmore get the money so fast?"

"I don't know, but he could be walking into an ambush. I'm twenty minutes out, but on my way."

"Text me the GPS coordinates," Cash said.

Maddox did, and Cash glanced at the map. "I can be there in ten minutes." He rushed back to the room to tell BJ he was leaving.

She gave Drew a hug. "I'll be back, sweetie. Hang in there, okay?"

"Okay." The kid hugged her with arms so frail they looked like they might break.

They rushed outside, barreled from the parking lot and flew toward the river. Trees swayed in the wind as they neared the section of land where the river forked. Cash slowed and rolled to a stop. He'd hike in on foot and hide while waiting.

A gunshot rent the air.

"Stay put!" He grabbed his pistol from behind the seat, jumped out of the truck and darted through the trees.

Another gunshot, and he spotted Elmore.

Dammit to hell. The man was lying on the embankment, his hand over his chest, blood oozing through his fingers.

Chapter Twenty-One

Cash quickly scanned the area near Elmore, and saw a figure darting up the hill on the opposite side of the river. He wanted to go after him.

But Elmore was bleeding.

Leaves rustled nearby. "I heard gunshots," BJ said, as she came up behind him.

"Elmore's hit," Cash said. "Call an ambulance. And get something to help stop the bleeding."

Cash jogged toward Elmore. His heart pounded as he scanned the hill where the shooter had disappeared. A car engine fired up in the distance, too far away for him to make it in time.

Dammit.

Elmore lay motionless, eyes closed, his bloody hand pressed over his chest. Cash checked for a pulse. Barely there, but Elmore was breathing.

He patted the man's face. "Mr. Elmore, who shot you?"

Elmore groaned, and his eyelids fluttered as if he was struggling to open them, but failed.

Footsteps crunched the dry earth. "Cash?"

"He's alive, but in bad shape. The ambulance?"

"On its way." She pressed a cloth to Elmore's wound.

"Elmore," Cash said again "Who did this to you?"

Elmore moaned again, and mumbled something, but Cash couldn't understand him.

A siren wailed, and BJ ran up the hill to meet the ambulance. Another siren followed, blue lights twirling and streaking the cloudy sky as Maddox approached.

Seconds later, Maddox and the medics scrambled down the hill. That damned Sheriff Jasper was on his heels.

"What the hell happened?" Jasper shouted.

The medics checked Elmore's vitals, tossed the bloody cloth aside and applied blood stoppers.

"When I got here, I heard gunshots." Cash pointed toward the right. "The shooter escaped up there. I heard the car take off but Elmore needed help."

"I told him to call me if he received another ransom demand. He should have let me go." Sheriff Jasper wiped sweat from the back of his neck. "What are you doing here anyway, Koker? Did you shoot him?"

Cash's temper rose. "No, I was with BJ."

"BJ?" Jasper asked.

Cash realized he'd used her first name. "My lawyer. She can verify my story."

"It's true," BJ said. "Cash tried to save Mr. Elmore."

Maddox cut in, "Did Elmore see the shooter?"

"I don't know," Cash said. "He hasn't regained consciousness."

"I'll ride with him in the ambulance," Maddox said.

"No, I will." Jasper squared his shoulders. "He trusts me."

Cash exchanged a wary look with Maddox, but Maddox agreed.

"The kidnapper escaped with the money," Cash said.

Despair nagged at him.

The ransom was paid—but still, no news of Tyler.

FEAR SEIZED BJ as the ambulance drove away.

Was Tyler with the kidnapper? If so, why wouldn't he have left the little boy? Because he'd never intended to return him to his grandfather?

The reasons that came to mind terrified her.

She and Cash drove toward the hospital in silence. Maddox was close behind.

By the time they parked at the emergency entrance, the medical staff was rushing Elmore to surgery. Maddox met them in the waiting room.

"Did he wake up?" BJ asked.

"No." Maddox looked grim-faced.

"What did you find out about Frannie Cooper's murder?" Cash asked.

"Not much. The sheriff who investigated gave me a copy of the notes he took during his interviews, but I haven't had time to go through them."

Jasper stalked toward Maddox, his jaw tight with anger. "I want to talk to you, McCullen."

Maddox gave a quick nod. "Of course. How about getting us some coffee?"

"I'm not your errand boy," Jasper snarled.

"I know that," Maddox said. "But we may be here a while. I have to call my deputy, then we'll talk. I'll meet you in the cafeteria."

Jasper stomped away and headed toward the cafeteria.

"You have your hands full, Maddox. Let me look at those files while you deal with Jasper," BJ said.

Maddox shrugged. "I guess it won't hurt."

Maddox hurried to his vehicle and returned a few minutes later with a file. "Let me know if you see anything." Then he headed down the hall to meet Jasper.

BJ carried the file to the seating area in the waiting room. Cash walked down the hall and returned with two cups of coffee. She handed him half the notes and she took the remainder.

"Frannie's mother was an alcoholic who hadn't spoken to her daughter in years," BJ said as she skimmed the notes. "She was in and out of rehab, graduated to cocaine and overdosed the year after Frannie was murdered."

"Sounds like Frannie had a rough life," Cash muttered.

BJ nodded. "Frannie lived in an apartment. According to her neighbors, she loved Drew and did her best to take care of him, but on a waitress's salary she couldn't make ends meet. When Drew became ill, she missed so many days of work the owner fired her."

Sympathy for Frannie engulfed BJ.

"Frannie found another job working the late shift at a brew pub, but one night she was shot in the alley behind the bar. The owner found her the next morning. Police determined the killer was probably a drunken customer, but never made an arrest."

"No security cameras?" Cash asked.

"Apparently they weren't working."

Cash cursed. "Dammit, BJ. Look at this." He angled a paper with a list of people interviewed.

BJ's heart raced when she zeroed in on a familiar name. Sheriff Jim Jasper.

CASH'S HEAD REELED. "Jasper was in the bar the night Frannie died."

"Seems too coincidental," BJ said.

"Damn right it does." Cash rifled through the notes to the interview with Jasper. "Says here that he was looking for a stolen car, and traced it to the bar."

BJ worried her bottom lip with her teeth, and glanced down the hall where Jasper had disappeared. "Did he know Frannie?"

"Said that she just waited on him."

Cash's mind raced. "Other than Tyler and Drew sharing the same father, Jasper is the only common factor between Frannie and Sondra."

BJ made a low sound in her throat. "Cash, what if Jasper fathered the boys?"

Cash's stomach knotted. He'd never liked Jasper. "I guess it's possible. Since Sondra's father and Jasper were friends, she probably thought it would cause trouble if Elmore knew they'd been together, especially if Jasper had taken advantage of her." The pieces began to fit in Cash's mind. "Jasper would also know how to frame me."

BJ drummed her fingers on the table. "That's true. He would also have access to criminals, someone he could have paid to drug you, kill Sondra and pose as you for that camera. Someone like Taft or Spillman."

"We have to let Maddox know," Cash said.

"Right now all we have is a theory," BJ said. "We can't accuse a sheriff of murder or kidnapping without more evidence."

She was right. Jasper would make Maddox's life hell if they made accusations.

"Let's talk to Jasper's deputy," BJ said. "Maybe he knows more about Jasper."

Going out on their own without telling Maddox was chancy. But Maddox had stood up for him. He didn't want to jeopardize Maddox's career—or his life.

BJ looked up as Maddox approached. "Did you find anything?" Maddox asked.

"Nothing concrete," BJ said. "Where's Jasper?"

"He insists on waiting here for Elmore to wake up. I'm going to do the same."

BJ handed Maddox the files. "All right. Let us know when he regains consciousness."

Cash followed BJ outside, feeling antsy. Jasper had been quick to arrest him.

Because he'd made the perfect patsy?

He was all alone. A man with no money and no way to defend himself. A man who was close to Sondra, and who Elmore thought was Tyler's father.

Jasper had also been friends with Elmore, so Elmore hadn't once suspected that his friend would betray him.

BJ DIDN'T LIKE where this case was going. But the elaborate way Cash had been framed was orchestrated by someone who knew what he was doing.

Dark clouds rolled in, a light rain drizzling down as they drove toward Jasper's office.

If Jasper was Tyler's father, he wouldn't have wanted

Elmore to know—why? Because he didn't love Sondra? Because he didn't want a child?

Because he had forced himself on Sondra and knew Elmore would kill him if he found out?

A deputy's vehicle sat in front of the building. She climbed from the truck, and they walked up the sidewalk together. In spite of his bad memories, Cash opened the door and strode in, shoulders squared.

She followed, her stomach clenching. If Jasper was as devious and coldhearted as she suspected, he had covered his own butt.

So why ask for a ransom? To make it appear that the kidnapping and Sondra's murder was about money?

The deputy looked up at her with a scowl as she entered, his frown deepening when Cash halted in front of him and crossed his arms.

"What the hell are you doing here?" the deputy asked.

BJ adopted a poker face. What if the deputy knew what Jasper had done and was covering for him?

ANGER COILED INSIDE CASH. He stepped forward, tempted to jerk a knot in the deputy's collar, but BJ placed a warning hand on his arm and he froze.

He had to keep his cool or he'd wind up locked up again.

"I have some questions," BJ said "Did you know Sondra Elmore?"

The young man shook his head. "I never met her, but her father and Jasper's father were friends."

"What about a woman named Frannie Cooper?" BJ asked.

"Can't say as I do. But I've only lived here three months. Moved here from Cheyenne."

"Did Jasper ever mention having a child?" Cash asked.

BJ shot Cash a dark look. The deputy's brows rose in a puzzled expression. "Where'd you get that idea? Jasper doesn't have any family. Heard him say he liked it that way. He was planning to run for Mayor and didn't want anything to get in the way."

An election could mean that someone might expose his secrets.

Having two illegitimate children, abandoning one who was sick, and possibly assault or rape charges against him would definitely have tainted his chances.

Sounded like a motive.

Cash glanced at the sheriff's desk. He'd like to take a look inside. Not that Jasper would be foolish enough to leave any evidence behind.

Except for the evidence he'd planted against Cash.

BJ thanked the deputy for his help, then they stepped outside. "It's time we let Maddox know what we learned."

Cash removed his phone from his pocket. "I'll call him." He punched Maddox's number and filled him in.

"Good god, that makes sense now," Maddox said. "Jasper's been behind everything."

"Is he still there?" Cash asked.

"He left a minute ago. Said he had a clue he was going to check out, but he refused to tell me what it was."

"He may be going to Tyler," Cash said. "Did Elmore wake up?"

"Not yet." Maddox muttered a sound of frustration. "I'll call Jasper's office and see if he's there."

"We're there now and the deputy hasn't seen him."

"Then I'll check his house," Maddox said. "You and BJ sit tight. I'll keep you posted."

Cash didn't like it, but he had to trust Maddox. Hard to do, but so far he'd been aboveboard with him.

He ended the call, then he and BJ walked over to the diner to get coffee. From there, they could see the sheriff's office and would know if he came back.

Thirty minutes passed with no news from Maddox. Jasper didn't show either.

"I can't stand this waiting," BJ said. "I'm going to talk to the deputy again."

Cash stood. "All right."

"Wait here, Cash," BJ said. "He might tell me more if I'm alone."

Cash exhaled. "Okay, but I'll be right outside the door if you need me."

They walked across the street and BJ went inside. Cash paced the sidewalk, every second increasing his anxiety as he waited.

Finally she came out, but she looked anxious. "Jasper owns a cabin in a desolate wooded area. He likes to go there and think sometimes."

Cash's heart pounded. "He might have Tyler there."

"That's what I was thinking."

Cash's keys jangled as they hurried to his truck.

"I'll call Maddox," BJ said.

Cash nodded, and she made the call while he entered the address the deputy had given her into his GPS.

BJ must have gotten Maddox's machine because she left a message.

He fought the fear eating at him as he drove. Twenty minutes later, they were in the wilderness when BJ's phone buzzed. Maddox.

She put him on the speaker.

"I got your message," Maddox said. "You may be right. Jasper isn't at his house so he may be at that cabin."

"We're on our way there now," BJ said.

"Dammit, I warned you two to let me handle this," Maddox said.

"I'm sorry, Maddox," Cash said. "BJ tried to reach you."

"Just wait on me when you get there. Jasper is dangerous," Maddox said.

"We know that," Cash said. But Tyler was worth it.

"Devon phoned about Sondra's computer," Maddox continued. "Jasper is Tyler's father. Sondra found out Jasper had another son, Drew, and started asking questions about his mother. One of Jasper's emails warned her to keep quiet or else."

Maddox hung up, and Cash accelerated as they crossed the rugged terrain. If Jasper was desperate, he might be planning an escape.

Cash clenched the steering wheel in a white-knuckled grip and veered down the graveled road. The truck rumbled over dirt and potholes, across rugged land that was untamed and so far off the grid a person could hide out for months.

Suddenly a burst of light illuminated the sky above, streaking the dark clouds.

"Oh, my God," BJ cried. "That's a fire."

Terror clawed at Cash, and he pressed the accelerator. Tyler...

Chapter Twenty-Two

Flames burst into the sky, lighting the dark clouds and sending panic through Cash. He rounded a curve, spotted a barn on fire and screeched to a stop.

"Tyler might be in there!" He vaulted from the truck "Call for help!"

Just as he neared the barn, Jasper ran out. Cash jerked him by the collar. Jasper raised his weapon at Cash, but Cash was fast, and knocked it from his grasp. The gun flew into the dirt a few feet away.

"Let me go, you son of a bitch!" Jasper yelled.

Cash slammed Jasper against the barn wall. Heat from the fire seared him. "You killed Sondra and took Tyler. Is he in that barn?"

Jasper's eyes flashed with rage. "She was going to ruin me!"

Cash squeezed the man's neck. "*Is* Tyler in there?"

Jasper slammed his fist into Cash's stomach. Cash grunted and threw the man to the ground, then punched him in the chest. Anger heated his blood, and he punched him again.

"Let him go, Cash," BJ said in a commanding tone.

She inched toward them, her hands gripping Jasper's gun. She aimed it at Jasper.

"Go get Tyler, Cash!" she shouted. "If he moves, I'll shoot him."

Cash dragged the sheriff to the wooden railing of the pen, grabbed the man's handcuffs and cuffed him to it. Then he turned and ran toward the burning barn.

Fire crackled and popped. Wood splintered. Flames danced from the rear of the barn and crawled along the straw on the floor. The fire hadn't yet reached the front door, but it was creeping toward it.

"Tyler, are you in here?"

Heat seared Cash's neck. A board from the roof splintered off and fell at his feet. He jumped over it, dodging fire as it crept up the wall.

"Tyler!" He weaved past two stalls, then made it to the last one. Tyler was hunched in a corner, tied to a post.

Rage fueled Cash's adrenaline. Flames were eating the wood, catching the straw near the little boy's feet. Tyler had been gagged, but he was trying to scream, and pulling at the ropes.

Cash ran to the tack room, grabbed one of the horse blankets, then darted back toward Tyler. The poor little boy's eyes were panicked and tears streaked his dirty cheeks. Smoke clogged the air.

Cash beat at the flames as he ran through them. He used his pocketknife to cut the ropes, wrapped the blanket around the little boy, then picked him up. Tyler sagged against him, trembling with fear.

Cash covered Tyler's head and body with the blanket, then ran through the barn. The front was just catching fire. He ducked his head against Tyler and hurried outside.

Flames licked at his arms and legs, but he beat them away with one hand, then carried Tyler to a tree several hundred feet away.

BJ was still standing guard over Jasper, who was growling and cursing.

She glanced over her shoulder at Cash and relief filled her face when she saw Tyler.

Sirens wailed in the distance. Maddox roared onto the scene along with an ambulance.

Tyler coughed, but clung to Cash. Cash rocked him back and forth until the medics reached them.

BJ DARED JASPER to make a move. She'd never shot a person before, but this coldhearted bastard had left an innocent little child in a barn to burn to death.

"How could you kill your own son?" BJ asked.

Jasper's harsh face hardened even more. "I didn't ask for a kid."

"You know how it happens and you didn't prevent it," BJ said, furious. "Even worse, you have two children, neither of which you've taken responsibility for."

"He's your son," Cash snapped. "How could you hurt him?"

"That's your fault," Jasper said. "If you two hadn't kept snooping around, I would have taken the money and gotten him back to Elmore. But you had to interfere."

BJ tightened her fingers around the gun. Poor little Tyler was crying in Cash's arms.

The big tough man's body was shaking as well, as if he was overcome with emotions. He was so tender with Tyler. He'd saved his life.

The medics knelt beside Cash and Tyler and began to examine Tyler.

Maddox approached slowly. "BJ, I've got it. You can put the gun down."

Her hand jerked, but Maddox gently pushed the weapon down with one hand. "I've got it, BJ. He's not going anywhere."

BJ released the breath she'd been holding and lowered the gun.

The next few hours passed in a blur as the medics transported Tyler to the hospital for observation. Cash rode with him, and she drove his truck. Whitefeather arrived to meet the crime team, with promises they would have all the evidence they'd need to put Jasper away for a long time.

Maddox was transferring him to jail to book him.

While Cash stayed with Tyler and they settled him into a room, BJ checked on Drew. Candace, his social worker, was sitting by the little guy's bed.

"How's he doing?" BJ asked.

A sad expression tugged at the woman's mouth. "Not very well, I'm afraid. We need a donor soon."

"We found his father." BJ's mind raced with the beginnings of a plan. "He needs to be tested to see if he's a match, right?"

"Right. Will he agree to it?"

BJ removed her phone from her purse. "I'll make sure he does."

She dropped a kiss on the sleeping little boy's head, then stepped into the hall to make a call.

CASH COULDN'T RELAX until he knew Tyler was all right.

But how could he be all right when his mother had been murdered and his father had tried to kill him?

How did a child overcome that kind of trauma?

He hadn't known his own parents, but at least they had wanted him. Neither one of them had tied him up in a burning building and left him to die.

Instead they'd died trying to find him and his brother. Maddox had filled him in when they were in the waiting room. The killer made it look like his mother crashed her car while she was drinking, but the accident hadn't been an accident at all. She'd been drugged.

And his father, Joe McCullen, had been poisoned.

The doctor who examined Tyler motioned for Cash to step into the hall.

"Is he going to be all right?" Cash asked.

"Physically, he's fine. But emotionally, he may have a hard time. Are you family?"

No, but he wished he was. He explained about Jasper and Sondra's murder. "His grandfather, Lester Elmore, was brought in suffering from gunshot wounds."

The doctor scratched his chin. "We're required to confer with Children and Family Services. Depending on his grandfather's condition, Tyler may be placed in foster care."

Cash fought a reaction. So many bad memories for him. He didn't want Tyler to suffer the way he had.

And what would happen to Tyler's half brother, Drew?

"If Tyler wakes, tell the nurse to assure him I'll be back."

He rode the elevator to Elmore's floor and stopped at the nurse's station. "I was with the ambulance that brought Lester Elmore's grandson in. How is Mr. Elmore?"

"He's in and out of consciousness. It's still touch and go."

"Can I see him?"

Maybe Tyler could stay with him until Elmore was released and feeling better. Would Elmore consider taking in Drew?

"Are you family?" the nurse asked.

Cash hesitated. "Not technically, but I'm close to his grandson. You know he was kidnapped?"

"Yes, I saw the story on the news. I've been praying for the little boy," the nurse said.

"Elmore was shot trying to pay that ransom," Cash said. "It might help him to know that we rescued Tyler and that he's safe."

"Of course it would." She led him to Elmore's room. "Just don't stay too long or upset him. He needs to rest."

Cash nodded. He had bad blood with Elmore. It was possible that his presence might agitate the man.

But…he needed to know that Tyler was safe.

That he had to fight to live.

Because Tyler needed his grandfather now more than ever.

BJ CLENCHED HER phone as she explained the situation with Jasper to her father.

"So Cash Koker is a McCullen?" her father asked.

"Yes, Dad, and he's innocent."

"Hmm." A pregnant pause. "I'm sure the McCullens are happy."

"They will be," BJ said. "Right now we're dealing with Sheriff Jasper."

"He's guilty. You've got the proof. He'll go to jail."

"Yes, but it's complicated. He had another son, a little boy named Drew, who needs a kidney transplant badly. Jasper may be a match, but he hasn't agreed to testing. I was thinking that if we had leverage, maybe offered him a deal, he might agree to donate his kidney."

"If he killed two women, kidnapped his son for ransom and tried to kill him, then he should rot in jail."

"I agree," BJ said. Jasper had admitted that Drew's mother had threatened to expose him if he didn't pay her. "But Drew may not make it without that transplant. Can you talk to the DA and ask him to take the death penalty off the table in exchange for a kidney? That is, if Jasper is a positive match to Drew."

Another hesitation. "I'll make the call."

BJ closed her eyes and said a silent prayer that her plan would work. Once Drew was healthy, it would be much easier for him to find a forever home.

She phoned Maddox and relayed her conversation with her father. Maddox agreed to coerce Jasper into taking the tests.

BJ went to check on Tyler and Cash. Maybe if Drew got well, he and Tyler could connect. Then neither little boy would have to be alone again.

Of course, that depended on Elmore...

CASH EASED INTO a chair beside Elmore. The astute man who'd made his life hell looked frail in the hospital bed, not so imposing.

Cash took a deep breath, determined to forget his animosity toward the older man. Nothing mattered now except Tyler.

"Mr. Elmore, it's Cash Koker," he said in a low voice. "I don't know if you can hear me, but Tyler is safe." He hesitated, waiting for a reaction.

Elmore's eyes fluttered open and he struggled to focus. He licked his lips and tried to make his voice work, but coughed instead.

Cash spotted the water on the tray, inserted a straw and pressed it to the man's lips. Elmore took a sip, his eyes fluttering again.

"Did you hear me, Elmore? Tyler is safe and alive."

"Thank God." Elmore groaned and slowly turned his head to face Cash. "Jasper?"

"Maddox—Sheriff McCullen—arrested him. He's going to prison."

"Did he hurt Tyler?" The question came out a croak.

"He's shaken up, but he'll be all right."

Regret racked Elmore's face. "I've wasted so much time with Sondra and Tyler."

Cash's throat thickened. "It's not too late for Tyler."

The man's lip quivered. "Thank you for...saving him."

"He needs you," Cash said. "You're all he has."

Elmore shook his head, then tried to lift his hand. "Tyler loves you."

Cash took the man's trembling hand in his. "I'll be around if he needs me. That is, if...you want."

Elmore nodded. "If I don't make it, promise me you'll take care of him."

Cash clenched his teeth. "You are going to make it, Mr. Elmore. You can't leave Tyler now."

For a weak man, his grip on Cash's hand grew stronger. "Promise me," Elmore said, his voice cracking.

Cash swallowed hard. "I promise."

A small smile tilted the corners of Elmore's mouth. Then he closed his eyes and drifted back to sleep.

Cash stood, dumbfounded. What the hell had just happened?

Had Elmore really asked him to take Tyler if something happened to him?

Suddenly, the heart monitor beeped and machines trilled. A nurse rushed in and waved him away from the bed. "Get a crash cart!" she shouted to another nurse.

Cash was pushed to the side while a team tried to revive Elmore. Several minutes passed.

But Elmore didn't respond.

Instead, he slipped into death.

Chapter Twenty-Three

Cash stared at the scene in the hospital room in shock.

A few minutes ago Elmore had asked him to take care of Tyler if something happened to him.

Now Elmore was dead.

"Cash?" BJ's voice barely registered through his dazed state. "What happened?"

"He's dead," Cash said in a gruff voice.

Her hand brushed his back. "My God, poor little Tyler. What's he going to do?"

Cash pivoted, heart aching. "I don't know. Elmore actually asked me to take care of him, but...I can't."

BJ's expression softened. "You could, Cash. Tyler loves you."

Cash shrugged. "I have nothing to offer the kid. No money. No home. I don't even have a damn job." He ran a hand over his rough, beard-stubbled jaw. "Besides, the law would never give him to me. I'm not blood kin."

Sympathy registered in her eyes. "I'm sorry. I...we'll talk to the social worker." She guided him away from the sight of Elmore lying dead in the bed.

They walked down the hall toward Tyler's room. "I spoke with Maddox about Drew and Jasper," BJ said. "He's going to pressure Jasper to be tested for the kidney transplant."

Anger threatened to make Cash explode. No man should have to be bribed to step up for his own kids. "You think he'll do it?"

"I put a call in to talk to the DA about a deal to take death row off the table if he cooperates."

A rock and a hard place. Jasper deserved to die. But Drew needed that kidney.

"How's Tyler?" BJ asked.

"Physically, he'll be fine." Cash pushed open the door

and they both stepped inside. The little boy was curled on his side, deep in sleep. He looked peaceful—but his life had been anything but peaceful lately.

His mama and grandfather were dead, and he was alone in the world.

"I'll call Candace," BJ said. "She's sitting with Drew. Maybe she can help."

Admiration for BJ flooded Cash, and he took her hand in his. "I don't know how to thank you for everything you've done, BJ. I...you're amazing."

Her eyes sparkled, the attraction simmering between them bursting to life. "So are you, Cash. So are you."

BJ's LUNGS SQUEEZED for air.

She wanted to say so much more to Cash. But the hospital wasn't the place.

Maybe when the legal issues were settled, when they returned to Horseshoe Creek, they could talk.

Although she wanted more than talk...

A nurse walked by, jarring her back to reality and the job she had to do.

Had Elmore told anyone other than Cash his wishes? If not, it would be difficult to prove that he'd actually asked Cash to raise the little boy.

Candace met her in the hallway outside Tyler's room. "Tyler's grandfather just died." She explained about Cash's conversation with Elmore.

"Unfortunately, we'll have to see what Sondra and her father stipulated in their wills," Candace said. "Until then, Tyler will be placed in a temporary foster home."

"He's already been through so much," BJ said, her heart aching. "Staying with strangers will only add to his trauma."

"I'll make arrangements to handle his case myself." Candace squeezed BJ's hand. "Try not to worry."

BJ went to join Cash while Candace made the phone call. Cash sat by Tyler's bed, his head bowed.

BJ remained still, giving him space and time, until he finally glanced back at her. He looked so tortured that she crossed the room to him and rubbed his back.

"Candace is going to help us, Cash."

She realized she'd said *us* and knew she'd lost her heart to Cash and the little boy.

Candace's heels clicked on the floor as she entered. "My supervisor agreed to let me handle Tyler's situation."

She joined them by Tyler's bed. "Mr. Koker, BJ explained what happened. I'll do everything I can to help you."

"Thanks. I appreciate that." He patted Tyler's hand. "I hate to see him suffer any more."

Candace offered him a smile. "You obviously love him. Both of you look wrung out. Why don't you go home, shower and get some rest? I'll stay here with Tyler in case he wakes up."

Cash looked torn. "I don't want to leave him."

"Who knows if he's slept at all these last couple of days?" She smiled softly. "You need to rest, too."

Cash hesitated again, but finally stood. "All right. I guess I do smell like smoke and could use a shower. Call me if he wakes up."

Candace promised she would.

BJ and Cash left the hospital together and drove in silence back to Horseshoe Creek.

Exhaustion lined his features as he parked at the cabin.

BJ wanted to console him, to assure him that everything would work out. But how could she do that?

Legally, he had no right to Tyler, not if Elmore hadn't specified it in his will.

He slid from the truck, walked around and opened her door. He made no invitation for her to join him at his cabin, and she reminded herself that he had a lot on his mind. That he was worn-out and needed a shower and sleep.

So she walked up the path to her cabin and watched him drive across the way to the one where he was staying.

It was best she not give in to her desires.

Sleeping with him would only complicate things.

He'd already stolen a piece of her heart. She needed to keep the remainder intact. If not, she wouldn't survive when they parted.

And now the case was over, she'd have to go back to her job and her life.

Besides, Cash had a new family. And she wasn't part of it.

CASH'S ARM ACHED like the devil from that flesh wound, smoke permeated his clothes and hair, and he felt as if his arms had been singed.

It didn't matter, though. Tyler was alive.

But that kid faced a tough road, losing his family in a violent way.

He'd probably have nightmares about the fire.

Did he even know that Jasper was the man who'd fathered him?

God, Cash hoped not. What would that realization do to a little kid?

Probably screw him up for life.

Tyler needed someone to love him, to help him through the grief he'd feel over his mother's loss.

Cash shucked his clothes and stepped under the warm water, then dunked his head. He quickly lathered and washed off, although when he closed his eyes, memories of BJ's sweet touch made his body ache.

Last night she'd kissed him. Not just kissed him, but really *kissed* him, like she wanted more. Like she wanted to be with him.

Like she enjoyed his hands touching her.

He wanted them on her now. Wanted to feel her delicate skin beneath his work-roughened fingers. To feel those gorgeous legs wrapped around him. To inhale her feminine scent and taste her, and slide his naked skin against hers.

His erection swelled to a throbbing need, and he turned the water to cold to tamp down his libido.

It didn't help.

Wanting her wasn't just about his body's hunger. Somewhere along the way he'd fallen for her soft heart and her stubbornness and her desire to help others. She'd defended him, and she would fight for Tyler and for his brother, Drew.

The world needed more people like her.

He needed her.

The thought sucker punched him.

He'd cared about Sondra, but as friends. He'd never wanted to be friends and lovers before.

He wanted both with BJ.

He dried off, yanked on clean jeans and a shirt and stared at the empty bed.

Rational thought fled. He didn't want to be alone.

He pivoted and headed outside. Only one way to find out if BJ wanted him, too.

The light was burning in her cabin. In the bedroom.

He walked across the grassy area, then hurried up the path to her door. One knock, and she opened it, her face a beautiful sight.

She'd showered and changed into pajama pants and a thin white camisole. No bra.

Her plump breasts pushed against the fabric, her nipples stiff peaks.

"BJ?"

Her eyes lit with desire, then she curled one hand around his head and pressed her lips to his. "I was hoping you'd come," she whispered against his cheek.

Her softly spoken words and the passion in her kiss ignited his hunger, and he pushed her backward into the room.

Her arms wound around his neck, her hands urgent as she raked her fingers through his hair.

He cupped her butt with one hand, pressing her against his thighs as he deepened the kiss.

Hunger ignited, raw and primal. He dragged his mouth from hers and planted frenzied kisses down her neck. She tasted like sweetness and hope and salvation, everything a man like him needed but didn't deserve.

He started to pull away.

But she cupped his face in her hands, looked into his eyes with need, and he forgot his reservations.

He needed her. And dammit, she wanted him, at least for the moment.

That would do for now.

BJ HAD NEVER craved a man's touch the way she craved Cash's. The emotional connection from working the case and finally saving Tyler intensified her desires.

His body was hard, his muscles thick from hard work, yet his hands gentle as he traced one finger down her jaw. She sucked in a sharp breath, his earlier hesitancy only fueling her growing feelings for him.

Cash was honorable. A man who fought for what was right. A man who'd saved a little boy's life.

A man who would protect a woman, as well.

She parted her lips and tasted the salty skin of his neck as he trailed his fingers over her breasts through the thin tank top. Her nipples beaded to stiff peaks, yearning for more.

She urged him closer with sweet whispers, and stroked his back down to his muscular backside, reveling in the pleasure in his moan.

"BJ?" he whispered against her ear.

She took his hand and guided him to the bedroom. He paused, raking his eyes over her with appreciation, stirring erotic sensations inside her. A come-hither smile curved her mouth.

There was no turning back now.

She was going to give herself to Cash Koker.

The pleasure would be worth whatever the price of her heartbreak when he left.

Chapter Twenty-Four

Cash wanted BJ naked. Skin to skin.

Bodies moving together.

He planted kisses along her jaw and neck, tasting sweetness and desire as he lifted the tank top over her head.

Her breasts spilled out, sending his erection straining against his jeans. Her nipples were rosy and stiff, begging for a man's touch.

He cupped her breasts in his hands, then lowered his mouth and sucked one taut bud into his mouth. She threw her head back and groaned, arousing him even more.

Her fingers tunneled through his hair as he laved one breast, then the other, and she pulled him toward the bed. He gently shoved her onto the quilt, but resisted when she reached for him.

Instead, he focused on her pajama pants. They were some kind of flimsy material and felt soft to his hands, but not as soft and satiny as her bare skin.

She wasn't wearing panties.

His breath caught at the blatant hunger in her eyes. She urged him closer, her whispered sigh a plea for more. But he didn't want to rush this.

He threaded his fingers in her hair, tilted her neck back and kissed the sensitive skin behind her ear. "Tell me what BJ stands for," he murmured.

She moaned his name.

He drove his tongue inside her ear and stroked one nipple between his fingers. "Tell me, BJ."

A soft sigh escaped from her, and she rubbed his back. "You'll laugh."

"No, I won't," he said, as he kissed her again. "I want to say your name when I'm inside you."

BJ shivered, shifting so she rubbed his thick length against her belly. "It's Brandy Jane," she murmured.

A smile tugged at his mouth as he looked into her eyes. "Brandy Alexander?"

She nodded, heat in her gaze. "My mother's favorite drink."

He chuckled and she slapped him playfully. "I told you you'd laugh."

He brushed her hair back and kissed her again, this time fervently. "I want you, Brandy Jane."

She tugged at his jeans. "I want you, too, Cash."

Instead of mounting her, he lowered himself to the floor, then spread her legs with his hands.

She whispered his name, her body trembling as he placed his tongue at her sweet center. He drove his mouth over her sensitive spot, teasing her with his tongue and savoring her honeyed taste.

She reached for his arms, silently urging him to enter her, but he held back. More than anything he wanted to give her pleasure, to make her feel special. Wanted.

To be the person she needed and deserved.

He shut out the doubts. He'd have time for those later.

He lifted her hips slightly, then closed his lips over her center, adding his finger to the madness to tease her. Her hips bucked and she trembled.

Her sigh of pleasure ended with a long groan and she came apart in his arms.

His need became more urgent, and he stripped off his clothes, braced himself above her and pressed his rigid length between her legs.

Rational sense intruded for a millisecond, long enough for him to roll on a condom.

Moaning his name, she clutched his hips as if she couldn't wait, then rubbed herself against his erection. She felt like heaven.

It would be hell to leave her when it was over.

But they both needed tonight.

He stroked her dampness with his throbbing sex, until his release burned inside him, begging for escape.

Murmuring how much he wanted her, he stroked her sex

with his. The first touch of her body quivering and clenching around him nearly made him shout.

He thrust inside her, filling her to the core, then drove himself in and out, teasing her until the urgency swept them both away.

Erotic sensations pummeled him as he came inside her.

She clawed his back with her hands as she joined him on the ride.

BJ SNUGGLED UP to Cash's chest and closed her eyes, the euphoria of making love with him triggering emotions that threatened to overflow.

She was in love with the man.

But she couldn't confess her feelings. He would think she was crazy and desperate. Besides, he didn't need his lawyer latching on to him like a lovesick teenager.

Hadn't she vowed not to get involved with another client? Her father had insisted on professionalism. She'd failed him once.

He'd never allowed her to forget it, either.

Cash slid from the bed and padded to the bathroom, and she instantly missed him. Was he going to leave and retreat to his cabin?

Her heart fluttered. He should leave.

But he returned, crawled in beside her and drew her to him again.

She curled against him and fell into a deep, exhausted sleep.

Hours later, the nightmares of her son's death woke her. Aaron's voice cried out, "Help me, Mommy. Save me."

Grief and anguish bombarded her, and she sobbed his name. She could see his little hand reaching out for her to pull him from the water. Hear him choking for a breath as his head bobbed up and down.

She screamed his name, but suddenly his face faded into the fog and little Drew's pale face appeared. Drew was so sick.

He needed help. Needed that kidney.

Tears blinded her and she jerked upright.

Cash sat up quickly and rubbed her arm. "BJ?"

"I couldn't save him," she cried. "I wanted to but I couldn't."

Cash made a low sound in his throat, then rubbed her back in small circles and pulled her into his arms. She closed her eyes, the pain as relentless as it had been the day she'd lost him.

That pain would never go away.

A hollow emptiness robbed her of breath, the same void she'd lived with for two years now.

"I'm sorry, BJ." Cash pressed a kiss to her hair. "So sorry."

She fought the urge to scream that he couldn't possibly understand.

No one could.

CASH DIDN'T KNOW what to do. One minute, BJ had been sleeping in his arms, content and purring his name.

The next she'd been screaming her son's.

Anger and frustration at her situation ripped through him. He had no idea how to help her.

"I'm sorry," BJ whispered through her tears.

"You have recurring nightmares?"

She nodded, then pulled on her robe. "I need to be alone, Cash. Please go."

He chewed the inside of his cheek, then stood and rubbed her arms. "Let me help you, BJ. Come back to bed—"

"No," she said sharply. "I can't, not when I see my dead son every time I close my eyes. When it was my fault he died."

A muscle jumped in Cash's cheek. "BJ, it wasn't your fault. You know that." Didn't she?

"It was. I knew my ex had a drinking problem. But I never thought he'd drink and drive, not with Aaron in the car."

"Had he done that before?"

"No, never." Her voice broke. "He loved Aaron and was always good with him."

"Then you couldn't have known, BJ," Cash said quietly. "Some things are just out of our control."

BJ swiped angrily at her tears. "Please, Cash, just go. I need to be alone."

Cash went still, his heart pounding. He'd thought they'd had a connection when they'd made love. That she might even…care about him.

But she'd simply needed comfort.

He didn't regret giving it to her.

He was a fool, though, for thinking that a relationship with her could be anything but temporary.

She had her demons to slay. And he had his own.

Tyler's face flashed in his mind. Tyler needed a parent. Someone who'd understand him.

He'd probably need therapy.

Self-doubts ate at Cash.

Even if the court granted him custody of Sondra's little boy, what did he know about being a father?

"Cash, please be gone when I come out." She hurried into the bathroom and closed the door with a resounding thud.

He yanked on his jeans.

Damn. He should be grateful she wasn't making demands, talking about the next time they'd see each other, wanting to be his girlfriend.

He'd never had a real girlfriend.

But something about her made him want to claim her as his.

Still, she wanted him gone. She was probably already regretting sleeping with him. After all, her father was a powerful attorney.

They were from different worlds.

And he had to accept it.

THE NEXT TWO DAYS BJ worked to wrangle in the ridiculous feelings she had for Cash. She'd met with her father again. He was proud of her for helping solve the case.

He'd also been inquisitive about the McCullens, but she hadn't let on that she'd fallen for Cash.

Disgust made her sigh as she let herself back into her

old apartment. The situation had drawn them together—that was simply all this attraction was.

The deafening quiet as she stepped into the entryway struck her.

The place seemed cold. Empty.

Lonely.

Just as she was.

She had been ever since she'd lost her son.

She remembered the smile on Drew's face when she'd dropped by the hospital, and her heart melted. Drew would survive.

But he had no place to go when he was released, except to another foster home.

She'd gotten the charges against Cash completely dropped. He was a free man—free to do whatever he wanted and make a life with whomever he wanted.

She made several calls to Elmore's attorney about Tyler's custody issue. Shockingly, the man had called a meeting with Cash and the McCullens to discuss the situation.

Jasper had confessed to murder and kidnapping, and accepted the DA's deal. The tests proved he was a match for Drew. They'd performed the surgery that night. Thankfully, Drew's body had accepted the match and he was recovering.

Rain pounded the roof outside and slashed the windowpanes. She dragged her rolling suitcase to her bedroom, the pristine white walls and comforter stark and almost depressing, just like the dark storm clouds outside.

She'd thrown away all the color in her life when Aaron had died, because he loved colors.

One of the many rainbow drawings she'd kept and framed still sat on her dresser, a reminder of him and the energy he'd had in life.

She went to the desk and removed the folder of his sketches. More rainbows, the sun shining, happy faces and horses. She'd promised to sign him up for horseback riding lessons, but she'd never gotten the chance.

Tears filled her eyes. A million years ago, she'd had

rainbows and laughter and a little boy's precious voice and smile in her house for a while.

Drew's face haunted her. Had he dreamed of rainbows or a future at all? Or had he just been waiting to die?

Sorrow for Aaron swelled inside her. She couldn't bring her son back or help him now.

But that other little boy needed love. A family. A mother. Someone to take care of him.

She grabbed her keys, jogged outside, then drove to the Memorial Gardens center where she'd laid Aaron to rest. Emotions pummeled her as she parked and crossed the grassy gardens to a tiny spot in a section marked Little Angels.

Padding softly to his tombstone, she knelt and ran her finger over the marker.

"I love you, buddy, I always will," she whispered. Then she began to tell him about Drew.

"You will always be my son, and you own my heart." She kissed her fingers, then pressed them on the plaque where his name was etched. "What would you think if I let this other little boy live with me? He doesn't have a mommy or anyone else." Except for Tyler, and they were still working out the details to see if Cash gained custody of the boy.

The wind ruffled the trees. A breeze tossed leaves around the grave.

Suddenly, a rainbow appeared, the brilliant colors shimmering across the stone marker and grass.

A seed of joy and hope burst inside her. She kissed her fingers again and laid them on the stone.

The rainbow was her answer, her wise and wonderful son's way of telling her that it was okay for her to love another child.

She stood, antsy to call the social worker.

Chapter Twenty-Five

Two days later

Cash's stomach tightened as he entered the lawyer's office. Conan Cambridge, Elmore's attorney, greeted him with a handshake. Maddox also shook the man's hand.

Having Maddox here meant more than Cash would ever have thought. When he'd relayed Elmore's last words to him, Maddox had insisted on accompanying him.

BJ was waiting inside, her hair tugged back in a bun, the professional mask in place. She wore a jacket and skirt, as if she thought dressing in a business suit would dull his desire for her.

But nothing could do that.

He wanted to strip the damn suit and make her writhe beneath him again, naked, hot and sweaty.

The thought disturbed him to the core.

"Have a seat, Mr. Koker," Cambridge said. "I've been talking with your lawyer, Miss Alexander."

BJ gave him a stiff smile, one that ticked him off, because she was acting like she didn't know him, as if he'd never been inside her and heard her cry his name in the throes of passion.

Cash and Maddox claimed the wing chairs across from BJ, who was perched on the leather love seat.

"We're here to discuss Mr. Elmore's wishes for his grandson, and his will," Cambridge said.

Cash chewed the inside of his cheek, his heart pounding.

"Miss Alexander informed me of your conversation with Mr. Elmore when he was on his deathbed," Cambridge said.

Here it was. That fancy lawyer would say it wasn't valid. No one else had heard it. Cash had made it up.

A muscle ticked in Cambridge's jaw. "Unfortunately, Elmore died without changing his will."

Cash shifted and started to say something, but BJ shook her head, indicating for him to hold his tongue.

"That said, I can tell you that Elmore left his estate to his daughter, Sondra, and her son, Tyler. I've reviewed Sondra's will, and surprisingly, she made stipulations that in the event of her death, she wanted you to raise Tyler, Mr. Koker."

Shock stole Cash's words. "She did?"

He nodded. "She also stipulated that she wanted Tyler to be with you, but she wanted her father to have access to the boy." He paused. "She wanted them to have a relationship."

The lawyer's words reverberated in Cash's ears. "What does this mean?"

Cambridge pulled at his tie. "It means that if you're agreeable, Tyler Elmore will be placed in your custody." A serious frown carved lines in the man's weathered face. "Of course, a social worker will be assigned to make home visits, check on the child's well-being and confirm that you are able to care for the boy."

Cash's head reeled in shock, but he nodded.

"One more thing, Mr. Koker," Cambridge said. "Lester phoned me the day you tried to make the ransom drop and were injured. He told me he'd been wrong about you."

Cash couldn't believe this was happening.

"According to his will, Tyler inherited Elmore's ranch," Cambridge continued. "You being his guardian, you and Tyler can live on his ranch."

"I don't think Elmore would like that," Cash said.

Cambridge crossed his hands on his desk. "You risked your life to save Tyler, Mr. Koker. Lester knew that. He told me he was going to offer you a job as his head foreman. With Lester gone and Tyler a minor, someone will have to take over."

The man paused. "How do you feel about all this?"

Cash pinched the bridge of his nose, emotions flooding him. Love. Relief. Worry. He'd never had a father. He didn't know if he could handle the job.

"You do want custody of Tyler, don't you, Cash?" BJ asked softly.

Cash's gaze met hers. "Yes."

The lawyer stepped outside the door for a moment, and more self-doubt pummeled Cash. He leaned close to BJ and spoke in a conspiratorial whisper. "But what do I know about being a father? What if I mess up?"

BJ squeezed his hand. "You love him. That's what he needs most." The McCullens were good people and would help their newfound brother raise the boy.

The social worker Cash had met at the hospital with Drew entered the room, Tyler's tiny hand tucked in hers.

The little boy looked up at him with worry and sadness, melting Cash's heart as he knelt before him. "Tyler?"

Tyler's lower lip quivered. "They said Mommy's gone."

"I'm sorry, bud." Cash wiped a tear from Tyler's cheek. "But you've got me."

"The lady said I can live with you, Cash," he said in a small voice.

"That's true." Cash's heart pounded. "I'd like that, Tyler. What do you think?"

Tyler nodded, then threw himself against Cash's chest. Cash wrapped his arms around the little boy, Tyler's tears mingling with his own. He might not know how to be a father. He might mess up.

But he'd do the best he could. And from now on, Tyler would be his son.

"ARE YOU SURE you want to do this, BJ?"

BJ squared her shoulders and faced her father. She wanted his blessing, but she didn't need it. She had to follow her heart. "I've never been so sure of anything in my life."

His stern face softened. "I understand. I know the last two years have been rough."

"They have," she admitted. "I made mistakes, Dad. My judgment wasn't always good."

"Everyone makes mistakes, honey," he said in an uncharacteristically thick voice. "You need to forgive yourself and move on."

BJ blinked, surprised at his comment. "I wanted to make you proud, Dad."

He left the chair behind his desk, walked over to her and captured her hands in his. "I am proud of you, sweetheart. I realize I haven't always shown it, and we disagreed sometimes. I didn't know how to help you after you lost Aaron." His voice warbled. "I…hated seeing you hurting, and didn't know what to do to make it right for you."

"You couldn't make it right," BJ said, her heart splintering at the sound of pain and helplessness in his voice. "No one could. I had to grieve. And…I still am grieving."

"I've grieved, too, baby. But you deserve to go on." He lifted her hands and kissed them. "All I want is for you to be happy, honey."

BJ inhaled a deep breath. "Giving Drew a home will make me happy."

He nodded, understanding softening his eyes. "Take all the time off you want. If you need anything, money—"

"Thanks, Dad, but I don't need money. I have savings," BJ said. "Once Drew's settled, I may come back, even if it's only part-time."

"You always have a place here." He hugged her, and BJ kissed his cheek. She hadn't expected him to take her news so well. Maybe in her grief and guilt, she'd been too hard on him.

Her phone buzzed. Candace. She connected the call.

"BJ, I have good news. You can take Drew home today."

Her heart fluttered with joy and relief. She would never hold her son again. But Drew needed her and a home, and she could give him that.

Five days later

CASH STOOD OUTSIDE the McCullen farmhouse, still in awe of the new family he'd found. They were having a barbecue celebration tonight in his honor. Mama Mary had cooked a feast of side dishes, while the McCullen men grilled steaks and burgers. The wives and kids gathered in the yard, talking and laughing, warmth exuding from them all.

Tyler didn't want to go back to the guesthouse or to Elmore's. Neither did Cash.

He would never feel at home there. So they were staying at Horseshoe Creek in the cabin. His brothers—it still felt weird to refer to them as that—planned to help him build a house of his own on the land.

Mama Mary had embraced him and Tyler, welcoming them into the family as if they'd always been around. Tyler followed Brett's son around like a puppy, and Sam had taken him in like a kid brother, showing him the ropes.

His brothers had given him a box of letters and cards their mother had written to him after his disappearance. She hadn't forgotten a single birthday or holiday and poured out her love, and her determination to find him and his twin.

He'd cried like a baby when he'd read them.

Cash made arrangements for Elmore's head foreman, a robust, friendly man named Wayne, to run the ranch. Maddox, Brett and Ray had heard good things about the ranch hand, whom they knew from the Cattleman's Club.

Mama Mary seemed taken with him, as well. According to Rose, she'd invited him to supper several times the past few months.

Tonight Roan Whitefeather and his wife, Megan, joined in the barbecue celebration.

The McCullens had had their problems, but they remained family and supported each other through thick and thin.

Cash wanted Tyler to grow up here.

"What are you going to do about BJ?" Maddox asked.

Cash tilted his hat against the waning sun as he watched Tyler toss a horseshoe. Brett and his little boy had quickly drawn Tyler into the game.

"What do you mean? I'll have to make payments on what I owe—"

"Her fee was taken care of," Maddox said. "I meant, what are you going to do personally?"

Cash gave him a dark look. He'd never told Maddox how he felt about BJ. Hadn't told anyone. "I was just a case to her," he said quietly.

Maddox grunted. "You weren't just a case, at least not toward the end. I saw the way the two of you looked at each other."

He shrugged. "You must have misunderstood."

"No, I didn't," Maddox said, his gaze straying to his wife, who was rocking their baby in the rocking chair on the porch. "Let me tell you something, little brother. Real love only comes along once."

His chest squeezed. "Maybe. But I've got Tyler now and nothing to offer a woman like her."

"That's BS," Maddox said. "You have part of our spread, and she adores Tyler."

Cash couldn't argue with that. But something else was bothering him. "I've been thinking about Drew. He's Tyler's half brother. I think the boys should be together, but I don't know if I can manage two kids and work a ranch."

"Mama Mary would be happy to watch the boys," Maddox said. "She made a great mama for me and Brett and Ray."

"I don't doubt that," Cash said, affection for the woman warming his heart.

The trouble was, he wanted BJ to be with them, too.

But she'd asked him to leave her alone.

Maddox patted Cash's back. "Don't be afraid to go after what you want."

Cash straightened. Was that his problem?

All his life he'd thought his mother and father hadn't wanted him. That no one had.

But he'd found the McCullens, and they'd embraced him with love and support.

Was it possible that BJ might want him, too?

BJ SETTLED DREW into bed. He was still recovering from the surgery and needed rest, but he was gaining strength every day. He'd seen Aaron's rainbow drawings and had wanted to paint one himself.

Now both boys' art hung on the walls.

She tucked the covers around him. "I'll be in the next room." She brushed his hair from his forehead. His eyelids were already heavy, drooping. He reminded her of her son. Yet he was different, his own little man. "Call me if you need anything, sweetie."

His eyes widened for a second. "Where am I going after here?"

BJ smiled. The poor little boy was so insecure. "You're not going anywhere, Drew. I want you to live with me. Forever."

"Forever?" he said in a tiny voice.

"Yes, sweetie." She planted a kiss on his forehead. "That is, if you want. I'll be your mommy."

"But what if you get tired of me?" he asked, big-eyed.

BJ pulled him into her arms and rubbed his back. "I'll never get tired of you, Drew. Never."

His little body trembled, but he sniffed and relaxed against her. She rocked him back and forth until his breathing evened and he fell asleep.

BJ gently tucked the blanket around him, and guided her son's stuffed lion into Drew's arms. The lion had given Aaron comfort when he woke in the night. It had given her comfort, too, during the last two years.

Now it was doing the same for Drew.

She could almost see Aaron smiling, running in the

yard, playing hide and seek, then curling with the lion at night as she read him a story.

Odd, how, since the accident, she'd remembered only the anguish of losing her son. Although her heart longed for him, and it felt bittersweet, she was finally able to remember the happy moments. To see him smiling, not crying out for her to save him from death. She'd even dreamed the night before that he was holding his father's hand and they were walking together in heaven.

She planted another kiss on Drew's forehead, then tiptoed from the room.

It would take time, patience and love for Drew to heal and accept that he had a permanent home.

His insecurities reminded her of Cash's childhood. Never having love or the comfort of a secure home.

Cash would give security to Tyler, though.

Maybe at some point, once she overcame her heartbreak over not being with him, they could get the boys together. Tyler and Drew both deserved to know they had a brother.

She showered and poured herself a glass of wine, then sank onto the sofa in her den. Tomorrow she'd start searching for a small house, someplace with a yard and trees to climb and acreage to run and play. Some place homey like the cabin where she'd stayed on Horseshoe Creek…

Her doorbell dinged, and she tensed. Ever since Candace had called with the news that she could keep Drew, she'd been afraid that something would happen and the courts would reverse the decision.

She took a deep breath and hurried to the door. Shock hit her when she saw Cash standing in the doorway, his expression strained.

Something was wrong.

"Did something happen with Tyler?"

He shook his head. "No, he's good. He's with Brett's boy. They've become fast friends. And Mama Mary is smothering him with love and food, just like he's a McCullen."

BJ couldn't help but smile at the reminder of the sweet, robust woman with the bigger-than-life heart. "She is special. Everyone ought to have a Mama Mary in their life."

Cash murmured agreement, then shifted as if he was suddenly uncomfortable. "The McCullens have all been great."

BJ smiled. "I'm glad, Cash. You deserve a family."

His gaze darkened. "It still feels weird. Like they might change their mind any day."

She understood that feeling. She was afraid of losing Drew. "I think you can count on them."

Cash sucked in a deep breath. "I want Tyler to feel that way about me."

The fear tinging his voice struck a chord.

She motioned for him to come in. "I'm glad you stopped by. I…wanted to talk to you."

He stepped into the entryway. "You did?"

She nodded. She wanted to tell him she loved him, but held her tongue. "I talked to Candace about Drew."

His eyes widened. "I was going to do that. I thought he should live with me and Tyler."

Her chest clenched. Was that the reason he was here? Because he wanted to take Drew away from her?

Chapter Twenty-Six

Cash hadn't meant to start out by talking about Drew, but if he and BJ had a chance, she had to accept him for the man he was, baggage included. No pretenses.

"How did you know Drew was here?" BJ asked.

Cash stared at BJ in surprise. "Drew is here?"

She nodded. "Did you talk to the social worker?"

"Not yet." He'd wanted to talk to her first. "What's going on?"

"I have temporary custody of Drew."

Cash was shocked. "You do?"

"Yes, I want to adopt him." She folded her arms across her chest. "Is that why you're here? To tell me you're going to fight me for him?"

"God, no," Cash said. Her raised brow reeked of suspicion, a reminder that she had trust issues. "I just wanted to see you."

Her expression softened as she ran a hand through her hair. The movement drew his gaze to the fact that it was still damp. She wore pajama pants and a tank, too, just as she had the night they'd made love. This tank was more modest, built with one of those bras inside it, but her cleavage spilled over, making his mouth water.

He wanted her again.

A blush stained her cheeks, as if she'd read his mind. "Then what are you doing here, Cash?"

A smile tugged at his mouth. The desire in her eyes gave him hope and courage. "I...miss you," he said gruffly.

She bit her lip, her expression wary. "If you came for a booty call, that's not going to happen. Not with Drew here."

"I'm not here for a booty call," he said gruffly. "I want more than that."

BJ's eyes narrowed, but she took a step toward him. "What do you mean, Cash?"

A rush of hunger shot through him, and he closed the distance between them. The scent of her feminine body wash suffused his senses, making him crazy. "I want you, BJ."

"Cash—"

"Let me finish. Yes, I want to sleep with you, but I want to sleep with you every night."

"Ahh, Cash," she said in a soft whisper.

Her hair lay in long waves around her shoulders, and he reached out and tucked one silky strand behind her ear. "For a long time, I didn't think I deserved to have someone like you in my life. That no one could love me."

Warmth and tenderness filled her eyes, and she pressed her hand against his jaw. "You're a brave, honorable man, Cash. You deserve the McCullens. And you deserve love."

"I want us to be together. To be a family. Forever."

"If this is about Drew—"

"It's not about Drew, although he and Tyler will be part of this." Cash traced a finger over her lips. "It's about you and me, BJ. I love you, Brandy Jane Alexander. I...want to build a life with you."

Yearning glowed in BJ's eyes, and she wrapped her arms around his neck. "I love you, too, Cash."

Then she tilted her head and fused her mouth with his. He yanked her to him, hungry and aching for her touch.

But most of all for her answer.

The kiss was erotic, teasing, promising more. But he needed the words.

"BJ?" he whispered. "Will you marry me?"

A sexy smile brightened her eyes, and she kissed him again, then whispered, "Yes."

Cash picked her up and swung her around. He'd gone

from being locked in a cell, accused of murder, from feeling all alone, to finding a bride and two kids.

Except for his missing twin, life was perfect. He had brothers and their families and Mama Mary.

And now he'd have a family of his own.

* * * * *

Look for the final story in USA TODAY *bestselling author Rita Herron's series* THE HEROES OF HORSESHOE CREEK *when THE LAST McCULLEN goes on sale next month.*

You'll find it wherever Mills & Boon Intrigue books are sold!

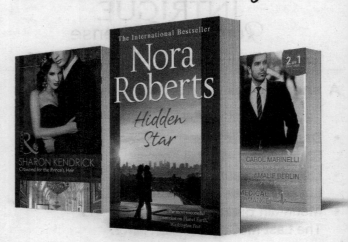